bronze age boogie ™

VOLUME ONE

SWORDS AGAINST DACRON!

STUART MOORE

ALBERTO PONTICELLI

GUILIA BRUSCO

SHAWN CRYSTAL

ROB STEEN

AHOY

BRONZE AGE BOOGIE

VOLUME ONE

SWORDS AGAINST DACRON!

STUART MOORE	WRITER
ALBERTO PONTICELLI	ARTIST
GUILIA BRUSCO	COLOR
SHAWN CRYSTAL	ARTIST (MOON-THING)
LEE LOUGHRIDGE	COLOR (MOON-THING)
ROB STEEN	LETTERS
ALBERTO PONTICELLI	
& GUILIA BRUSCO	COVER
BRETT EVANS	LOGO
JOHN J. HILL	DESIGN
STUART MOORE	EDITOR
CORY SEDLMEIER	COLLECTION EDITOR

CREATED BY STUART MOORE AND ALBERTO PONTICELLI

COMICSAHOY.COM 🐦 @ AHOYCOMICMAGS

HART SEELY - PUBLISHER
TOM PEYER - EDITOR-IN-CHIEF
FRANK CAMMUSO - CHIEF CREATIVE OFFICER
STUART MOORE - OPS
SARAH LITT - EDITOR-AT-LARGE

DAVID HYDE - PUBLICITY
DERON BENNETT - PRODUCTION COORDINATOR
KIT CAOAGAS - MARKETING ASSOCIATE
LILLIAN LASERSON - LEGAL
RUSSELL NATHERSON SR. - BUSINESS

PRINTED IN THE U.S.A. - FIRST PRINTING - NOVEMBER 2019 - ISBN: 978-0-9980442-5-5

C O N T E N T S

BRONZE AGE BOOGIE

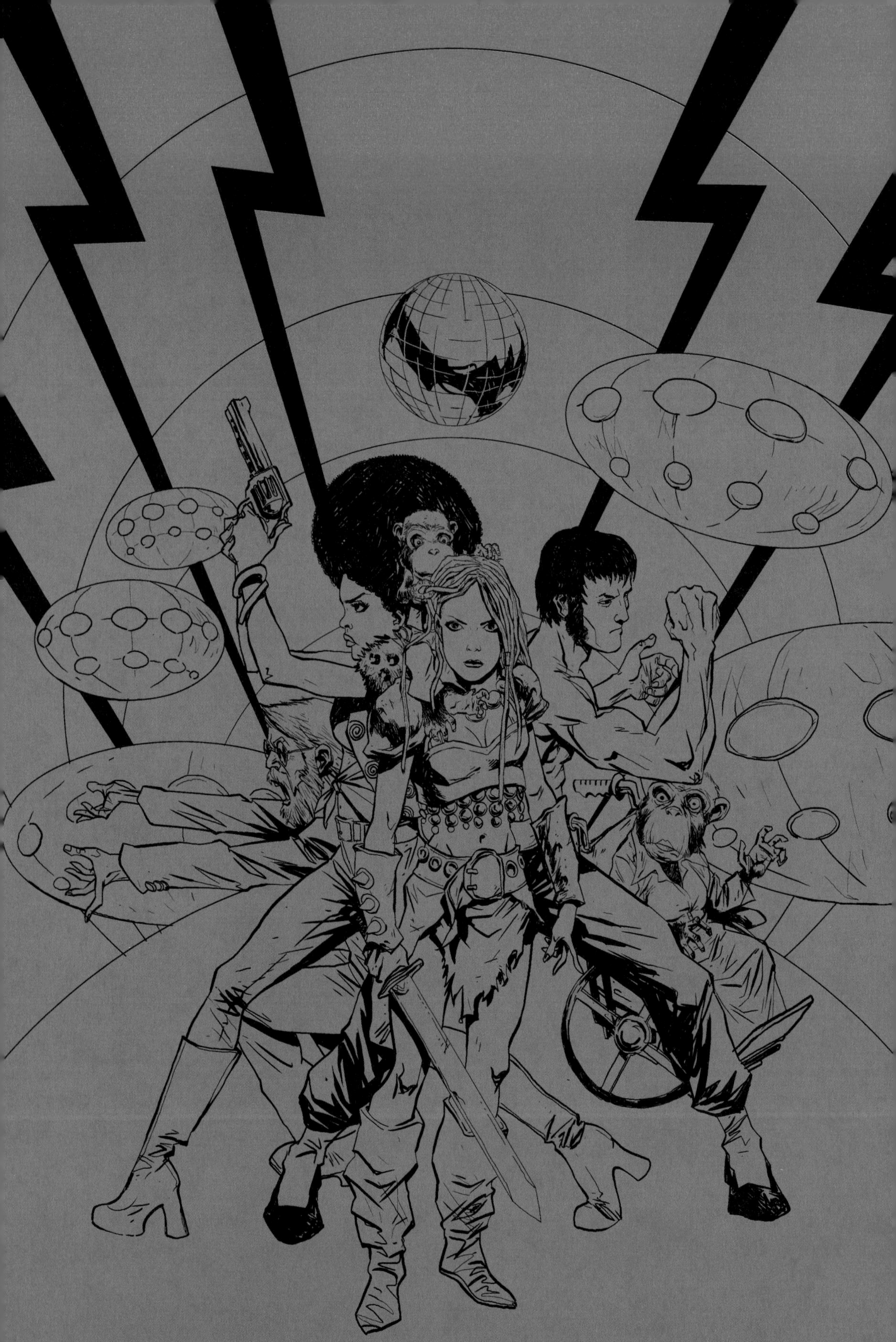

I SAY IT'S NOSTALGIA AN

Her name wasn't Roxane, but let's call her that. She was two years older than me—a glamorous high school junior—and I'd met her in the American Studies class they'd accelerated me into. She was smart, kind of shy, and having grown up part of the time in France, she had two native languages. I thought that was the coolest thing I'd ever heard.

Roxane and I weren't close—I don't think we ever actually hung out together. But I had that affection for her, just short of a crush, that a nerdy adolescent feels when someone older accepts them for who they are. I liked it when she worked shifts at Tiger's Deli. We'd exchange awkward hellos while I scavenged through the shelves for the latest science fiction magazine that some poor publisher had decided to cast out into a dying market.

One day she sold me a copy of *Marvel Preview* #4. I was a little embarrassed. The character on the cover, "Star-Lord," looked pretty silly. I was into *Analog, Fantasy and Science Fiction*, that sort of thing. I'd cut way back on comic books in the past year. They seemed childish, like something I'd outgrown.

Something about this book called to me, though. And inside was an editorial by the late Archie Goodwin that echoed my own reservations. It was called "I Say It's Space Opera and I Say to Hell With It!" and in it, Archie talked about his disdain for shoot-em-up, western-fiction-derived science fiction. "Guys running around in ridiculous costumes, usually tights," he wrote, "with fishbowls on their heads—zapping crazed BEMs with their ray guns. Intolerable!"

But then Archie went on to explain that he'd inherited editorial duties on this book, with the title character, Star-Lord, already in place. He'd also recently been introduced to the space-opera fiction of Jack Vance which, he said, "opened up a whole area of enjoyable reading I'd been too snobbish to sample."

I read that magazine over and over again. And it was a magazine, large-sized in black and white, with two mind-blowing features—Star-Lord and the short-lived Sword in the Star—as well as articles and features. It looked very different from the format we're using at AHOY, but in their way, those Marvel magazines were an inspiration for our own comic magazines.

And now I've written/edited/co-created a comic book series inspired, in a more direct way, by *Marvel Preview* and its ilk: *Savage Sword of Conan*, of course, but also the various Kung Fu and horror 'zines from a variety of publishers. The phrase BRONZE AGE, which comics historians use to refer to the comics of the '70s and '80s, is actually in our title.

Which brings up an awkward question: Is this book an exercise in nostalgia?

That may not sound like an awkward question—to you, anyway. But I'm deeply suspicious of nostalgia. I think of it as a bit of a trap: a warm, sad feeling that ultimately leaves you cold and alone. I've always preferred to look forward, to move on to the next project, the new challenge.

Nostalgia is also a very personal experience, which makes it a tricky exercise for a writer. Old comics, old movies, mean something very different to every person who's read or seen them. There's nothing wrong with that. But trying to evoke a period—to recreate a *feeling*—is a difficult game. You're likely to miss the mark with most of your audience, because that feeling is different for everyone.

So yeah, I'm suspicious of nostalgia. In fact, I'm probably as suspicious of it as Archie Goodwin was of monsters, blasters, and space westerns.

Yet here I am, writing an foreword for a book awash in 1970s cultural concepts, and getting misty about high school friends and buying comics at Tiger's Deli.

All I can say is: I think this book is more than *just* nostalgia. Yes, we're playing with certain types of characters and plot devices that have largely dropped out of the cultural conversation. I've also sprinkled in a few narrative techniques you don't see so much in modern comics, like those crazy illustrated-text pages that characterized some of the more literate Marvel books of the '70s. But all that is used sparingly, only when it serves the story.

I hope.

One thing's for sure: I am incredibly lucky to have Alberto Ponticelli and Giulia Brusco in the VW microbus with me. They make *BOOGIE* look like what it should be: a modern comic *about* the 1970s (and other time periods), a title that looks at home next to *Saga* and *Seeds* and *Seven for Eternity*. Alberto's characters are expressive and evocative; his settings seem incredibly real. And I couldn't believe it when he told me he was a longtime martial arts teacher. You're about to see that expertise in full-color action.

I've known Giulia for a long time, but never worked with her before. I knew she was good, but the first pages she sent took my damn breath away. I've been doing this for a while, and I'm not easily impressed. But wow. WOW.

So I hope you enjoy *BRONZE AGE BOOGIE*. But meanwhile, I'm left sitting here in 2019, a time incalculably different from 1975, with the same question: Is this nostalgia?

A classmate once asked Roxane, who (remember) was fluent in both English and French, which language she *thought* in. She paused, blushed, and shook her head. I don't know, she said. Both?

Maybe that's the answer to my question. BOOGIE is nostalgia, and it isn't. It exists, it lives, in both the world of 1975 and the world of today. If your taste in comics runs to *Maneaters* and Tom King's *Mister Miracle* (mine sure does!), then I encourage you to experience our book for what it is. On the other hand, if you're a fan of *Savage Tales* and the *original* (Kirby) *Mister Miracle*, I hope you'll get an extra charge out of the period references and occasional Easter eggs.

As for me: I was fortunate enough to get to know Archie Goodwin a little, in a time roughly equidistant from then and now. He was an amazing guy—funny, smart, down to Earth, liked and respected by virtually everyone in the comics industry. He is much missed, and I still laugh when I think of some of the stories he told me. I'm rambling. What I'm trying to say is, if Archie could get over his snobbishness toward space opera...

...maybe I can make peace with nostalgia.

Keep dancing!

Stuart Moore
2019

I SAY THE HELL WITH IT!

1

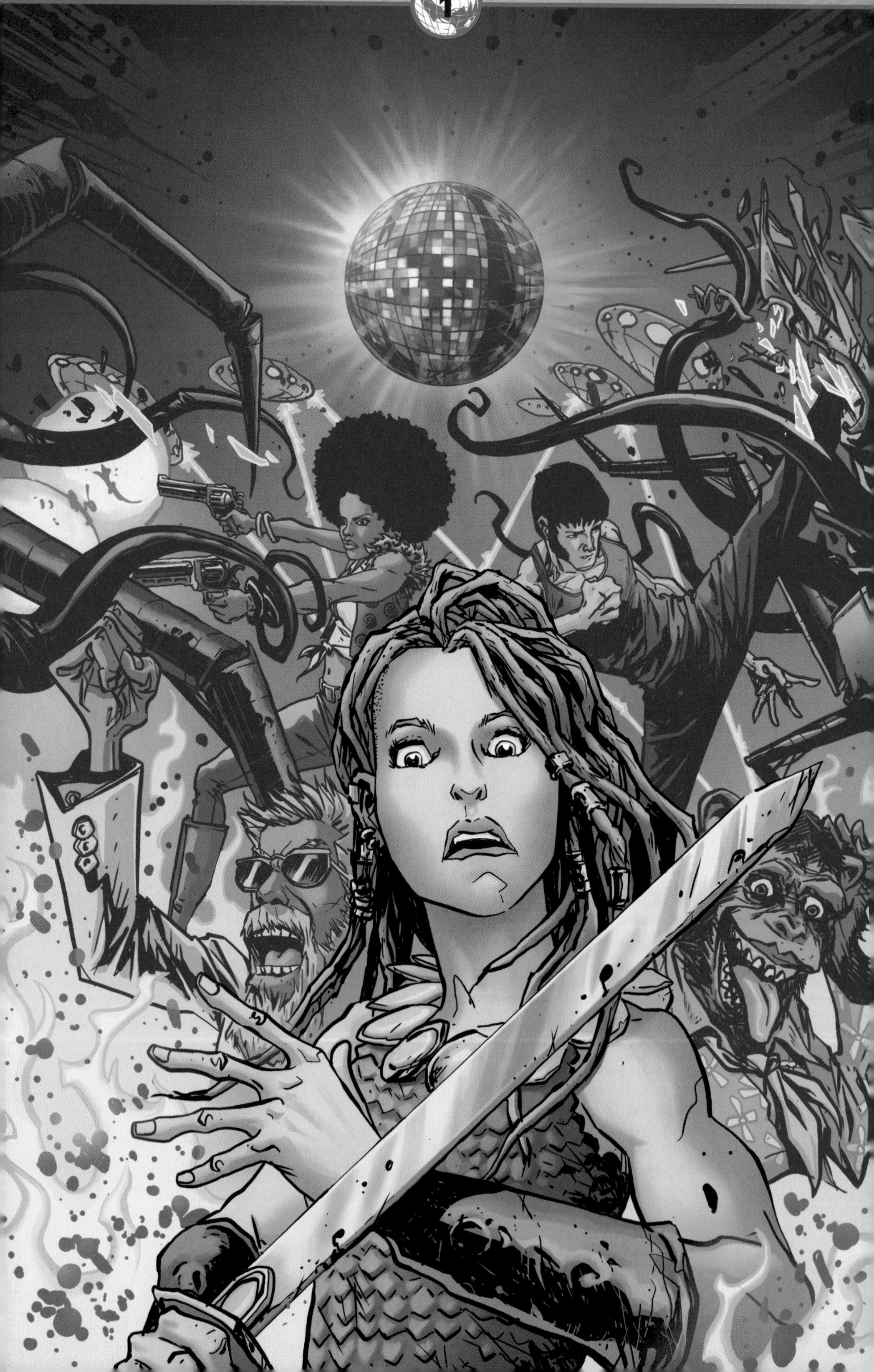

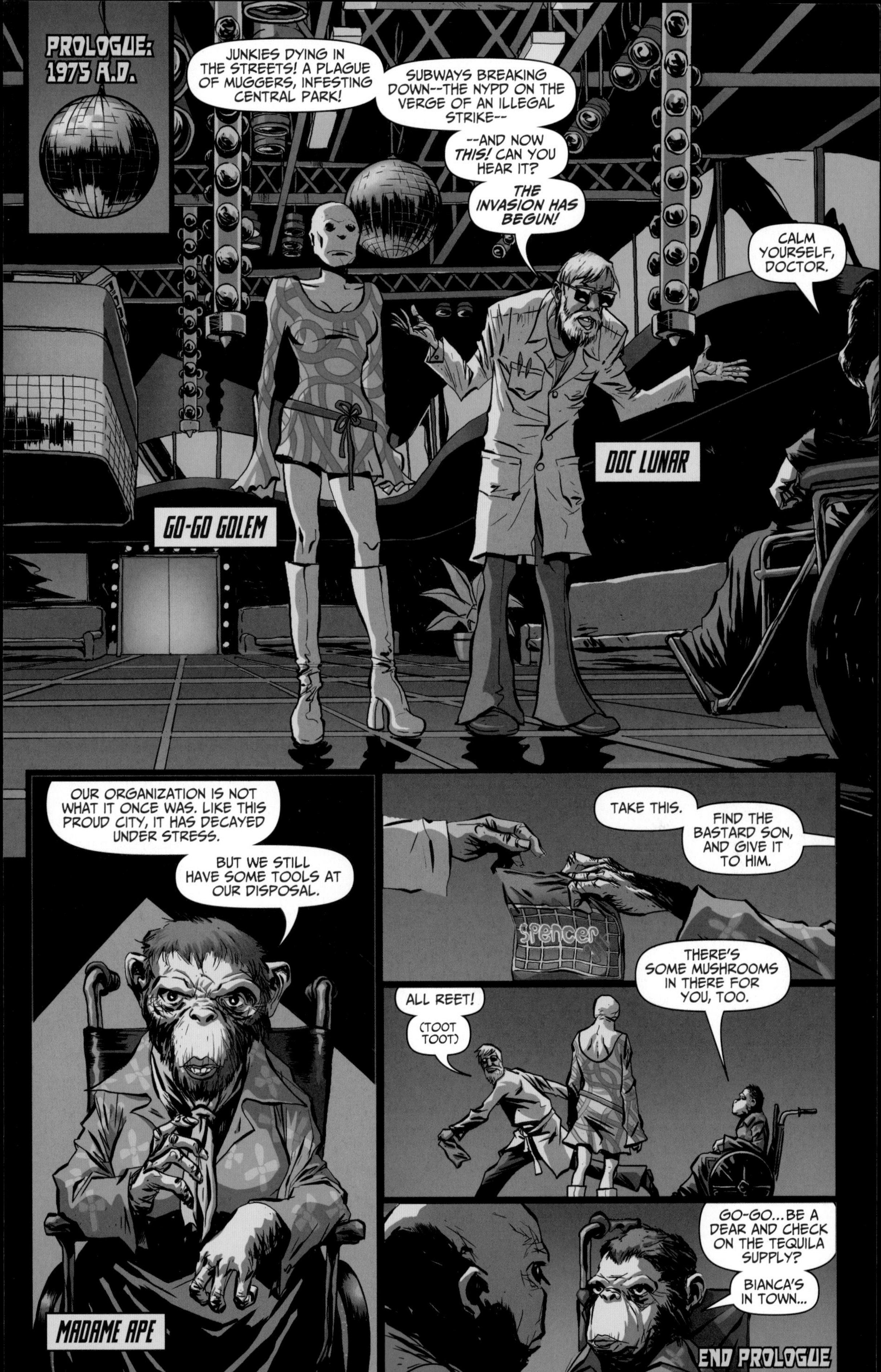
PROLOGUE: 1975 A.D.
JUNKIES DYING IN THE STREETS! A PLAGUE OF MUGGERS, INFESTING CENTRAL PARK!
SUBWAYS BREAKING DOWN--THE NYPD ON THE VERGE OF AN ILLEGAL STRIKE--
--AND NOW THIS! CAN YOU HEAR IT?
THE INVASION HAS BEGUN!
CALM YOURSELF, DOCTOR.
DOC LUNAR
GO-GO GOLEM
OUR ORGANIZATION IS NOT WHAT IT ONCE WAS. LIKE THIS PROUD CITY, IT HAS DECAYED UNDER STRESS.
BUT WE STILL HAVE SOME TOOLS AT OUR DISPOSAL.
MADAME APE
TAKE THIS.
FIND THE BASTARD SON, AND GIVE IT TO HIM.
Spencer
THERE'S SOME MUSHROOMS IN THERE FOR YOU, TOO.
ALL REET!
(TOOT TOOT)
GO-GO...BE A DEAR AND CHECK ON THE TEQUILA SUPPLY?
BIANCA'S IN TOWN...
END PROLOGUE

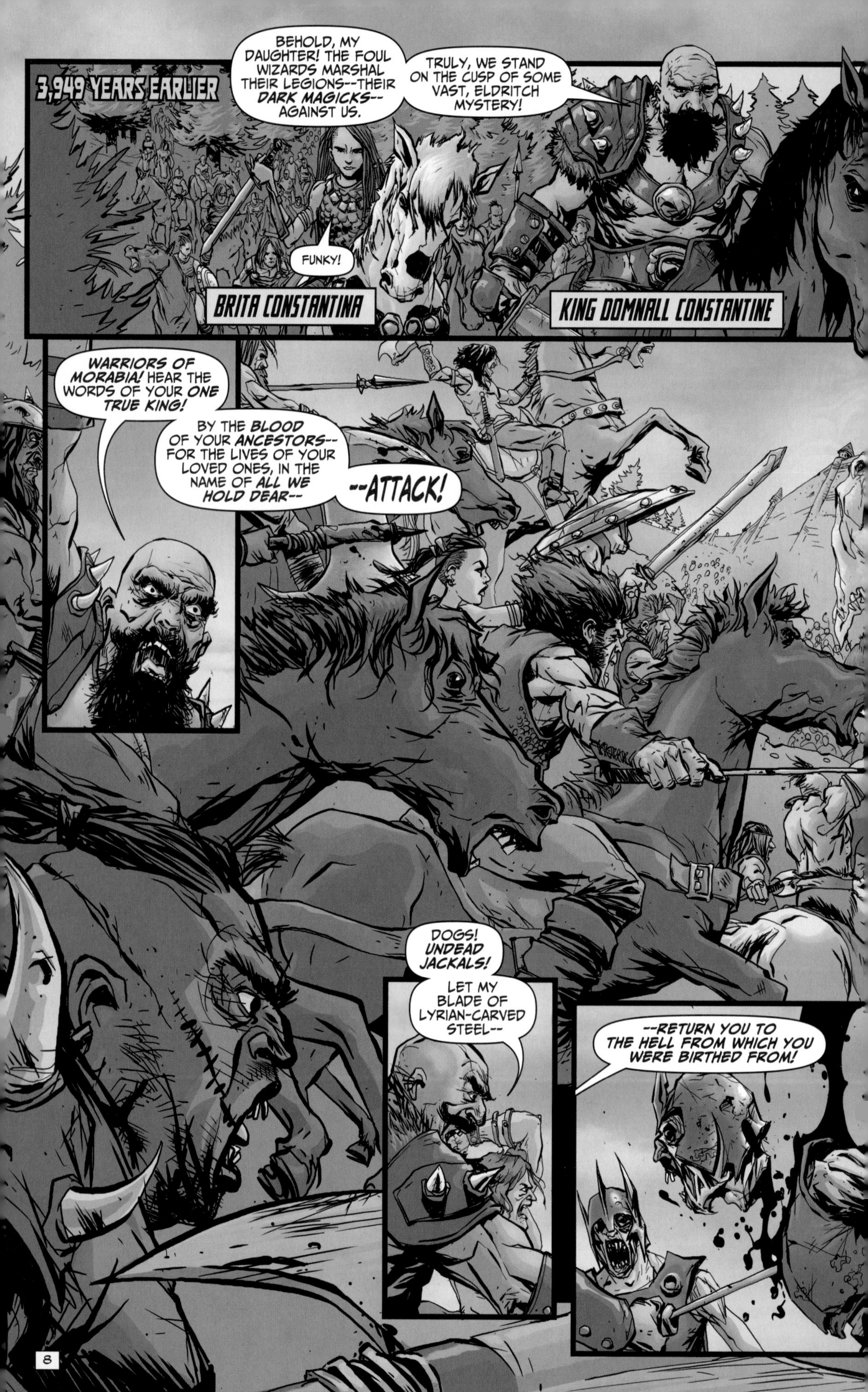
3,949 YEARS EARLIER
BEHOLD, MY DAUGHTER! THE FOUL WIZARDS MARSHAL THEIR LEGIONS--THEIR DARK MAGICKS--AGAINST US.
TRULY, WE STAND ON THE CUSP OF SOME VAST, ELDRITCH MYSTERY!
FUNKY!
BRITA CONSTANTINA
KING DOMNALL CONSTANTINE
WARRIORS OF MORABIA! HEAR THE WORDS OF YOUR ONE TRUE KING!
BY THE BLOOD OF YOUR ANCESTORS--FOR THE LIVES OF YOUR LOVED ONES, IN THE NAME OF ALL WE HOLD DEAR--
--ATTACK!
DOGS! UNDEAD JACKALS!
LET MY BLADE OF LYRIAN-CARVED STEEL--
--RETURN YOU TO THE HELL FROM WHICH YOU WERE BIRTHED FROM!

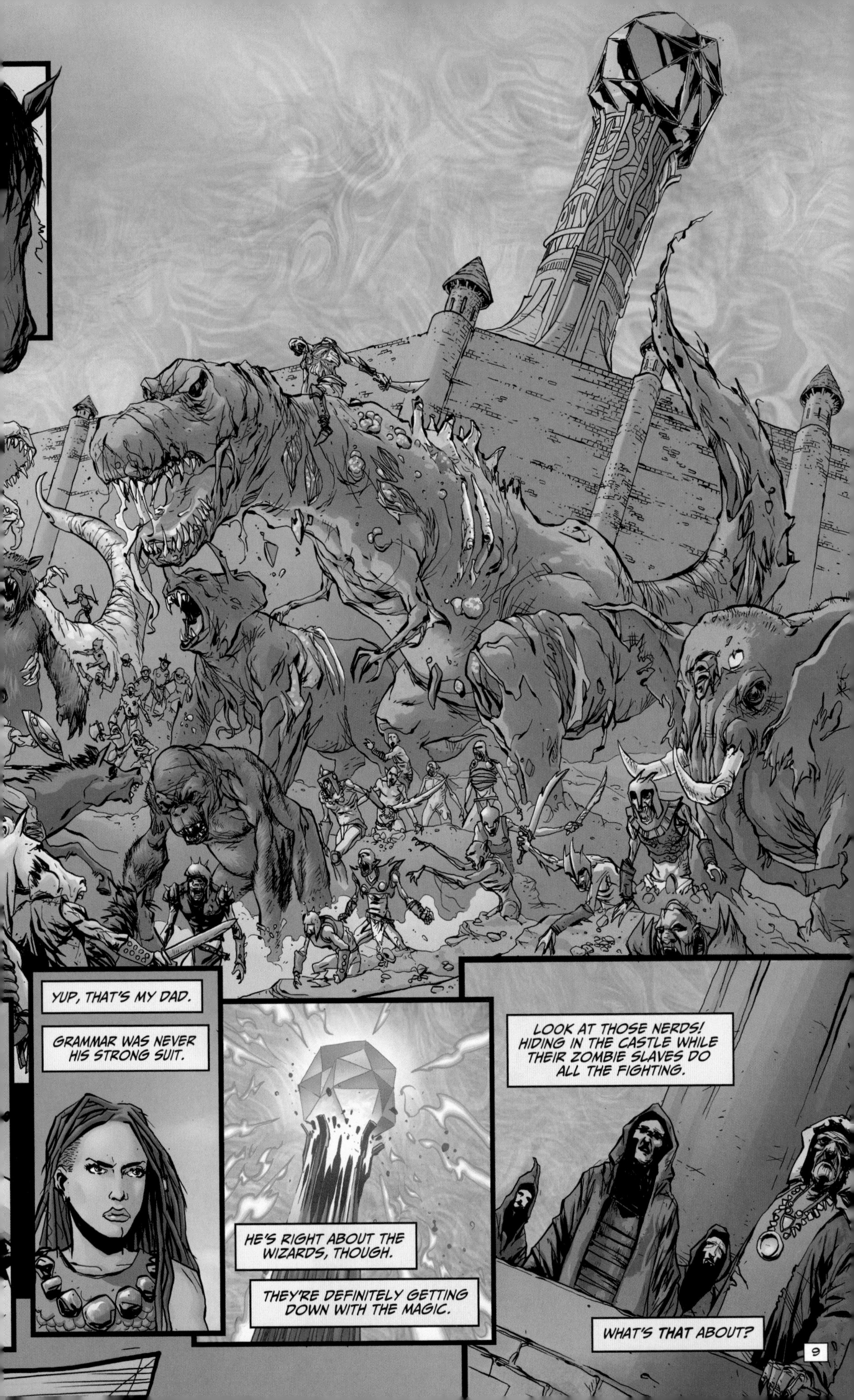
YUP, THAT'S MY DAD.
GRAMMAR WAS NEVER HIS STRONG SUIT.
HE'S RIGHT ABOUT THE WIZARDS, THOUGH.
THEY'RE DEFINITELY GETTING DOWN WITH THE MAGIC.
LOOK AT THOSE NERDS! HIDING IN THE CASTLE WHILE THEIR ZOMBIE SLAVES DO ALL THE FIGHTING.
WHAT'S THAT ABOUT?

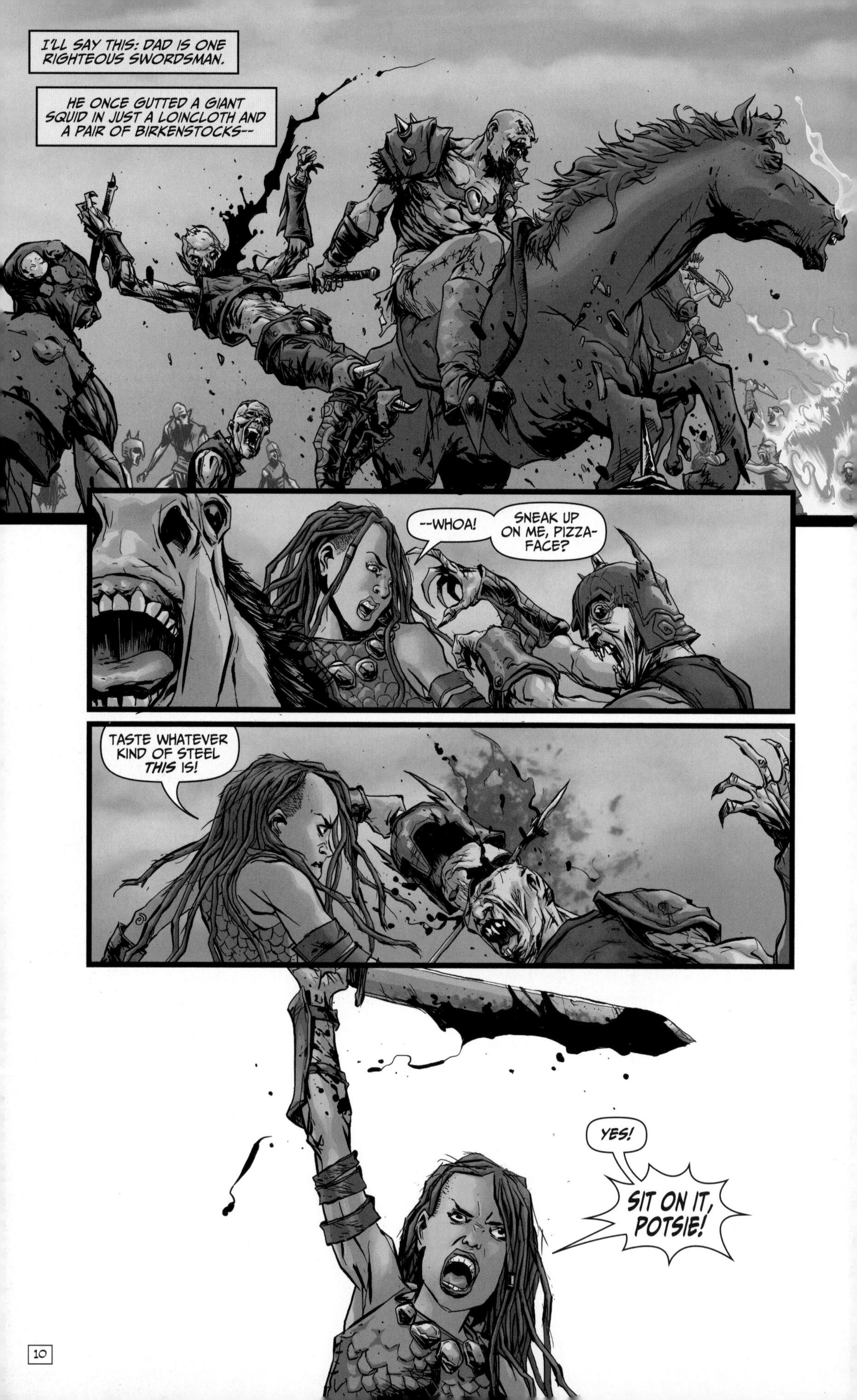

I'LL SAY THIS: DAD IS ONE RIGHTEOUS SWORDSMAN.
HE ONCE GUTTED A GIANT SQUID IN JUST A LOINCLOTH AND A PAIR OF BIRKENSTOCKS--
--WHOA!
SNEAK UP ON ME, PIZZA-FACE?
TASTE WHATEVER KIND OF STEEL THIS IS!
YES!
SIT ON IT, POTSIE!

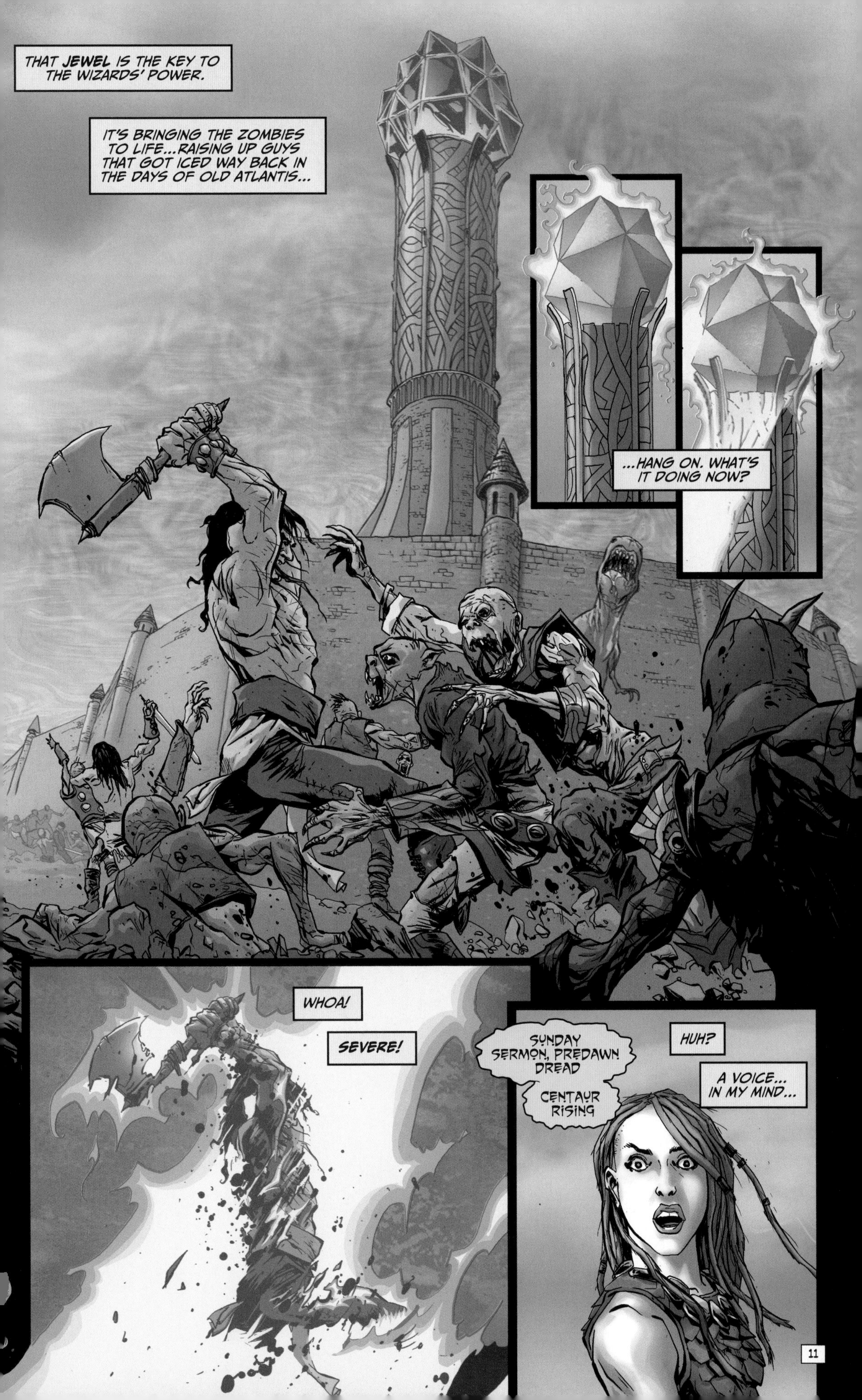
THAT **JEWEL** IS THE KEY TO THE WIZARDS' POWER.
IT'S BRINGING THE ZOMBIES TO LIFE...RAISING UP GUYS THAT GOT ICED WAY BACK IN THE DAYS OF OLD ATLANTIS...
...HANG ON. WHAT'S IT DOING NOW?
WHOA!
SEVERE!
SUNDAY SERMON, PREDAWN DREAD
CENTAUR RISING
HUH?
A VOICE... IN MY MIND...

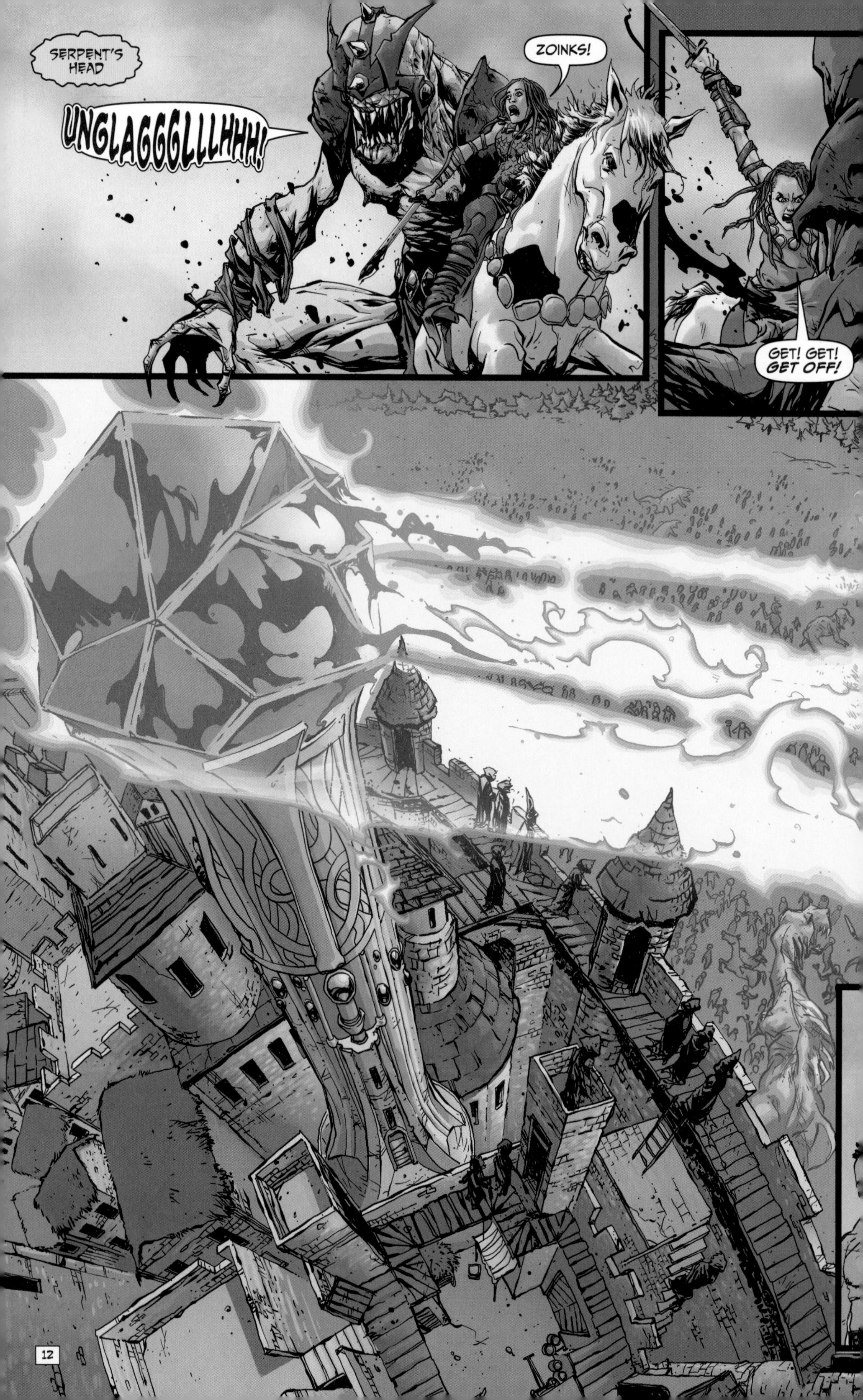
SERPENT'S HEAD
UNGLAGGGLLLHHH!
ZOINKS!
GET! GET! GET OFF!

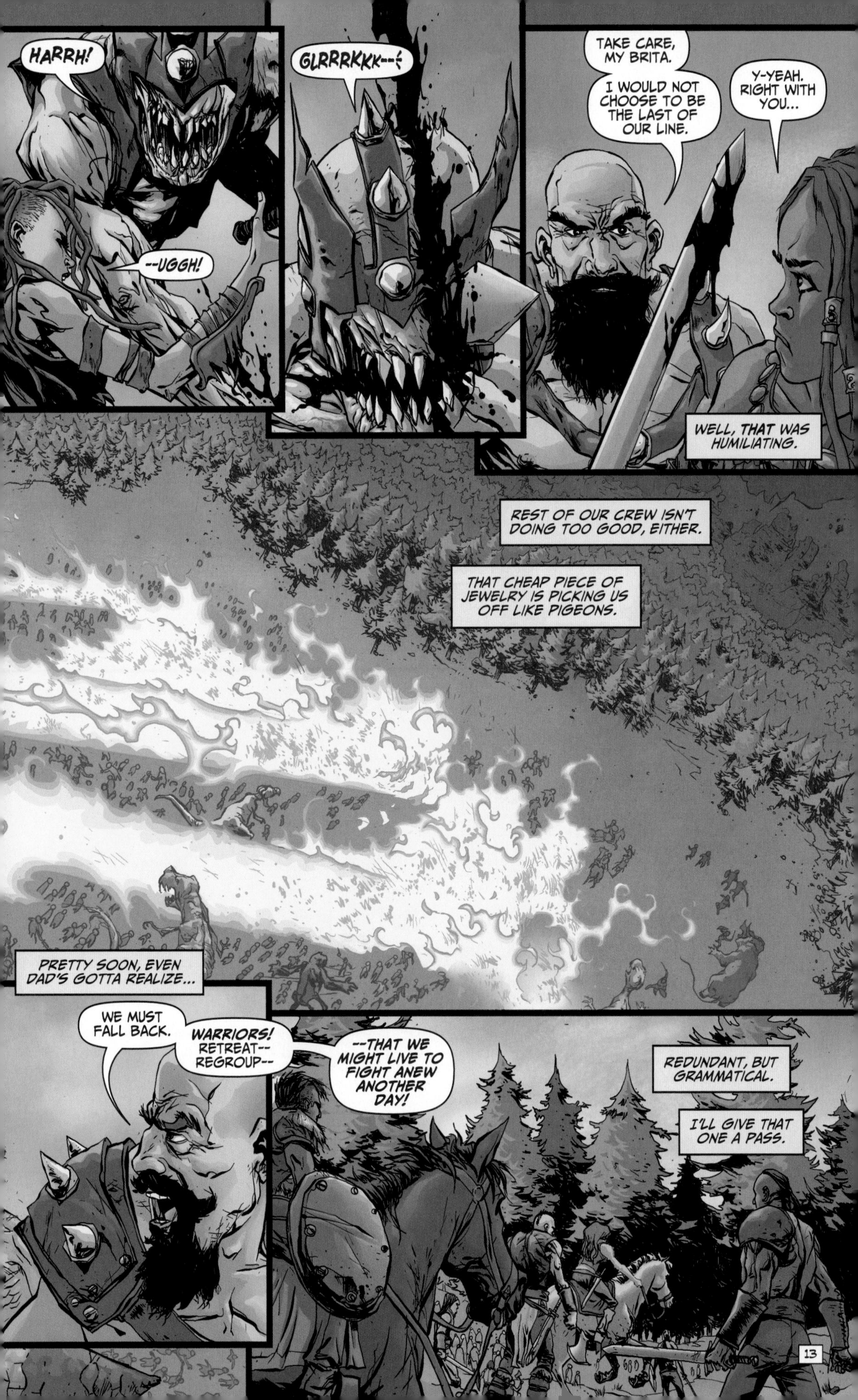
HARRH!
--UGGH!
GLRRRKKK--!
TAKE CARE, MY BRITA.
I WOULD NOT CHOOSE TO BE THE LAST OF OUR LINE.
Y-YEAH. RIGHT WITH YOU...
WELL, THAT WAS HUMILIATING.
REST OF OUR CREW ISN'T DOING TOO GOOD, EITHER.
THAT CHEAP PIECE OF JEWELRY IS PICKING US OFF LIKE PIGEONS.
PRETTY SOON, EVEN DAD'S GOTTA REALIZE...
WE MUST FALL BACK.
WARRIORS! RETREAT-- REGROUP--
--THAT WE MIGHT LIVE TO FIGHT ANEW ANOTHER DAY!
REDUNDANT, BUT GRAMMATICAL.
I'LL GIVE THAT ONE A PASS.

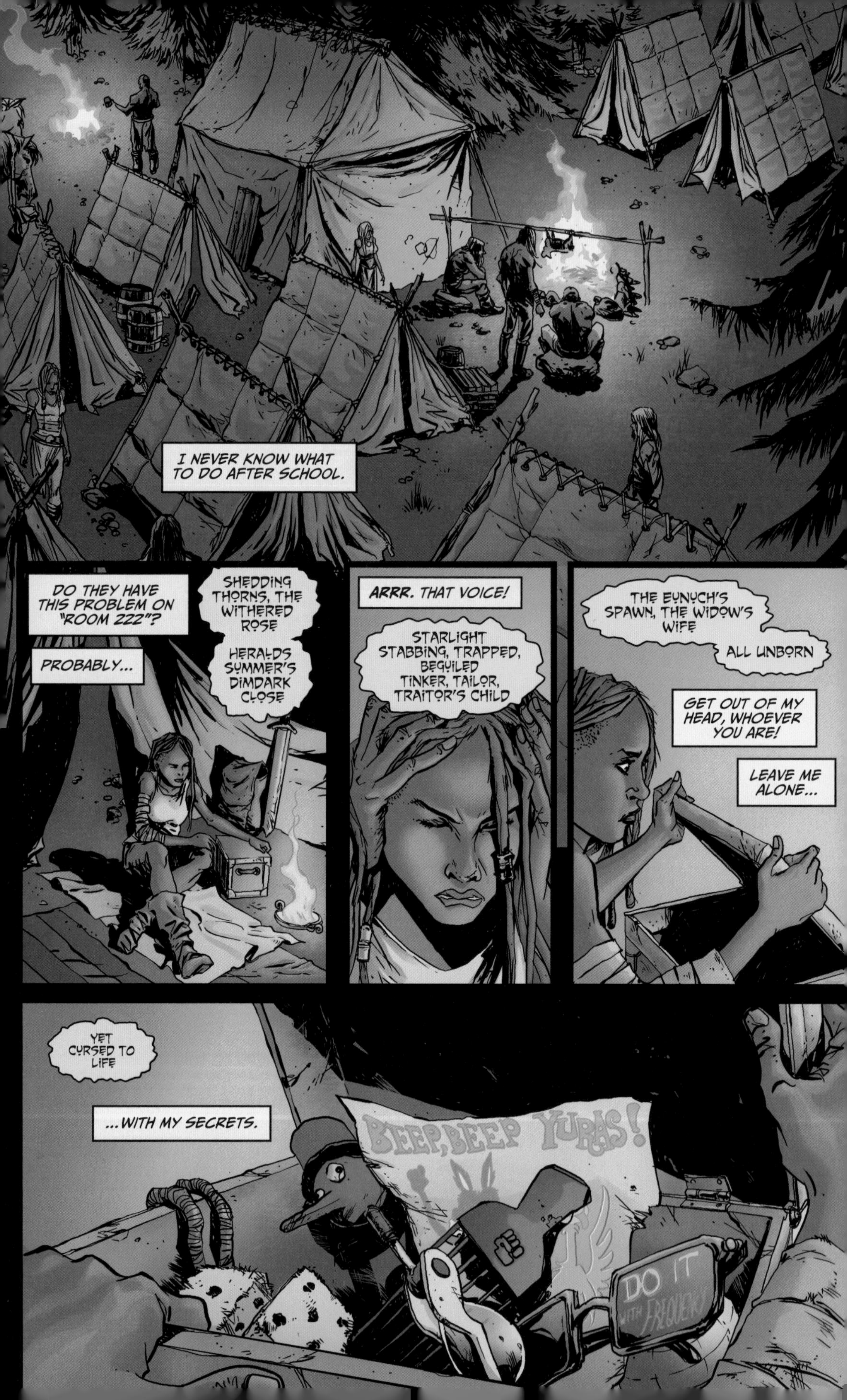
I NEVER KNOW WHAT TO DO AFTER SCHOOL.
DO THEY HAVE THIS PROBLEM ON "ROOM ZZZ"?
PROBABLY...
SHEDDING THORNS, THE WITHERED ROSE
HERALDS SUMMER'S DIMDARK CLOSE
ARRR. THAT VOICE!
STARLIGHT STABBING, TRAPPED, BEGUILED TINKER, TAILOR, TRAITOR'S CHILD
THE EUNUCH'S SPAWN, THE WIDOW'S WIFE
ALL UNBORN
GET OUT OF MY HEAD, WHOEVER YOU ARE!
LEAVE ME ALONE...
YET CURSED TO LIFE
...WITH MY SECRETS.
BEEP, BEEP YURAS!
DO IT with FREQUENCY

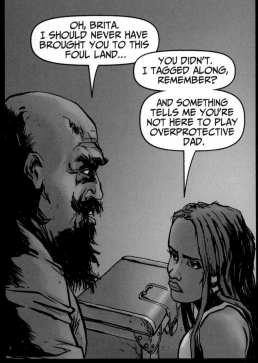

THRICE-DAMNED WIZARDS! RAISING THE DEAD...

ARE YOU INJURED, DAUGHTER?

YEAH! I MEAN NO!

JUST, UH, EMBARRASSED.

OH, BRITA. I SHOULD NEVER HAVE BROUGHT YOU TO THIS FOUL LAND...

YOU DIDN'T. I TAGGED ALONG, REMEMBER?

AND SOMETHING TELLS ME YOU'RE NOT HERE TO PLAY OVERPROTECTIVE DAD.

YOU KNOW ME WELL, DAUGHTER.

AND YET WE ARE VERY DIFFERENT. AT TIMES, YOU SEE THINGS I CANNOT.

I WOULD SEEK YOUR COUNSEL.

15

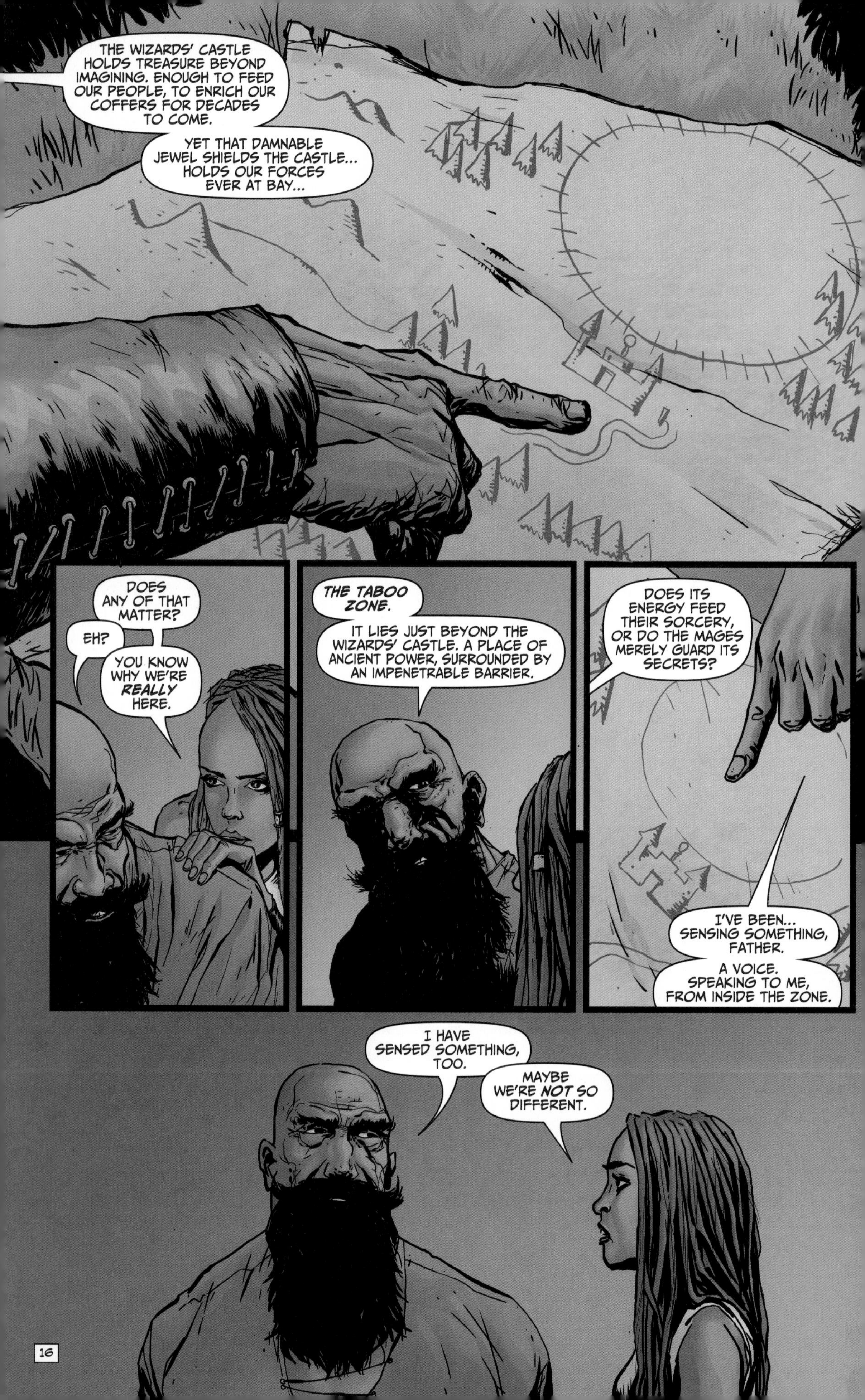
THE WIZARDS' CASTLE HOLDS TREASURE BEYOND IMAGINING. ENOUGH TO FEED OUR PEOPLE, TO ENRICH OUR COFFERS FOR DECADES TO COME.
YET THAT DAMNABLE JEWEL SHIELDS THE CASTLE... HOLDS OUR FORCES EVER AT BAY...
DOES ANY OF THAT MATTER?
EH?
YOU KNOW WHY WE'RE *REALLY* HERE.
THE TABOO ZONE.
IT LIES JUST BEYOND THE WIZARDS' CASTLE. A PLACE OF ANCIENT POWER, SURROUNDED BY AN IMPENETRABLE BARRIER.
DOES ITS ENERGY FEED THEIR SORCERY, OR DO THE MAGES MERELY GUARD ITS SECRETS?
I'VE BEEN... SENSING SOMETHING, FATHER.
A VOICE. SPEAKING TO ME, FROM INSIDE THE ZONE.
I HAVE SENSED SOMETHING, TOO.
MAYBE WE'RE ***NOT*** SO DIFFERENT.

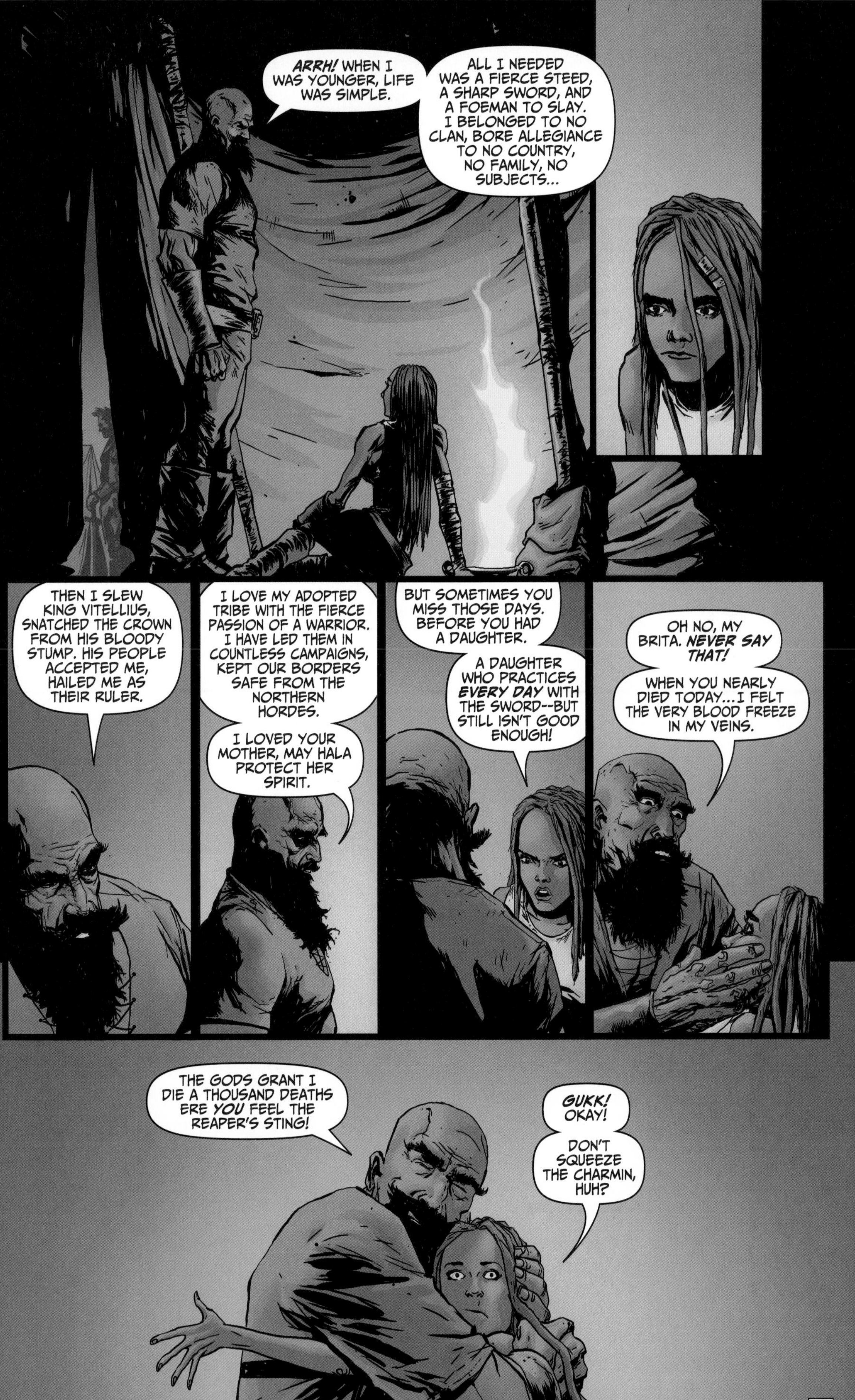
ARRH! WHEN I WAS YOUNGER, LIFE WAS SIMPLE.
ALL I NEEDED WAS A FIERCE STEED, A SHARP SWORD, AND A FOEMAN TO SLAY. I BELONGED TO NO CLAN, BORE ALLEGIANCE TO NO COUNTRY, NO FAMILY, NO SUBJECTS...
THEN I SLEW KING VITELLIUS, SNATCHED THE CROWN FROM HIS BLOODY STUMP. HIS PEOPLE ACCEPTED ME, HAILED ME AS THEIR RULER.
I LOVE MY ADOPTED TRIBE WITH THE FIERCE PASSION OF A WARRIOR. I HAVE LED THEM IN COUNTLESS CAMPAIGNS, KEPT OUR BORDERS SAFE FROM THE NORTHERN HORDES.
I LOVED YOUR MOTHER, MAY HALA PROTECT HER SPIRIT.
BUT SOMETIMES YOU MISS THOSE DAYS. BEFORE YOU HAD A DAUGHTER.
A DAUGHTER WHO PRACTICES EVERY DAY WITH THE SWORD--BUT STILL ISN'T GOOD ENOUGH!
OH NO, MY BRITA. NEVER SAY THAT!
WHEN YOU NEARLY DIED TODAY...I FELT THE VERY BLOOD FREEZE IN MY VEINS.
THE GODS GRANT I DIE A THOUSAND DEATHS ERE YOU FEEL THE REAPER'S STING!
GUKK! OKAY!
DON'T SQUEEZE THE CHARMIN, HUH?

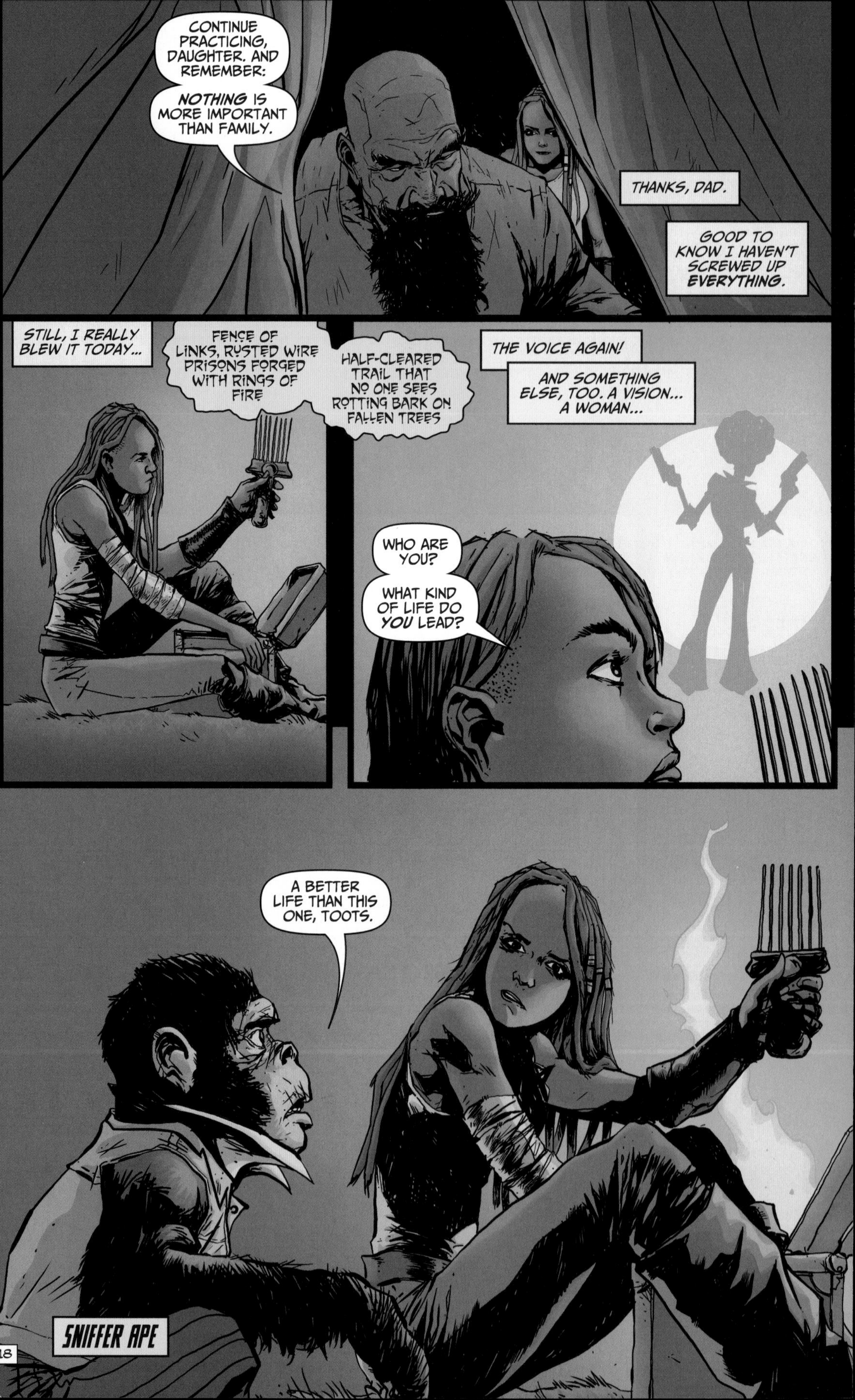
CONTINUE PRACTICING, DAUGHTER. AND REMEMBER:
NOTHING IS MORE IMPORTANT THAN FAMILY.
THANKS, DAD.
GOOD TO KNOW I HAVEN'T SCREWED UP EVERYTHING.
STILL, I REALLY BLEW IT TODAY...
FENCE OF LINKS, RUSTED WIRE PRISONS FORGED WITH RINGS OF FIRE
HALF-CLEARED TRAIL THAT NO ONE SEES ROTTING BARK ON FALLEN TREES
THE VOICE AGAIN!
AND SOMETHING ELSE, TOO. A VISION... A WOMAN...
WHO ARE YOU?
WHAT KIND OF LIFE DO YOU LEAD?
A BETTER LIFE THAN THIS ONE, TOOTS.
SNIFFER APE

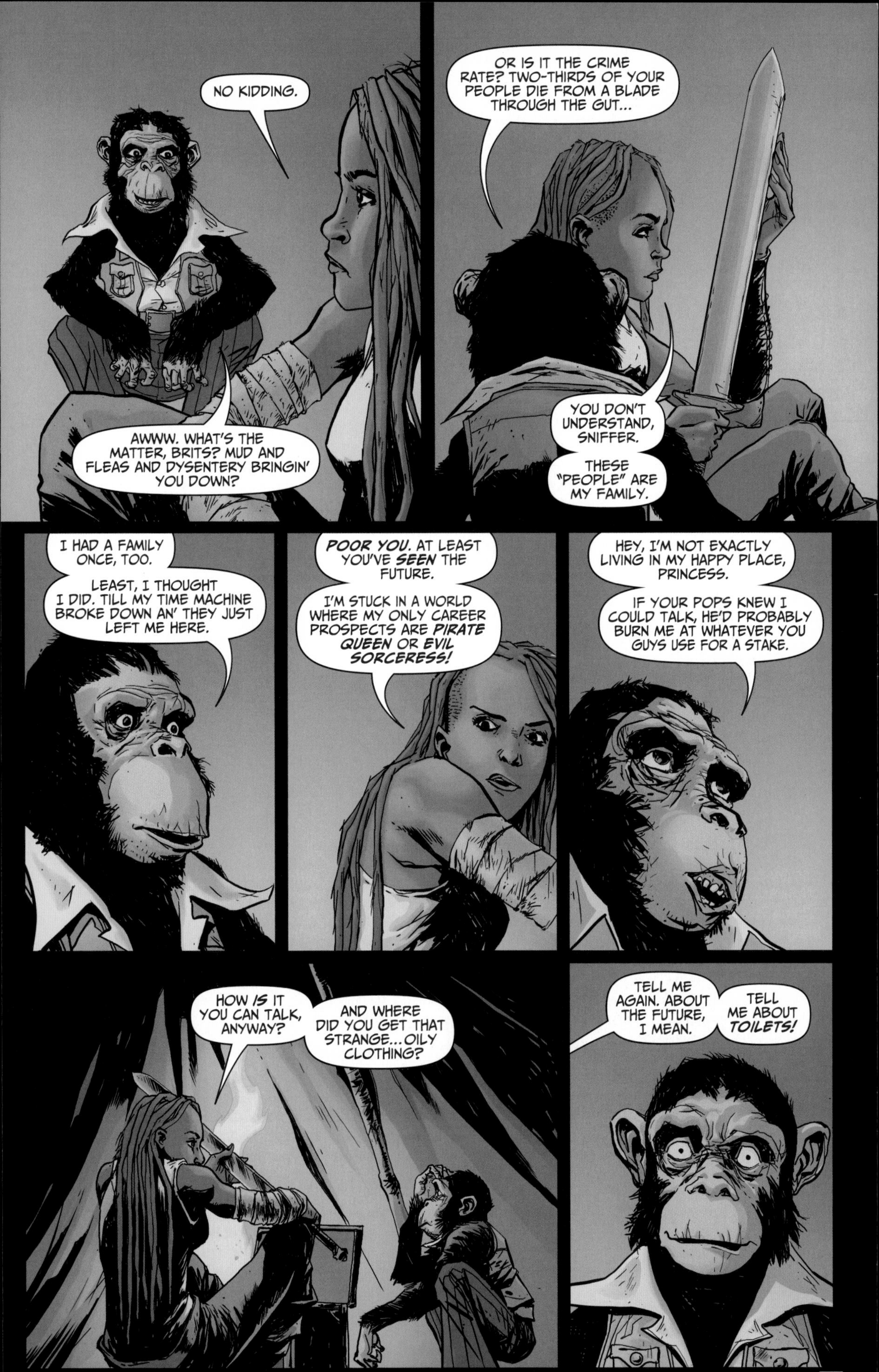
NO KIDDING.
AWWW. WHAT'S THE MATTER, BRITS? MUD AND FLEAS AND DYSENTERY BRINGIN' YOU DOWN?
OR IS IT THE CRIME RATE? TWO-THIRDS OF YOUR PEOPLE DIE FROM A BLADE THROUGH THE GUT...
YOU DON'T UNDERSTAND, SNIFFER.
THESE "PEOPLE" ARE MY FAMILY.
I HAD A FAMILY ONCE, TOO.
LEAST, I THOUGHT I DID. TILL MY TIME MACHINE BROKE DOWN AN' THEY JUST LEFT ME HERE.
POOR YOU. AT LEAST YOU'VE SEEN THE FUTURE.
I'M STUCK IN A WORLD WHERE MY ONLY CAREER PROSPECTS ARE PIRATE QUEEN OR EVIL SORCERESS!
HEY, I'M NOT EXACTLY LIVING IN MY HAPPY PLACE, PRINCESS.
IF YOUR POPS KNEW I COULD TALK, HE'D PROBABLY BURN ME AT WHATEVER YOU GUYS USE FOR A STAKE.
HOW IS IT YOU CAN TALK, ANYWAY?
AND WHERE DID YOU GET THAT STRANGE...OILY CLOTHING?
TELL ME AGAIN. ABOUT THE FUTURE, I MEAN.
TELL ME ABOUT TOILETS!

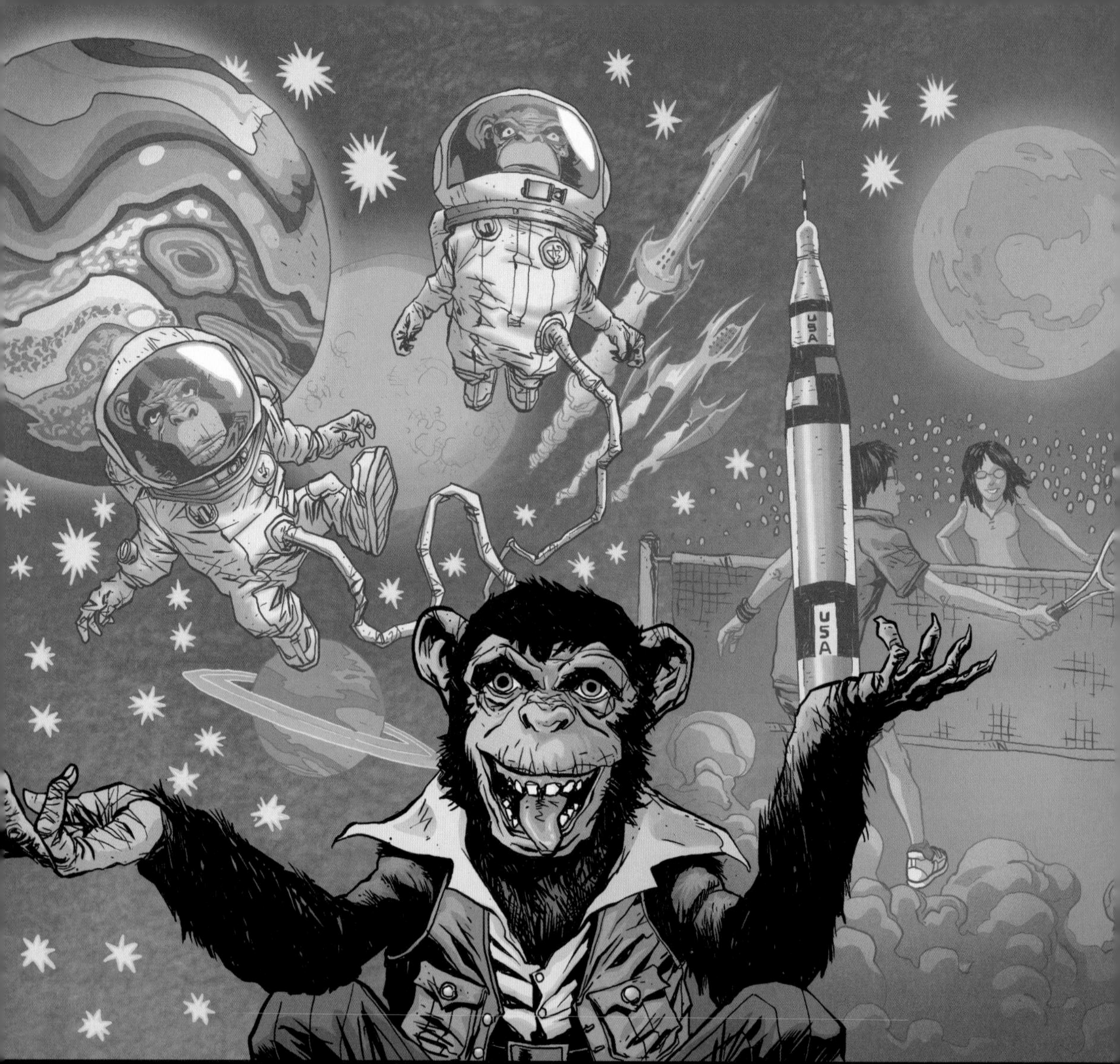

USA
USA

Sniffer Ape flashes a grin. Settles himself on the floor of the tent, winces, and turns to pick a small insect off his ass.

Brita sits back, a smile creeping across her face. Sniffer's stories are always worth the wait.

"In my time, apes are the dominant form of life throughout the galaxy," he begins—as if it's the most natural thing in the world to say. "We got ape explorers, ape soldiers, ape space pirates. Even an Ape Federation, though that was havin' some trouble, last I heard. Turns out the banana might not be an ideal standard of currency."

Brita giggles.

"On some worlds, though…evolution took kind of a funny turn." Sniffer reaches forward, pinches her on the cheek. "Yours, f'rinstance."

She bats his hand away.

"As for these fab, polyester threads…" He opens his vest, pulls his wide collars even wider. "I got 'em the same place I got those trinkets of yours. The glam, glitzy, glittery future."

Brita glances at her box. The treasures she keeps secret, even from her father.

"The future is…" Sniffer looks away, then, a trace of pain crossing his face. "It's hard to describe, toots. It's faster, harsher, brighter than here. And yet, it's full of things to dull your senses, make you *feel* less." He rubs a rough finger across his nose. "I had a little problem there, for a while. How I got my nickname, actually."

"Are you okay now?" she asks.

"Yeah, I been clean for months. Helps that there ain't a lot of refined benzoylmethylecgonine in this century."

Brita nods, as if she understands. So many strange concepts, in the future. So many long words!

"But you gotta stop dreamin' about that stuff, kid. I keep tellin' you: You're needed *here*."

He sounds very serious now. Sniffer is always going on about her destiny, about how important she is. Trouble is, she doesn't feel important.

"And god's truth, Brits: You're the best thirteen-year-old I ever seen with a sword. Or are you fourteen? Sixteen? You nomads ain't much with the birth certificates."

She waves that thought away, suddenly impatient. "What have you got for me?"

Sniffer grimaces, as if disappointed. Then he looks away and reaches into his pocket.

"… bottom of my stash, chica. But here…"

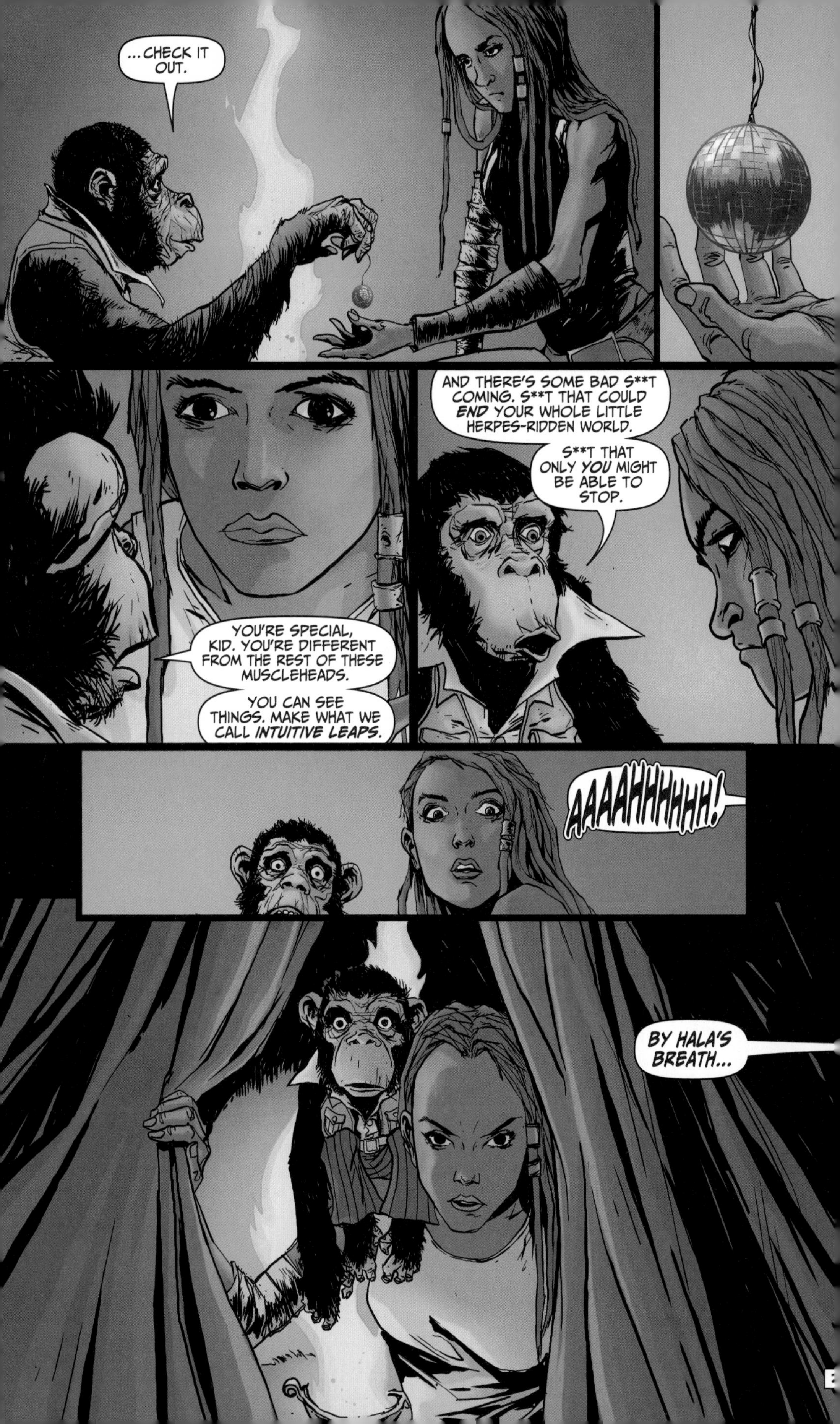
...CHECK IT OUT.
YOU'RE SPECIAL, KID. YOU'RE DIFFERENT FROM THE REST OF THESE MUSCLEHEADS.
YOU CAN SEE THINGS. MAKE WHAT WE CALL *INTUITIVE LEAPS*.
AND THERE'S SOME BAD S**T COMING. S**T THAT COULD *END* YOUR WHOLE LITTLE HERPES-RIDDEN WORLD.
S**T THAT ONLY *YOU* MIGHT BE ABLE TO STOP.
AAAAHHHHHH!
BY HALA'S BREATH...

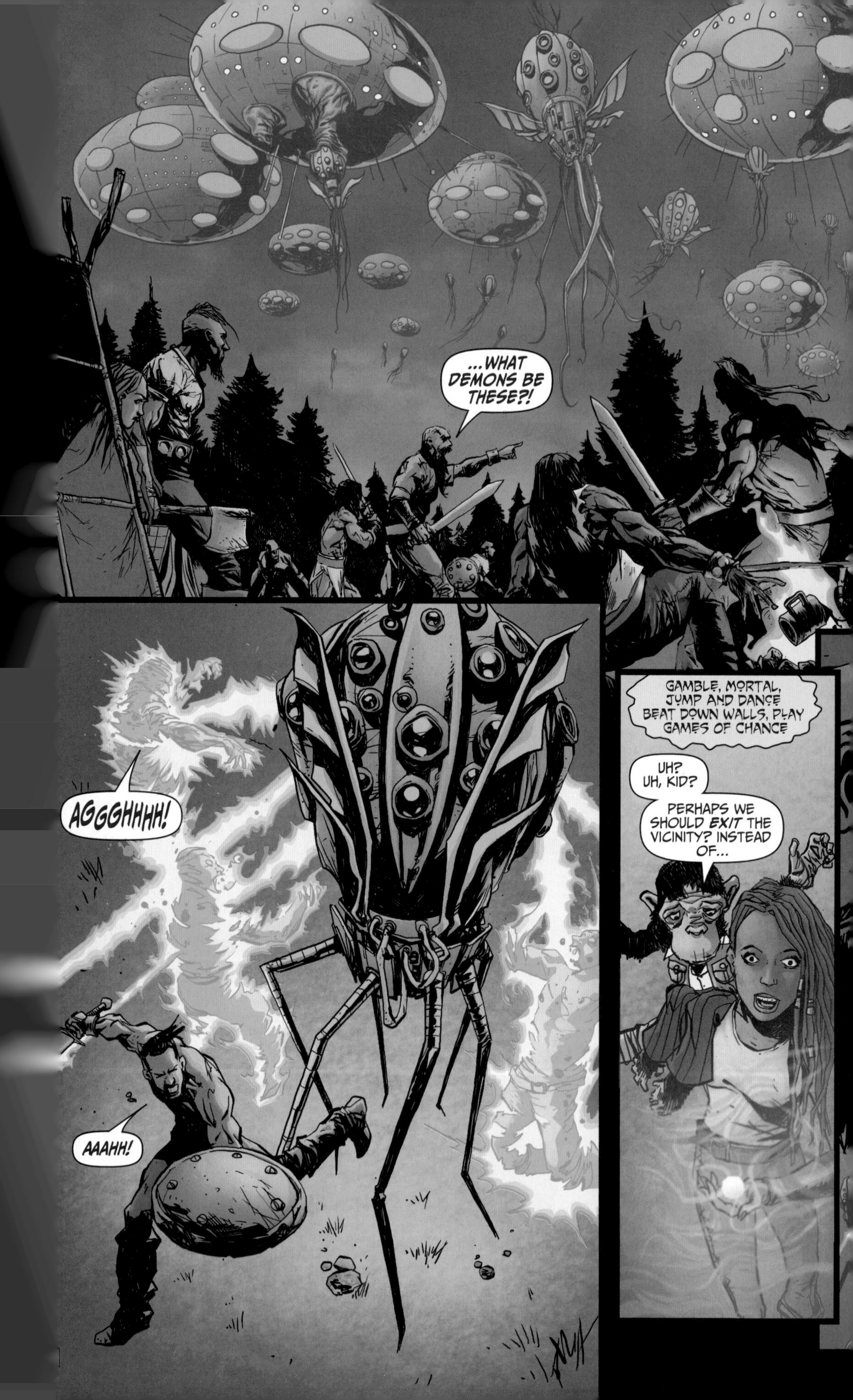
...WHAT DEMONS BE THESE?!
AGGGHHHH!
AAAHH!
GAMBLE, MORTAL, JUMP AND DANCE BEAT DOWN WALLS, PLAY GAMES OF CHANCE
UH? UH, KID?
PERHAPS WE SHOULD EXIT THE VICINITY? INSTEAD OF...

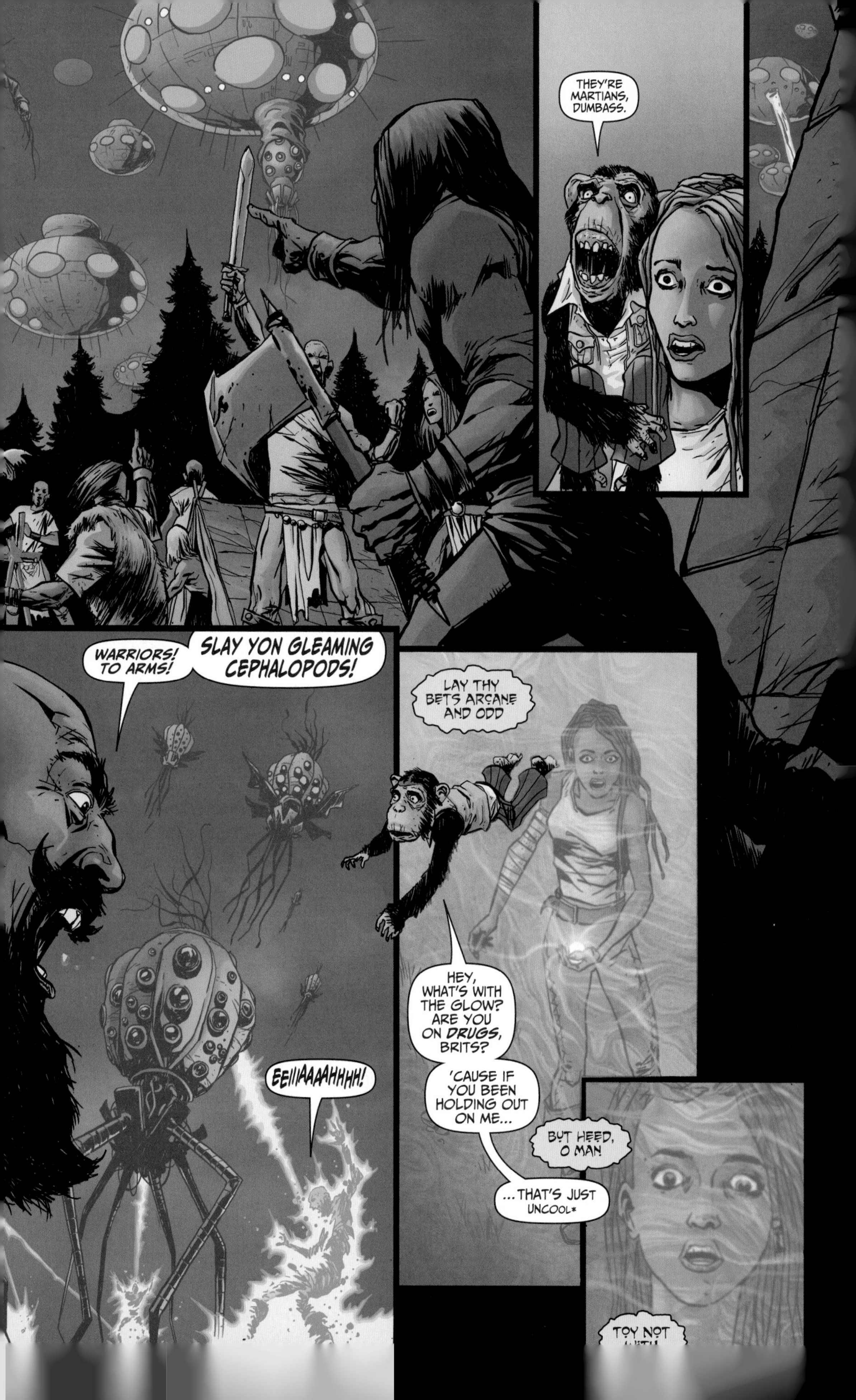
THEY'RE MARTIANS, DUMBASS.
WARRIORS! TO ARMS!
SLAY YON GLEAMING CEPHALOPODS!
EEIIIAAAAHHHH!
LAY THY BETS ARCANE AND ODD
HEY, WHAT'S WITH THE GLOW? ARE YOU ON *DRUGS*, BRITS?
'CAUSE IF YOU BEEN HOLDING OUT ON ME...
...THAT'S JUST UNCOOL*
BUT HEED, O MAN
TOY NOT

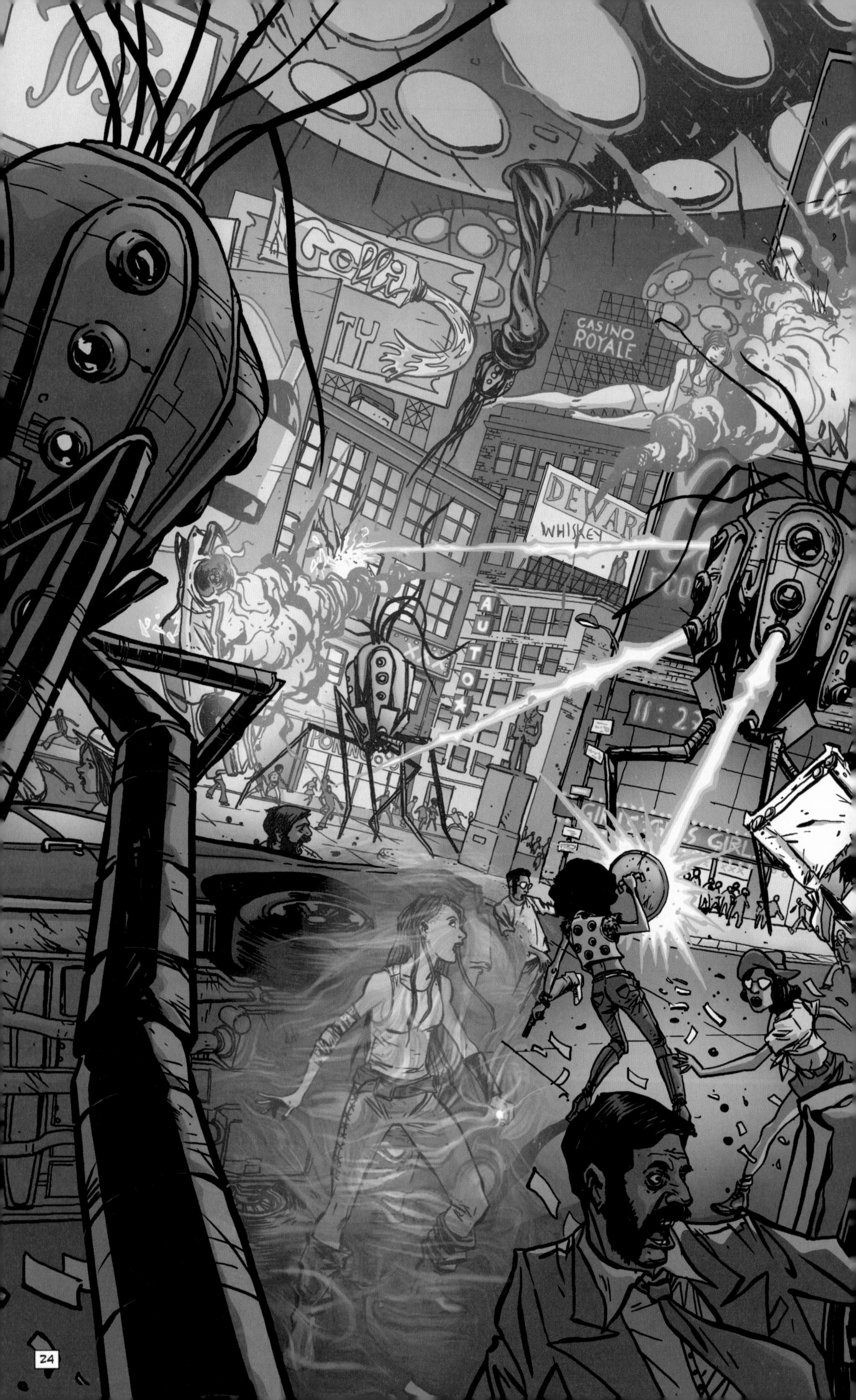
CASINO ROYALE
DEWAR
WHISKEY
AUTO

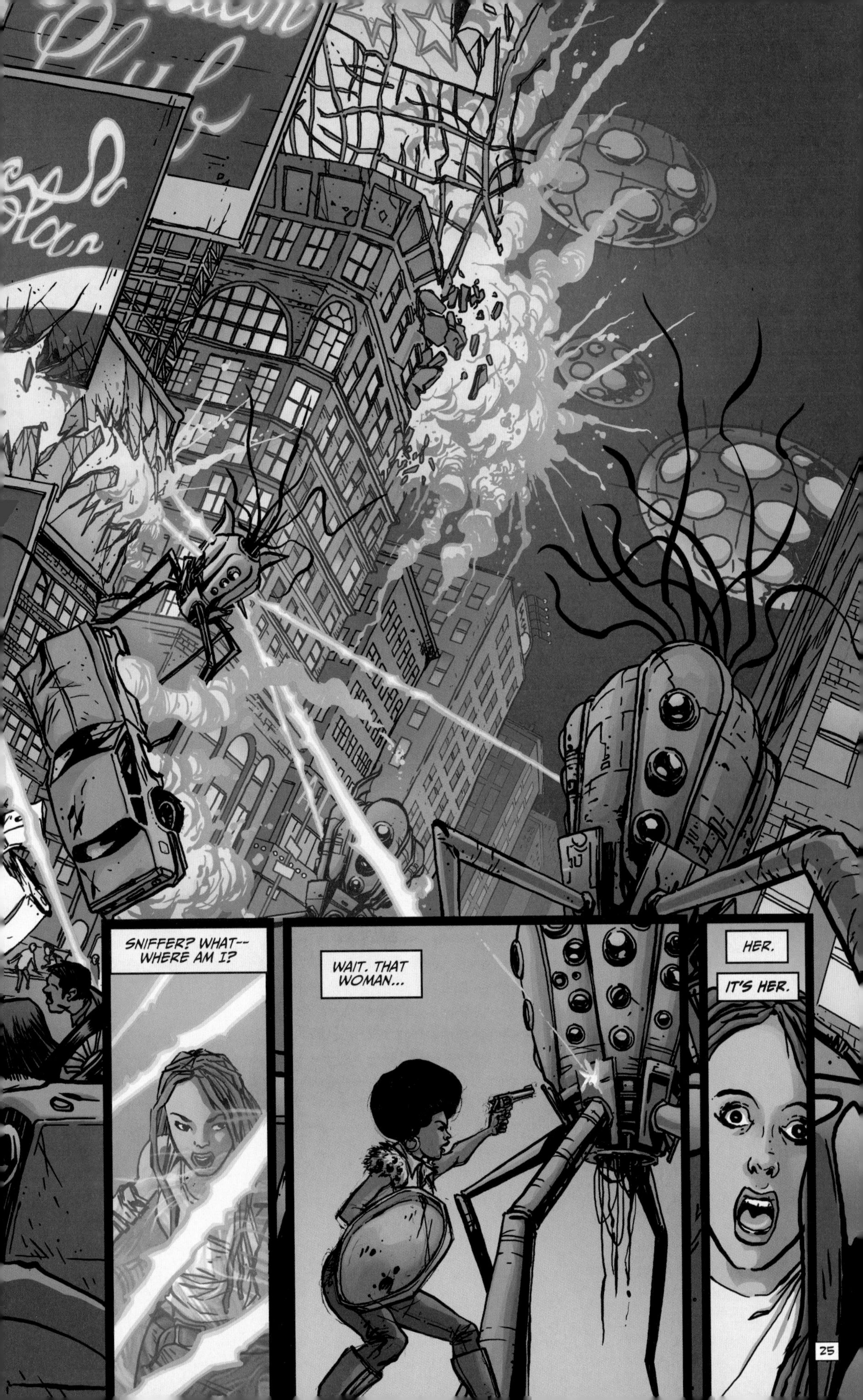
SNIFFER? WHAT--
WHERE AM I?
WAIT. THAT
WOMAN...
HER.
IT'S HER.

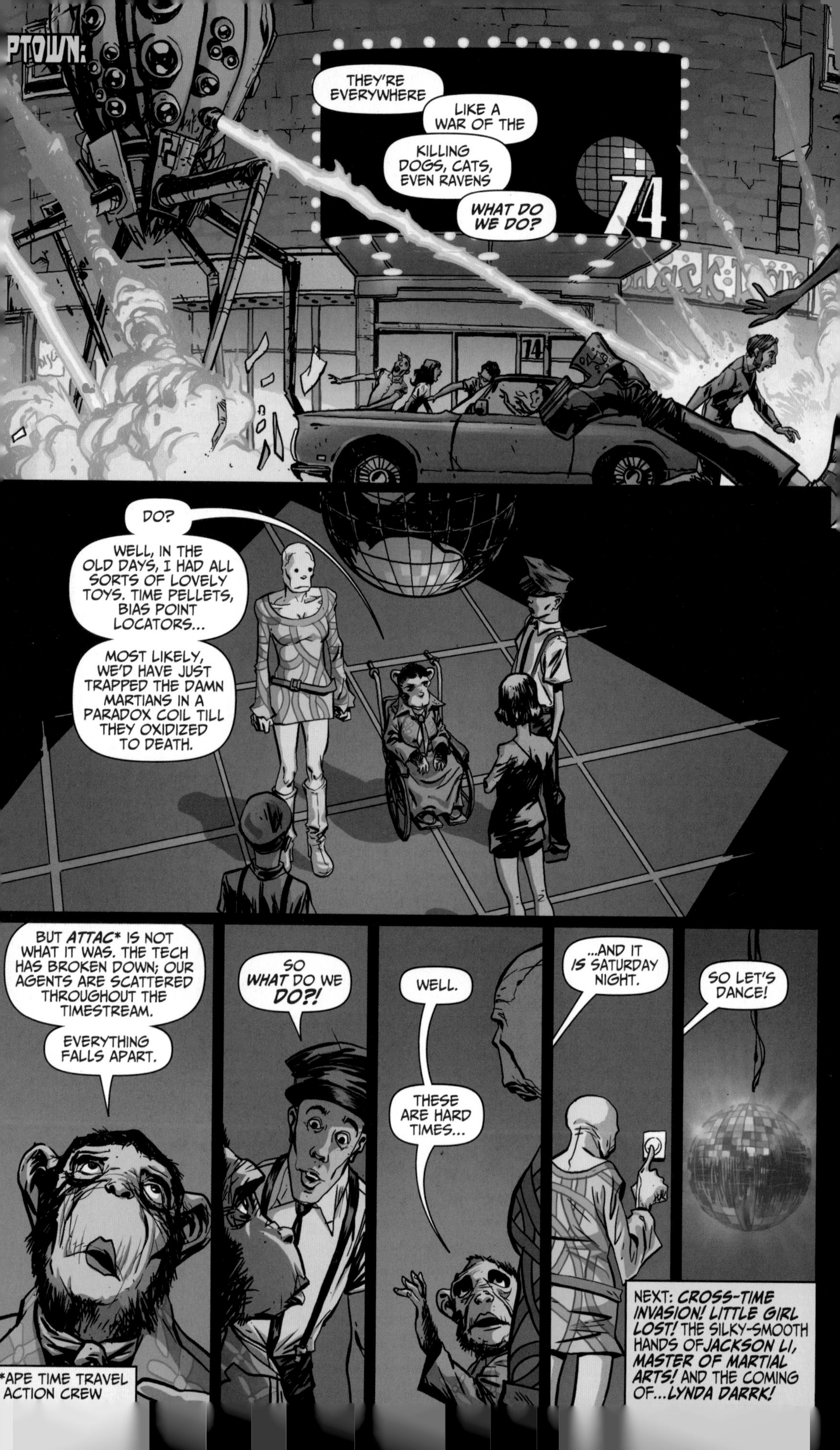
PTOWN:
THEY'RE EVERYWHERE
LIKE A WAR OF THE
KILLING DOGS, CATS, EVEN RAVENS
WHAT DO WE DO?
74
74
DO?
WELL, IN THE OLD DAYS, I HAD ALL SORTS OF LOVELY TOYS. TIME PELLETS, BIAS POINT LOCATORS...
MOST LIKELY, WE'D HAVE JUST TRAPPED THE DAMN MARTIANS IN A PARADOX COIL TILL THEY OXIDIZED TO DEATH.
BUT ATTAC* IS NOT WHAT IT WAS. THE TECH HAS BROKEN DOWN; OUR AGENTS ARE SCATTERED THROUGHOUT THE TIMESTREAM.
EVERYTHING FALLS APART.
*APE TIME TRAVEL ACTION CREW
SO WHAT DO WE DO?!
WELL.
THESE ARE HARD TIMES...
...AND IT IS SATURDAY NIGHT.
SO LET'S DANCE!
NEXT: CROSS-TIME INVASION! LITTLE GIRL LOST! THE SILKY-SMOOTH HANDS OFJACKSON LI, MASTER OF MARTIAL ARTS! AND THE COMING OF...LYNDA DARRK!

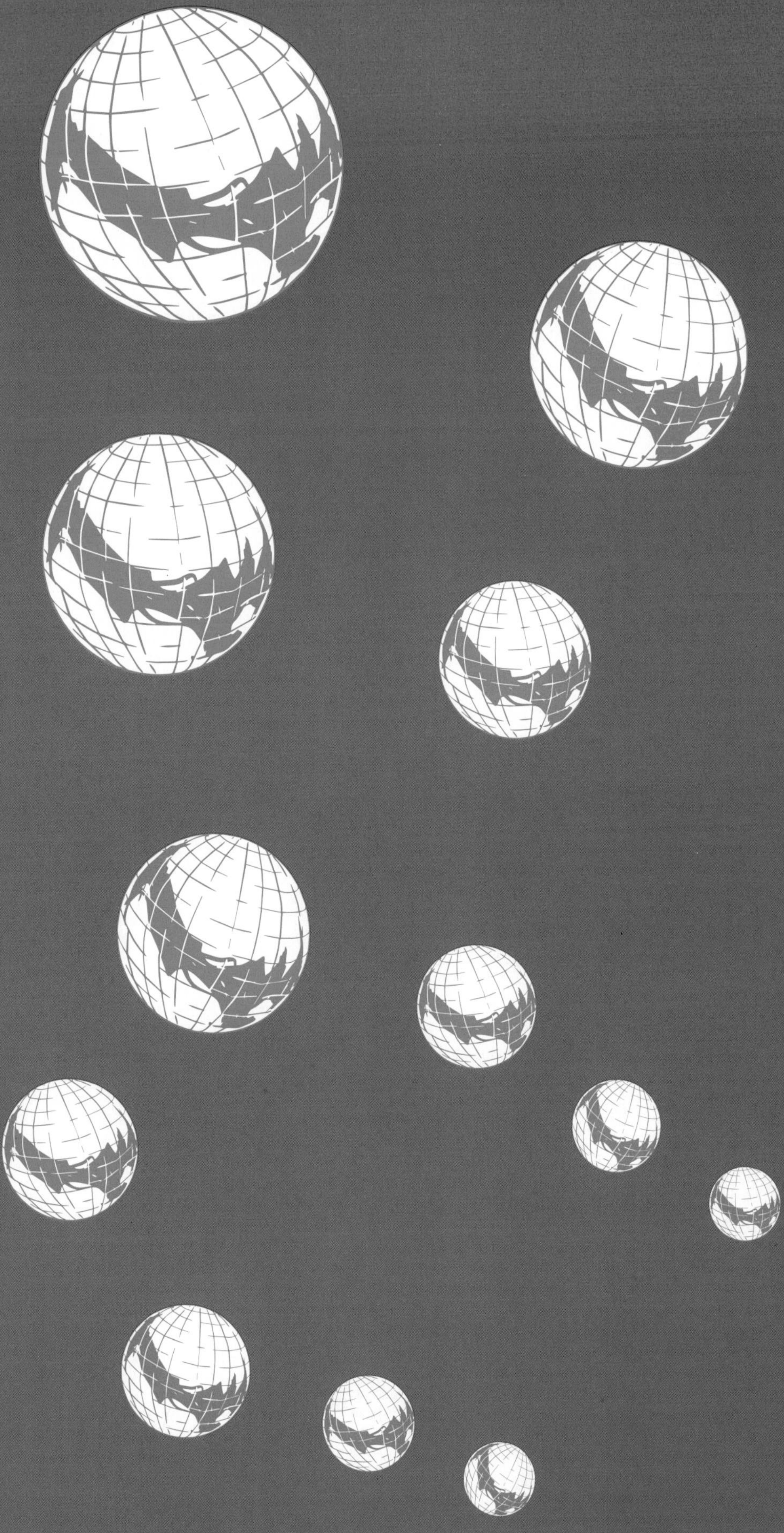

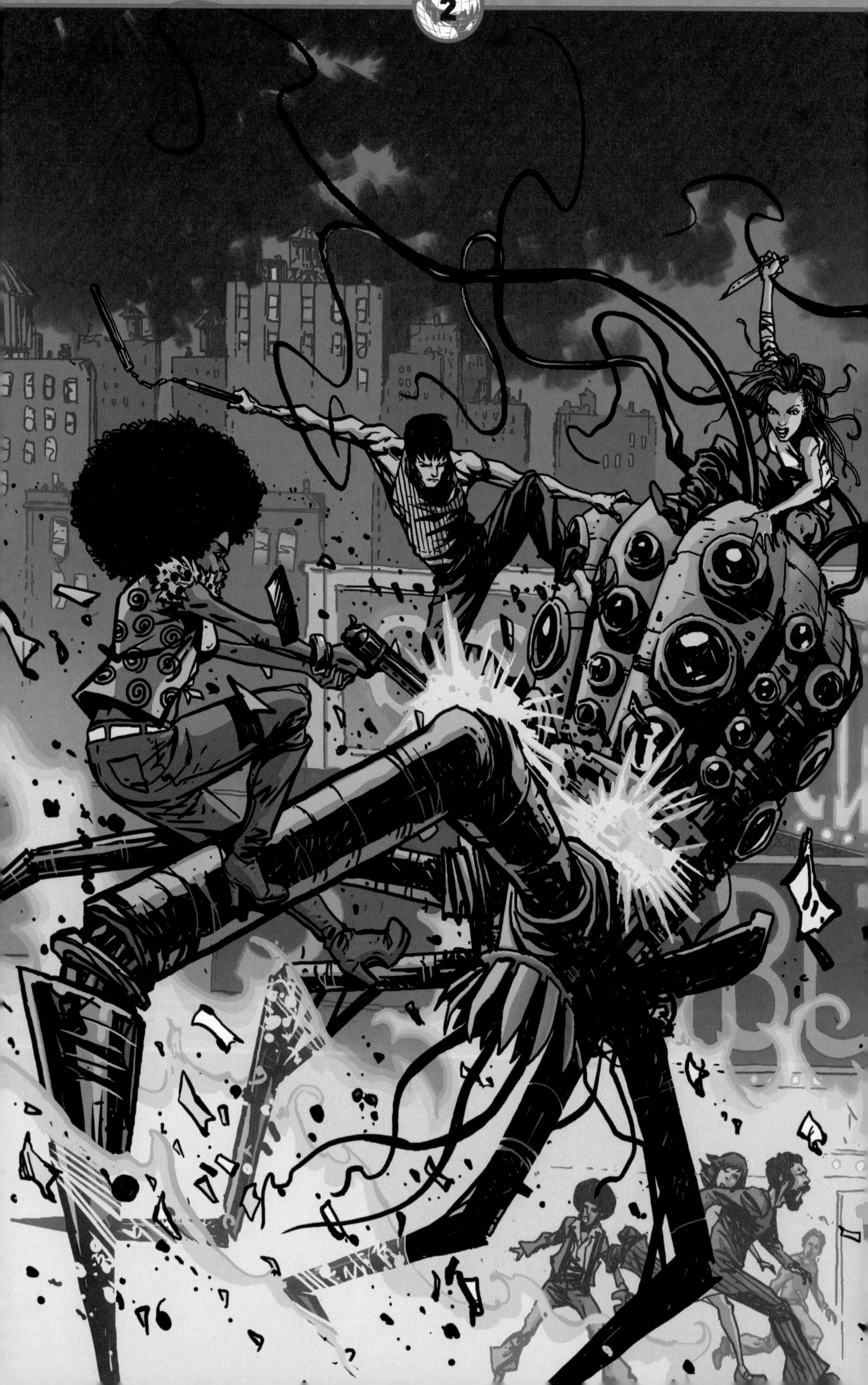

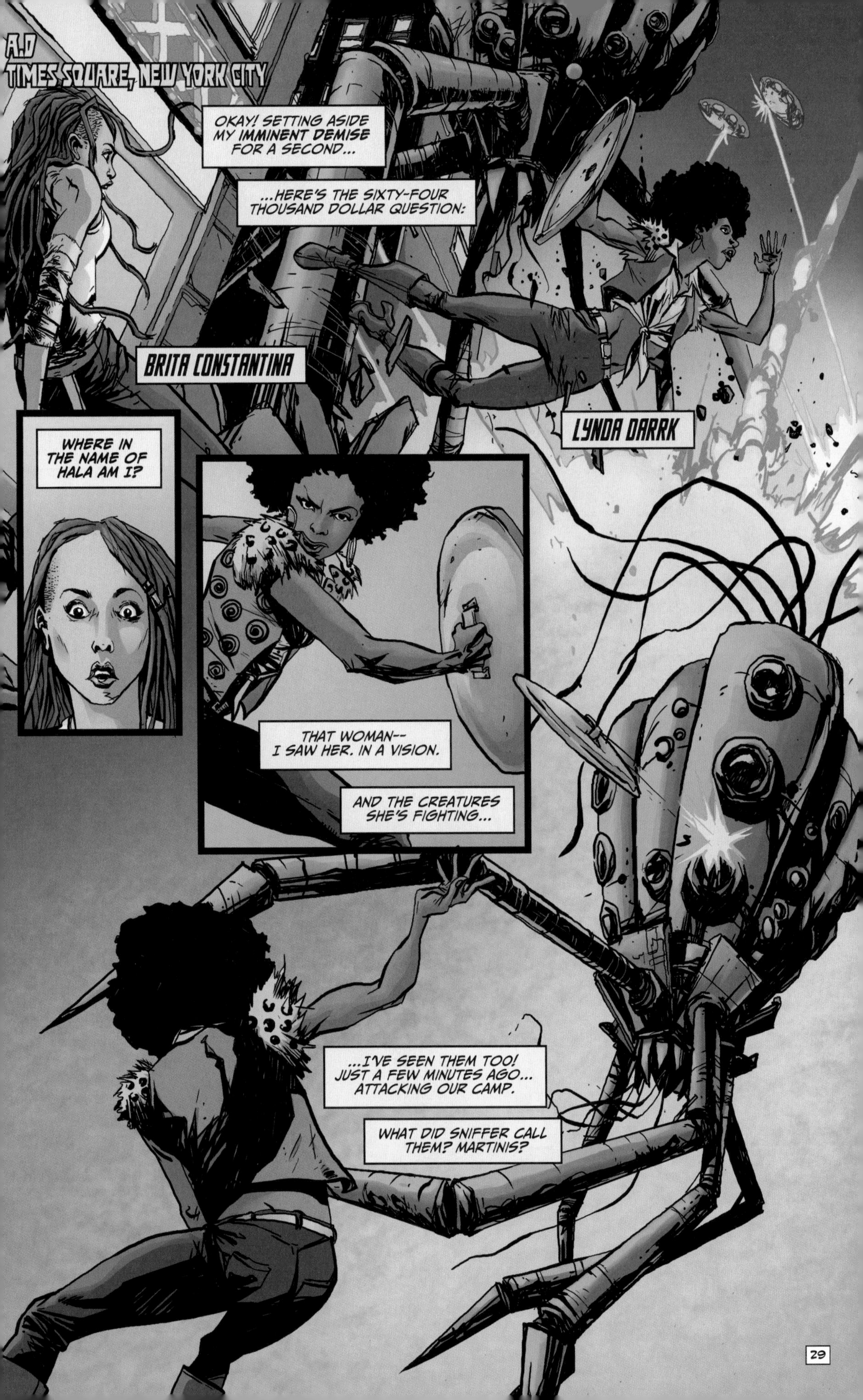
A.D
TIMES SQUARE, NEW YORK CITY
OKAY! SETTING ASIDE MY IMMINENT DEMISE FOR A SECOND...
...HERE'S THE SIXTY-FOUR THOUSAND DOLLAR QUESTION:
BRITA CONSTANTINA
LYNDA DARRK
WHERE IN THE NAME OF HALA AM I?
THAT WOMAN-- I SAW HER. IN A VISION.
AND THE CREATURES SHE'S FIGHTING...
...I'VE SEEN THEM TOO! JUST A FEW MINUTES AGO... ATTACKING OUR CAMP.
WHAT DID SNIFFER CALL THEM? MARTINIS?

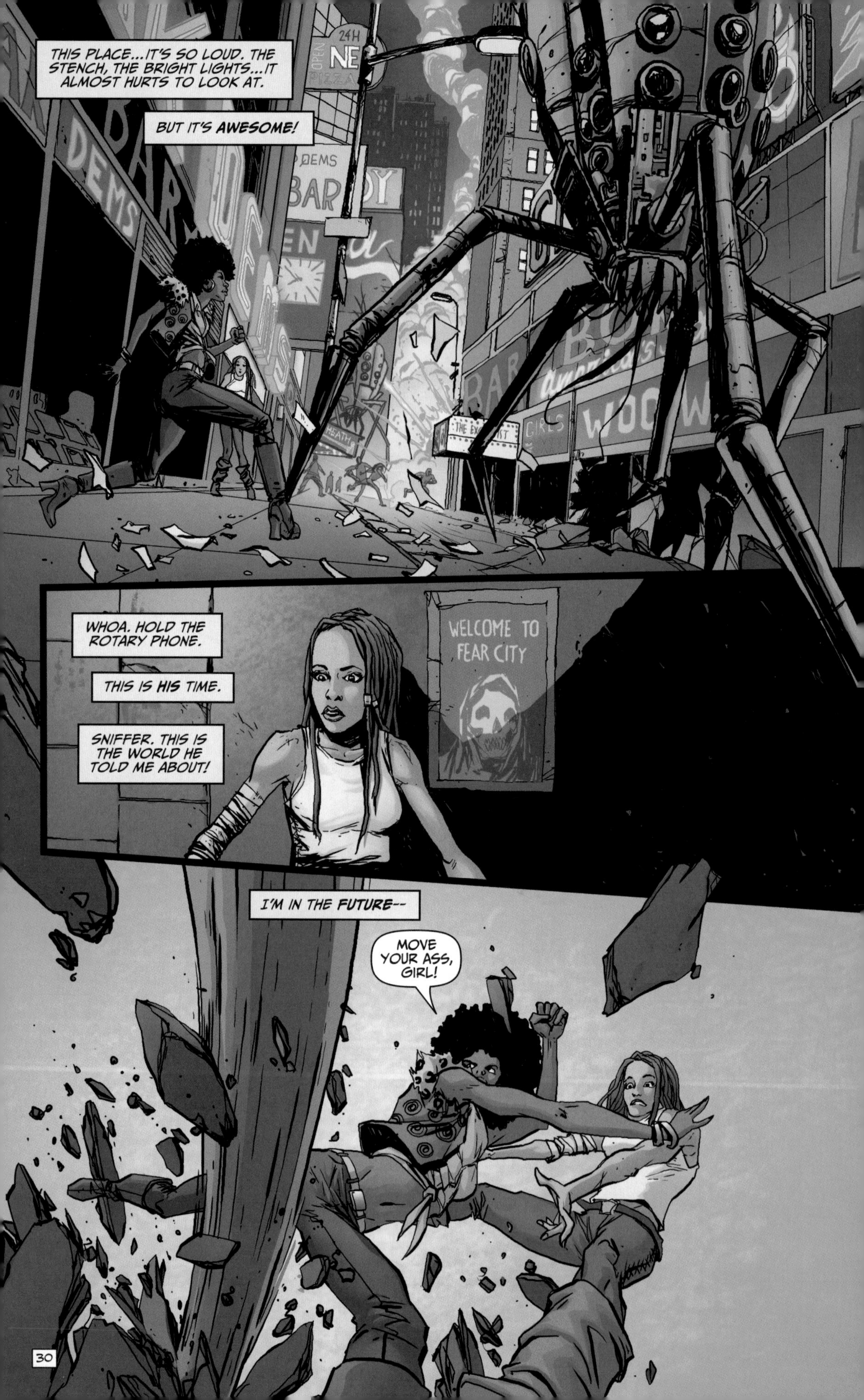
THIS PLACE...IT'S SO LOUD. THE STENCH, THE BRIGHT LIGHTS...IT ALMOST HURTS TO LOOK AT.
BUT IT'S AWESOME!
WHOA. HOLD THE ROTARY PHONE.
THIS IS HIS TIME.
SNIFFER. THIS IS THE WORLD HE TOLD ME ABOUT!
WELCOME TO FEAR CITY
I'M IN THE FUTURE--
MOVE YOUR ASS, GIRL!

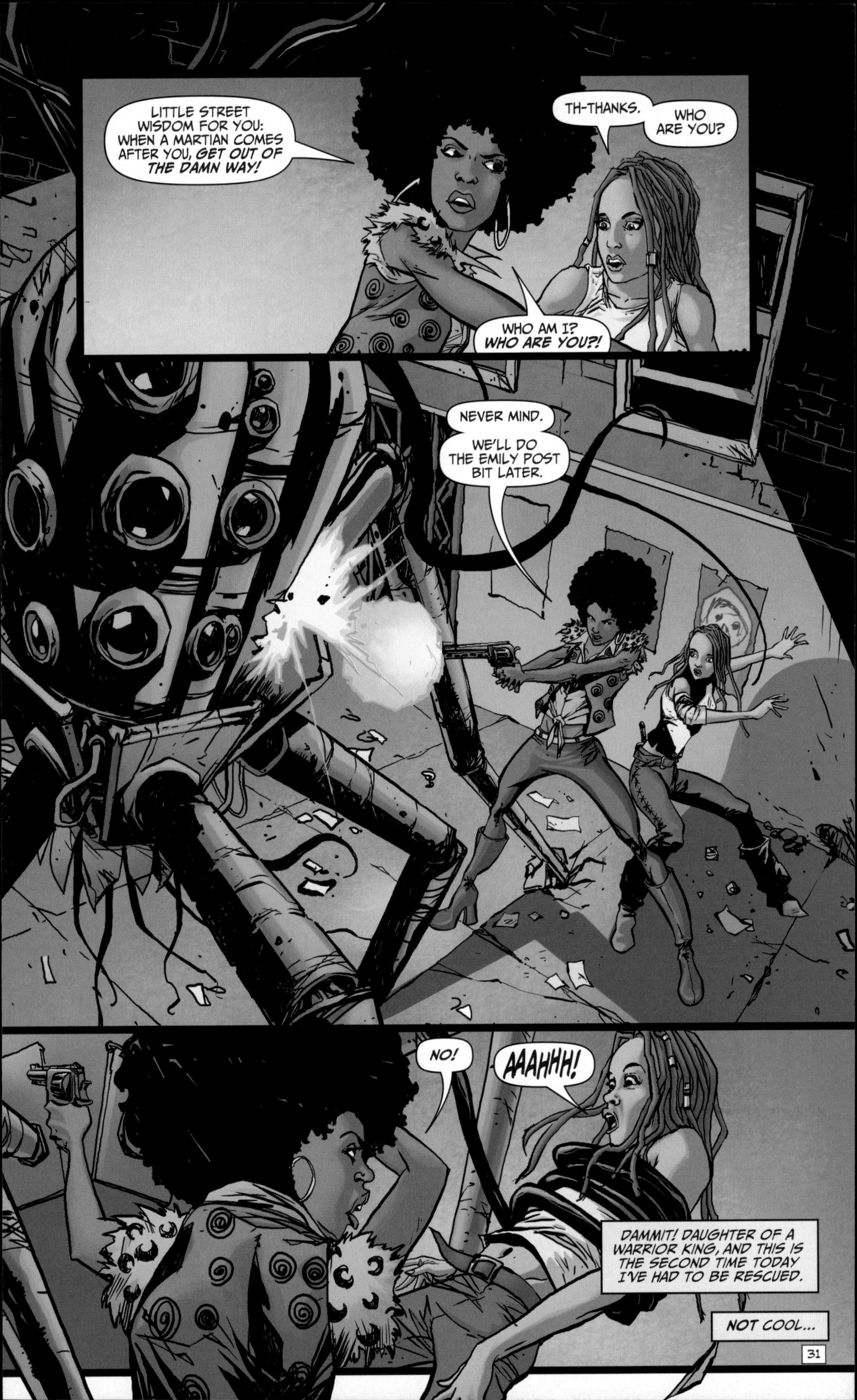
LITTLE STREET WISDOM FOR YOU: WHEN A MARTIAN COMES AFTER YOU, GET OUT OF THE DAMN WAY!
TH-THANKS.
WHO ARE YOU?
WHO AM I? WHO ARE YOU?!
NEVER MIND.
WE'LL DO THE EMILY POST BIT LATER.
NO!
AAAHHH!
DAMMIT! DAUGHTER OF A WARRIOR KING, AND THIS IS THE SECOND TIME TODAY I'VE HAD TO BE RESCUED.
NOT COOL...

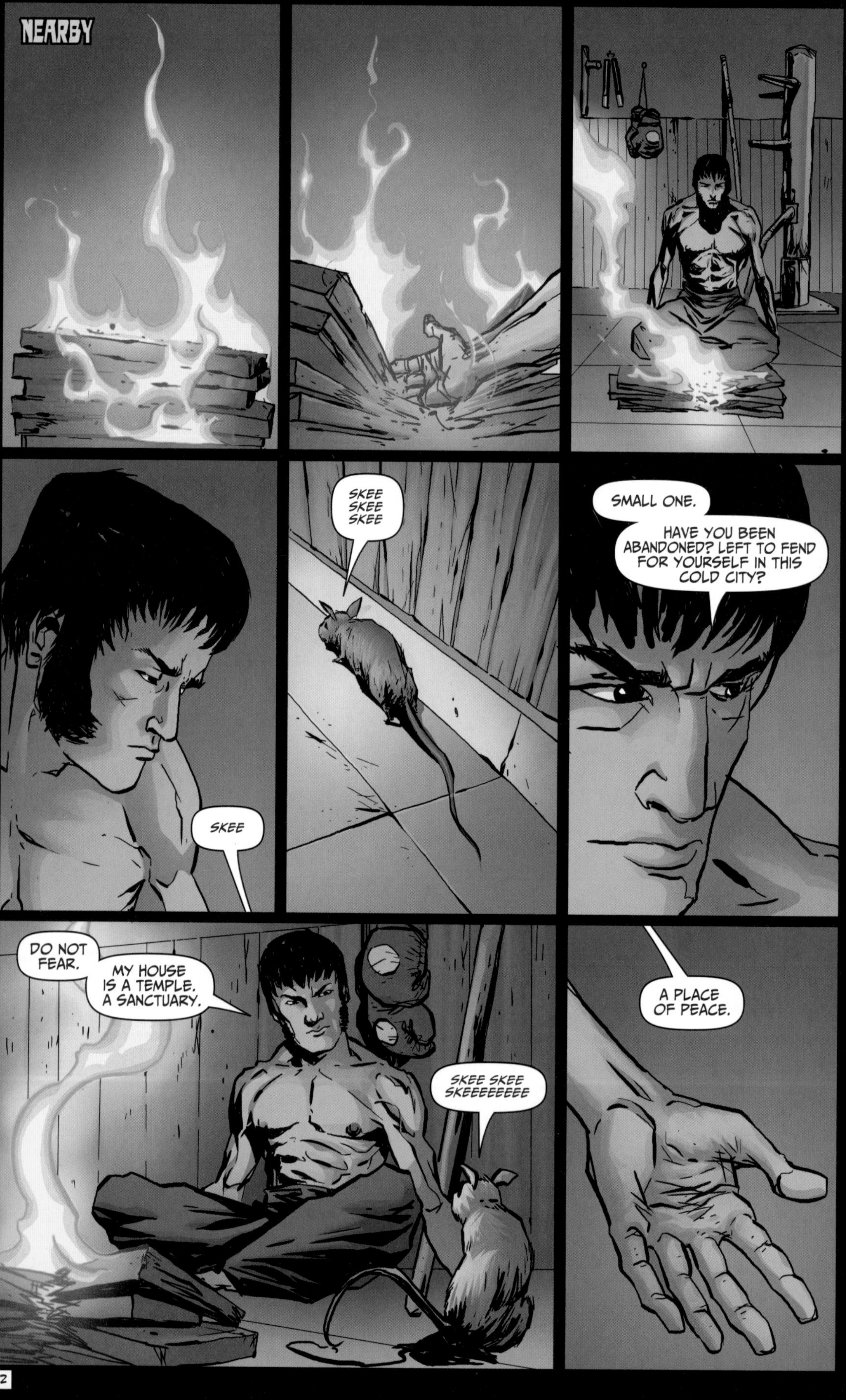
NEARBY
SKEE
SKEE
SKEE
SKEE
SMALL ONE.
HAVE YOU BEEN ABANDONED? LEFT TO FEND FOR YOURSELF IN THIS COLD CITY?
DO NOT FEAR.
MY HOUSE IS A TEMPLE. A SANCTUARY.
SKEE SKEE SKEEEEEEEE
A PLACE OF PEACE.

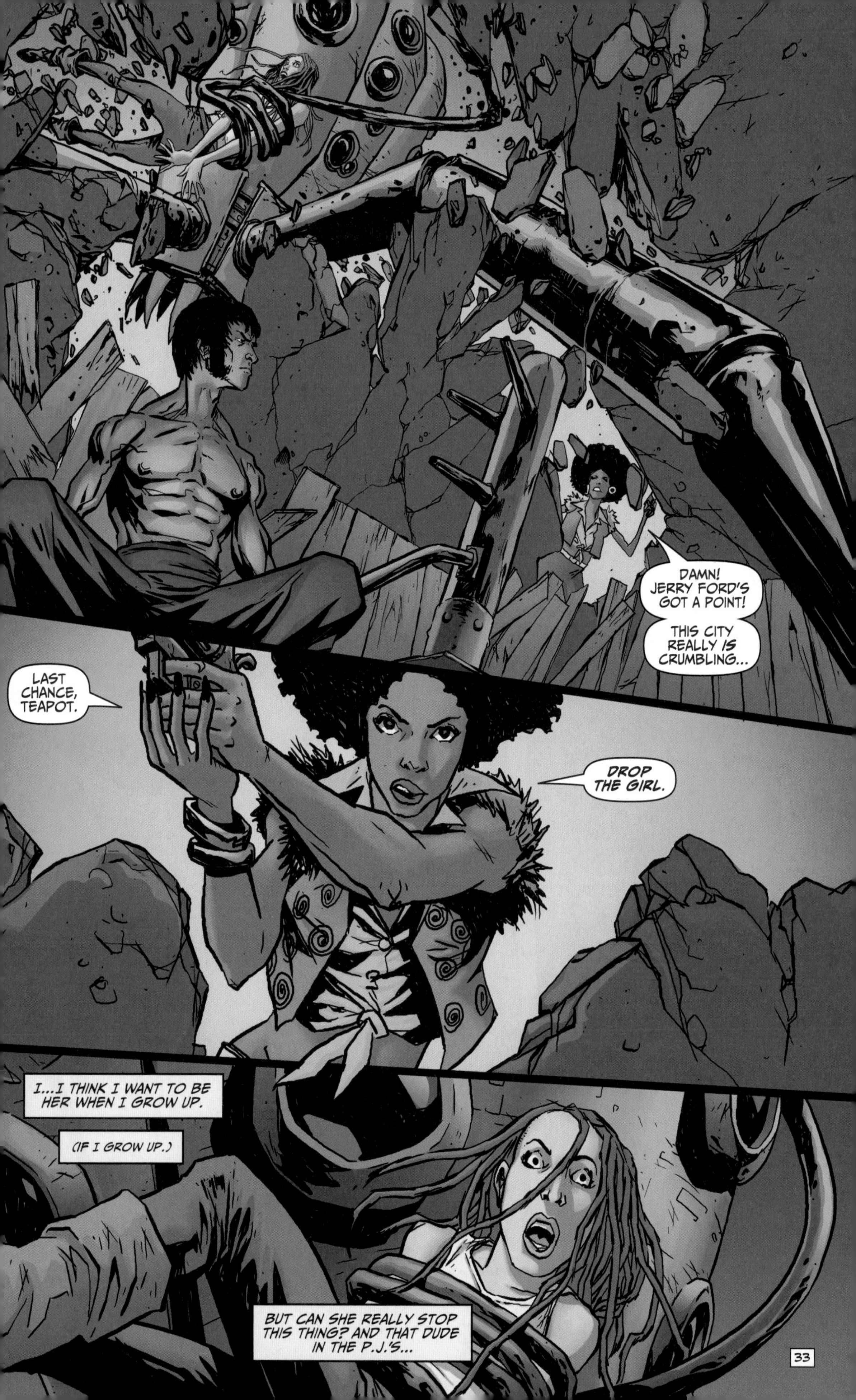
DAMN! JERRY FORD'S GOT A POINT!
THIS CITY REALLY *IS* CRUMBLING...
LAST CHANCE, TEAPOT.
DROP THE GIRL.
I...I THINK I WANT TO BE HER WHEN I GROW UP.
(IF I GROW UP.)
BUT CAN SHE REALLY STOP THIS THING? AND THAT DUDE IN THE P.J.'S...

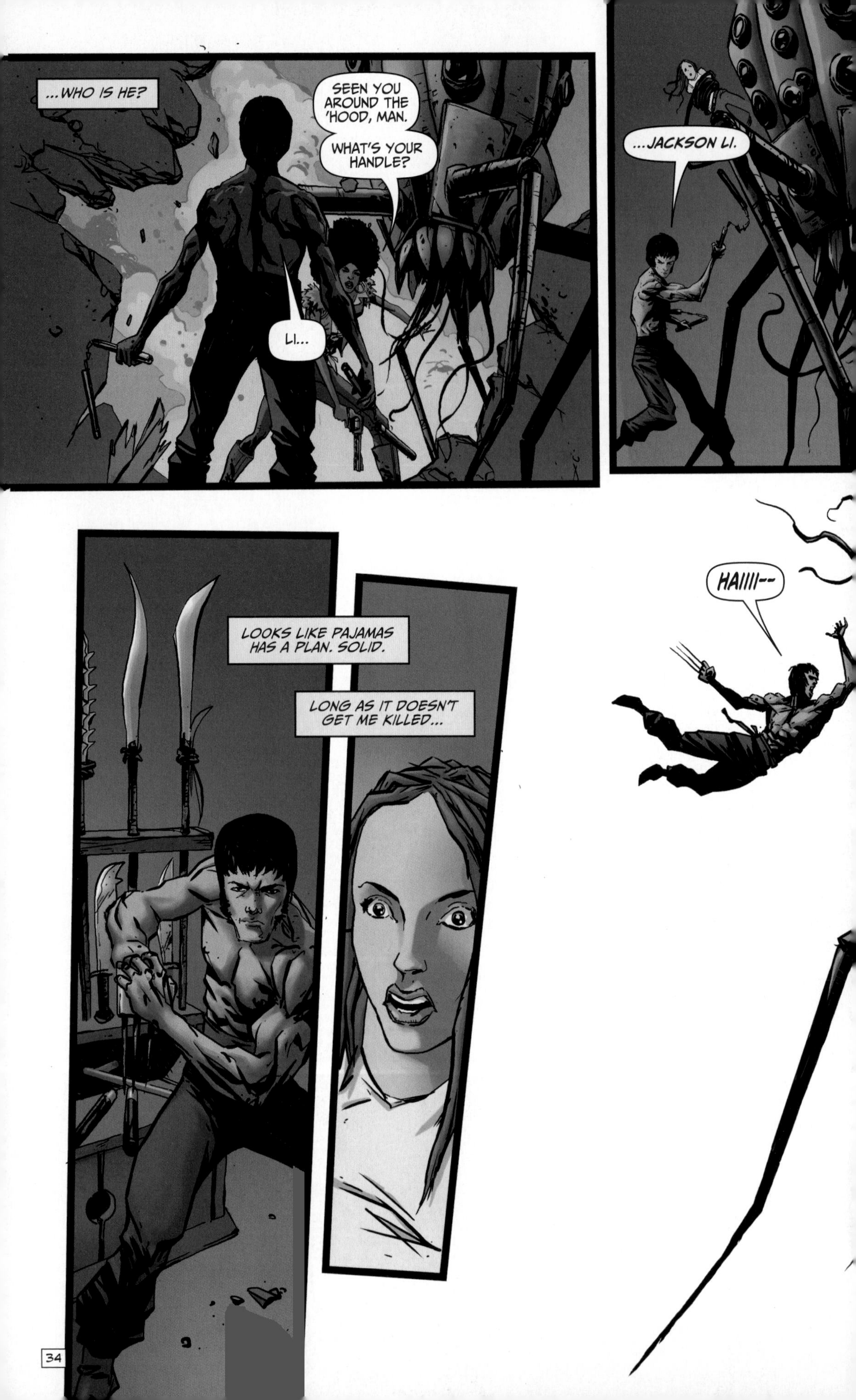
...WHO IS HE?
SEEN YOU AROUND THE 'HOOD, MAN.
WHAT'S YOUR HANDLE?
LI...
...JACKSON LI.
LOOKS LIKE PAJAMAS HAS A PLAN. SOLID.
LONG AS IT DOESN'T GET ME KILLED...
HAIIII--

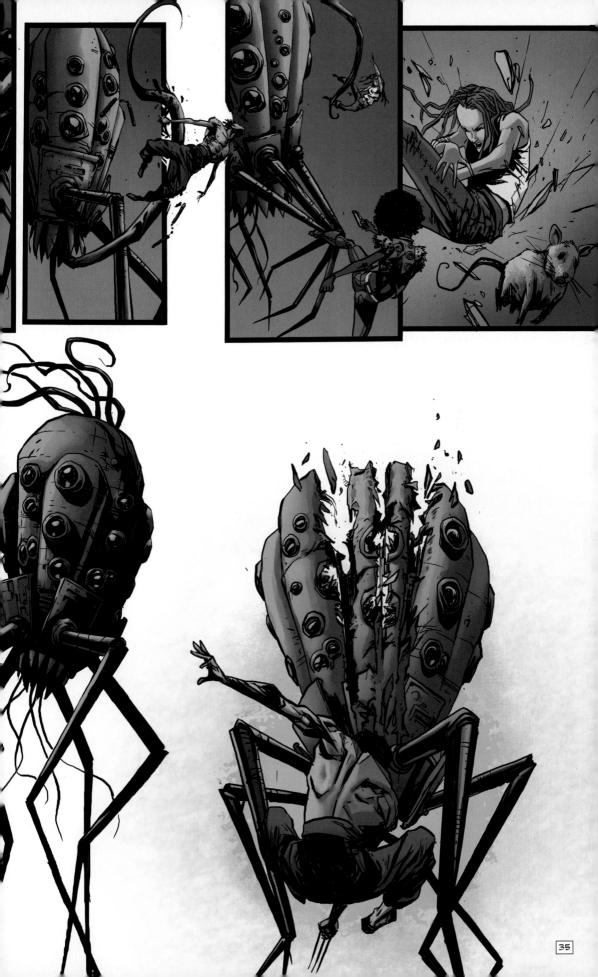

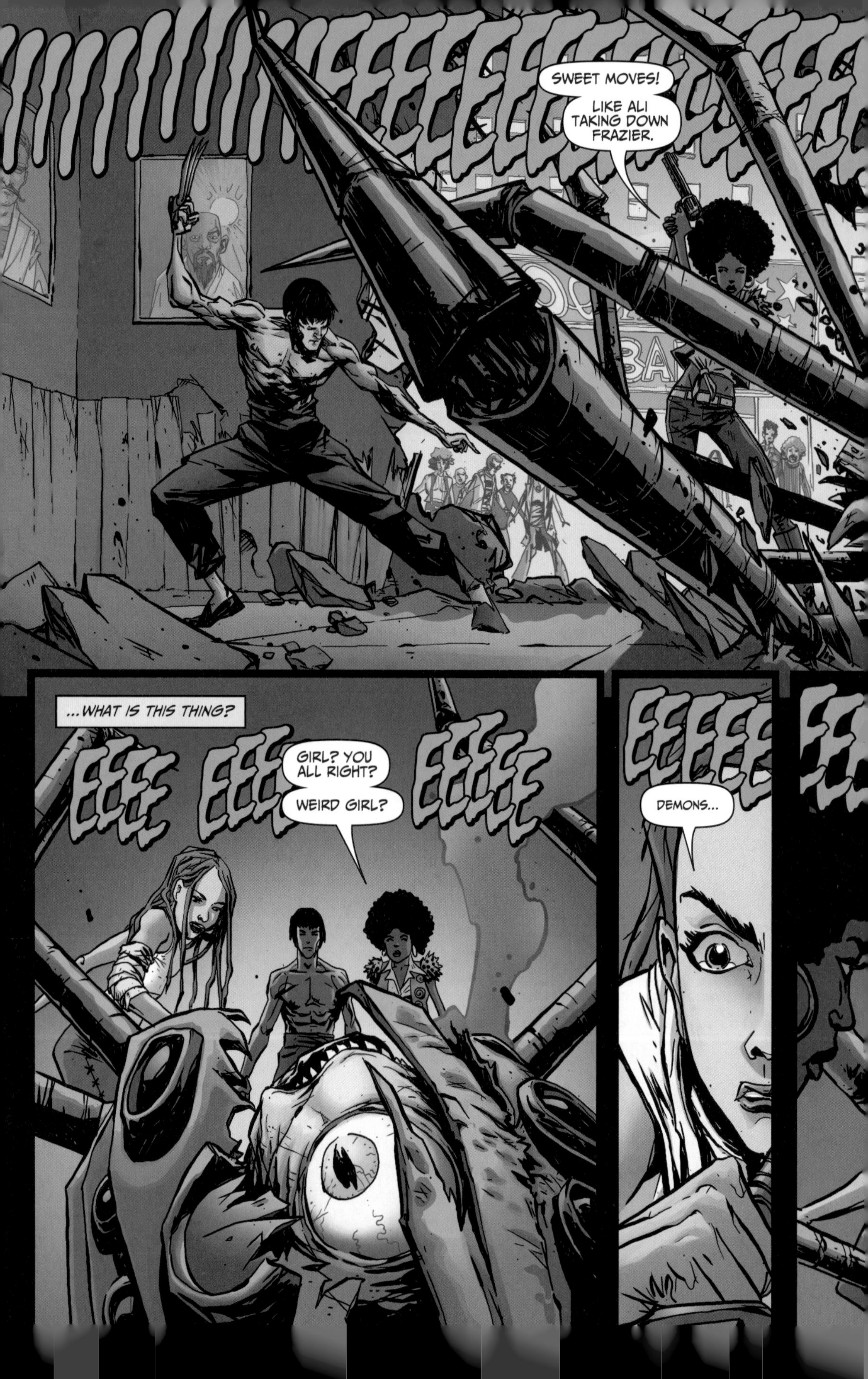
IIIIIIIIIIIEEEEEEEEEEEEEEEEEEEEE
SWEET MOVES!
LIKE ALI TAKING DOWN FRAZIER.
...WHAT IS THIS THING?
EEEE EEEE EEEEE
GIRL? YOU ALL RIGHT?
WEIRD GIRL?
EEEEE EEE
DEMONS...

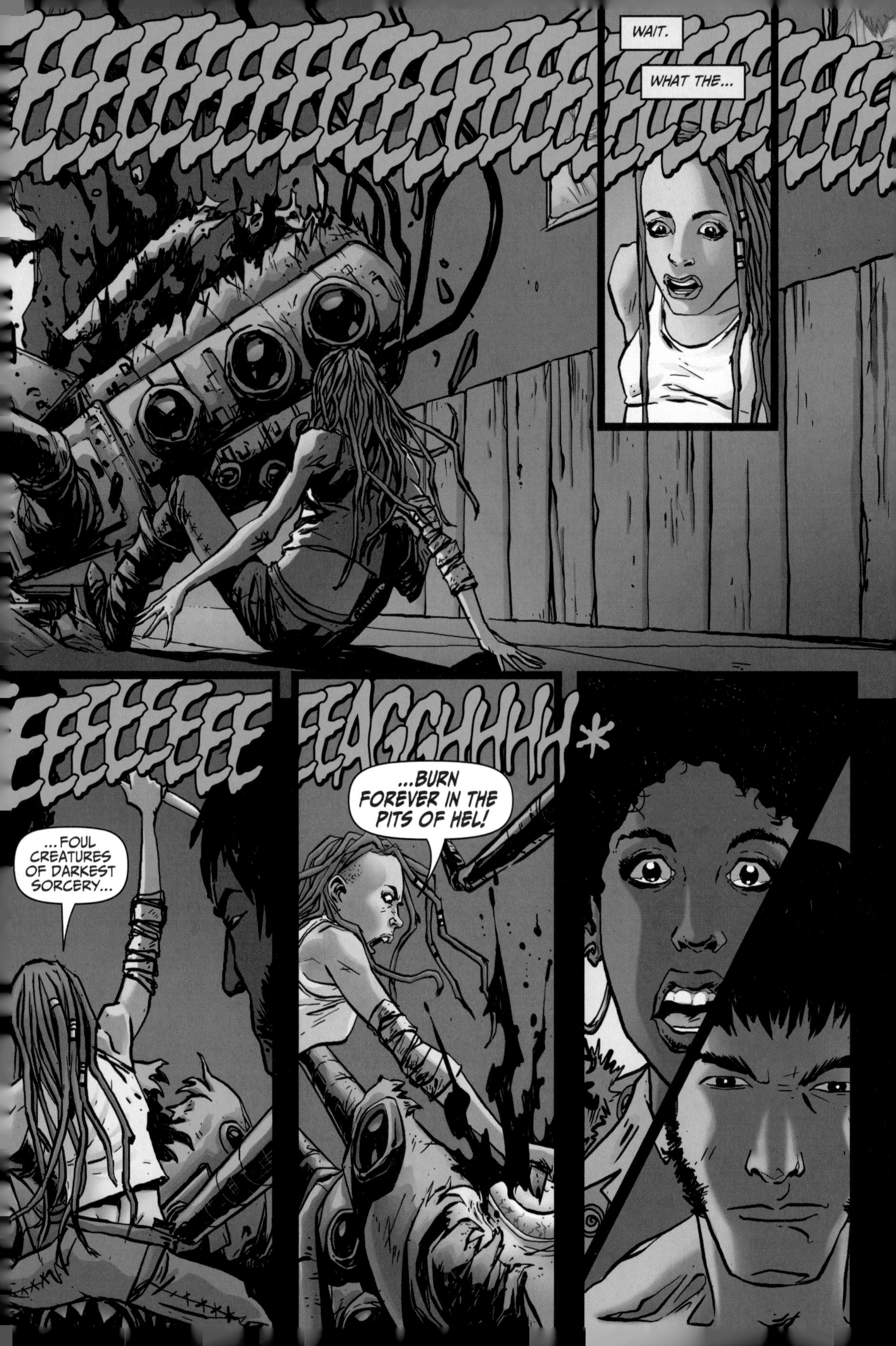

EEEEEEEEEEEEEEEEEEEE
WAIT.
WHAT THE...
EEEEEEEE
EEAGCHHHH*
...FOUL CREATURES OF DARKEST SORCERY...
...BURN FOREVER IN THE PITS OF HEL!

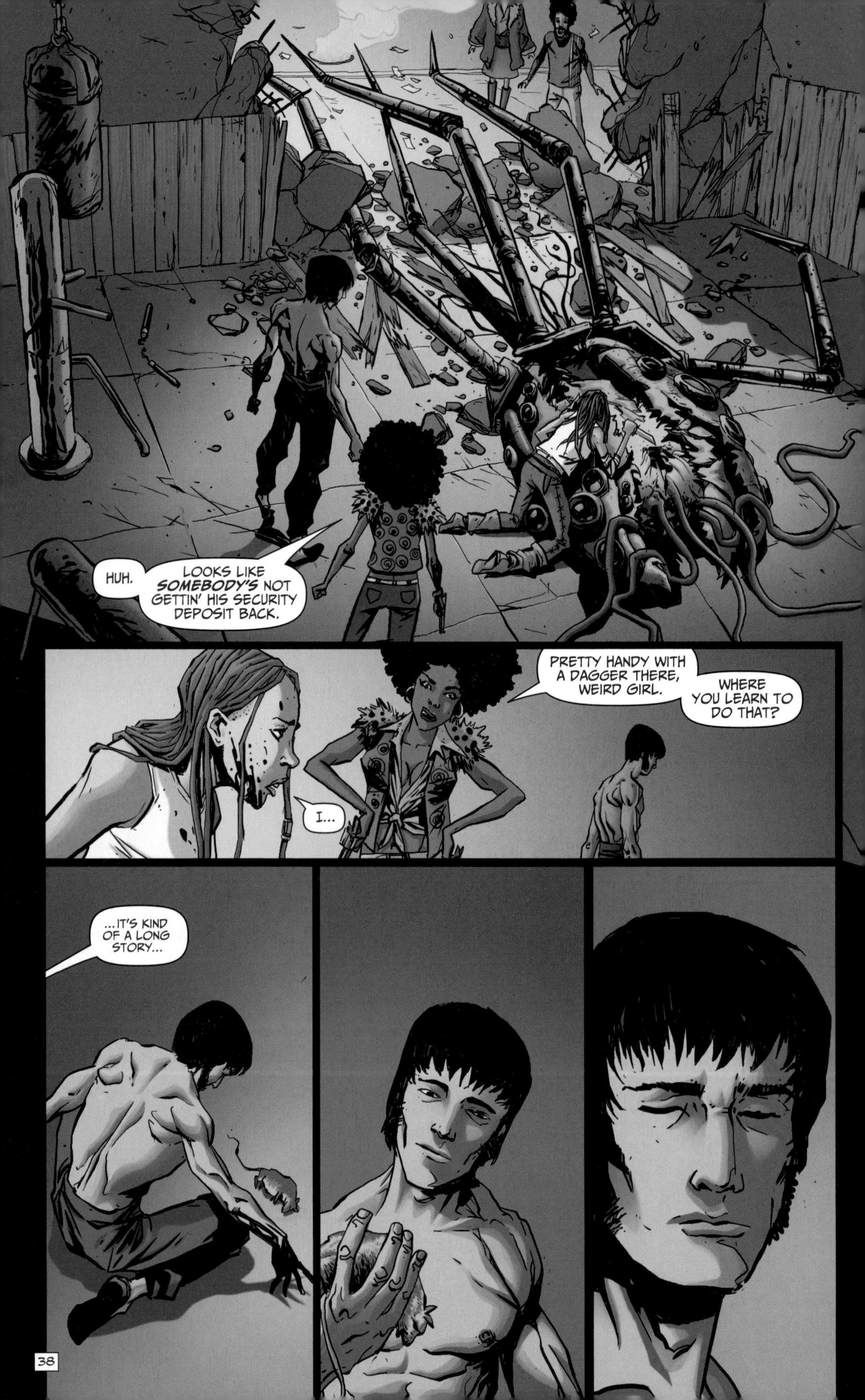
HUH.
LOOKS LIKE SOMEBODY'S NOT GETTIN' HIS SECURITY DEPOSIT BACK.
PRETTY HANDY WITH A DAGGER THERE, WEIRD GIRL.
WHERE YOU LEARN TO DO THAT?
I...
...IT'S KIND OF A LONG STORY...

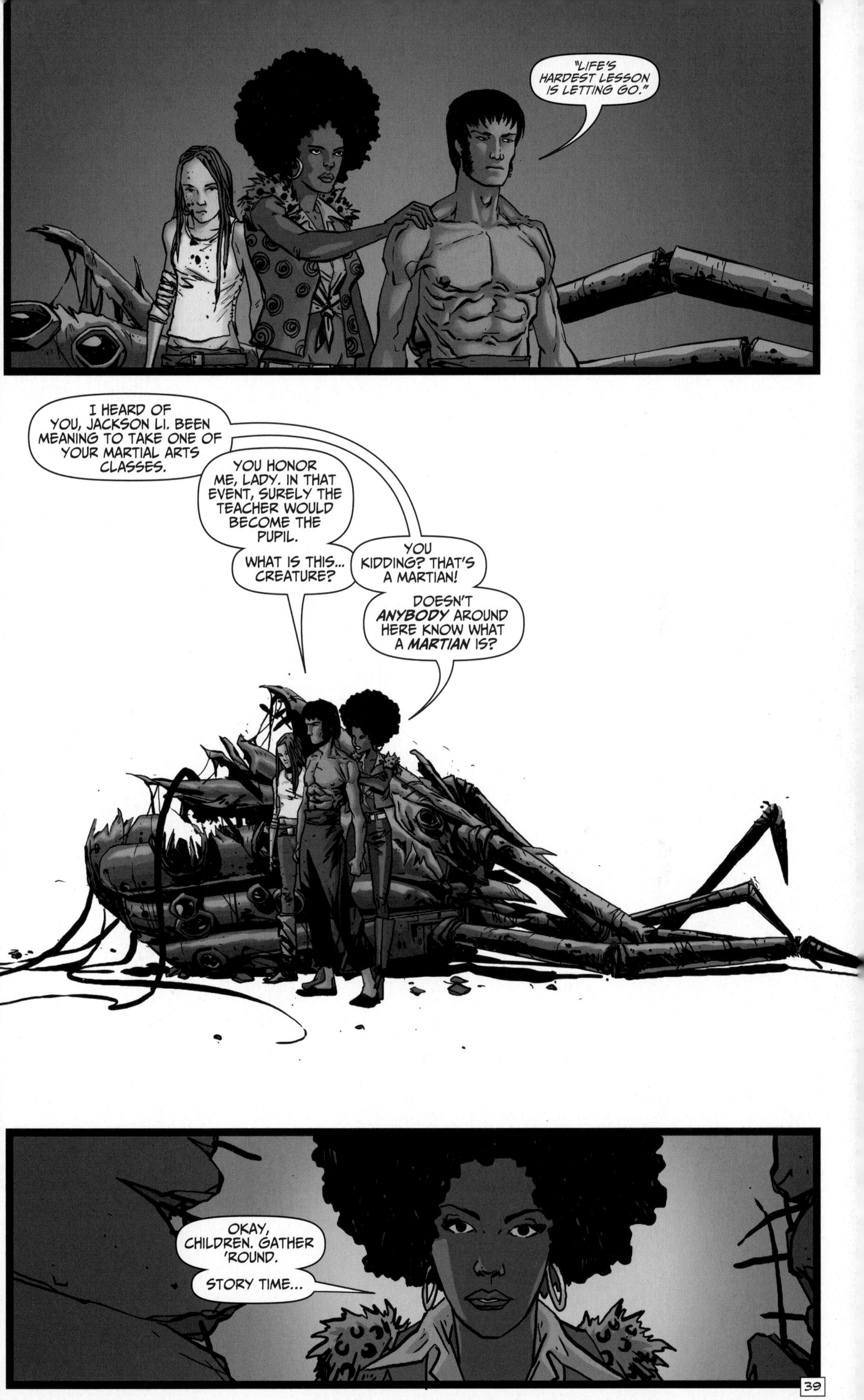
"LIFE'S HARDEST LESSON IS LETTING GO."
I HEARD OF YOU, JACKSON LI. BEEN MEANING TO TAKE ONE OF YOUR MARTIAL ARTS CLASSES.
YOU HONOR ME, LADY. IN THAT EVENT, SURELY THE TEACHER WOULD BECOME THE PUPIL.
WHAT IS THIS... CREATURE?
YOU KIDDING? THAT'S A MARTIAN!
DOESN'T *ANYBODY* AROUND HERE KNOW WHAT A *MARTIAN* IS?
OKAY, CHILDREN. GATHER 'ROUND.
STORY TIME...

Lynda Darrk plants herself down on the cracked floor, brushing away bits of debris. Jackson Li folds his muscular legs and drops down beside her. The girl—the weird girl in the animal-skin clothes—follows reluctantly, crouching on her knees like a cat.

Lynda closes her eyes for a moment. She breathes in the smoke of distant fires, the smog of the city—mixed now with the sharp, metallic tang of the invaders.

"Martians been softening us up for a long time," she begins. "Some people say they been at it since the last invasion, eighty years ago…infiltrating the government, screwing with the economy. Causing energy shortages, holes in the ozone layer, stagflation.

"I don't know much about that. I do know that last week, they showed up live and in person. A fleet of saucers, just—"

"Blanketing the sky," the girl interrupts.

Lynda gives her a sharp look.

"I saw 'em," the girl continues, glancing at the dead creature behind them. "They invaded my home, too."

Li says nothing. His eyes are sharp dots, flashing from one woman to the other, pausing briefly to study the crushed metal shell of the invader.

"Where *is* your home?" Lynda asks the girl. "Where were you born?"

"On a battlefield." The girl turns away. "Dad says I was ripped from my dying mother's womb."

"That's…intense," Lynda says.

"No, it's *gross!*" The girl looks around, as if suddenly aware of her surroundings. "I love my dad…my people. But I like it a lot better here, Martinis and all."

"Martians," Lynda says.

All at once, a profound exhaustion comes over her. *I'm tired*, she realizes. *Tired of fighting the Martians, tired of trying to save this city. Tired of looking for a piece of myself that just might be gone forever.*

She feels a soft hand on hers. Looks up, startled, to see Li staring into her eyes.

"You must resist despair, Lynda Darrk," he says. "It is the only true foe, the enemy that cannot be vanquished."

She nods. A phrase comes to mind…something her long-lost sister used to say. Her sister with the sharp laugh, the eyes that could light up a room. The reason Lynda came back to New York after so many years away; the missing piece she can never, ever, abandon hope of finding.

"Solid gold, baby," she whispers.

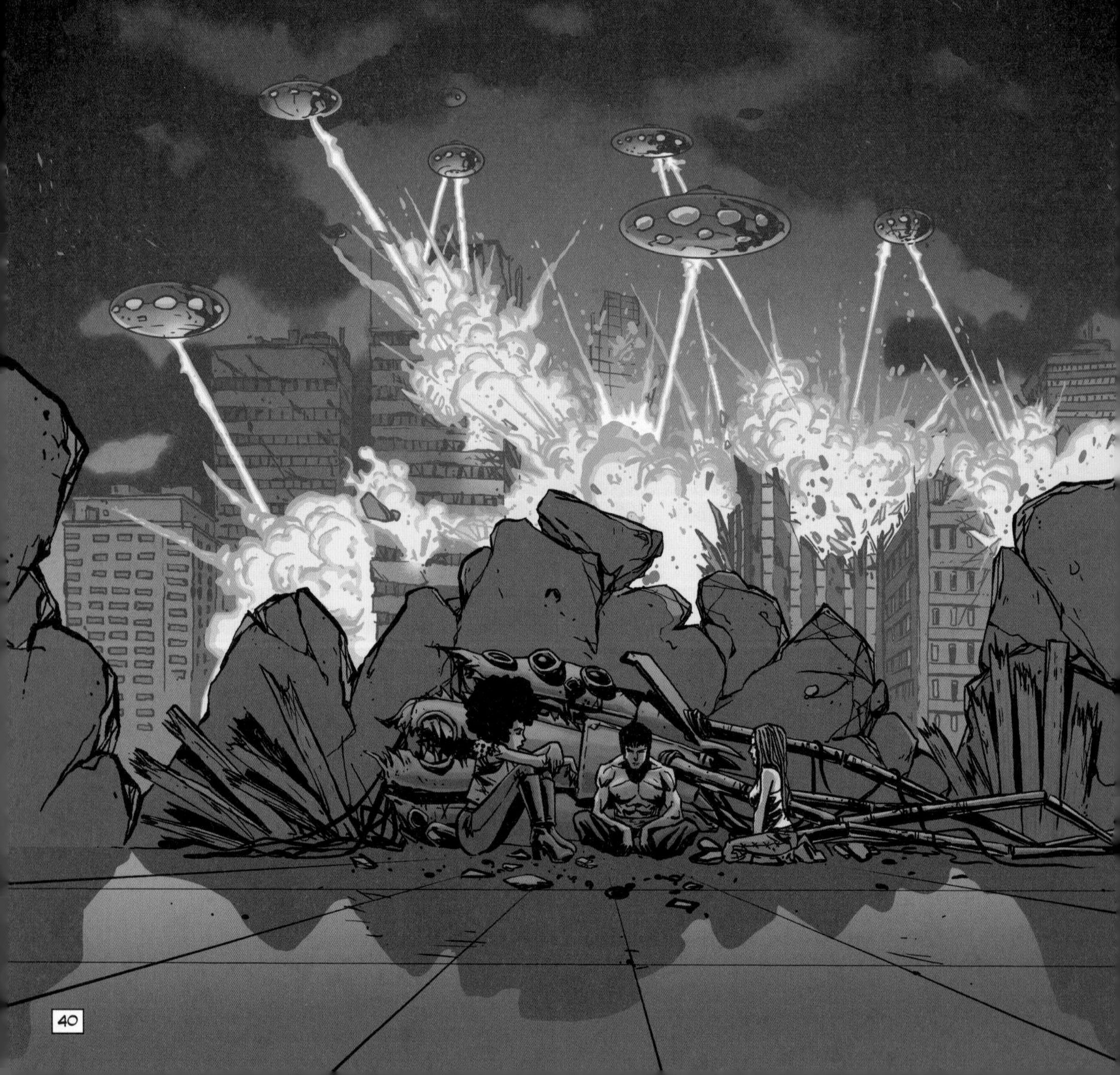

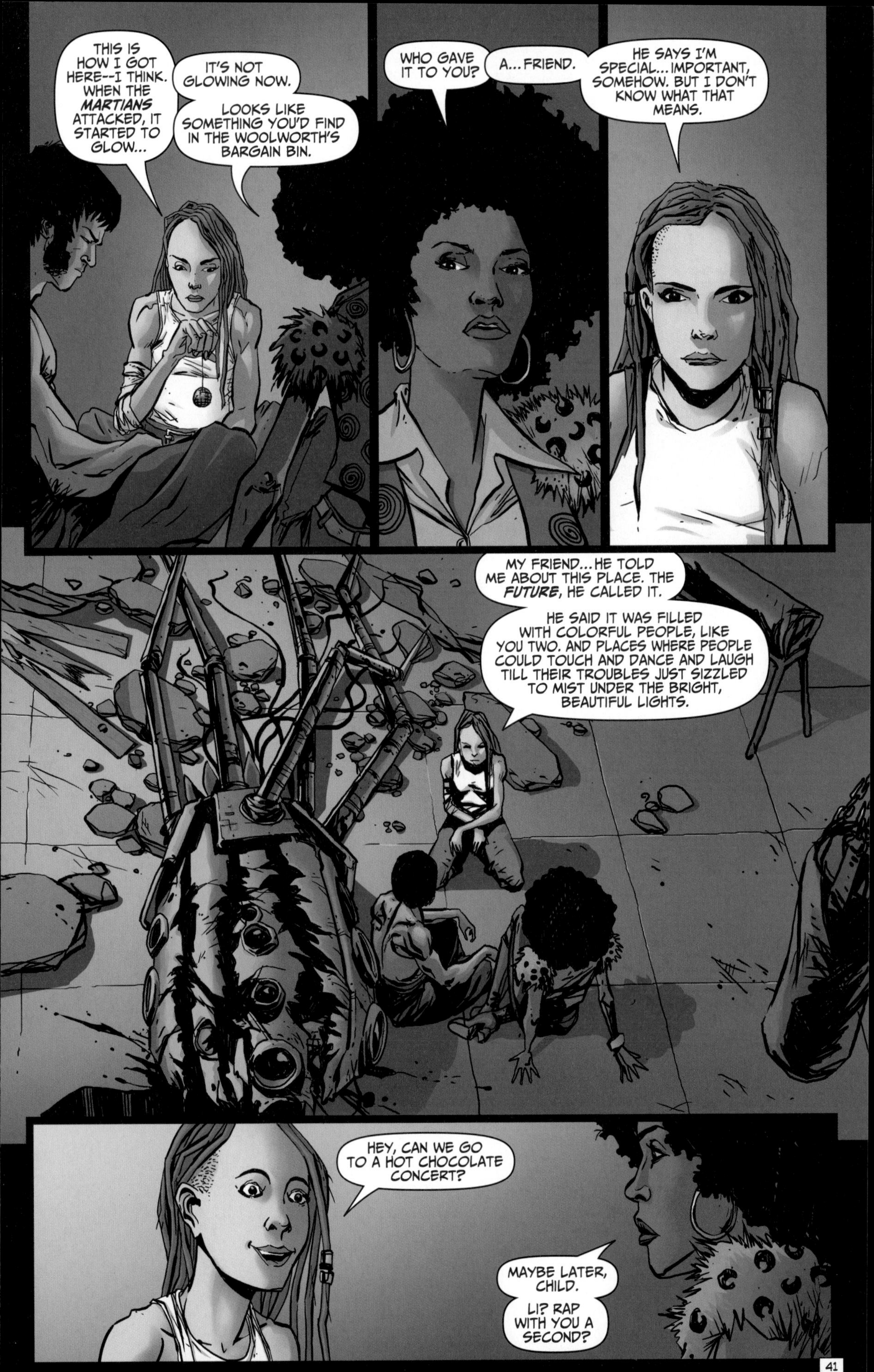
THIS IS HOW I GOT HERE--I THINK. WHEN THE *MARTIANS* ATTACKED, IT STARTED TO GLOW...
IT'S NOT GLOWING NOW.
LOOKS LIKE SOMETHING YOU'D FIND IN THE WOOLWORTH'S BARGAIN BIN.
WHO GAVE IT TO YOU?
A...FRIEND.
HE SAYS I'M SPECIAL...IMPORTANT, SOMEHOW. BUT I DON'T KNOW WHAT THAT MEANS.
MY FRIEND...HE TOLD ME ABOUT THIS PLACE. THE *FUTURE*, HE CALLED IT.
HE SAID IT WAS FILLED WITH COLORFUL PEOPLE, LIKE YOU TWO. AND PLACES WHERE PEOPLE COULD TOUCH AND DANCE AND LAUGH TILL THEIR TROUBLES JUST SIZZLED TO MIST UNDER THE BRIGHT, BEAUTIFUL LIGHTS.
HEY, CAN WE GO TO A HOT CHOCOLATE CONCERT?
MAYBE LATER, CHILD.
LI? RAP WITH YOU A SECOND?

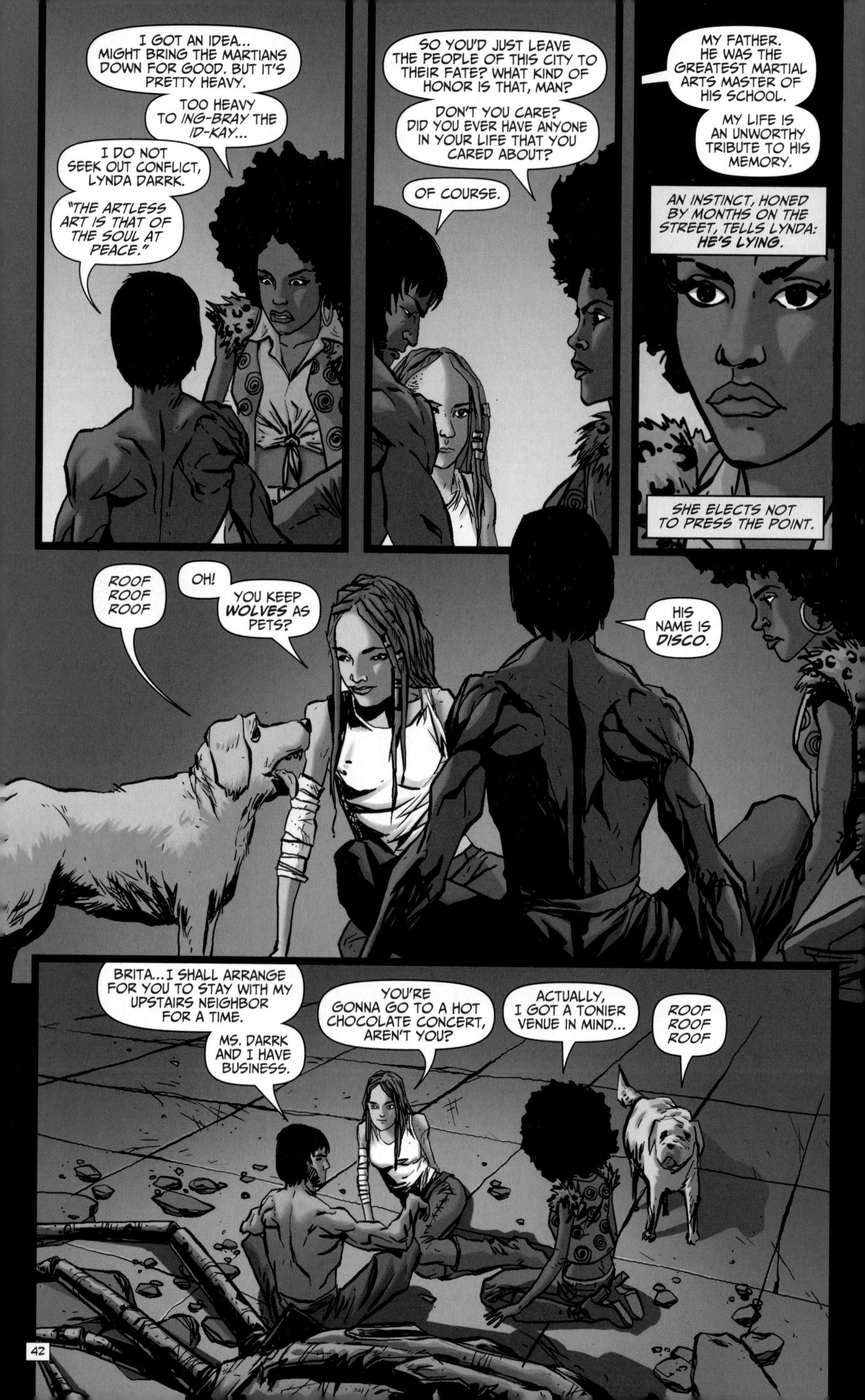

I GOT AN IDEA... MIGHT BRING THE MARTIANS DOWN FOR GOOD. BUT IT'S PRETTY HEAVY.
TOO HEAVY TO *ING-BRAY* THE *ID-KAY*...
I DO NOT SEEK OUT CONFLICT, LYNDA DARRK.
"THE ARTLESS ART IS THAT OF THE SOUL AT PEACE."
SO YOU'D JUST LEAVE THE PEOPLE OF THIS CITY TO THEIR FATE? WHAT KIND OF HONOR IS THAT, MAN?
DON'T YOU CARE? DID YOU EVER HAVE ANYONE IN YOUR LIFE THAT YOU CARED ABOUT?
OF COURSE.
MY FATHER. HE WAS THE GREATEST MARTIAL ARTS MASTER OF HIS SCHOOL.
MY LIFE IS AN UNWORTHY TRIBUTE TO HIS MEMORY.
*AN INSTINCT, HONED BY MONTHS ON THE STREET, TELLS LYNDA: **HE'S LYING.***
SHE ELECTS NOT TO PRESS THE POINT.
ROOF ROOF ROOF
OH!
YOU KEEP ***WOLVES*** AS PETS?
HIS NAME IS ***DISCO.***
BRITA...I SHALL ARRANGE FOR YOU TO STAY WITH MY UPSTAIRS NEIGHBOR FOR A TIME.
MS. DARRK AND I HAVE BUSINESS.
YOU'RE GONNA GO TO A HOT CHOCOLATE CONCERT, AREN'T YOU?
ACTUALLY, I GOT A TONIER VENUE IN MIND...
ROOF ROOF ROOF

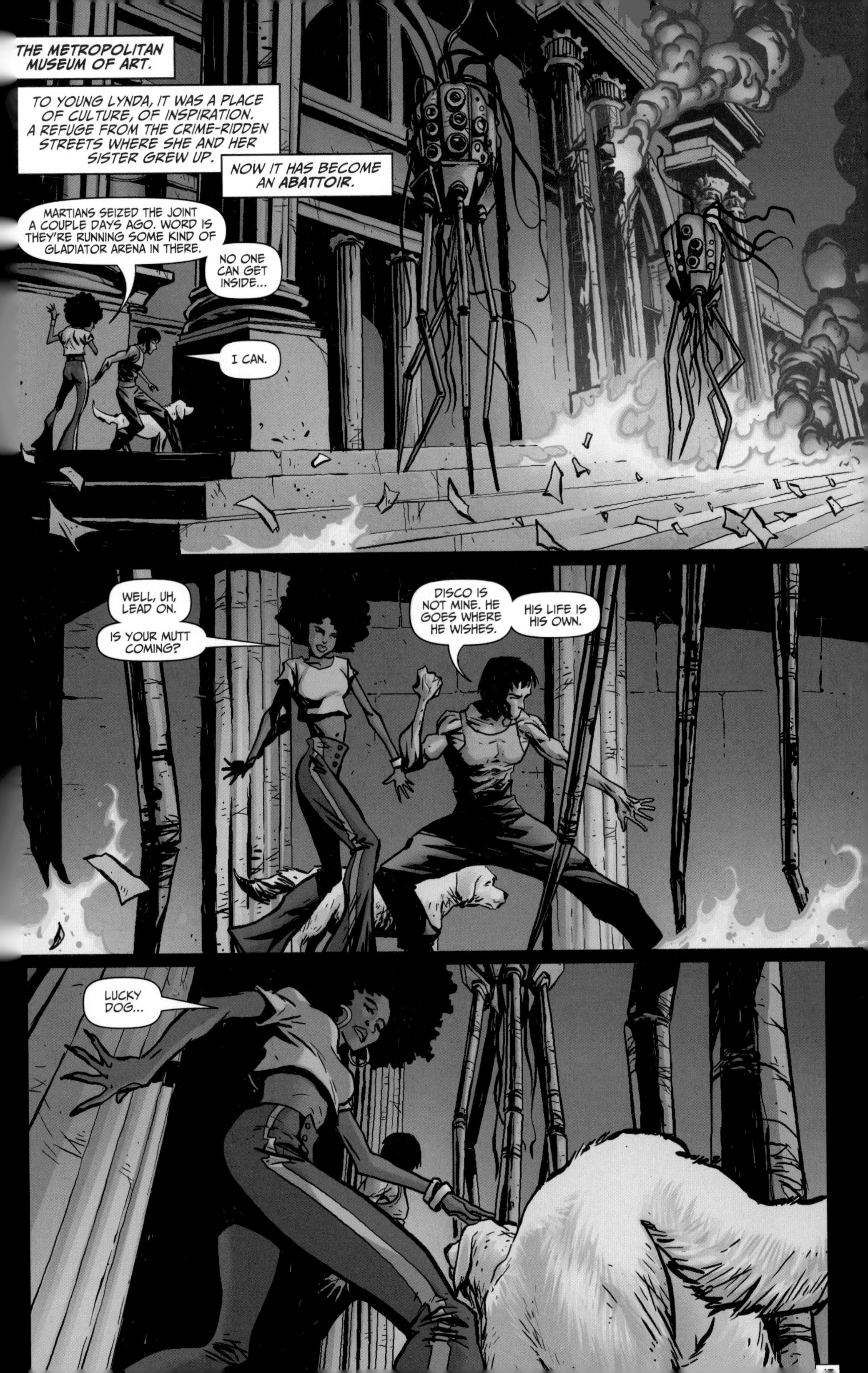
THE METROPOLITAN MUSEUM OF ART.
TO YOUNG LYNDA, IT WAS A PLACE OF CULTURE, OF INSPIRATION. A REFUGE FROM THE CRIME-RIDDEN STREETS WHERE SHE AND HER SISTER GREW UP.
NOW IT HAS BECOME AN ABATTOIR.
MARTIANS SEIZED THE JOINT A COUPLE DAYS AGO. WORD IS THEY'RE RUNNING SOME KIND OF GLADIATOR ARENA IN THERE.
NO ONE CAN GET INSIDE...
I CAN.
WELL, UH, LEAD ON.
IS YOUR MUTT COMING?
DISCO IS NOT MINE. HE GOES WHERE HE WISHES.
HIS LIFE IS HIS OWN.
LUCKY DOG...

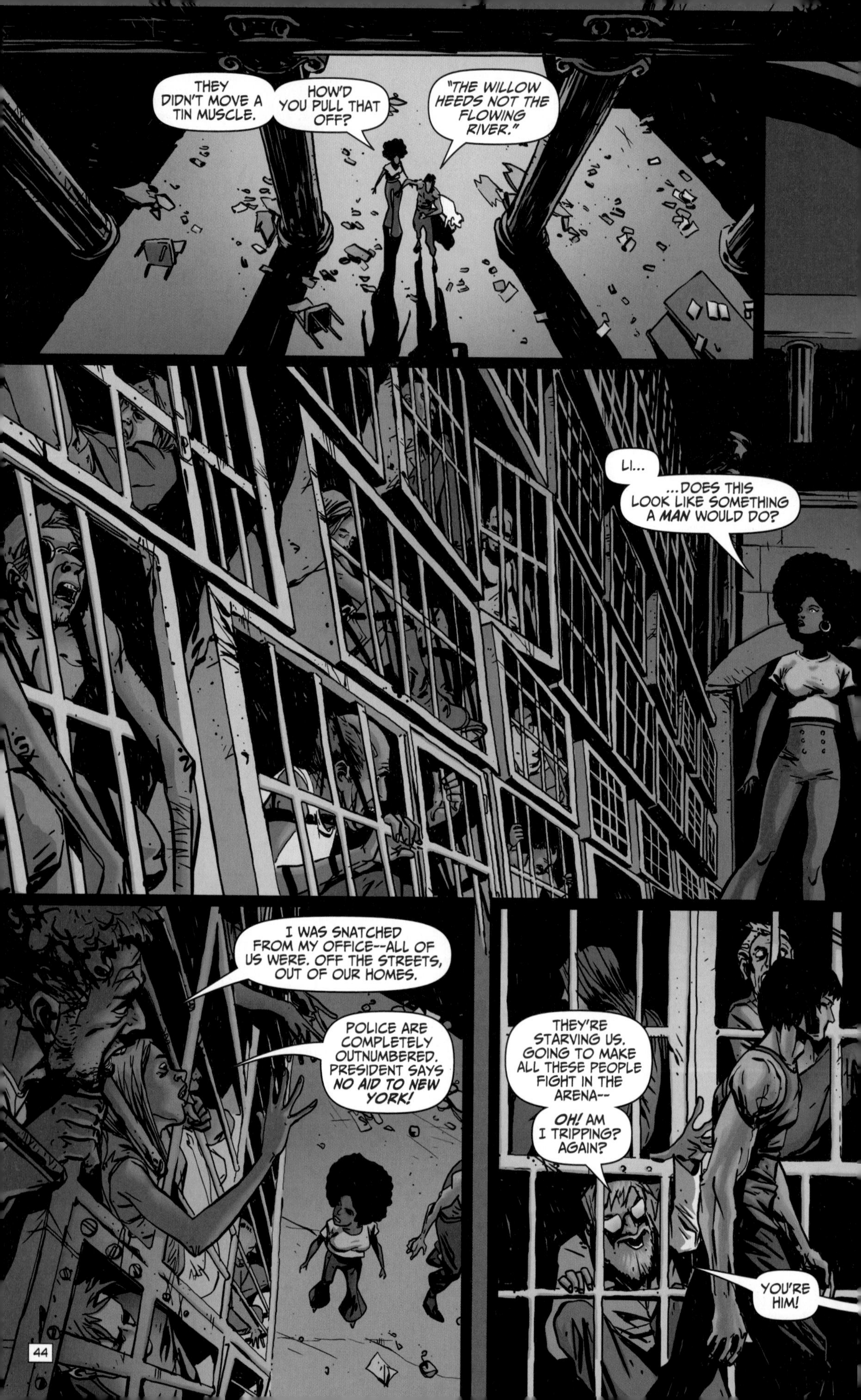
THEY DIDN'T MOVE A TIN MUSCLE.
HOW'D YOU PULL THAT OFF?
"THE WILLOW HEEDS NOT THE FLOWING RIVER."
LI...
...DOES THIS LOOK LIKE SOMETHING A MAN WOULD DO?
I WAS SNATCHED FROM MY OFFICE--ALL OF US WERE. OFF THE STREETS, OUT OF OUR HOMES.
POLICE ARE COMPLETELY OUTNUMBERED. PRESIDENT SAYS NO AID TO NEW YORK!
THEY'RE STARVING US. GOING TO MAKE ALL THESE PEOPLE FIGHT IN THE ARENA--
OH! AM I TRIPPING? AGAIN?
YOU'RE HIM!

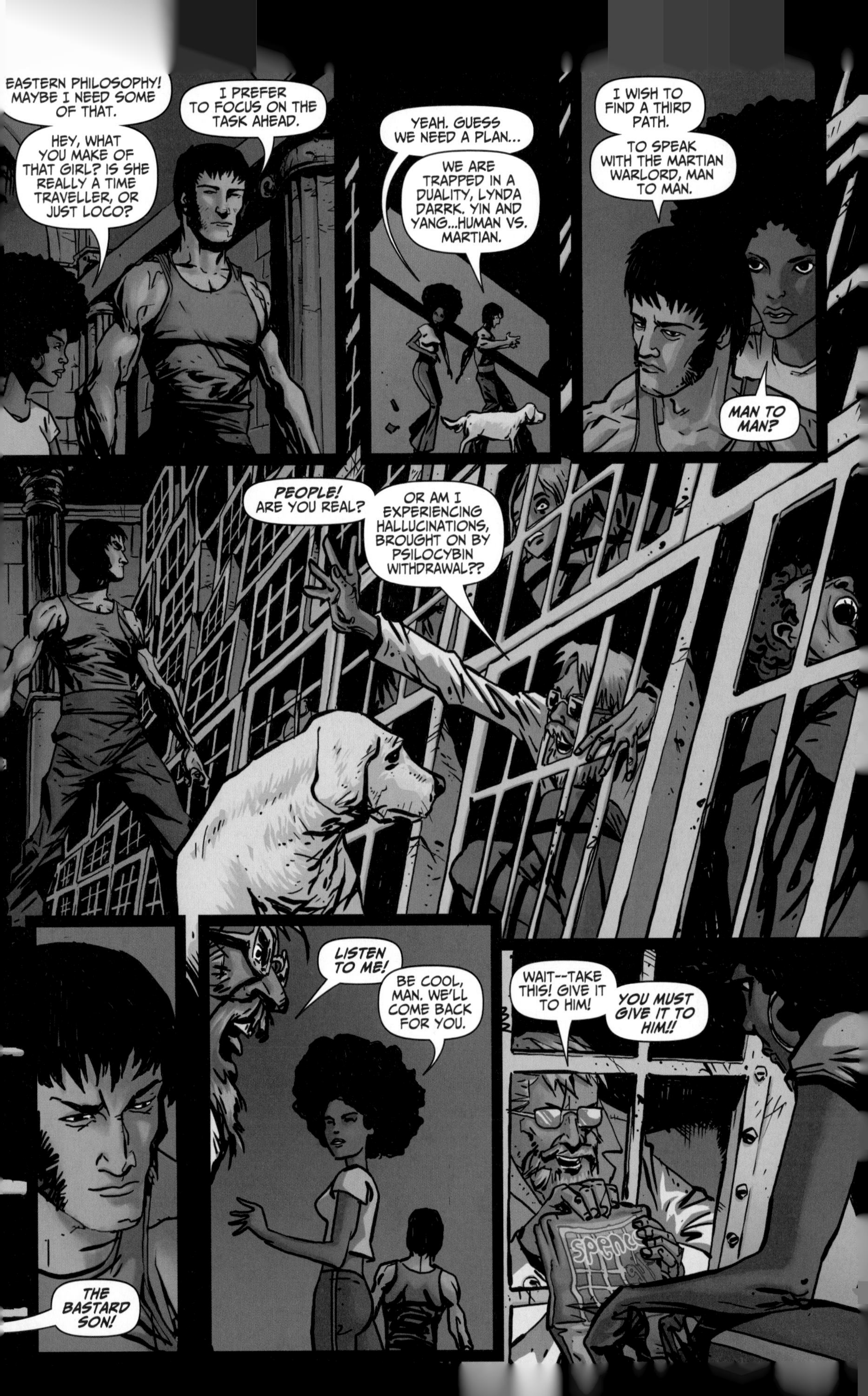
EASTERN PHILOSOPHY! MAYBE I NEED SOME OF THAT.
HEY, WHAT YOU MAKE OF THAT GIRL? IS SHE REALLY A TIME TRAVELLER, OR JUST LOCO?
I PREFER TO FOCUS ON THE TASK AHEAD.
YEAH. GUESS WE NEED A PLAN...
WE ARE TRAPPED IN A DUALITY, LYNDA DARRK. YIN AND YANG...HUMAN VS. MARTIAN.
I WISH TO FIND A THIRD PATH.
TO SPEAK WITH THE MARTIAN WARLORD, MAN TO MAN.
MAN TO MAN?
PEOPLE! ARE YOU REAL?
OR AM I EXPERIENCING HALLUCINATIONS, BROUGHT ON BY PSILOCYBIN WITHDRAWAL??
THE BASTARD SON!
LISTEN TO ME!
BE COOL, MAN. WE'LL COME BACK FOR YOU.
WAIT--TAKE THIS! GIVE IT TO HIM!
YOU MUST GIVE IT TO HIM!!

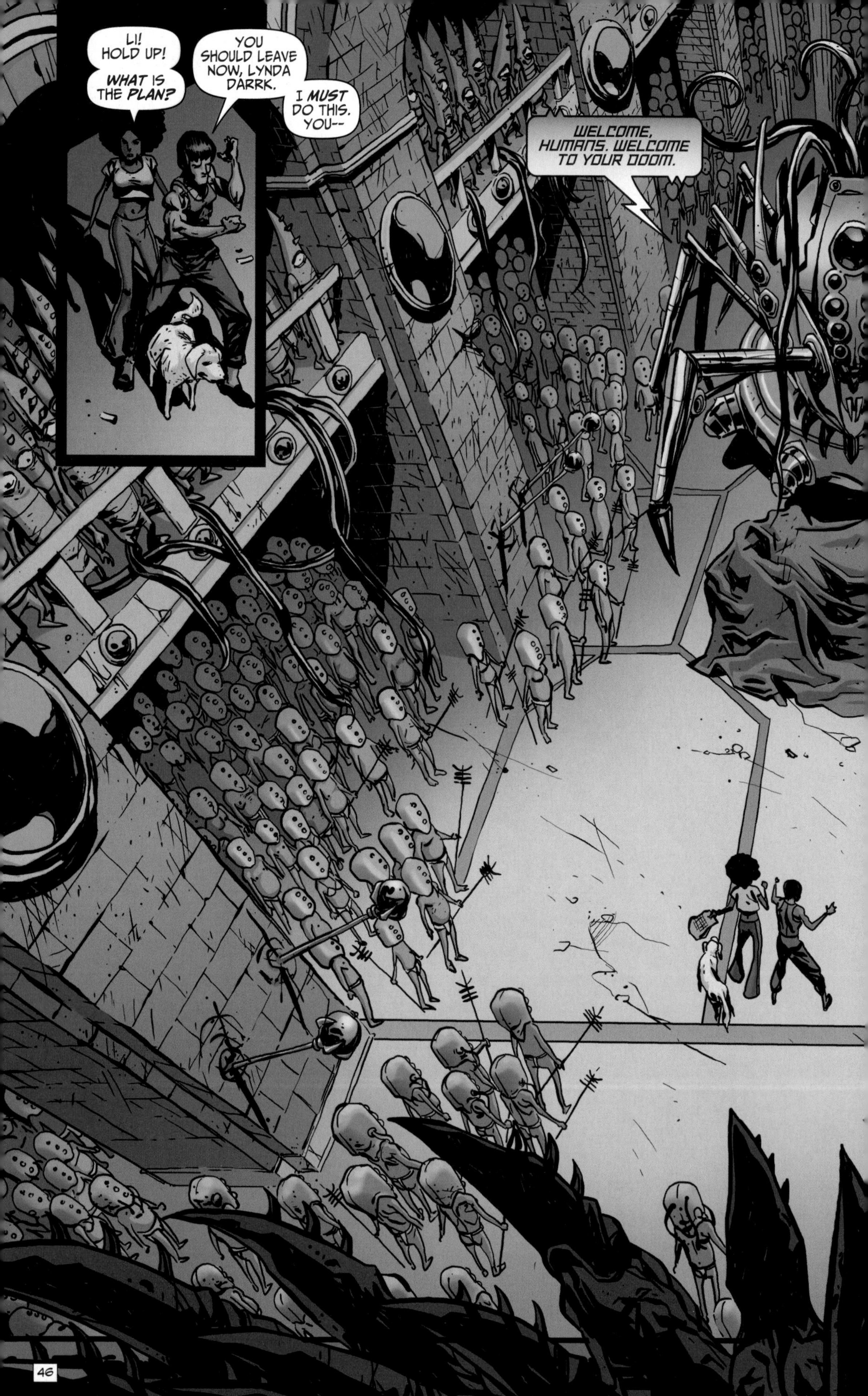
LI! HOLD UP! WHAT IS THE PLAN?
YOU SHOULD LEAVE NOW, LYNDA DARRK.
I MUST DO THIS. YOU--
WELCOME, HUMANS. WELCOME TO YOUR DOOM.

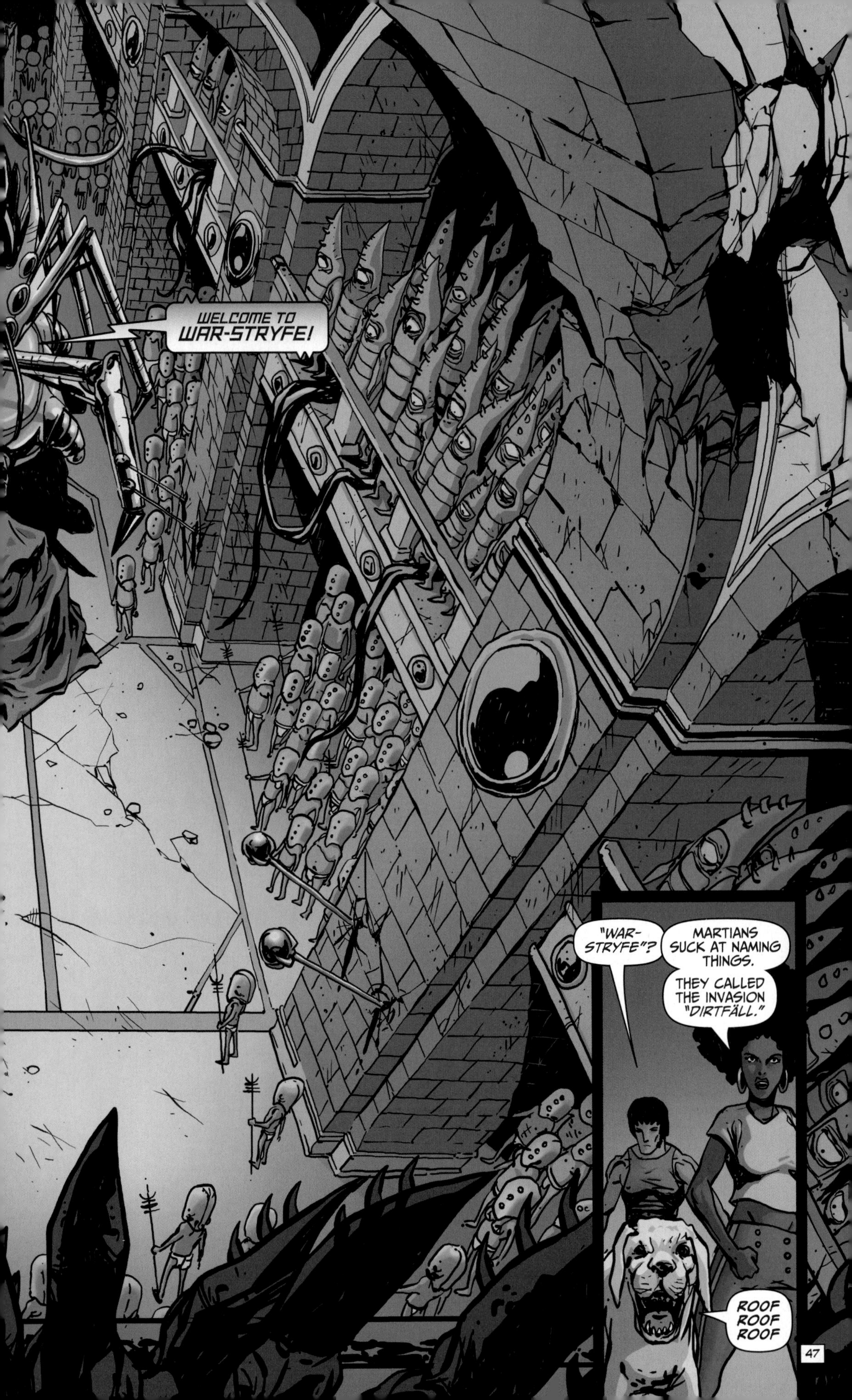

WELCOME TO WAR-STRYFE!
"WAR-STRYFE"?
MARTIANS SUCK AT NAMING THINGS.
THEY CALLED THE INVASION "DIRTFÄLL."
ROOF ROOF ROOF

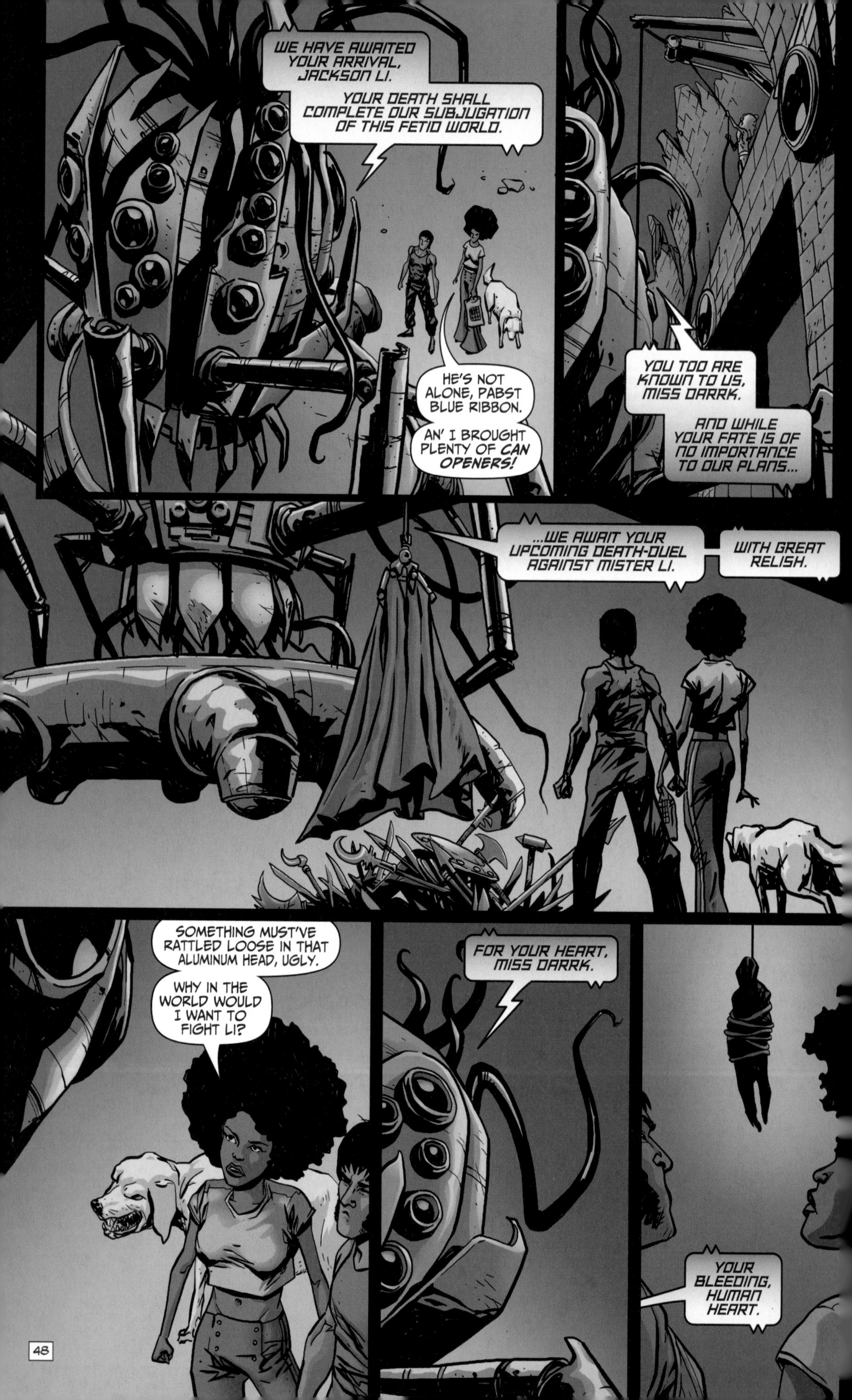
WE HAVE AWAITED YOUR ARRIVAL, JACKSON LI.
YOUR DEATH SHALL COMPLETE OUR SUBJUGATION OF THIS FETID WORLD.
HE'S NOT ALONE, PABST BLUE RIBBON.
AN' I BROUGHT PLENTY OF CAN OPENERS!
YOU TOO ARE KNOWN TO US, MISS DARRK.
AND WHILE YOUR FATE IS OF NO IMPORTANCE TO OUR PLANS...
...WE AWAIT YOUR UPCOMING DEATH-DUEL AGAINST MISTER LI.
WITH GREAT RELISH.
SOMETHING MUST'VE RATTLED LOOSE IN THAT ALUMINUM HEAD, UGLY.
WHY IN THE WORLD WOULD I WANT TO FIGHT LI?
FOR YOUR HEART, MISS DARRK.
YOUR BLEEDING, HUMAN HEART.

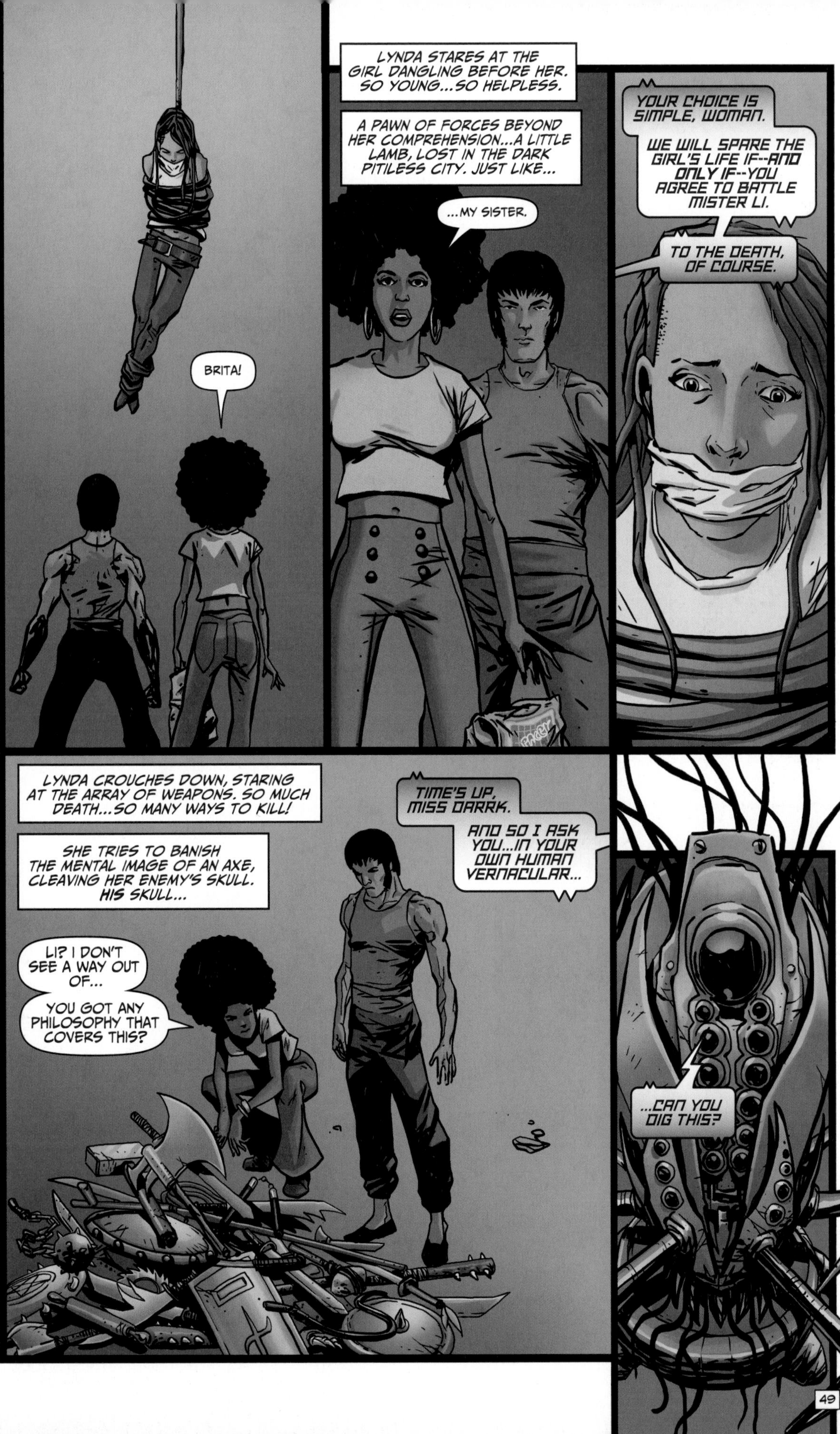
BRITA!
LYNDA STARES AT THE GIRL DANGLING BEFORE HER. SO YOUNG...SO HELPLESS.
A PAWN OF FORCES BEYOND HER COMPREHENSION...A LITTLE LAMB, LOST IN THE DARK PITILESS CITY. JUST LIKE...
...MY SISTER.
YOUR CHOICE IS SIMPLE, WOMAN.
WE WILL SPARE THE GIRL'S LIFE IF--AND ONLY IF--YOU AGREE TO BATTLE MISTER LI.
TO THE DEATH, OF COURSE.
LYNDA CROUCHES DOWN, STARING AT THE ARRAY OF WEAPONS. SO MUCH DEATH...SO MANY WAYS TO KILL!
SHE TRIES TO BANISH THE MENTAL IMAGE OF AN AXE, CLEAVING HER ENEMY'S SKULL. HIS SKULL...
LI? I DON'T SEE A WAY OUT OF...
YOU GOT ANY PHILOSOPHY THAT COVERS THIS?
TIME'S UP, MISS DARRK.
AND SO I ASK YOU...IN YOUR OWN HUMAN VERNACULAR...
...CAN YOU DIG THIS?

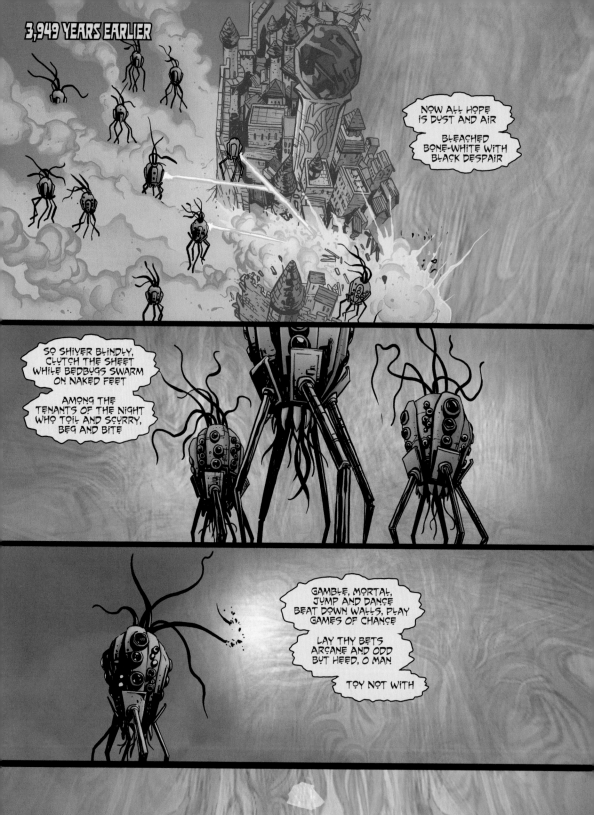

3,949 YEARS EARLIER

NOW ALL HOPE IS DUST AND AIR

BLEACHED BONE-WHITE WITH BLACK DESPAIR

SO SHIVER BLINDLY, CLUTCH THE SHEET WHILE BEDBUGS SWARM ON NAKED FEET

AMONG THE TENANTS OF THE NIGHT WHO TOIL AND SCURRY, BEG AND BITE

GAMBLE, MORTAL, JUMP AND DANCE BEAT DOWN WALLS, PLAY GAMES OF CHANCE

LAY THY BETS ARCANE AND ODD BUT HEED, O MAN

TOY NOT WITH

GODD

NEXT: *APE TREACHERY! DEATH-DUEL IN THE RUINS! THE FATE OF BRITA CONSTANTINA!* AND WHAT'S IN THAT *BAG,* ANYWAY? YOU'LL REALLY FEEL THE MUSIC... IN *THIRTY DAYS!*

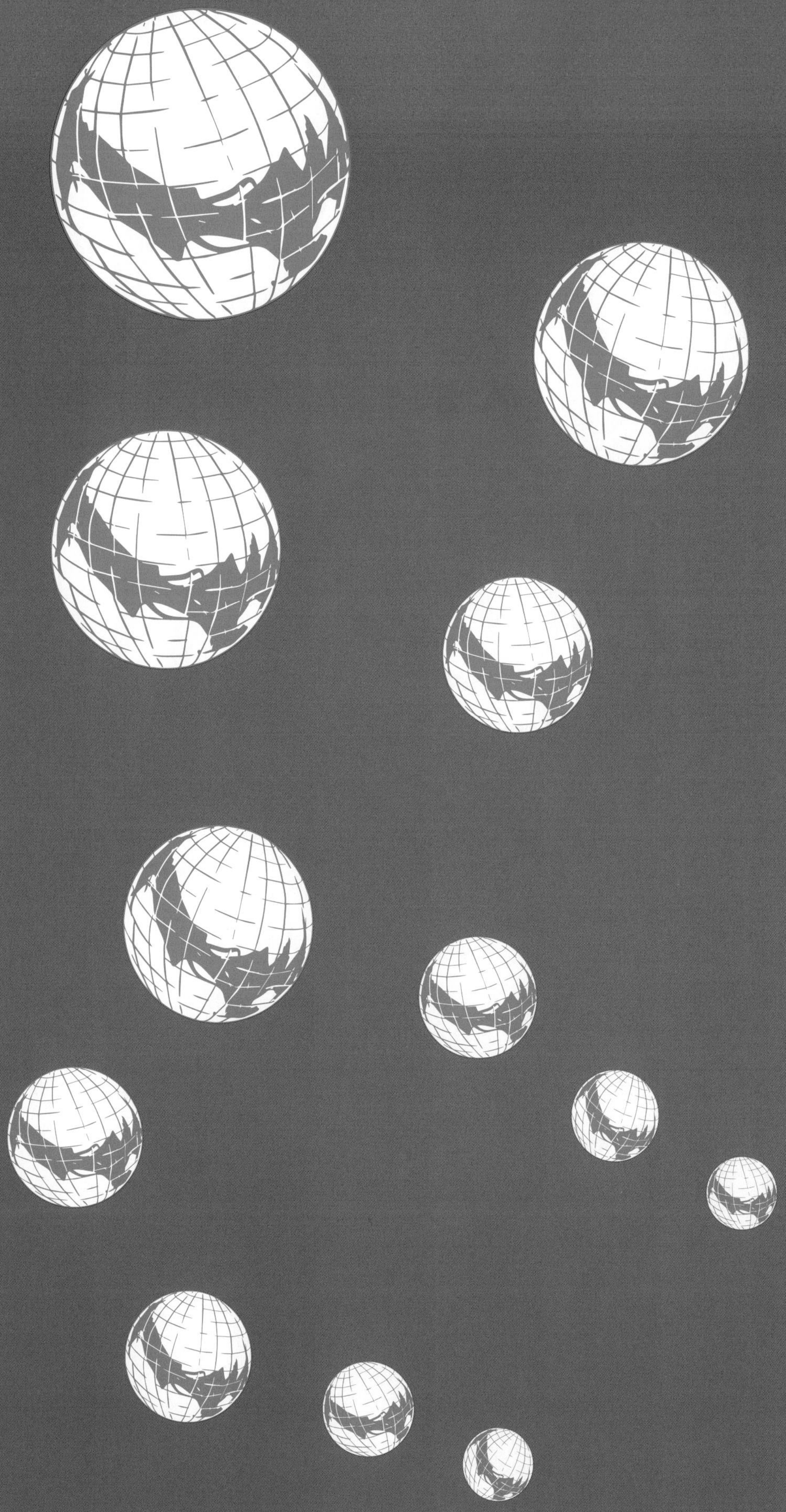

3

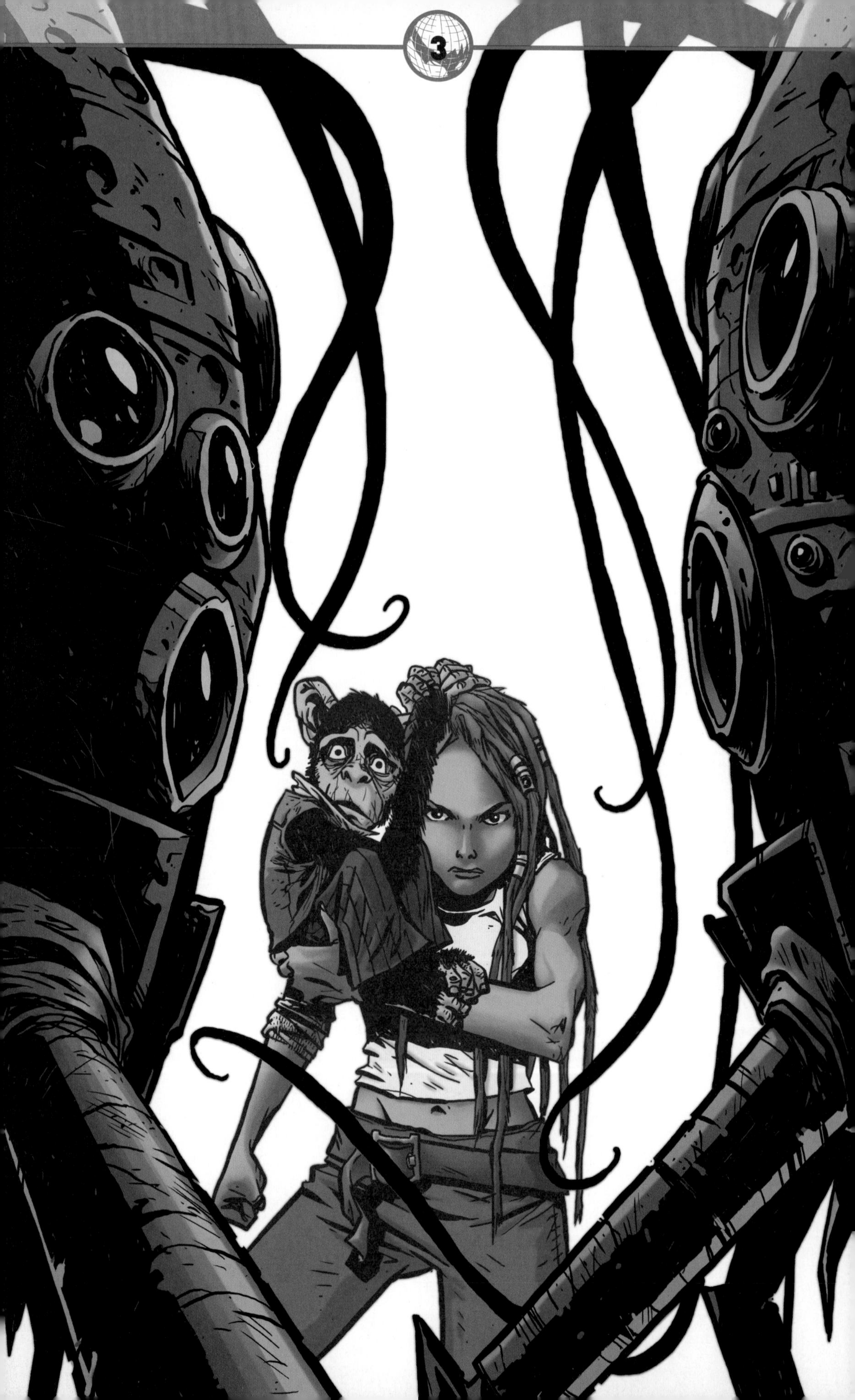

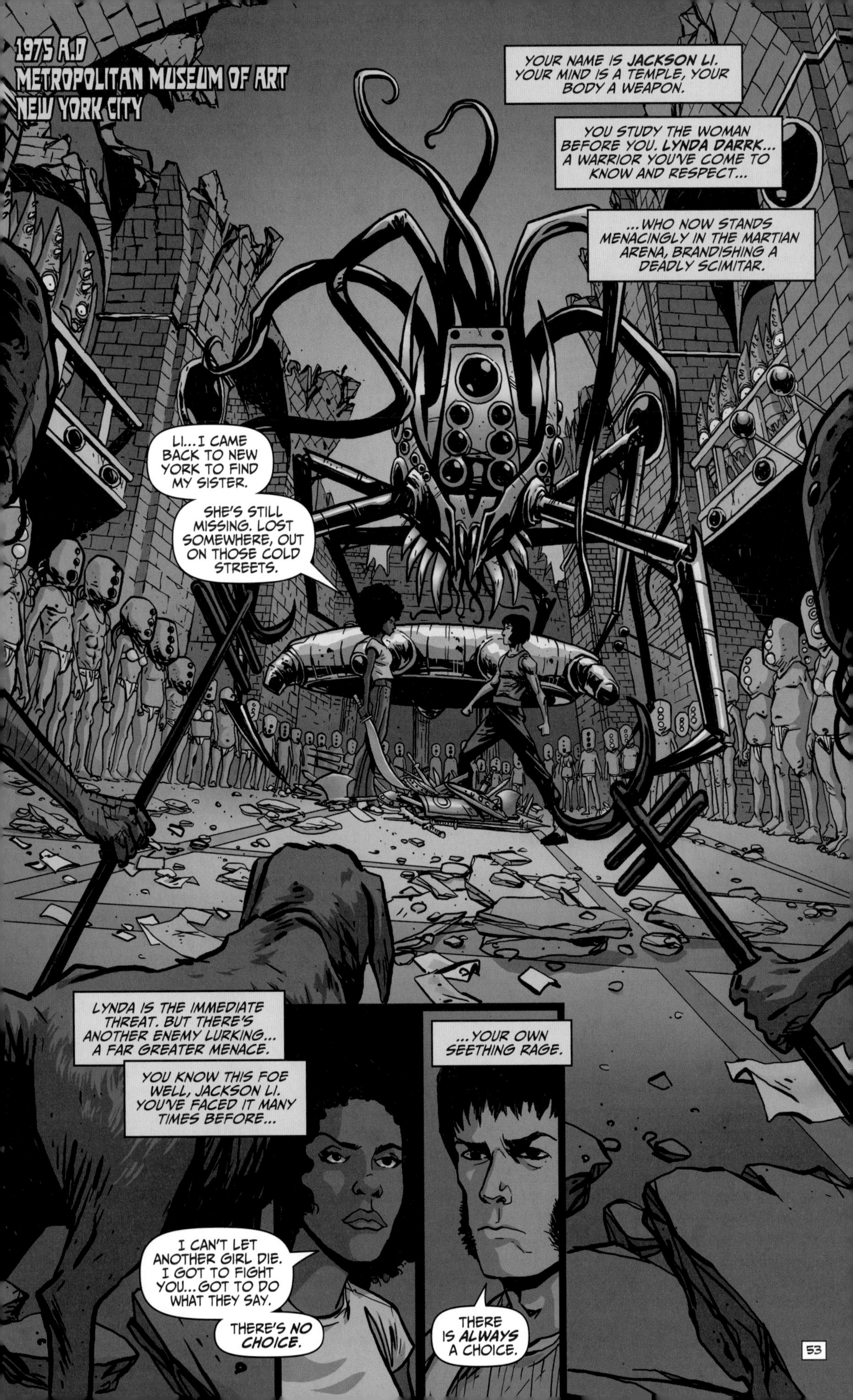
1975 A.D
METROPOLITAN MUSEUM OF ART
NEW YORK CITY
YOUR NAME IS JACKSON LI. YOUR MIND IS A TEMPLE, YOUR BODY A WEAPON.
YOU STUDY THE WOMAN BEFORE YOU. LYNDA DARRK... A WARRIOR YOU'VE COME TO KNOW AND RESPECT...
...WHO NOW STANDS MENACINGLY IN THE MARTIAN ARENA, BRANDISHING A DEADLY SCIMITAR.
LI...I CAME BACK TO NEW YORK TO FIND MY SISTER.
SHE'S STILL MISSING. LOST SOMEWHERE, OUT ON THOSE COLD STREETS.
LYNDA IS THE IMMEDIATE THREAT. BUT THERE'S ANOTHER ENEMY LURKING... A FAR GREATER MENACE.
YOU KNOW THIS FOE WELL, JACKSON LI. YOU'VE FACED IT MANY TIMES BEFORE...
I CAN'T LET ANOTHER GIRL DIE. I GOT TO FIGHT YOU...GOT TO DO WHAT THEY SAY.
THERE'S NO CHOICE.
...YOUR OWN SEETHING RAGE.
THERE IS ALWAYS A CHOICE.

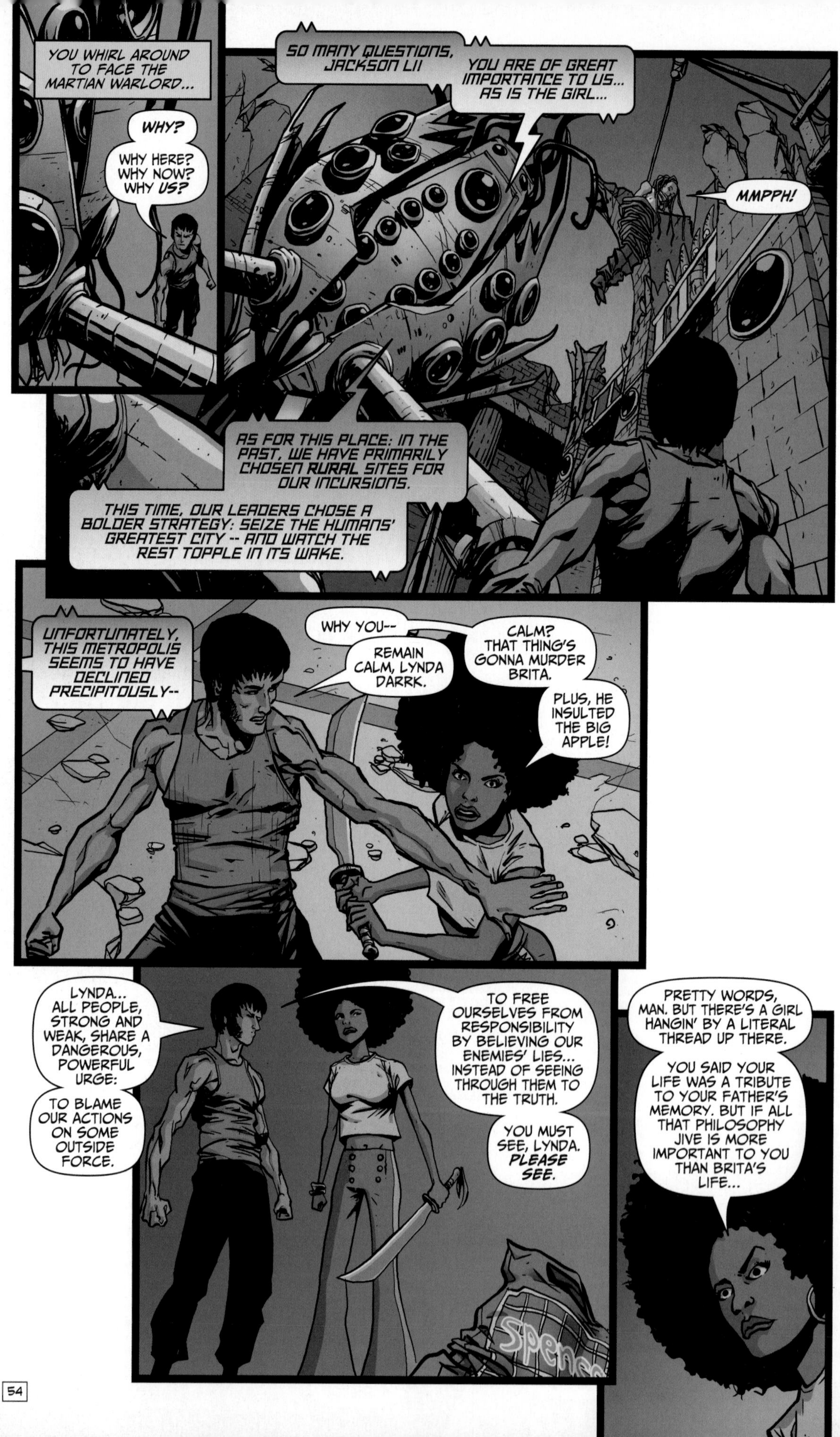
YOU WHIRL AROUND TO FACE THE MARTIAN WARLORD...
WHY?
WHY HERE? WHY NOW? WHY US?
SO MANY QUESTIONS, JACKSON LII
YOU ARE OF GREAT IMPORTANCE TO US... AS IS THE GIRL...
MMPPH!
AS FOR THIS PLACE: IN THE PAST, WE HAVE PRIMARILY CHOSEN RURAL SITES FOR OUR INCURSIONS.
THIS TIME, OUR LEADERS CHOSE A BOLDER STRATEGY: SEIZE THE HUMANS' GREATEST CITY -- AND WATCH THE REST TOPPLE IN ITS WAKE.
UNFORTUNATELY, THIS METROPOLIS SEEMS TO HAVE DECLINED PRECIPITOUSLY--
WHY YOU--
REMAIN CALM, LYNDA DARRK.
CALM? THAT THING'S GONNA MURDER BRITA.
PLUS, HE INSULTED THE BIG APPLE!
LYNDA... ALL PEOPLE, STRONG AND WEAK, SHARE A DANGEROUS, POWERFUL URGE:
TO BLAME OUR ACTIONS ON SOME OUTSIDE FORCE.
TO FREE OURSELVES FROM RESPONSIBILITY BY BELIEVING OUR ENEMIES' LIES... INSTEAD OF SEEING THROUGH THEM TO THE TRUTH.
YOU MUST SEE, LYNDA. PLEASE SEE.
PRETTY WORDS, MAN. BUT THERE'S A GIRL HANGIN' BY A LITERAL THREAD UP THERE.
YOU SAID YOUR LIFE WAS A TRIBUTE TO YOUR FATHER'S MEMORY. BUT IF ALL THAT PHILOSOPHY JIVE IS MORE IMPORTANT TO YOU THAN BRITA'S LIFE...

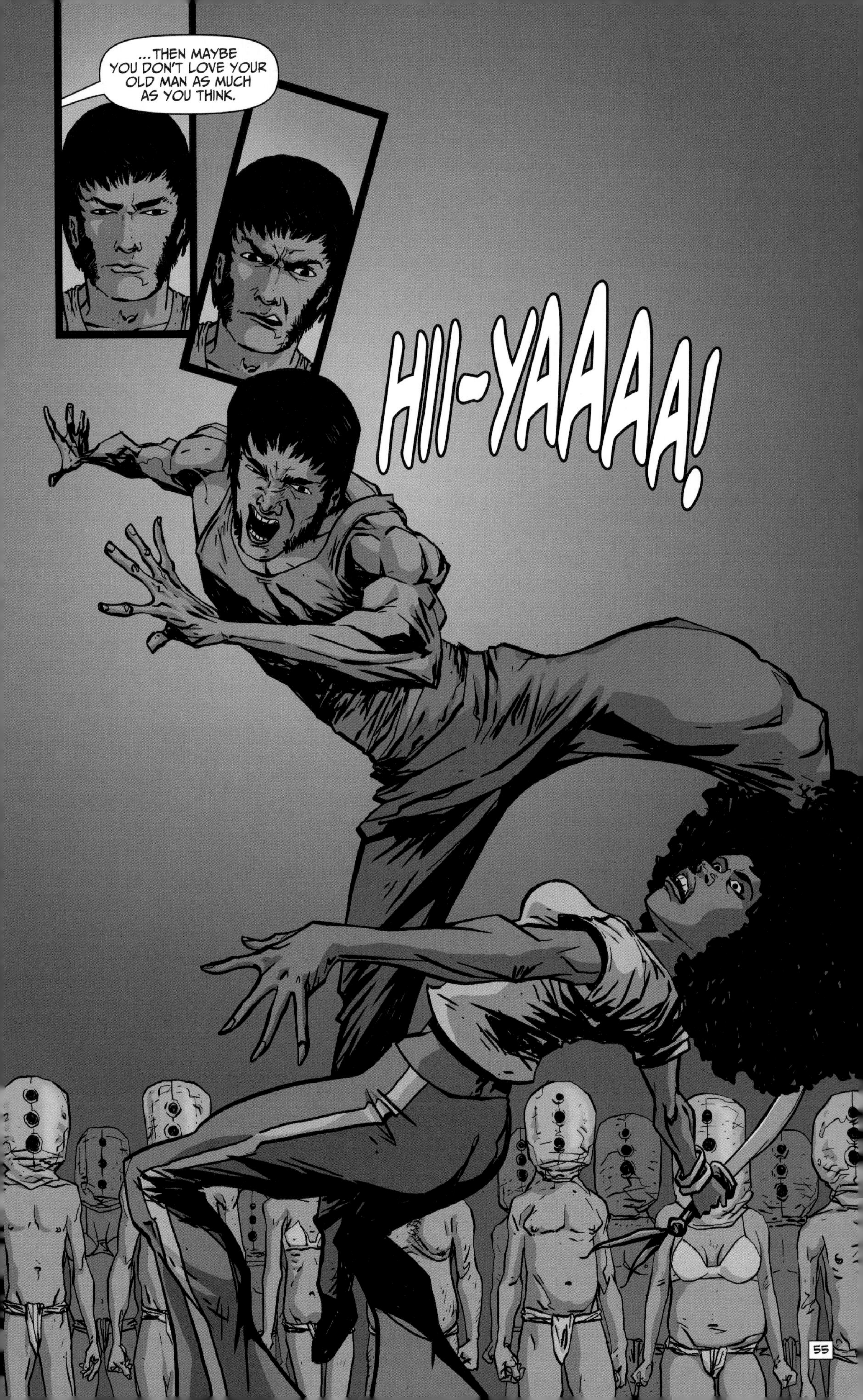
...THEN MAYBE YOU DON'T LOVE YOUR OLD MAN AS MUCH AS YOU THINK.
HII-YAAAAA!

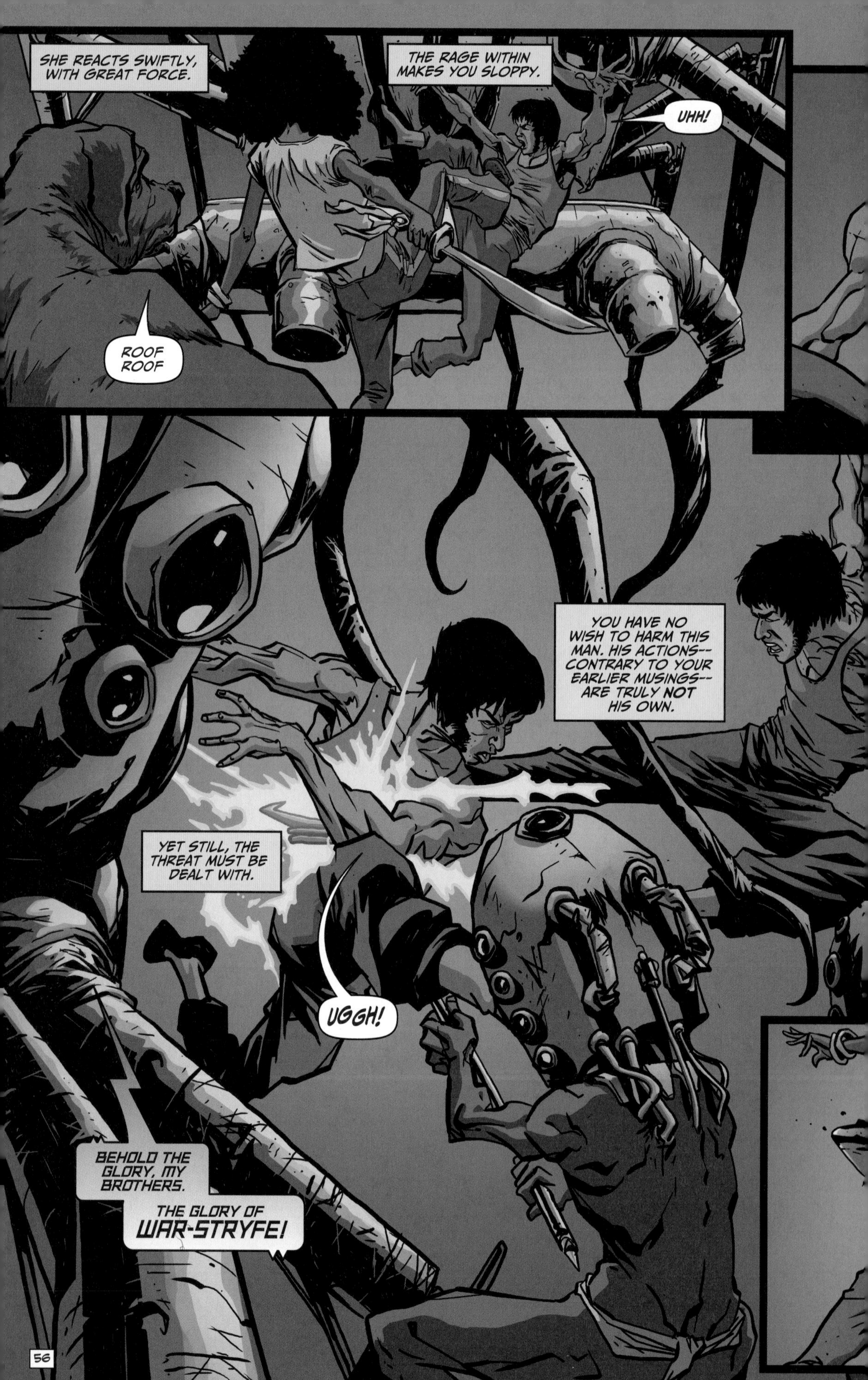
SHE REACTS SWIFTLY, WITH GREAT FORCE.
THE RAGE WITHIN MAKES YOU SLOPPY.
UHH!
ROOF ROOF
YOU HAVE NO WISH TO HARM THIS MAN. HIS ACTIONS-- CONTRARY TO YOUR EARLIER MUSINGS-- ARE TRULY NOT HIS OWN.
YET STILL, THE THREAT MUST BE DEALT WITH.
UGGH!
BEHOLD THE GLORY, MY BROTHERS.
THE GLORY OF WAR-STRYFE!

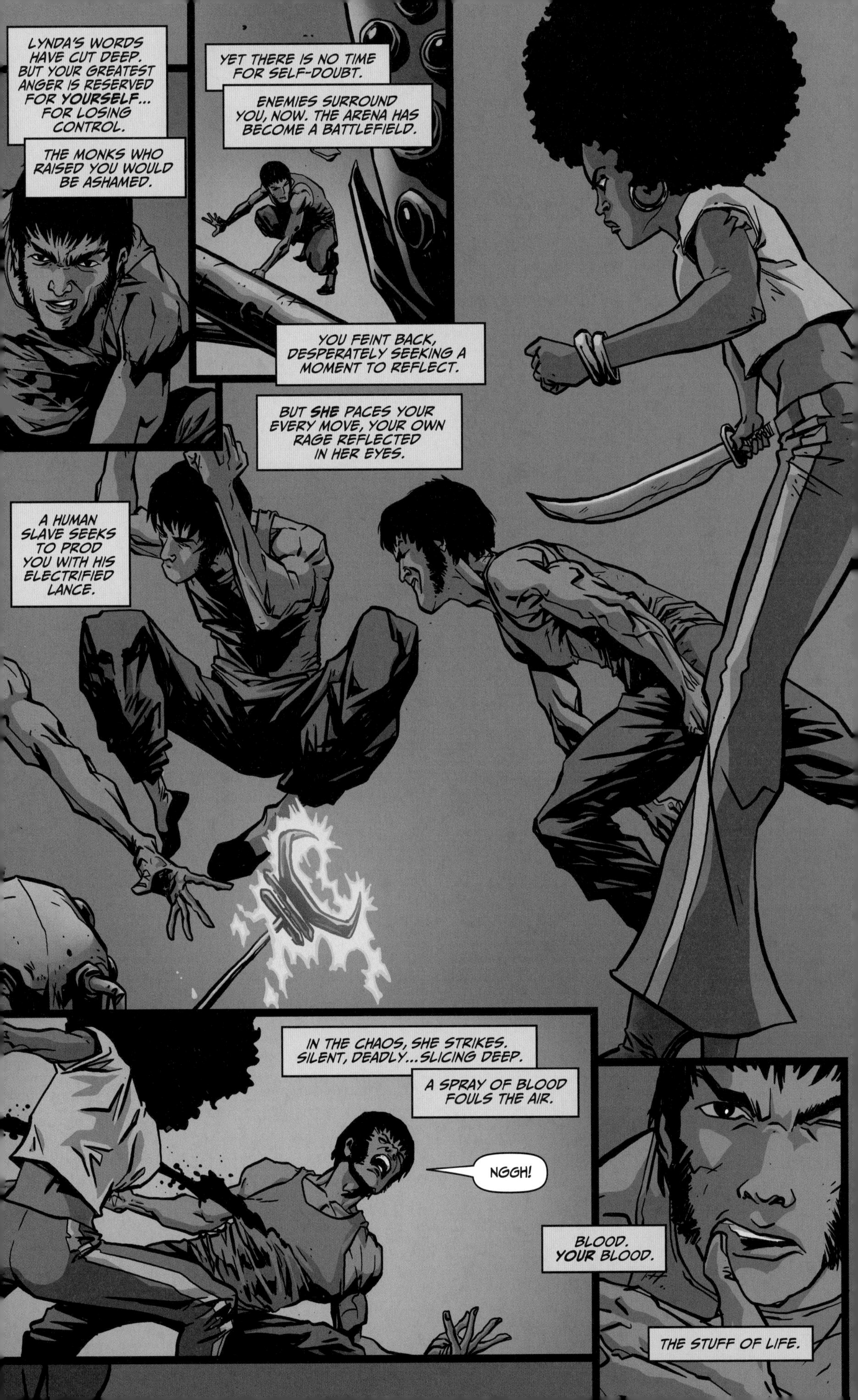
LYNDA'S WORDS HAVE CUT DEEP. BUT YOUR GREATEST ANGER IS RESERVED FOR YOURSELF... FOR LOSING CONTROL.
THE MONKS WHO RAISED YOU WOULD BE ASHAMED.
YET THERE IS NO TIME FOR SELF-DOUBT.
ENEMIES SURROUND YOU, NOW. THE ARENA HAS BECOME A BATTLEFIELD.
YOU FEINT BACK, DESPERATELY SEEKING A MOMENT TO REFLECT.
BUT SHE PACES YOUR EVERY MOVE, YOUR OWN RAGE REFLECTED IN HER EYES.
A HUMAN SLAVE SEEKS TO PROD YOU WITH HIS ELECTRIFIED LANCE.
IN THE CHAOS, SHE STRIKES. SILENT, DEADLY...SLICING DEEP.
A SPRAY OF BLOOD FOULS THE AIR.
NGGH!
BLOOD. YOUR BLOOD.
THE STUFF OF LIFE.

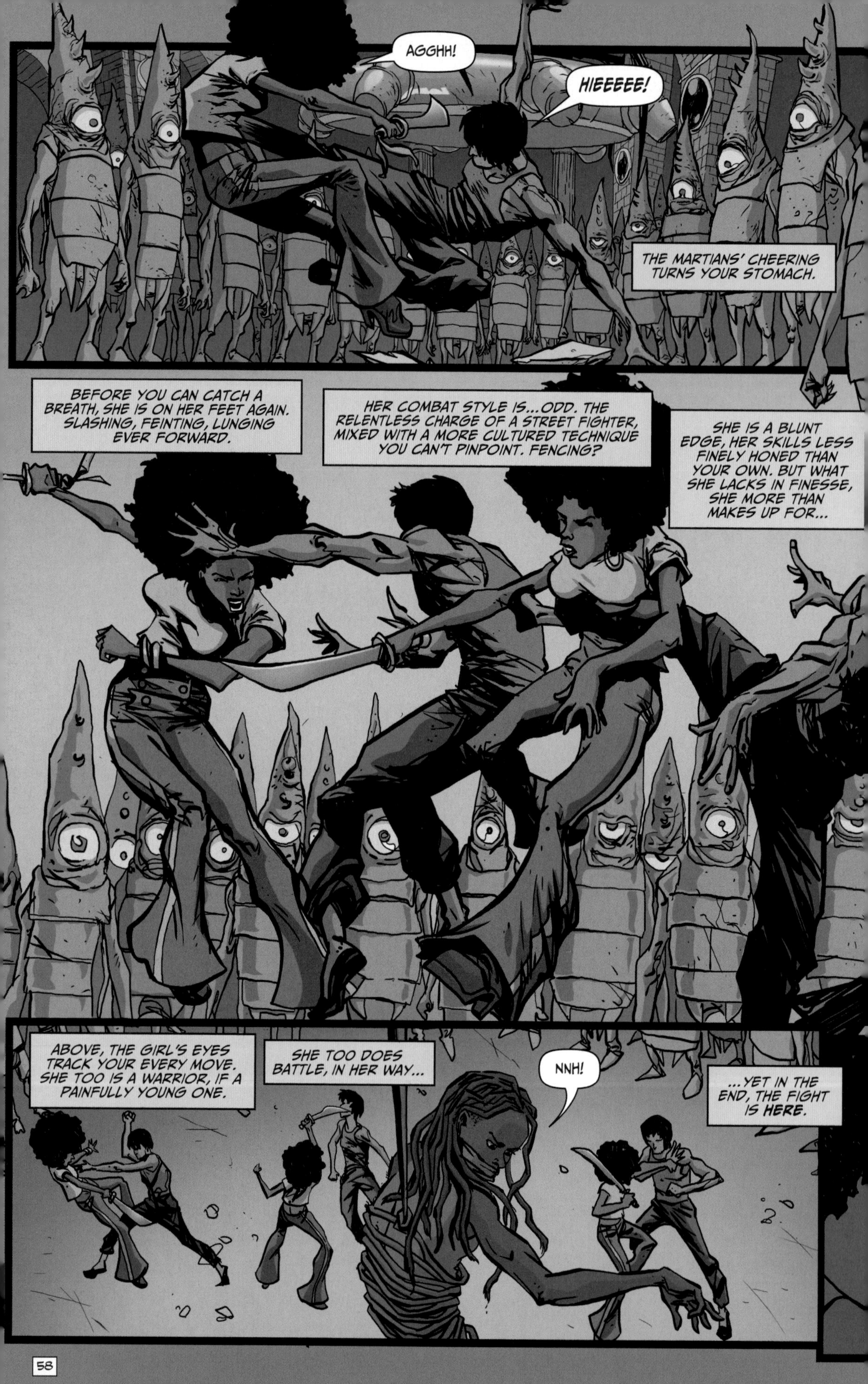
AGGHH!
HIEEEEE!
THE MARTIANS' CHEERING TURNS YOUR STOMACH.
BEFORE YOU CAN CATCH A BREATH, SHE IS ON HER FEET AGAIN. SLASHING, FEINTING, LUNGING EVER FORWARD.
HER COMBAT STYLE IS...ODD. THE RELENTLESS CHARGE OF A STREET FIGHTER, MIXED WITH A MORE CULTURED TECHNIQUE YOU CAN'T PINPOINT. FENCING?
SHE IS A BLUNT EDGE, HER SKILLS LESS FINELY HONED THAN YOUR OWN. BUT WHAT SHE LACKS IN FINESSE, SHE MORE THAN MAKES UP FOR...
ABOVE, THE GIRL'S EYES TRACK YOUR EVERY MOVE. SHE TOO IS A WARRIOR, IF A PAINFULLY YOUNG ONE.
SHE TOO DOES BATTLE, IN HER WAY...
NNH!
...YET IN THE END, THE FIGHT IS **HERE**.

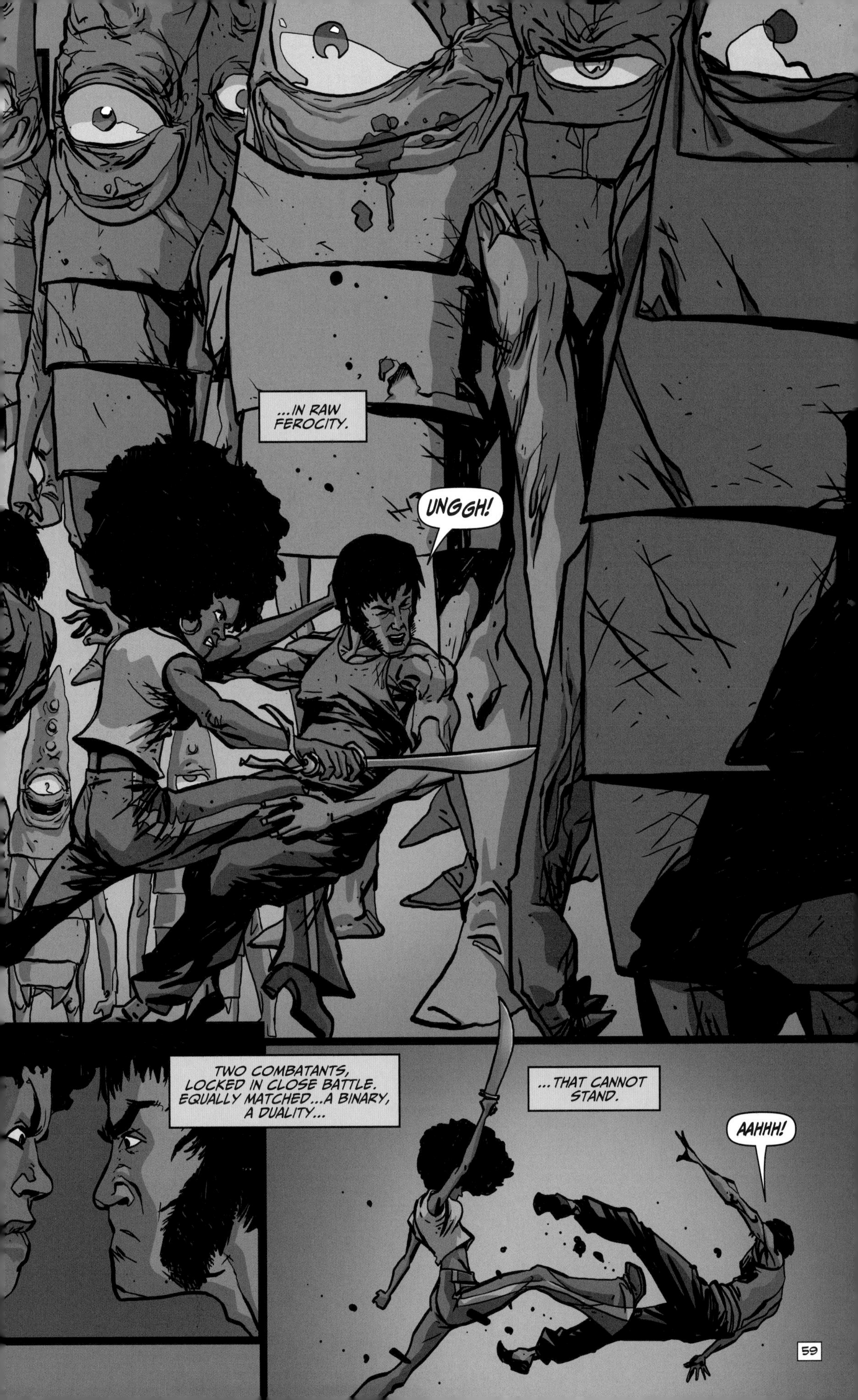
...IN RAW FEROCITY.
UNGGH!
TWO COMBATANTS, LOCKED IN CLOSE BATTLE. EQUALLY MATCHED...A BINARY, A DUALITY...
...THAT CANNOT STAND.
AAHHH!

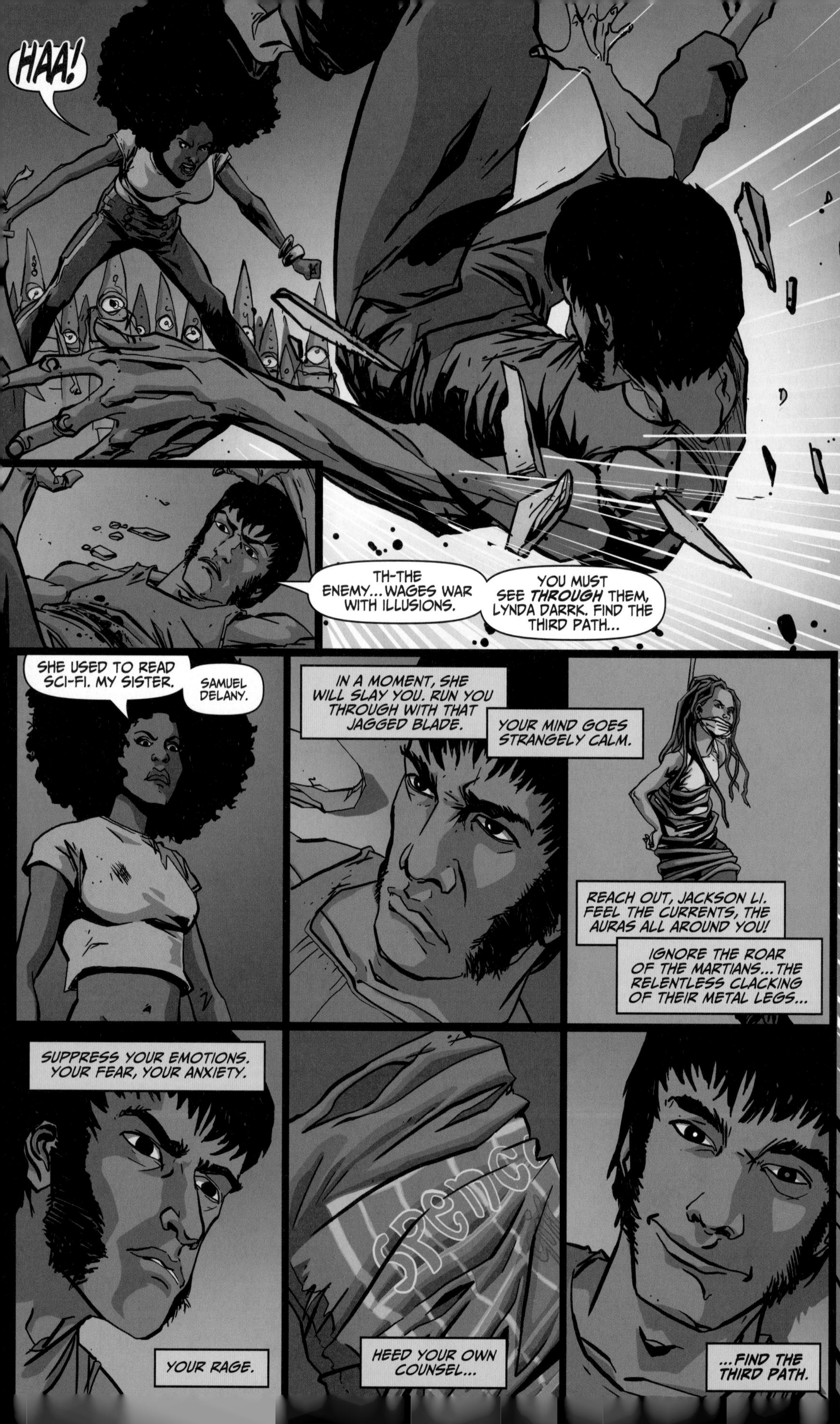
HAA!
TH-THE ENEMY... WAGES WAR WITH ILLUSIONS.
YOU MUST SEE *THROUGH* THEM, LYNDA DARRK. FIND THE THIRD PATH...
SHE USED TO READ SCI-FI. MY SISTER.
SAMUEL DELANY.
IN A MOMENT, SHE WILL SLAY YOU. RUN YOU THROUGH WITH THAT JAGGED BLADE.
YOUR MIND GOES STRANGELY CALM.
REACH OUT, JACKSON LI. FEEL THE CURRENTS, THE AURAS ALL AROUND YOU!
IGNORE THE ROAR OF THE MARTIANS... THE RELENTLESS CLACKING OF THEIR METAL LEGS...
SUPPRESS YOUR EMOTIONS. YOUR FEAR, YOUR ANXIETY.
YOUR RAGE.
HEED YOUR OWN COUNSEL...
...FIND THE THIRD PATH.

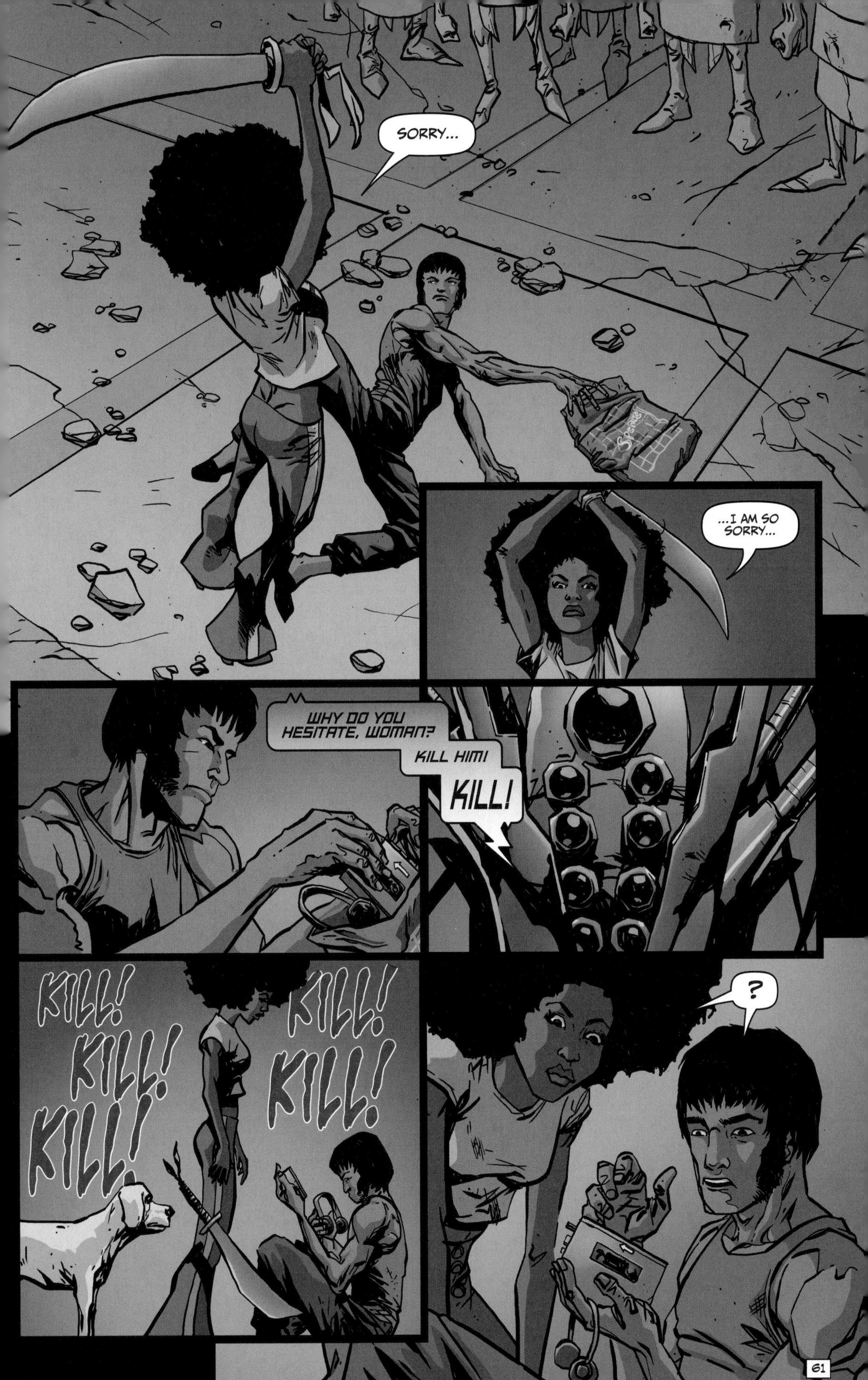
SORRY...
...I AM SO SORRY...
WHY DO YOU HESITATE, WOMAN?
KILL HIM!
KILL!
KILL!
KILL!
KILL!
KILL!
KILL!
?

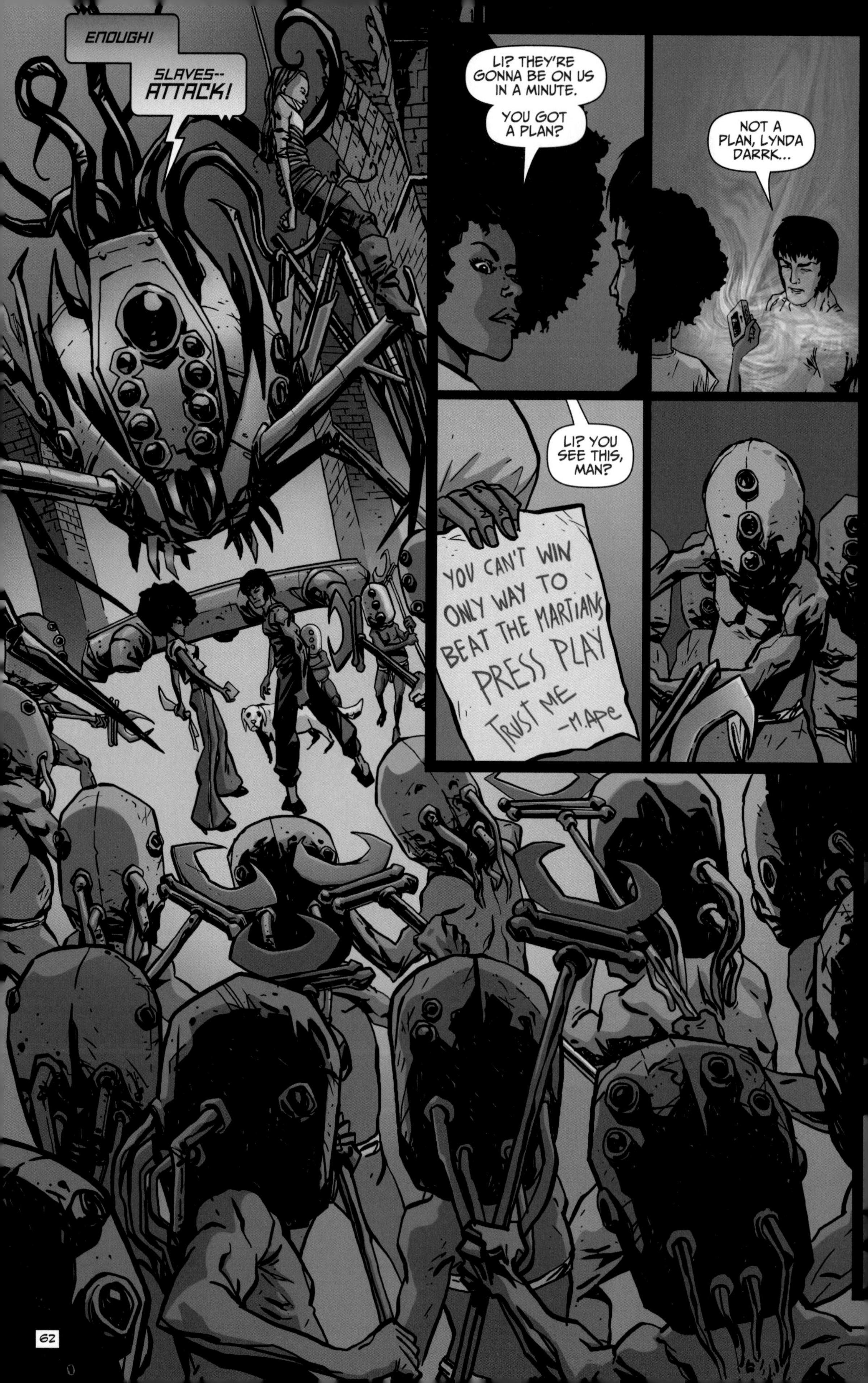
ENOUGH!
SLAVES-- ATTACK!
LI? THEY'RE GONNA BE ON US IN A MINUTE.
YOU GOT A PLAN?
NOT A PLAN, LYNDA DARRK...
LI? YOU SEE THIS, MAN?
YOU CAN'T WIN ONLY WAY TO BEAT THE MARTIANS PRESS PLAY TRUST ME -M.Ape

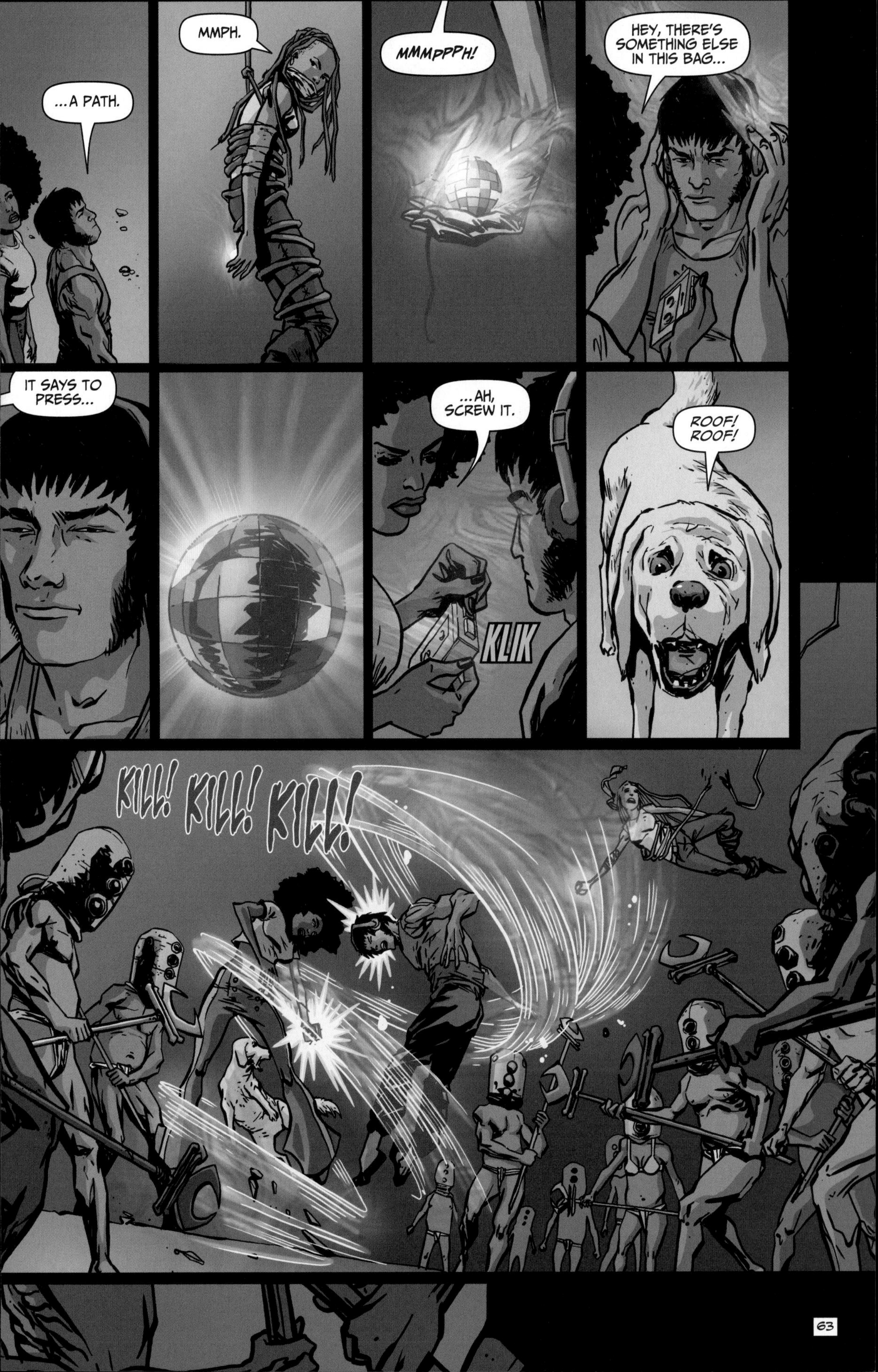

...A PATH.
MMPH.
MMMPPPH!
HEY, THERE'S SOMETHING ELSE IN THIS BAG...
IT SAYS TO PRESS...
...AH, SCREW IT.
KLIK
ROOF! ROOF!
KILL! KILL! KILL!

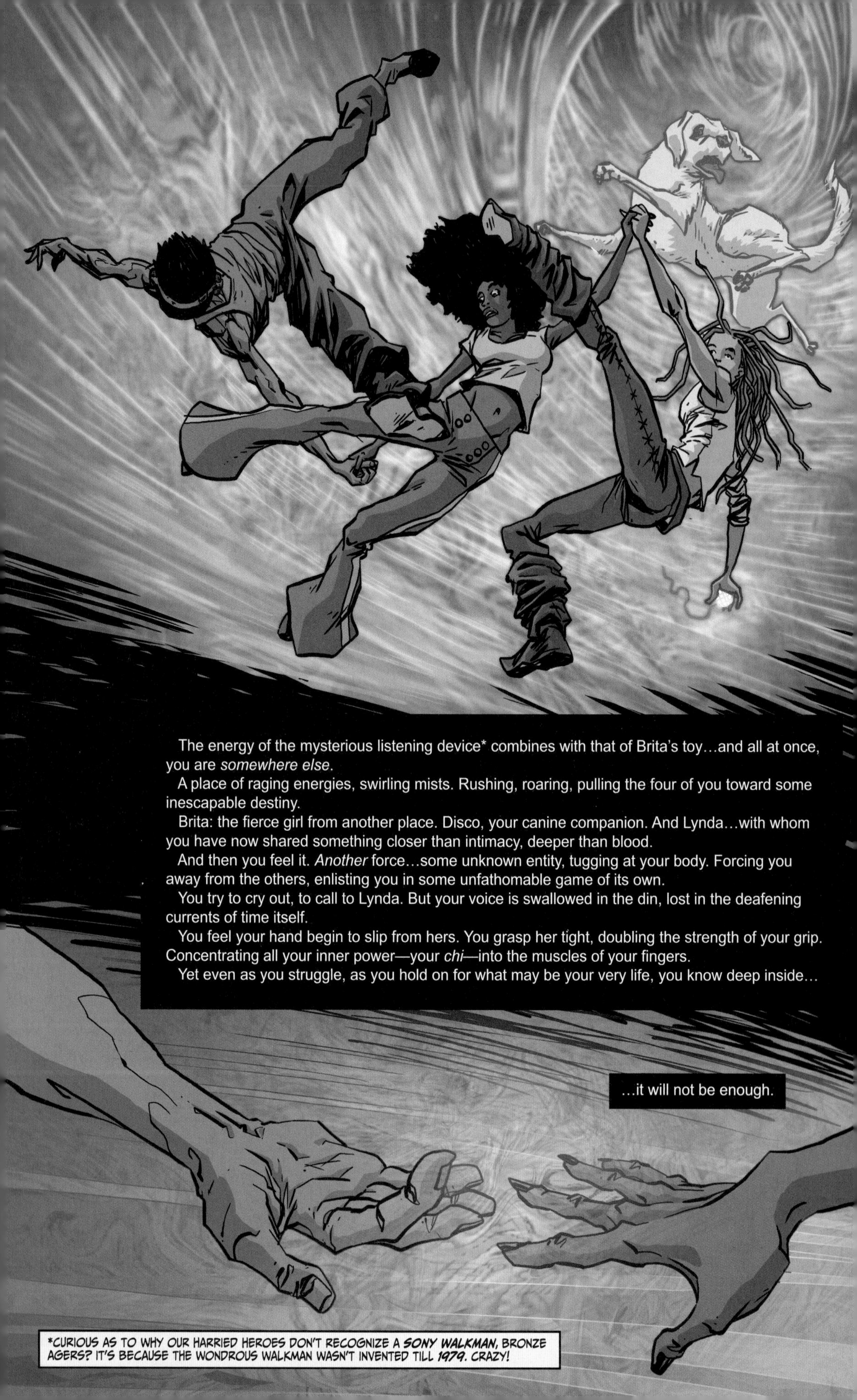
The energy of the mysterious listening device* combines with that of Brita's toy…and all at once, you are *somewhere else*.
A place of raging energies, swirling mists. Rushing, roaring, pulling the four of you toward some inescapable destiny.
Brita: the fierce girl from another place. Disco, your canine companion. And Lynda…with whom you have now shared something closer than intimacy, deeper than blood.
And then you feel it. *Another* force…some unknown entity, tugging at your body. Forcing you away from the others, enlisting you in some unfathomable game of its own.
You try to cry out, to call to Lynda. But your voice is swallowed in the din, lost in the deafening currents of time itself.
You feel your hand begin to slip from hers. You grasp her tight, doubling the strength of your grip. Concentrating all your inner power—your *chi*—into the muscles of your fingers.
Yet even as you struggle, as you hold on for what may be your very life, you know deep inside…
…it will not be enough.
*CURIOUS AS TO WHY OUR HARRIED HEROES DON'T RECOGNIZE A **SONY WALKMAN**, BRONZE AGERS? IT'S BECAUSE THE WONDROUS WALKMAN WASN'T INVENTED TILL **1979**. CRAZY!

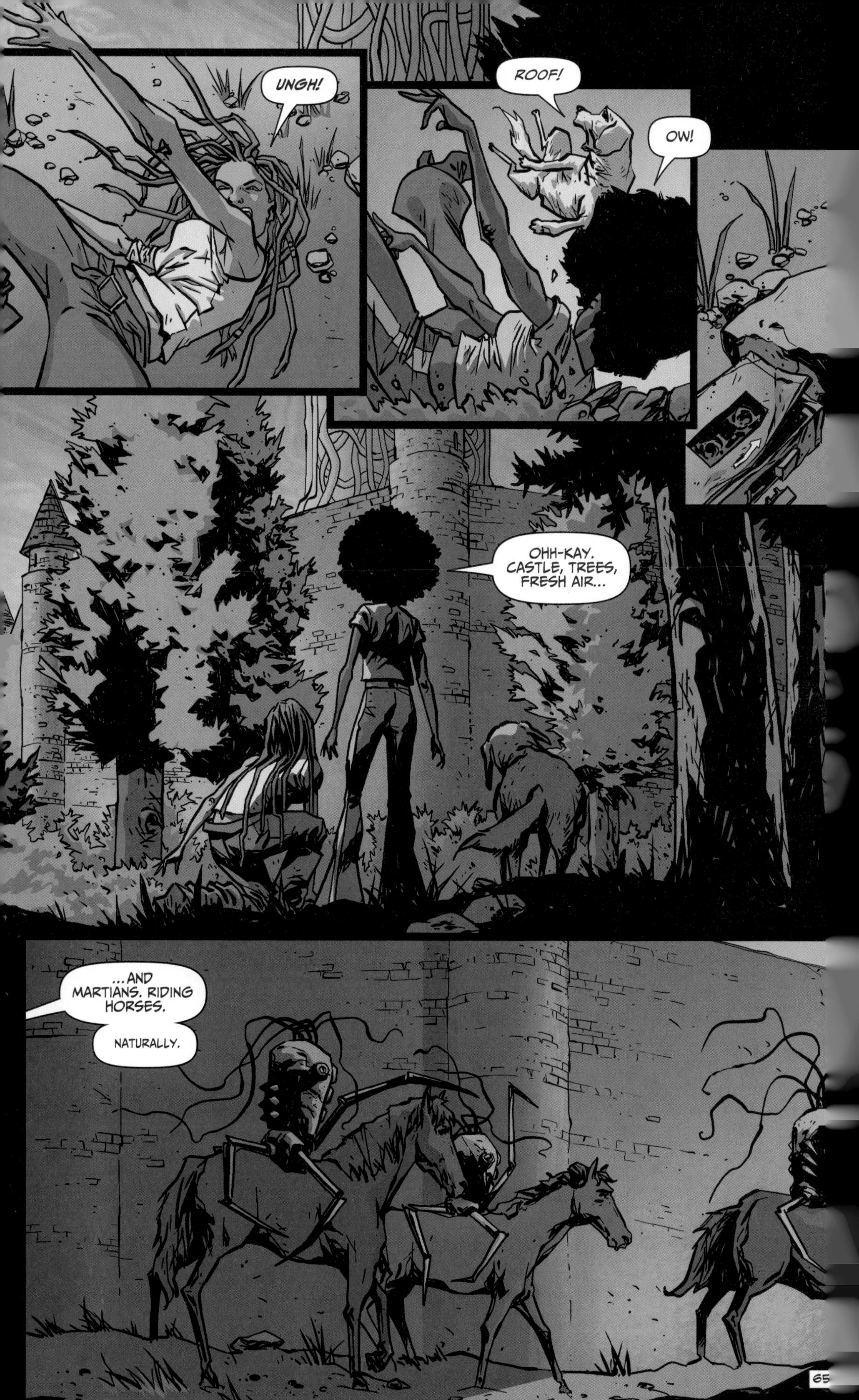
UNGH!
ROOF!
OW!
OHH-KAY. CASTLE, TREES, FRESH AIR...
...AND MARTIANS. RIDING HORSES.
NATURALLY.

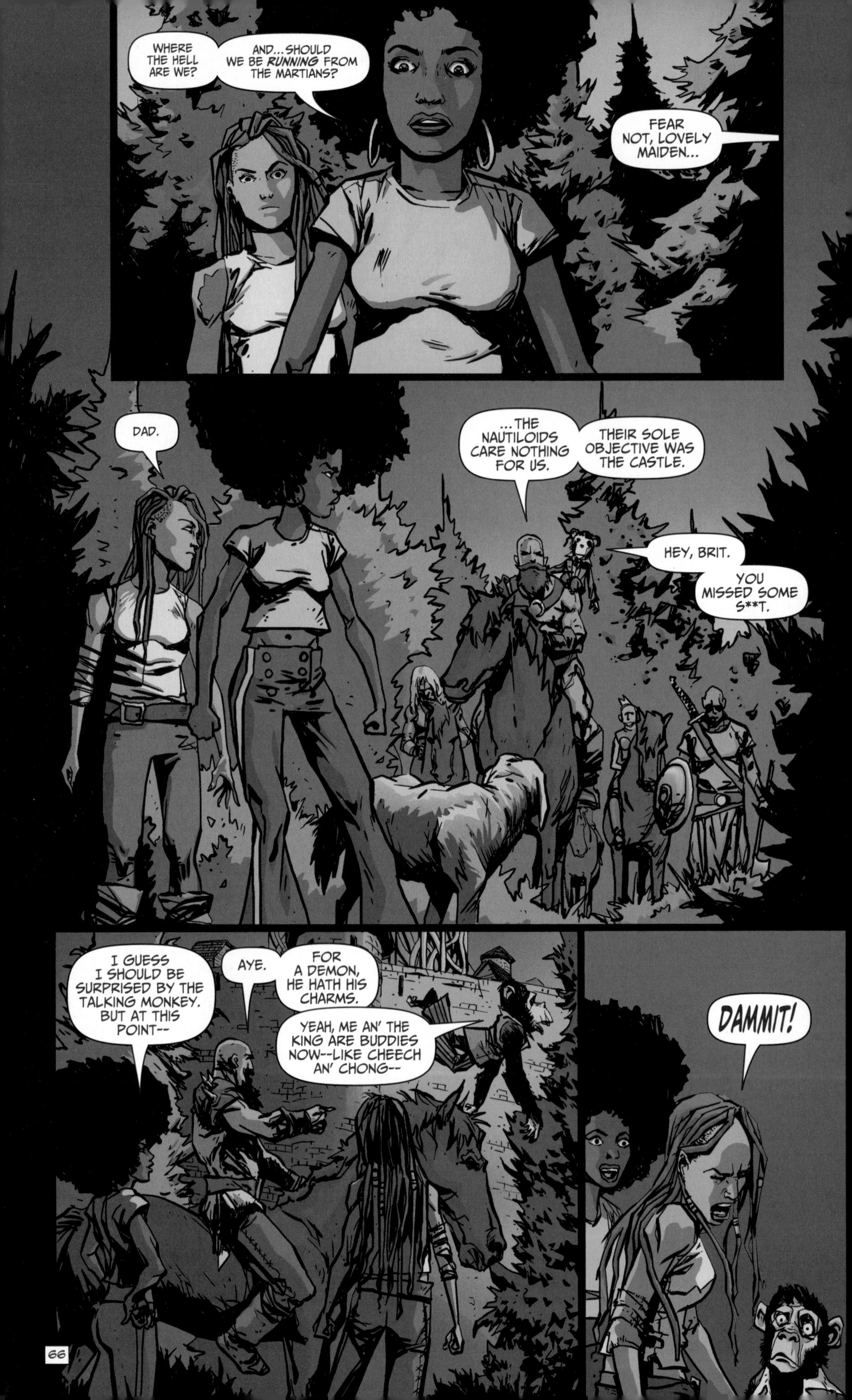
WHERE THE HELL ARE WE?
AND...SHOULD WE BE *RUNNING* FROM THE MARTIANS?
FEAR NOT, LOVELY MAIDEN...
DAD.
...THE NAUTILOIDS CARE NOTHING FOR US.
THEIR SOLE OBJECTIVE WAS THE CASTLE.
HEY, BRIT.
YOU MISSED SOME S**T.
I GUESS I SHOULD BE SURPRISED BY THE TALKING MONKEY. BUT AT THIS POINT--
AYE.
FOR A DEMON, HE HATH HIS CHARMS.
YEAH, ME AN' THE KING ARE BUDDIES NOW--LIKE CHEECH AN' CHONG--
DAMMIT!

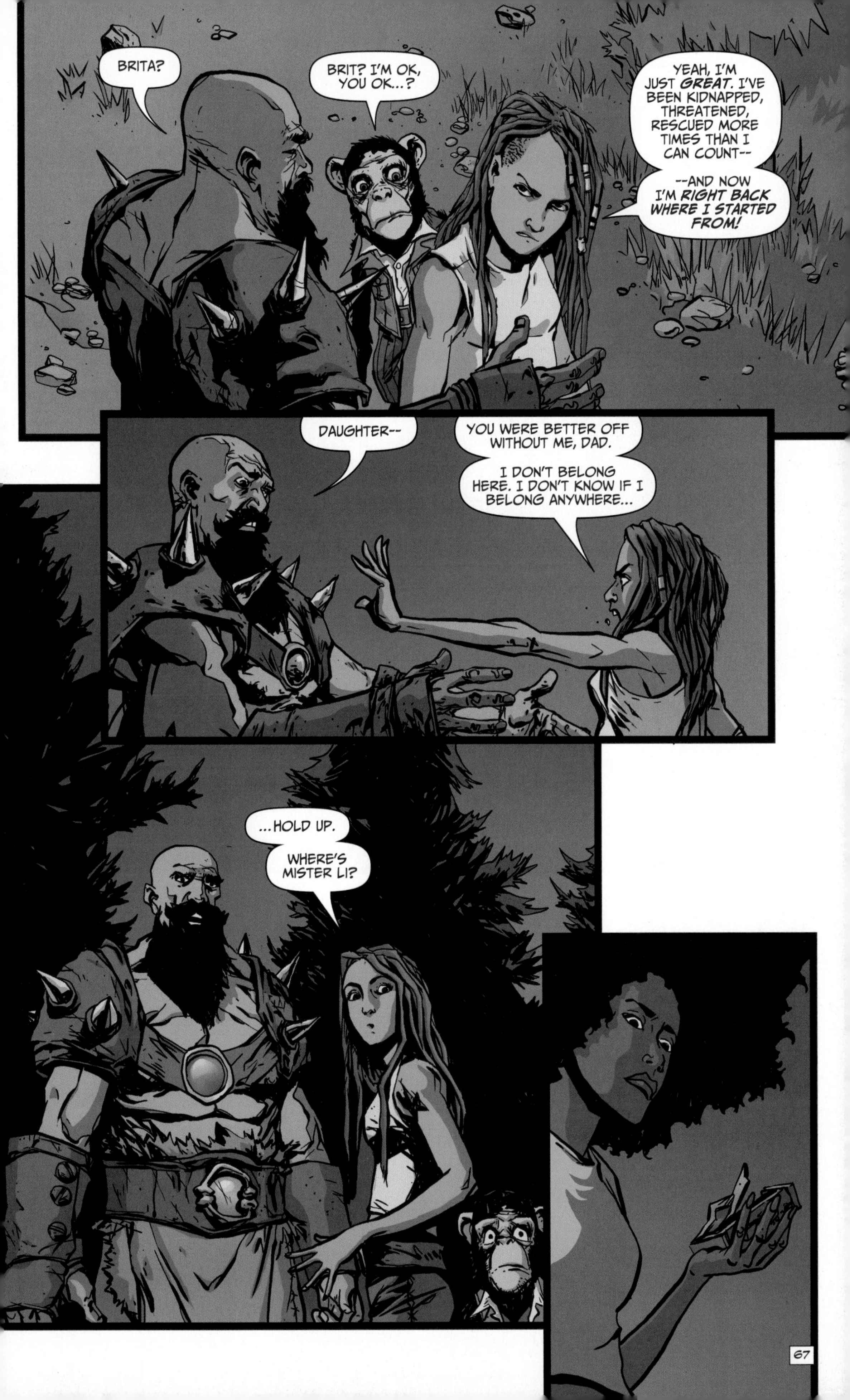
BRITA?
BRIT? I'M OK, YOU OK...?
YEAH, I'M JUST GREAT. I'VE BEEN KIDNAPPED, THREATENED, RESCUED MORE TIMES THAN I CAN COUNT--
--AND NOW I'M RIGHT BACK WHERE I STARTED FROM!
DAUGHTER--
YOU WERE BETTER OFF WITHOUT ME, DAD.
I DON'T BELONG HERE. I DON'T KNOW IF I BELONG ANYWHERE...
...HOLD UP.
WHERE'S MISTER LI?

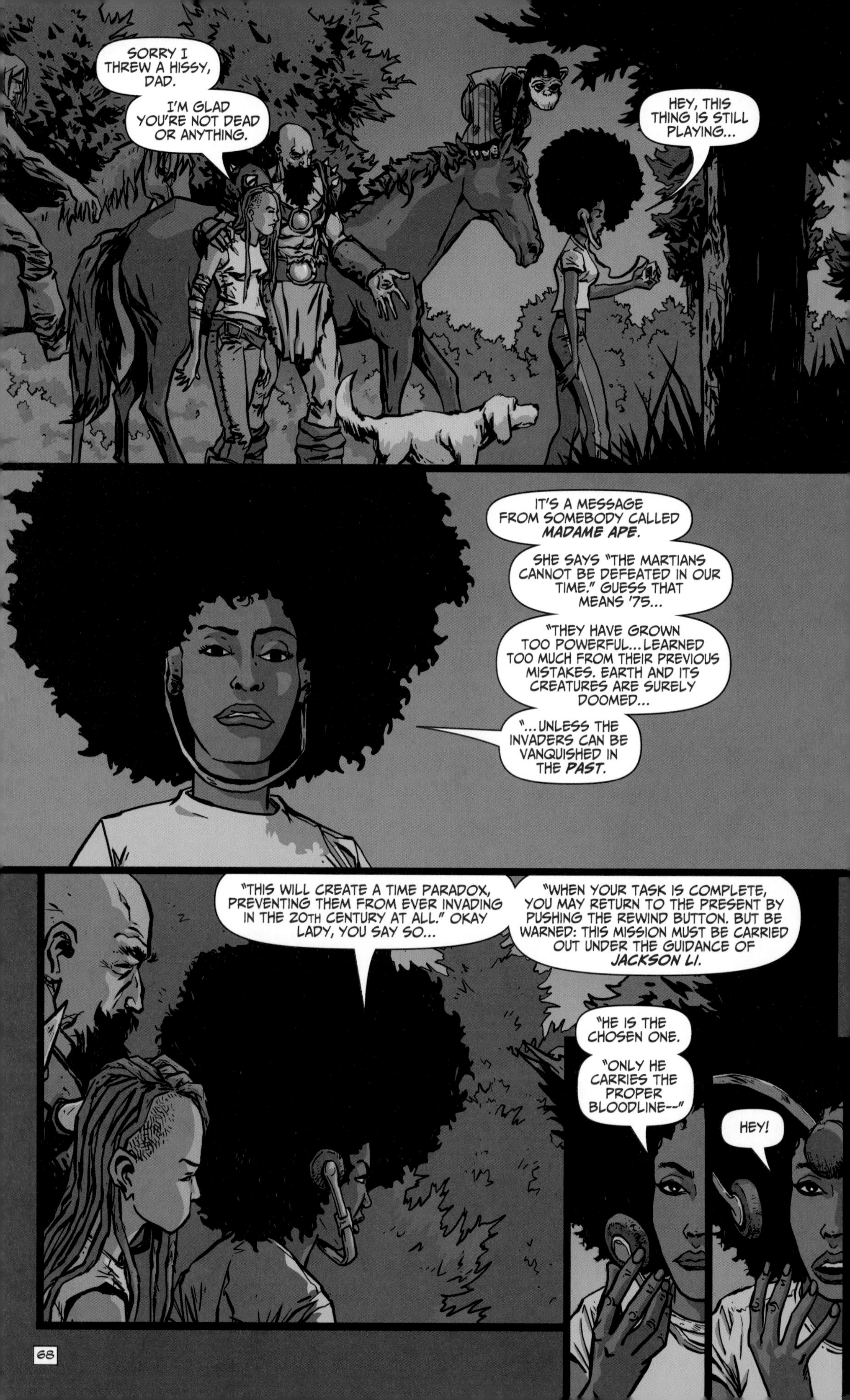
SORRY I THREW A HISSY, DAD.
I'M GLAD YOU'RE NOT DEAD OR ANYTHING.
HEY, THIS THING IS STILL PLAYING...
IT'S A MESSAGE FROM SOMEBODY CALLED MADAME APE.
SHE SAYS "THE MARTIANS CANNOT BE DEFEATED IN OUR TIME." GUESS THAT MEANS '75...
"THEY HAVE GROWN TOO POWERFUL...LEARNED TOO MUCH FROM THEIR PREVIOUS MISTAKES. EARTH AND ITS CREATURES ARE SURELY DOOMED...
"...UNLESS THE INVADERS CAN BE VANQUISHED IN THE PAST.
"THIS WILL CREATE A TIME PARADOX, PREVENTING THEM FROM EVER INVADING IN THE 20TH CENTURY AT ALL." OKAY LADY, YOU SAY SO...
"WHEN YOUR TASK IS COMPLETE, YOU MAY RETURN TO THE PRESENT BY PUSHING THE REWIND BUTTON. BUT BE WARNED: THIS MISSION MUST BE CARRIED OUT UNDER THE GUIDANCE OF JACKSON LI.
"HE IS THE CHOSEN ONE.
"ONLY HE CARRIES THE PROPER BLOODLINE--"
HEY!

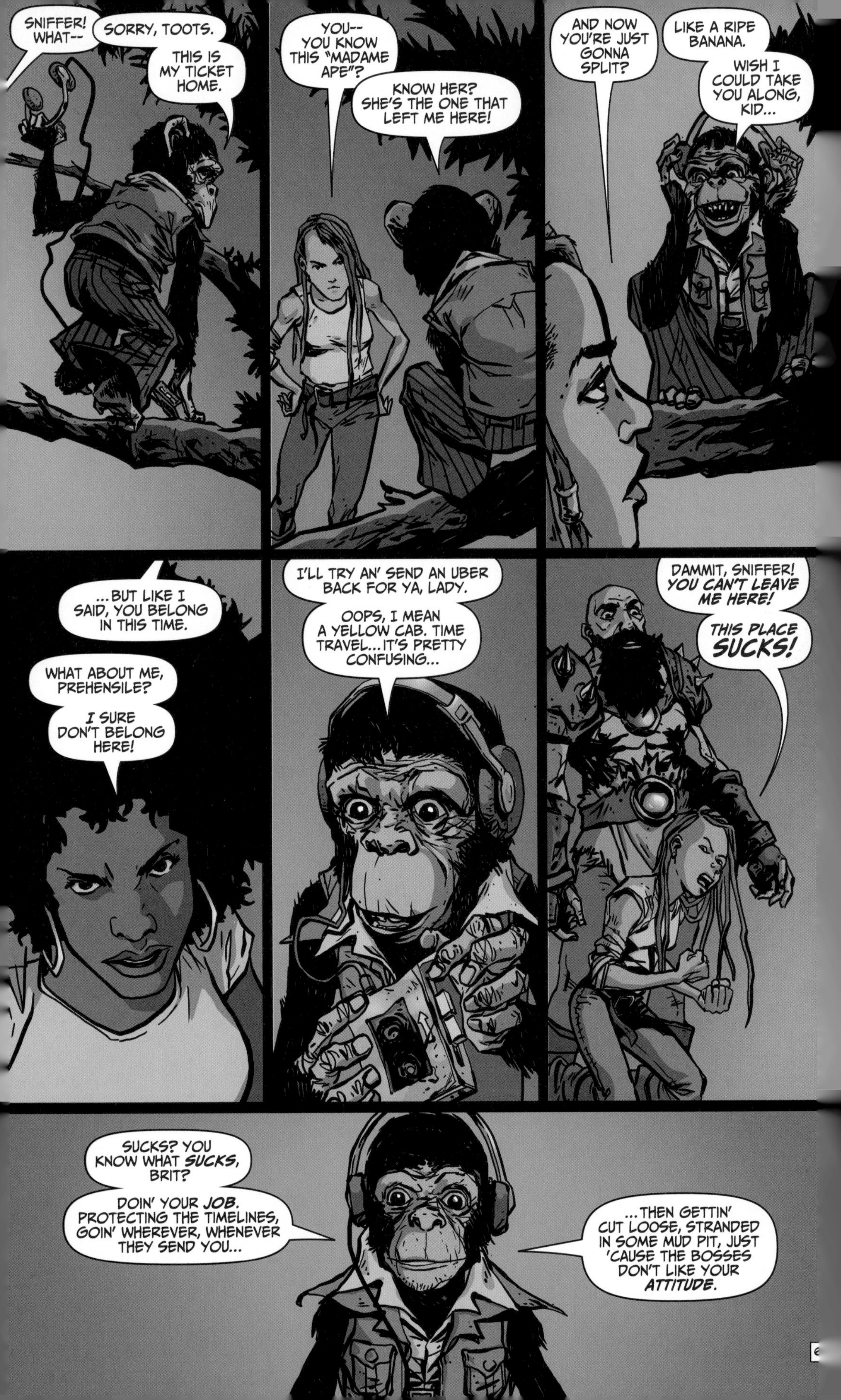
SNIFFER! WHAT--
SORRY, TOOTS.
THIS IS MY TICKET HOME.
YOU-- YOU KNOW THIS "MADAME APE"?
KNOW HER? SHE'S THE ONE THAT LEFT ME HERE!
AND NOW YOU'RE JUST GONNA SPLIT?
LIKE A RIPE BANANA.
WISH I COULD TAKE YOU ALONG, KID...
...BUT LIKE I SAID, YOU BELONG IN THIS TIME.
WHAT ABOUT ME, PREHENSILE?
I SURE DON'T BELONG HERE!
I'LL TRY AN' SEND AN UBER BACK FOR YA, LADY.
OOPS, I MEAN A YELLOW CAB. TIME TRAVEL...IT'S PRETTY CONFUSING...
DAMMIT, SNIFFER! YOU CAN'T LEAVE ME HERE!
THIS PLACE SUCKS!
SUCKS? YOU KNOW WHAT SUCKS, BRIT?
DOIN' YOUR JOB. PROTECTING THE TIMELINES, GOIN' WHEREVER, WHENEVER THEY SEND YOU...
...THEN GETTIN' CUT LOOSE, STRANDED IN SOME MUD PIT, JUST 'CAUSE THE BOSSES DON'T LIKE YOUR ATTITUDE.

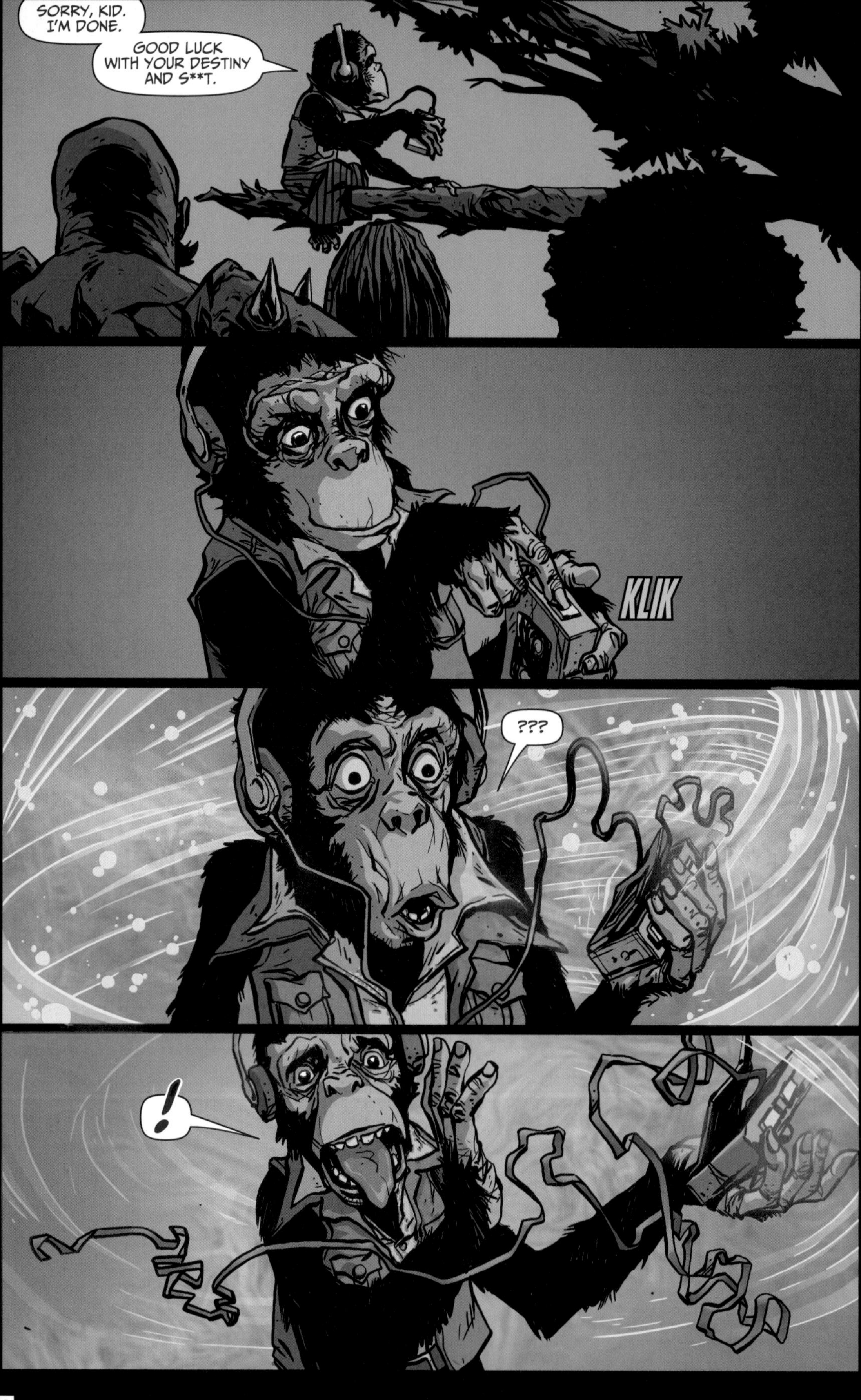
SORRY, KID. I'M DONE.
GOOD LUCK WITH YOUR DESTINY AND S**T.
KLIK
???
!

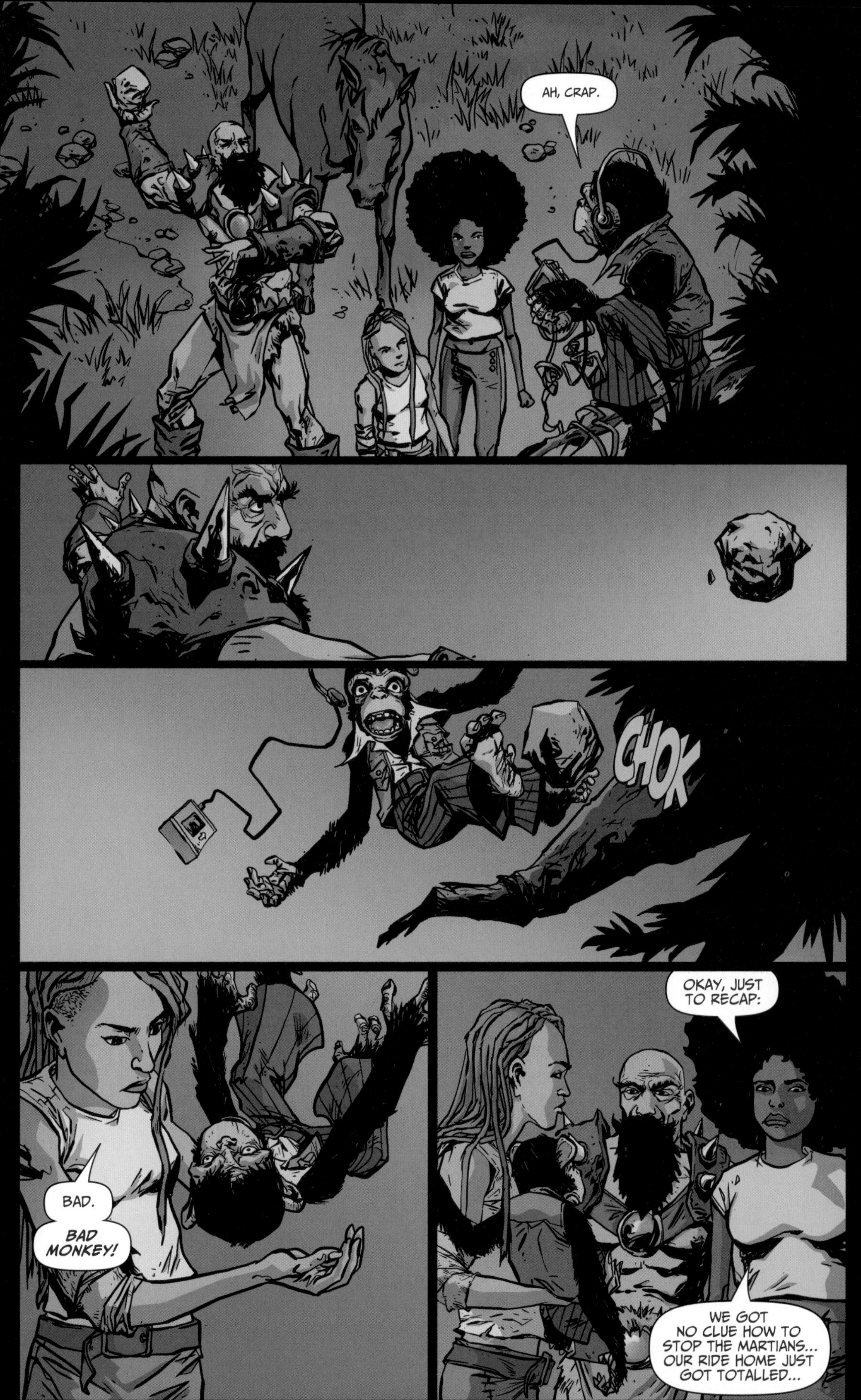
AH, CRAP.
CHOK
BAD.
BAD MONKEY!
OKAY, JUST TO RECAP:
WE GOT NO CLUE HOW TO STOP THE MARTIANS... OUR RIDE HOME JUST GOT TOTALLED...

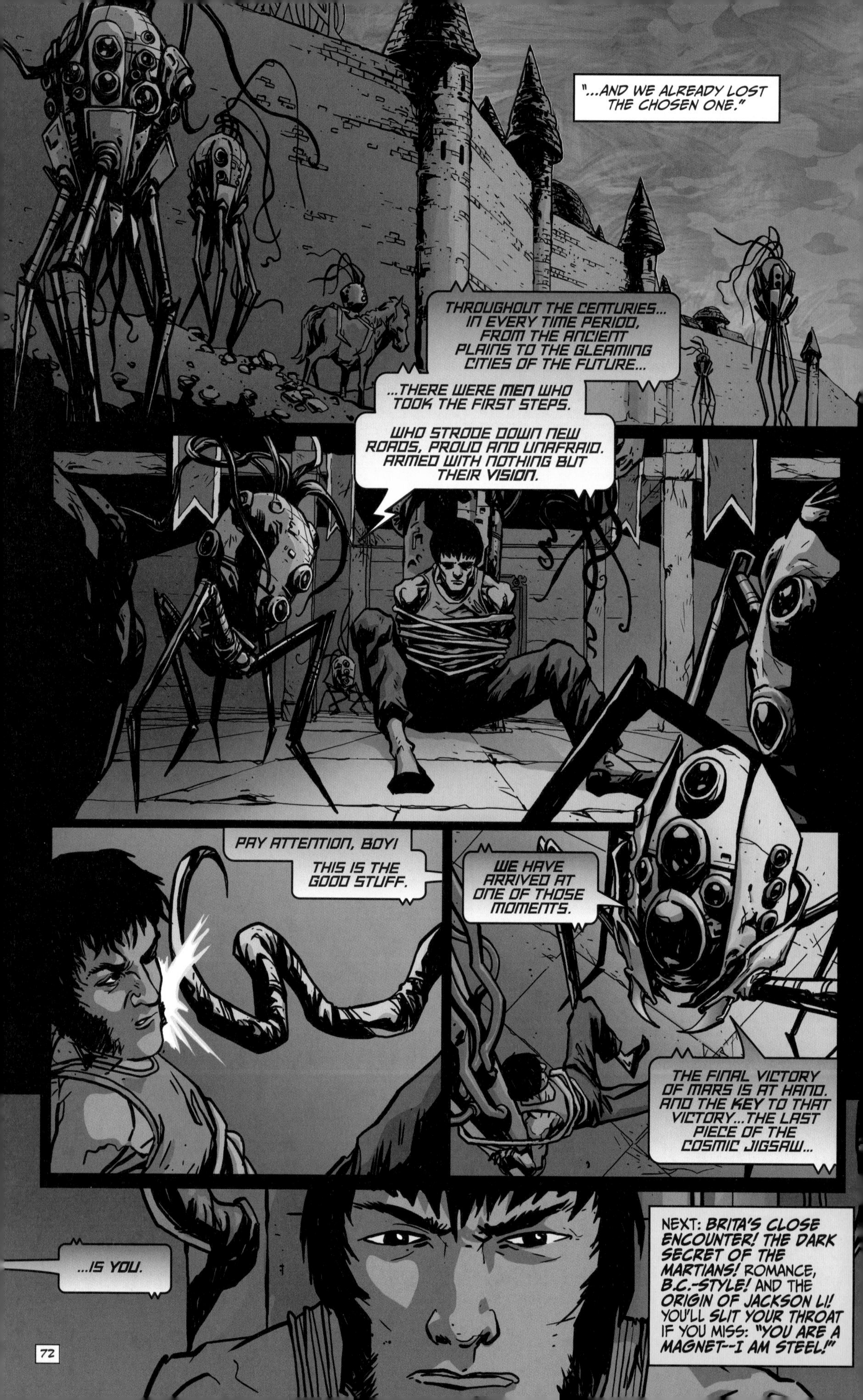
"...AND WE ALREADY LOST THE CHOSEN ONE."
THROUGHOUT THE CENTURIES... IN EVERY TIME PERIOD, FROM THE ANCIENT PLAINS TO THE GLEAMING CITIES OF THE FUTURE...
...THERE WERE MEN WHO TOOK THE FIRST STEPS.
WHO STRODE DOWN NEW ROADS, PROUD AND UNAFRAID. ARMED WITH NOTHING BUT THEIR VISION.
PAY ATTENTION, BOY!
THIS IS THE GOOD STUFF.
WE HAVE ARRIVED AT ONE OF THOSE MOMENTS.
THE FINAL VICTORY OF MARS IS AT HAND, AND THE KEY TO THAT VICTORY...THE LAST PIECE OF THE COSMIC JIGSAW...
...IS YOU.
NEXT: BRITA'S CLOSE ENCOUNTER! THE DARK SECRET OF THE MARTIANS! ROMANCE, B.C.-STYLE! AND THE ORIGIN OF JACKSON LI! YOU'LL SLIT YOUR THROAT IF YOU MISS: "YOU ARE A MAGNET--I AM STEEL!"

INTERMISSION

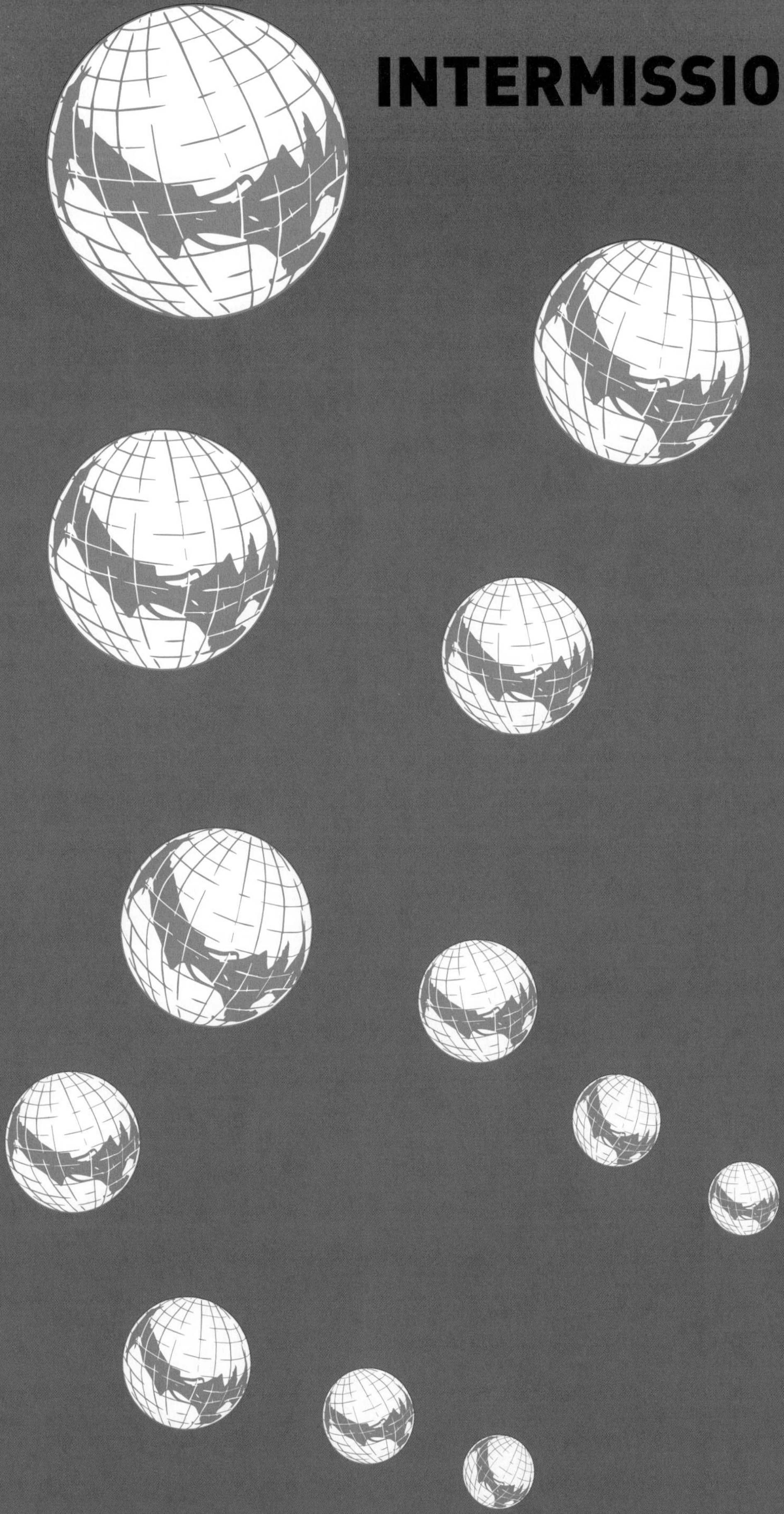

I HAVEN'T SPENT MUCH OF MY LIFE...WHAT'S THE WORD I'M LOOKING FOR...

SOBER?

AAAOOOWWWW!

FACT IS, I'VE PUT A LOT OF WORK INTO JUSTIFYING SOME PRETTY BAD HABITS.

I'M GUESSING THIS REJECT FROM A KNITTING FACTORY HAS, TOO.

IT'S NOT REALLY MY FAULT. NOT ANYMORE.

LEAST THAT'S WHAT I TELL MYSELF.

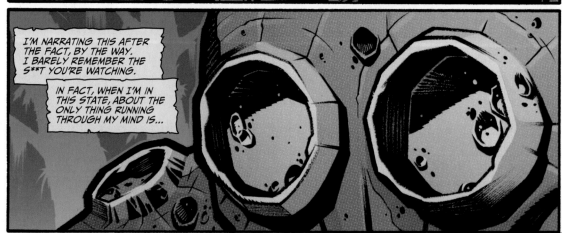

I'M NARRATING THIS AFTER THE FACT, BY THE WAY. I BARELY REMEMBER THE S**T YOU'RE WATCHING.

IN FACT, WHEN I'M IN THIS STATE, ABOUT THE ONLY THING RUNNING THROUGH MY MIND IS...

Tom Peyer PRESENTS: THE MIASMIC MOON-THING!

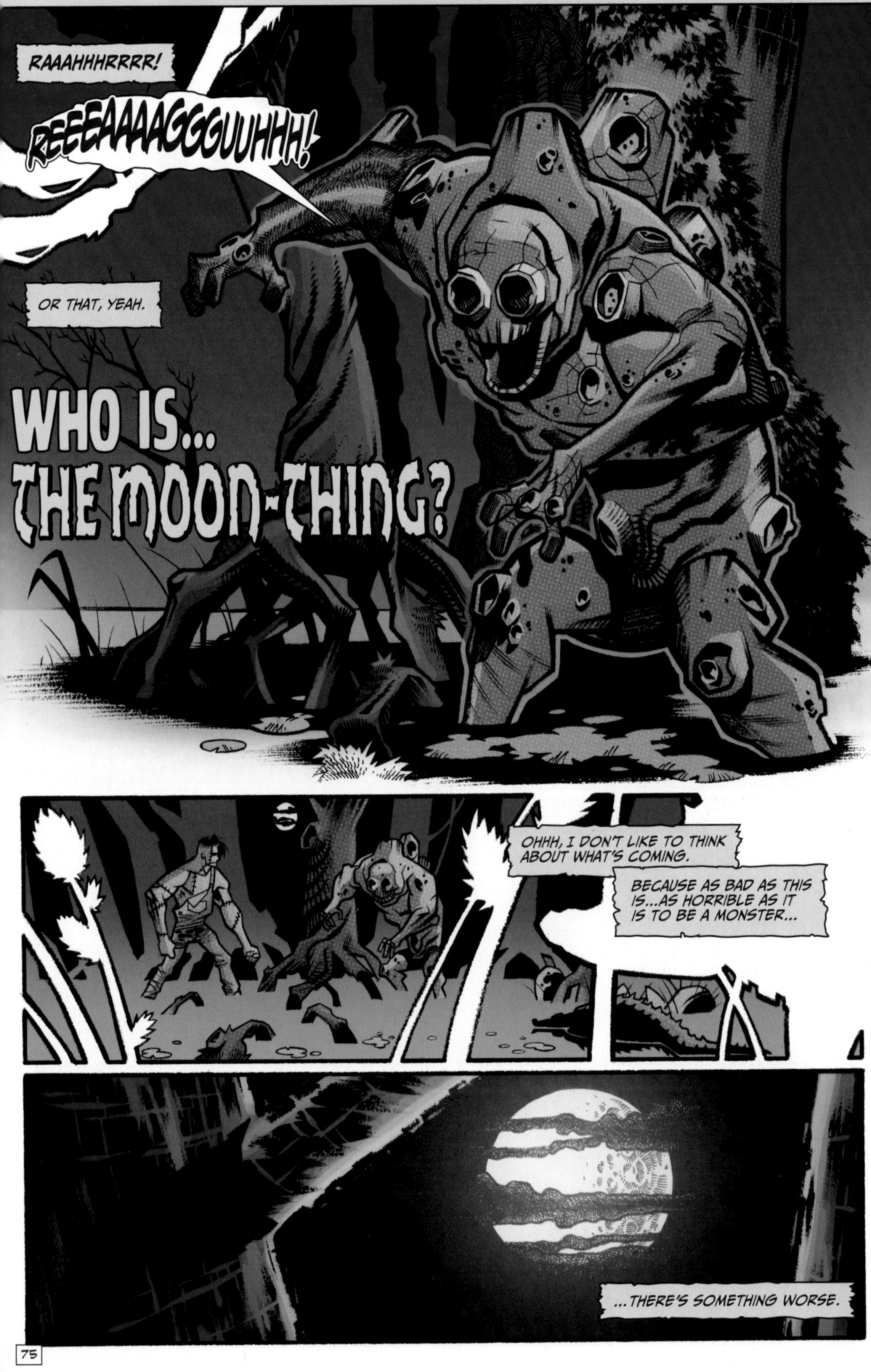

RAAAHHHRRRR!
REEEAAAAGGGUUHHH!
OR THAT, YEAH.
WHO IS... THE MOON-THING?
OHHH, I DON'T LIKE TO THINK ABOUT WHAT'S COMING.
BECAUSE AS BAD AS THIS IS...AS HORRIBLE AS IT IS TO BE A MONSTER...
...THERE'S SOMETHING WORSE.

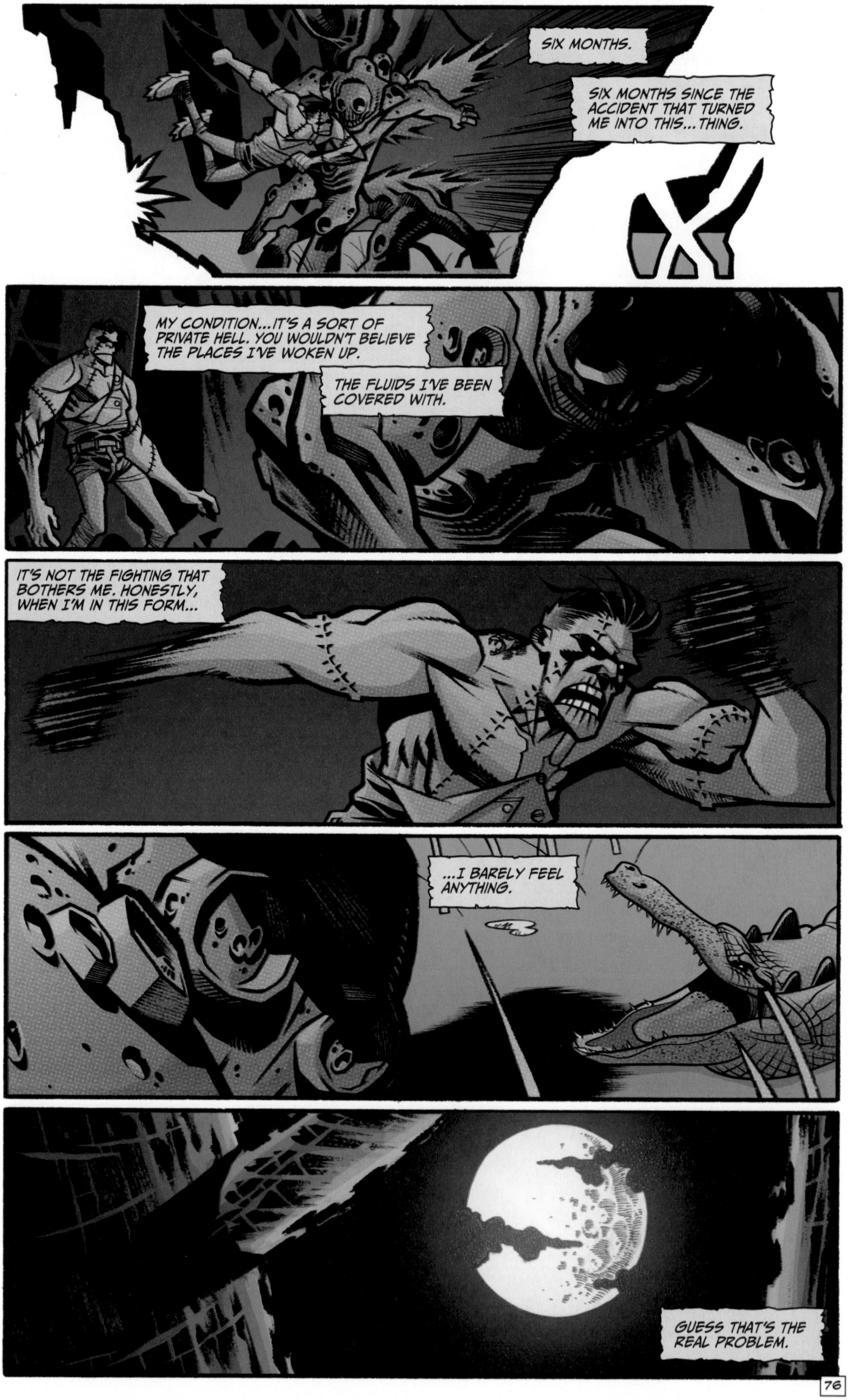
SIX MONTHS.
SIX MONTHS SINCE THE ACCIDENT THAT TURNED ME INTO THIS...THING.
MY CONDITION...IT'S A SORT OF PRIVATE HELL. YOU WOULDN'T BELIEVE THE PLACES I'VE WOKEN UP.
THE FLUIDS I'VE BEEN COVERED WITH.
IT'S NOT THE FIGHTING THAT BOTHERS ME. HONESTLY, WHEN I'M IN THIS FORM...
...I BARELY FEEL ANYTHING.
GUESS THAT'S THE REAL PROBLEM.

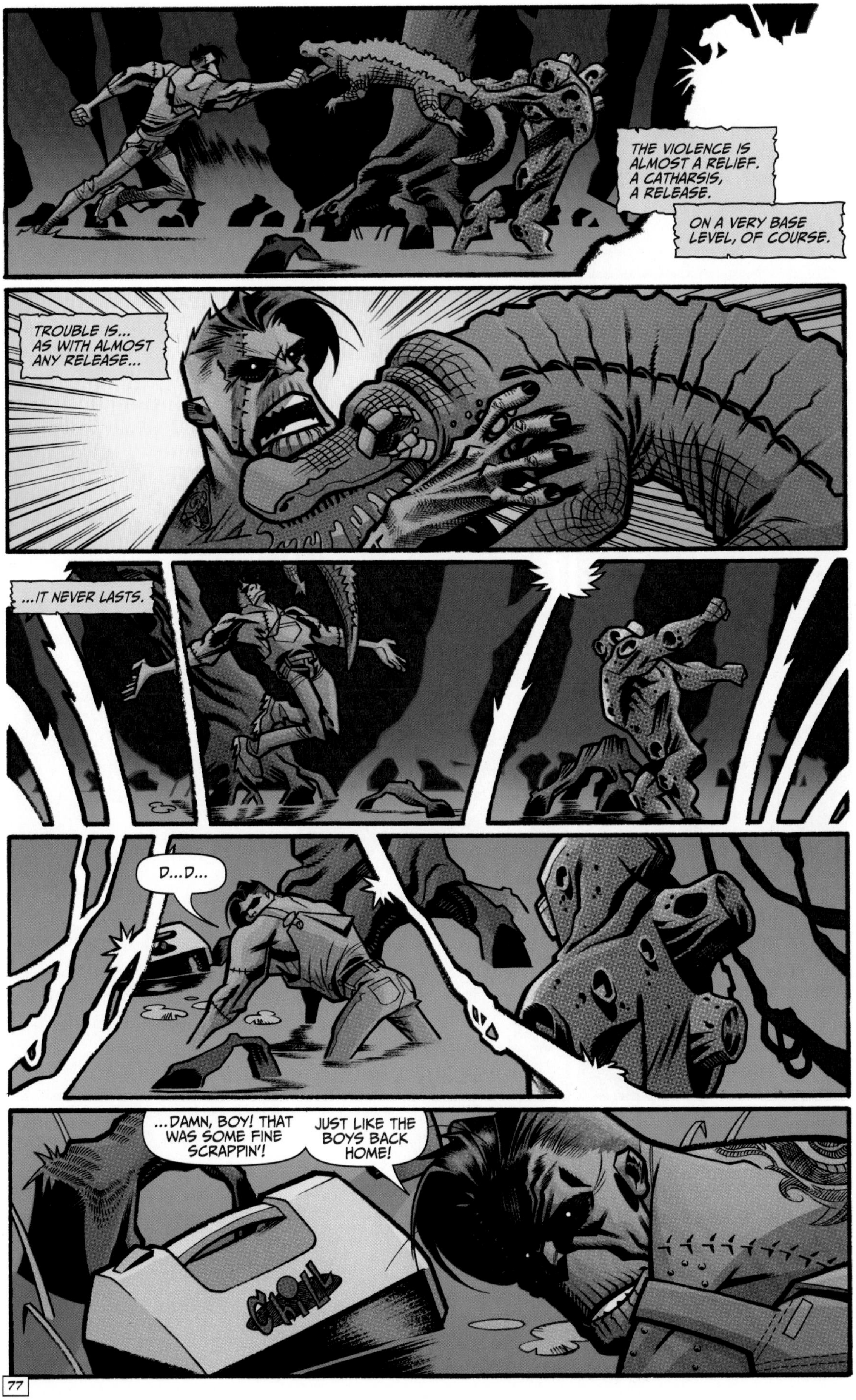
THE VIOLENCE IS ALMOST A RELIEF. A CATHARSIS, A RELEASE.
ON A VERY BASE LEVEL, OF COURSE.
TROUBLE IS... AS WITH ALMOST ANY RELEASE...
...IT NEVER LASTS.
D...D...
...DAMN, BOY! THAT WAS SOME FINE SCRAPPIN'!
JUST LIKE THE BOYS BACK HOME!

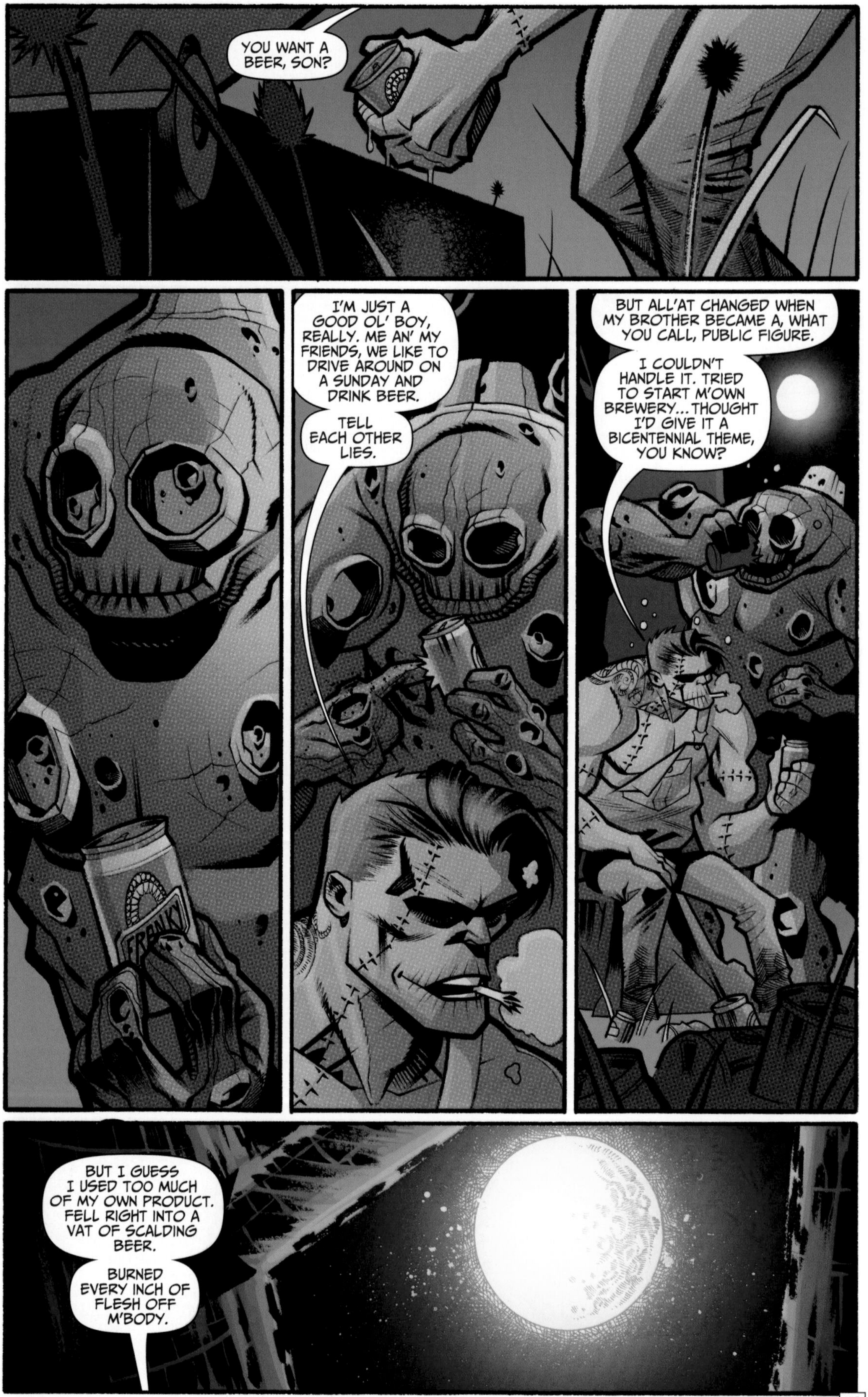
YOU WANT A BEER, SON?
I'M JUST A GOOD OL' BOY, REALLY. ME AN' MY FRIENDS, WE LIKE TO DRIVE AROUND ON A SUNDAY AND DRINK BEER.
TELL EACH OTHER LIES.
BUT ALL'AT CHANGED WHEN MY BROTHER BECAME A, WHAT YOU CALL, PUBLIC FIGURE.
I COULDN'T HANDLE IT. TRIED TO START M'OWN BREWERY... THOUGHT I'D GIVE IT A BICENTENNIAL THEME, YOU KNOW?
BUT I GUESS I USED TOO MUCH OF MY OWN PRODUCT. FELL RIGHT INTO A VAT OF SCALDING BEER.
BURNED EVERY INCH OF FLESH OFF M'BODY.

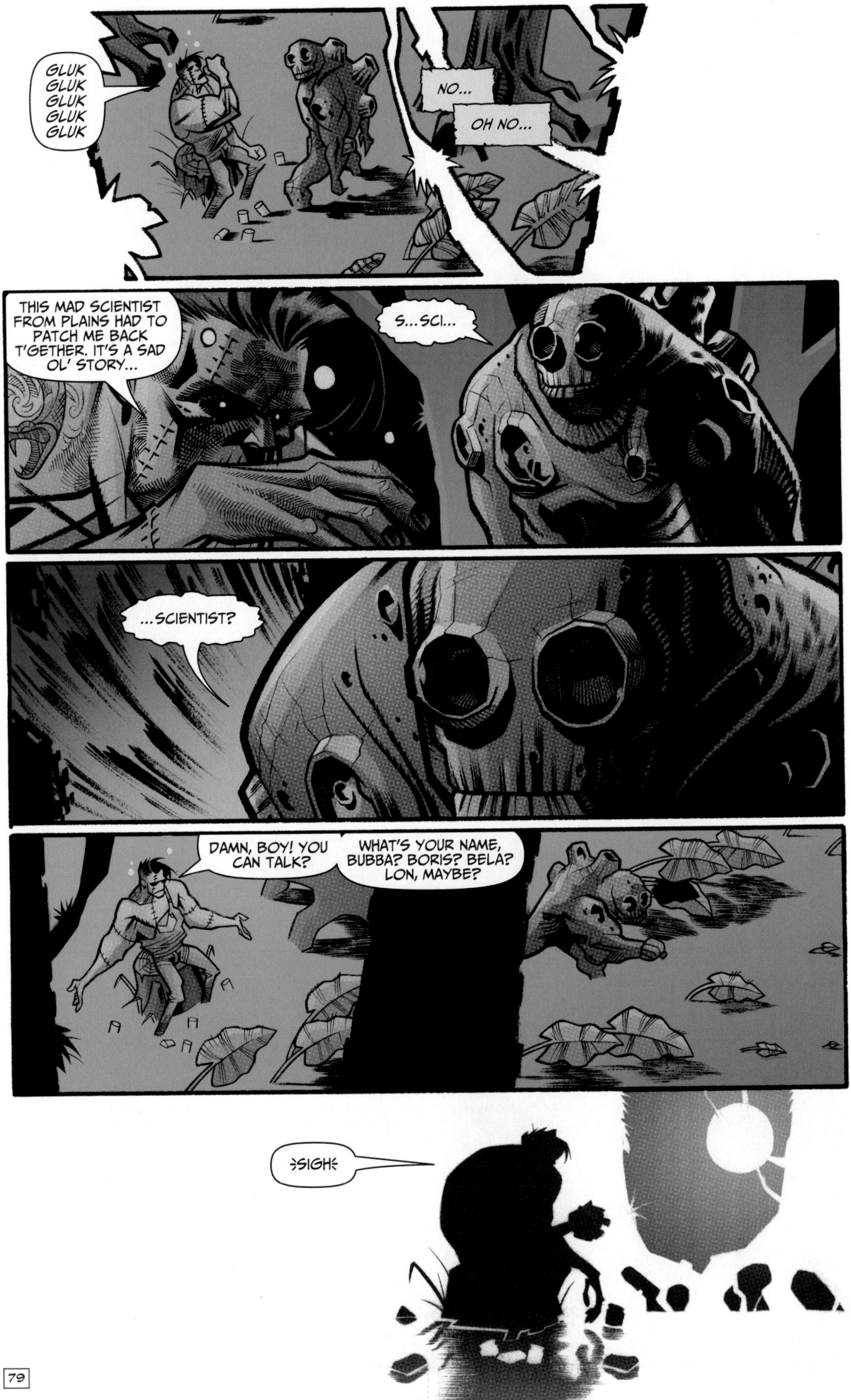
GLUK GLUK GLUK GLUK GLUK
NO...
OH NO...
THIS MAD SCIENTIST FROM PLAINS HAD TO PATCH ME BACK T'GETHER. IT'S A SAD OL' STORY...
S...SCI...
...SCIENTIST?
DAMN, BOY! YOU CAN TALK?
WHAT'S YOUR NAME, BUBBA? BORIS? BELA? LON, MAYBE?
SIGH

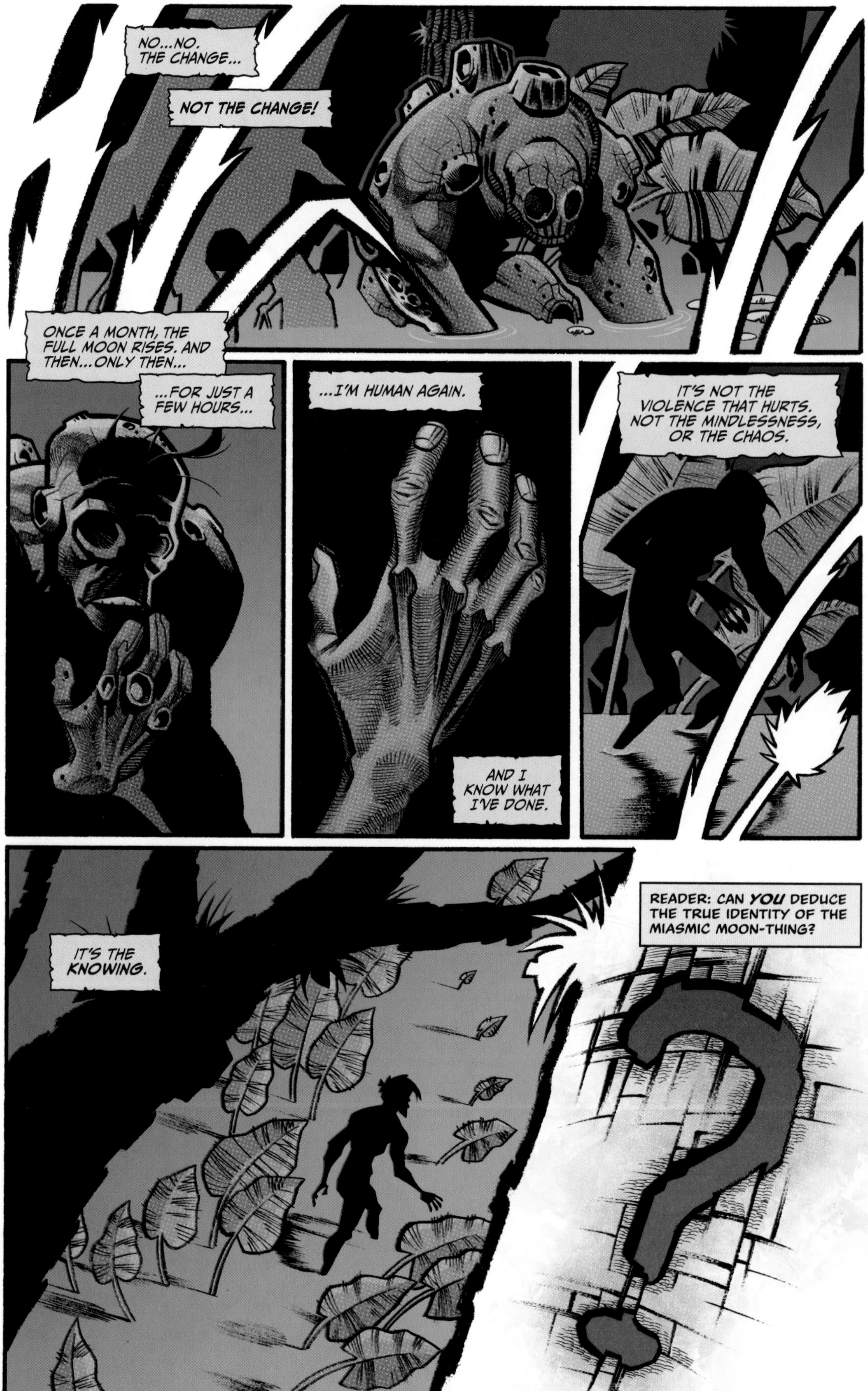

NO...NO. THE CHANGE...
NOT THE CHANGE!
ONCE A MONTH, THE FULL MOON RISES. AND THEN...ONLY THEN...
...FOR JUST A FEW HOURS...
...I'M HUMAN AGAIN.
AND I KNOW WHAT I'VE DONE.
IT'S NOT THE VIOLENCE THAT HURTS. NOT THE MINDLESSNESS, OR THE CHAOS.
IT'S THE KNOWING.
READER: CAN YOU DEDUCE THE TRUE IDENTITY OF THE MIASMIC MOON-THING?

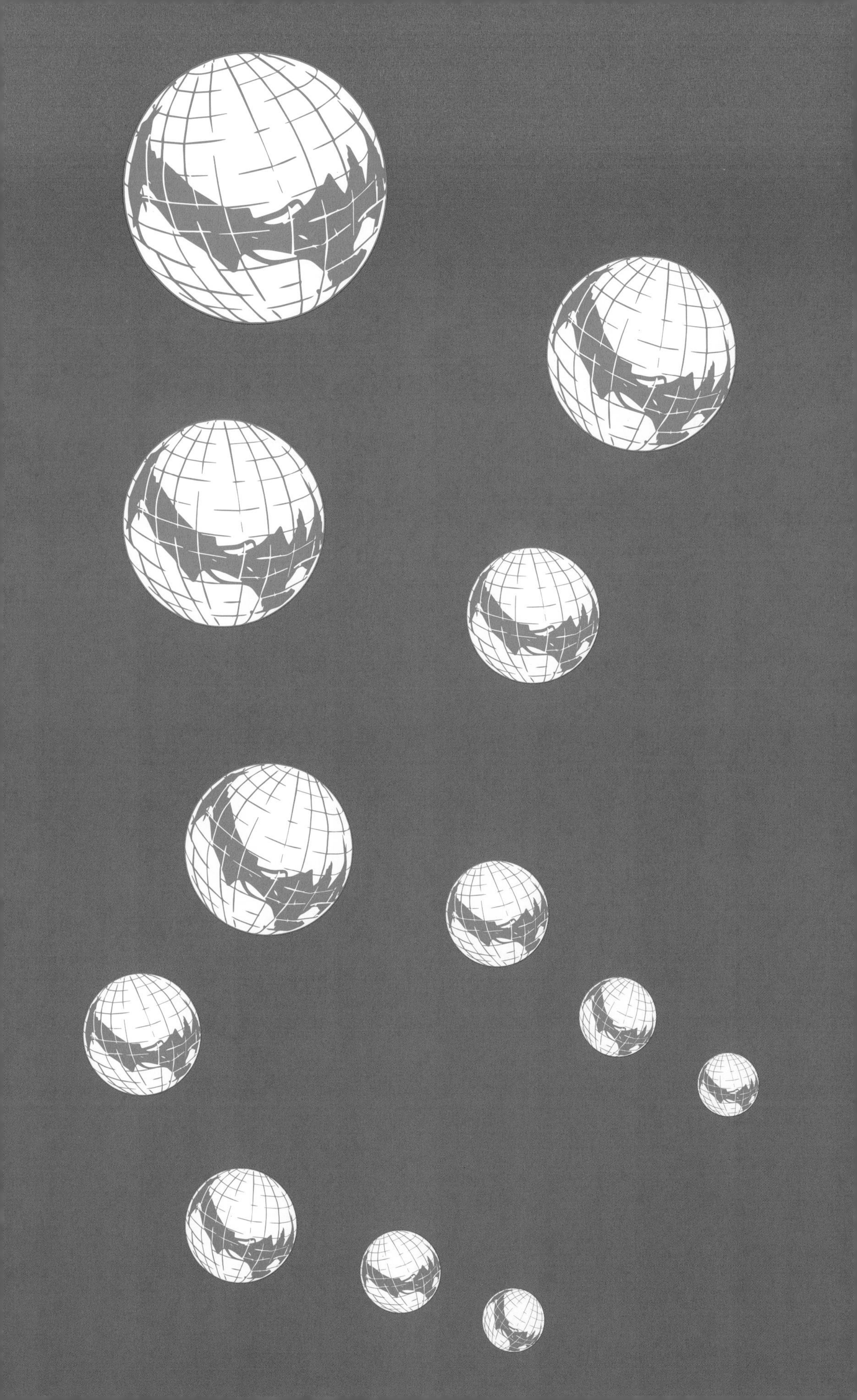

4

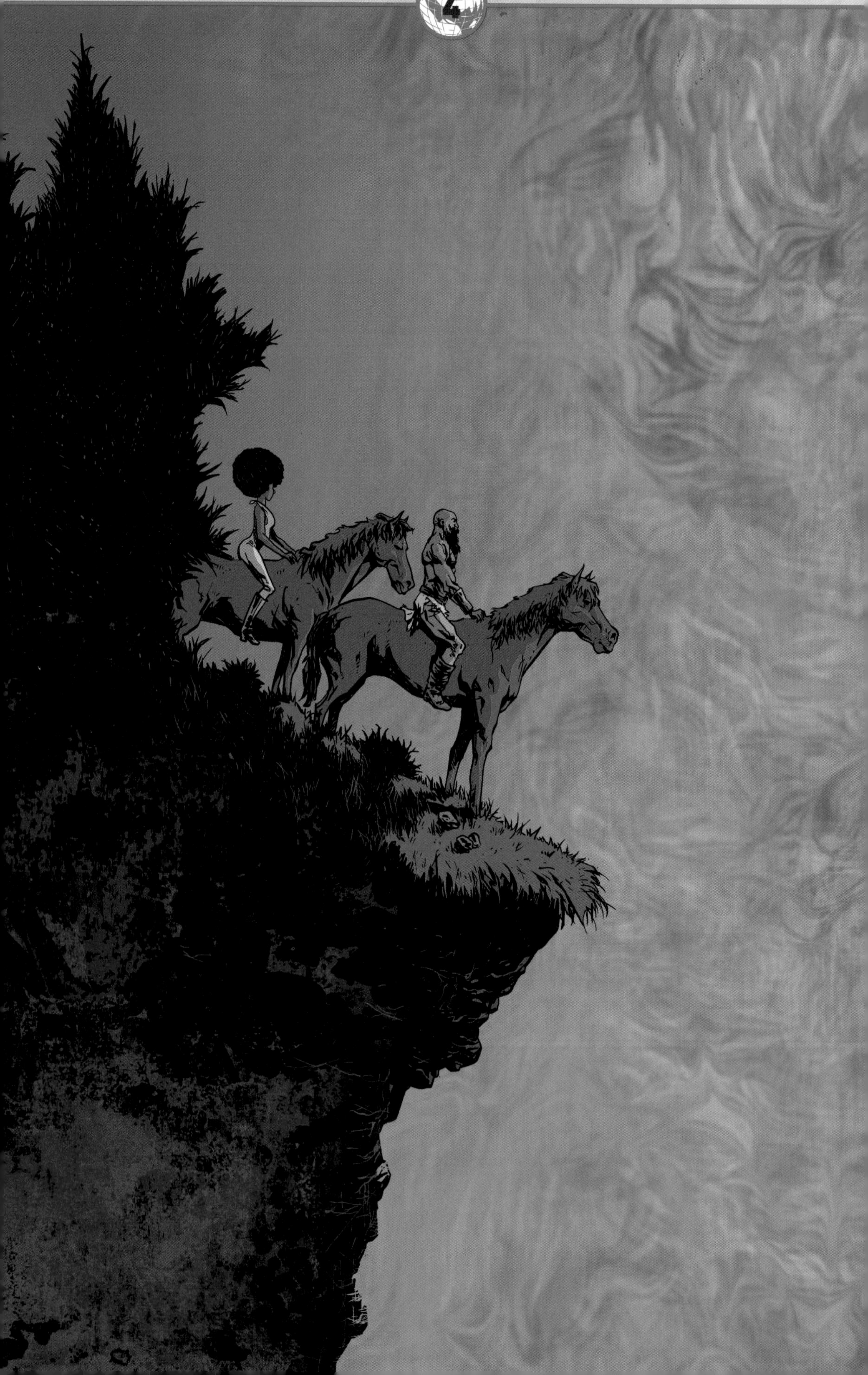

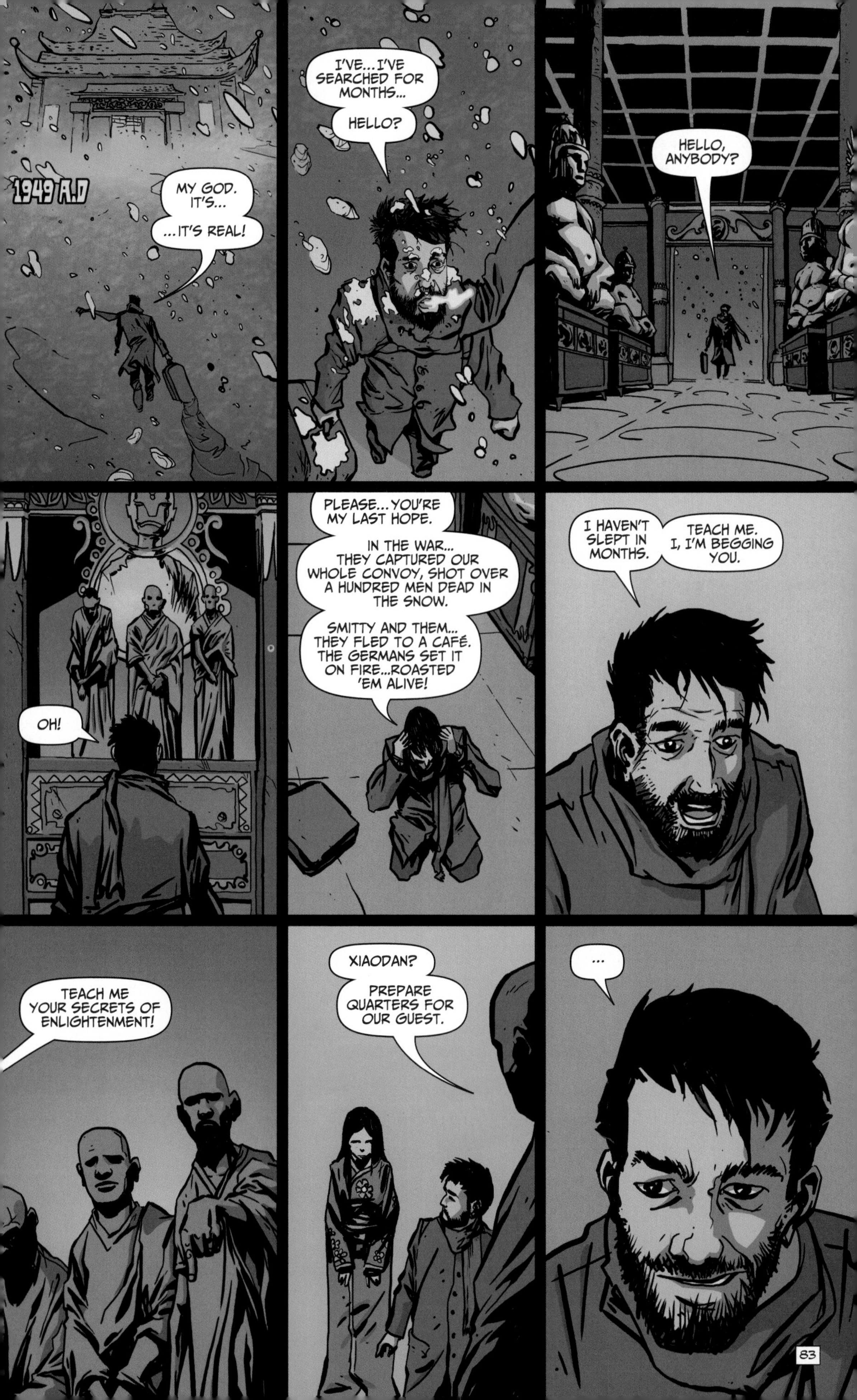
1949 A.D
MY GOD. IT'S...
...IT'S REAL!
I'VE...I'VE SEARCHED FOR MONTHS...
HELLO?
HELLO, ANYBODY?
OH!
PLEASE...YOU'RE MY LAST HOPE.
IN THE WAR... THEY CAPTURED OUR WHOLE CONVOY, SHOT OVER A HUNDRED MEN DEAD IN THE SNOW.
SMITTY AND THEM... THEY FLED TO A CAFÉ. THE GERMANS SET IT ON FIRE...ROASTED 'EM ALIVE!
I HAVEN'T SLEPT IN MONTHS.
TEACH ME. I, I'M BEGGING YOU.
TEACH ME YOUR SECRETS OF ENLIGHTENMENT!
XIAODAN?
PREPARE QUARTERS FOR OUR GUEST.
...
83

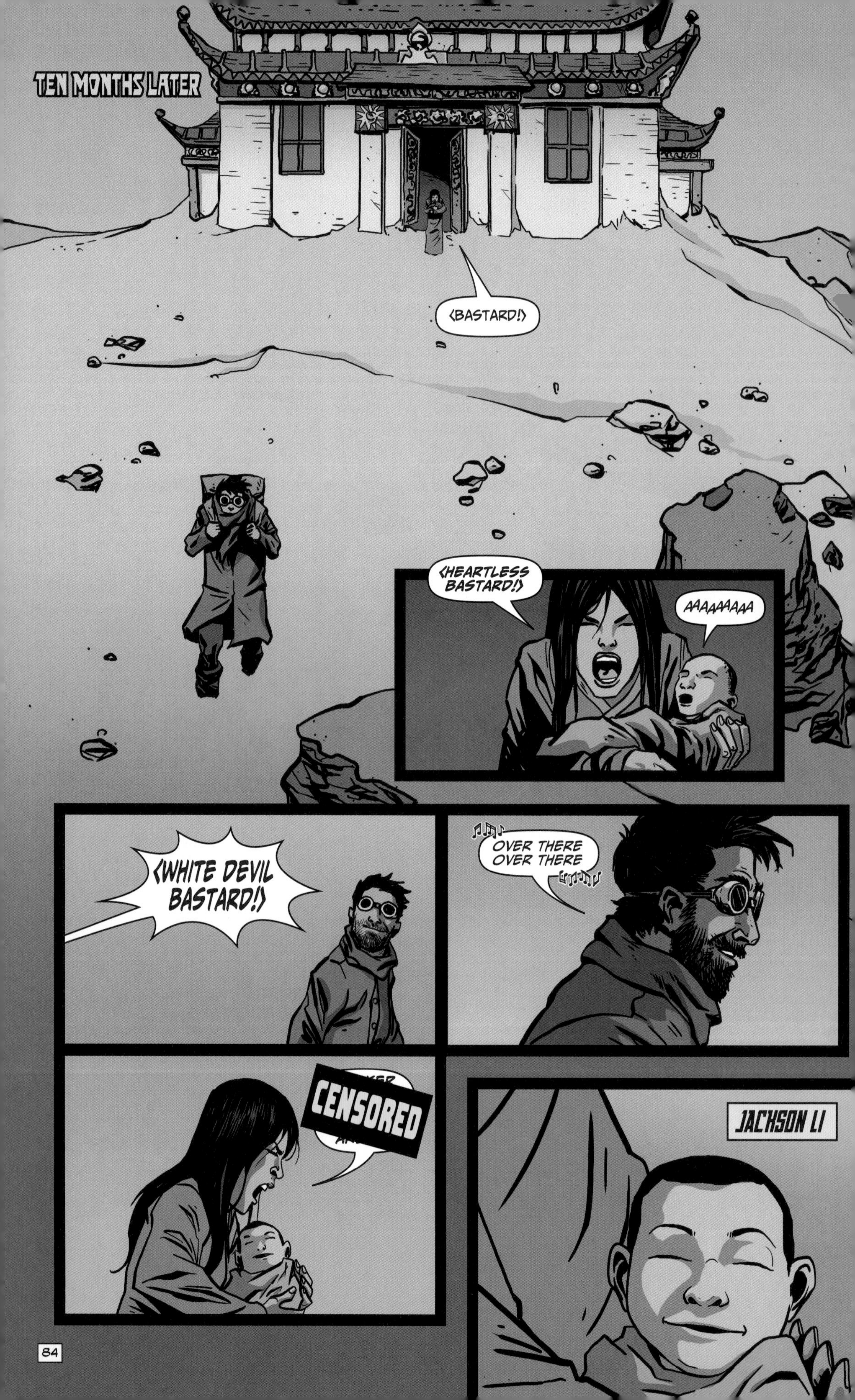
TEN MONTHS LATER
‹BASTARD!›
‹HEARTLESS BASTARD!›
AAAAAAAAA
‹WHITE DEVIL BASTARD!›
OVER THERE OVER THERE
CENSORED
JACKSON LI

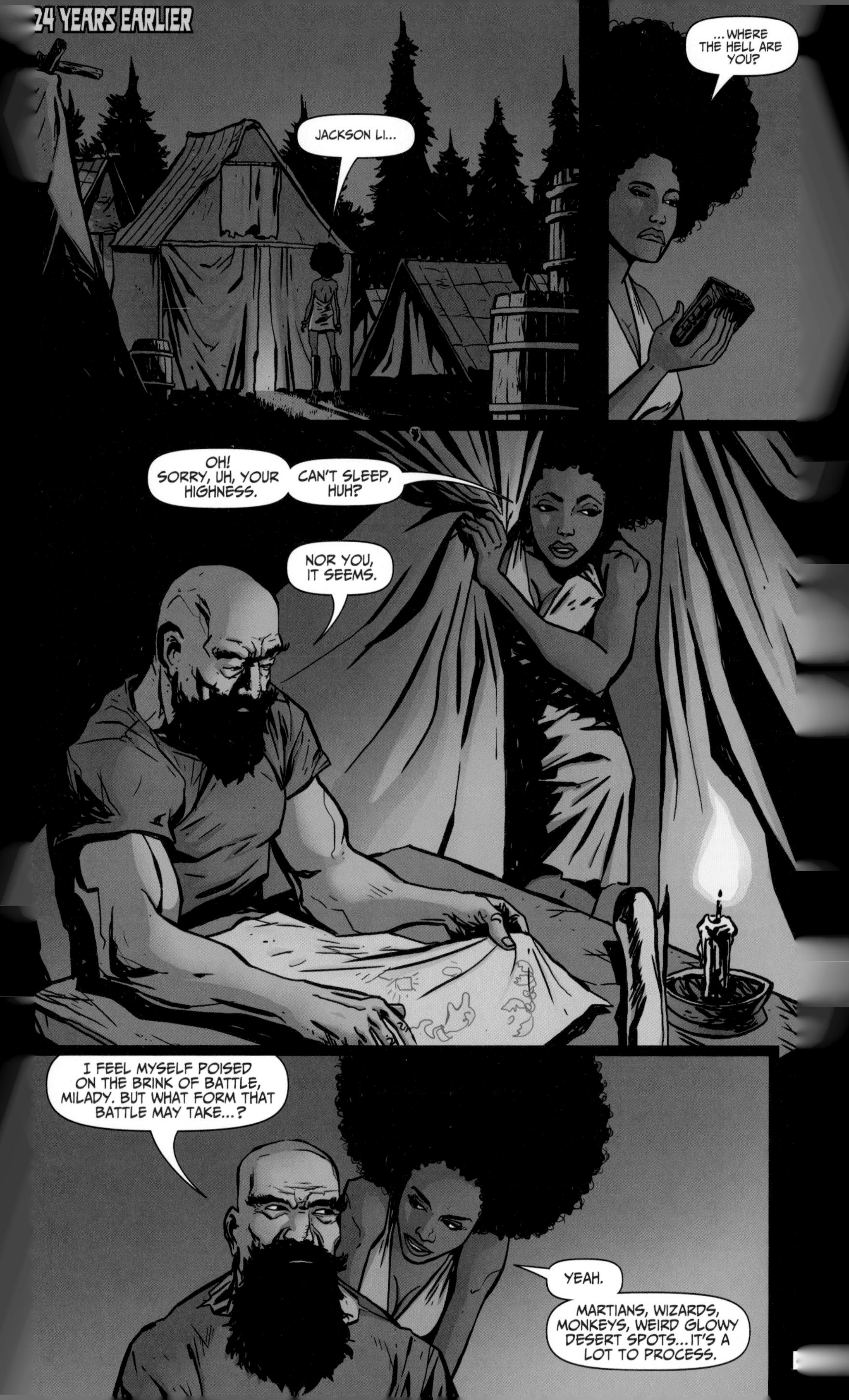
24 YEARS EARLIER
JACKSON LI...
...WHERE THE HELL ARE YOU?
OH! SORRY, UH, YOUR HIGHNESS.
CAN'T SLEEP, HUH?
NOR YOU, IT SEEMS.
I FEEL MYSELF POISED ON THE BRINK OF BATTLE, MILADY. BUT WHAT FORM THAT BATTLE MAY TAKE...?
YEAH.
MARTIANS, WIZARDS, MONKEYS, WEIRD GLOWY DESERT SPOTS...IT'S A LOT TO PROCESS.

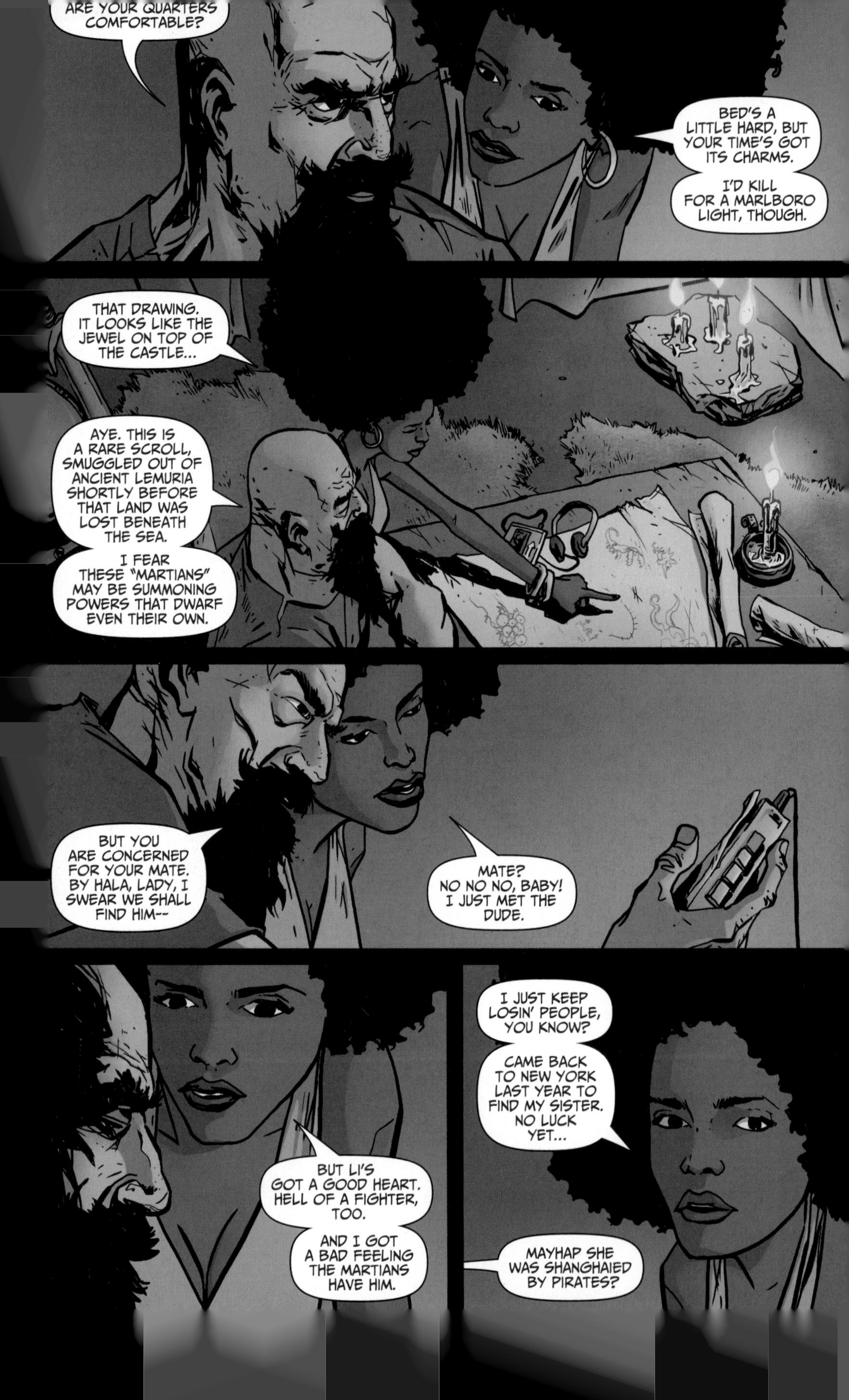
ARE YOUR QUARTERS COMFORTABLE?
BED'S A LITTLE HARD, BUT YOUR TIME'S GOT ITS CHARMS.
I'D KILL FOR A MARLBORO LIGHT, THOUGH.
THAT DRAWING. IT LOOKS LIKE THE JEWEL ON TOP OF THE CASTLE...
AYE. THIS IS A RARE SCROLL, SMUGGLED OUT OF ANCIENT LEMURIA SHORTLY BEFORE THAT LAND WAS LOST BENEATH THE SEA.
I FEAR THESE "MARTIANS" MAY BE SUMMONING POWERS THAT DWARF EVEN THEIR OWN.
BUT YOU ARE CONCERNED FOR YOUR MATE. BY HALA, LADY, I SWEAR WE SHALL FIND HIM--
MATE? NO NO NO, BABY! I JUST MET THE DUDE.
BUT LI'S GOT A GOOD HEART. HELL OF A FIGHTER, TOO.
AND I GOT A BAD FEELING THE MARTIANS HAVE HIM.
I JUST KEEP LOSIN' PEOPLE, YOU KNOW?
CAME BACK TO NEW YORK LAST YEAR TO FIND MY SISTER. NO LUCK YET...
MAYHAP SHE WAS SHANGHAIED BY PIRATES?

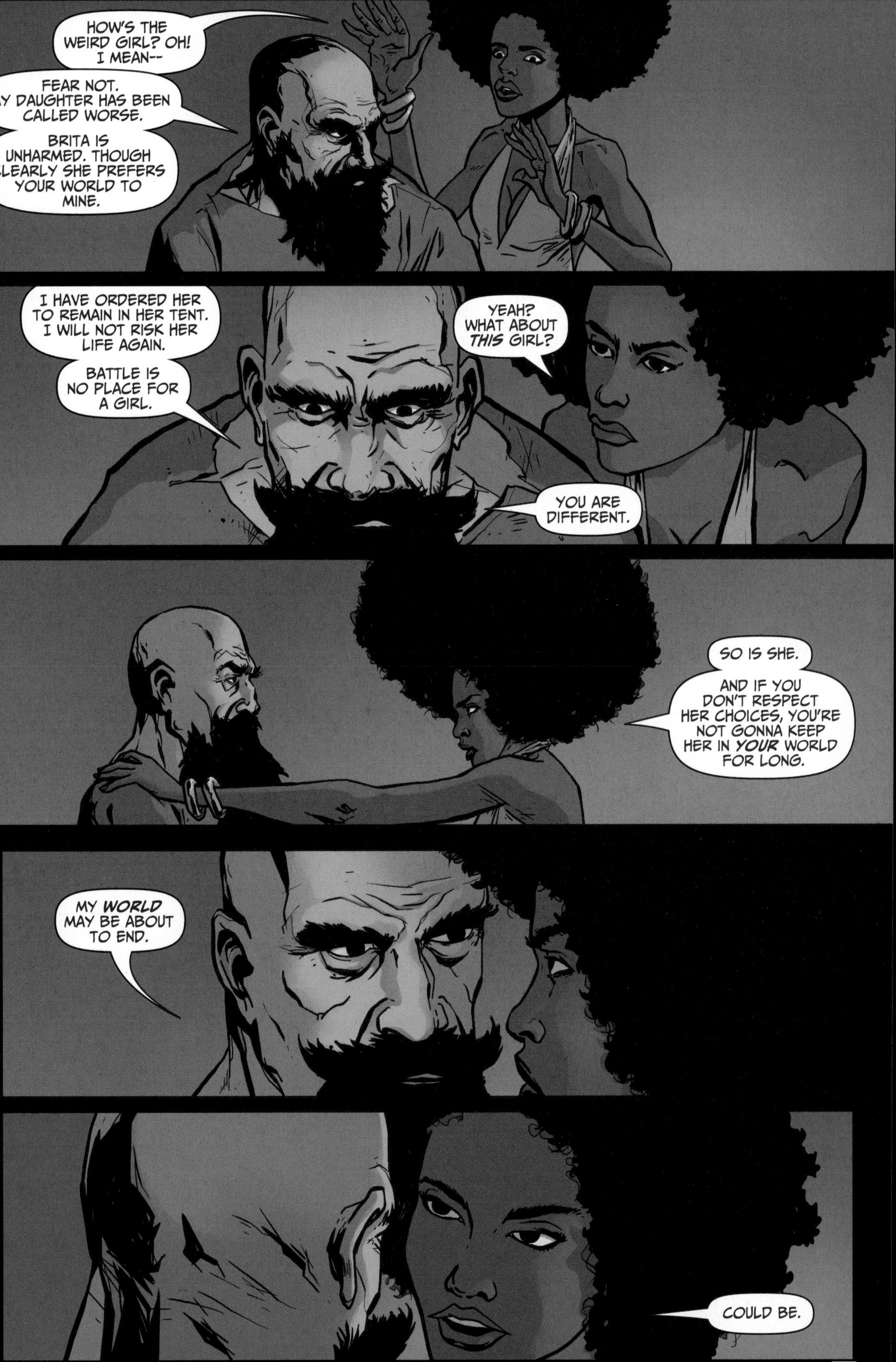
HOW'S THE WEIRD GIRL? OH! I MEAN--
FEAR NOT. MY DAUGHTER HAS BEEN CALLED WORSE.
BRITA IS UNHARMED. THOUGH CLEARLY SHE PREFERS YOUR WORLD TO MINE.
I HAVE ORDERED HER TO REMAIN IN HER TENT. I WILL NOT RISK HER LIFE AGAIN.
BATTLE IS NO PLACE FOR A GIRL.
YEAH? WHAT ABOUT *THIS* GIRL?
YOU ARE DIFFERENT.
SO IS SHE.
AND IF YOU DON'T RESPECT HER CHOICES, YOU'RE NOT GONNA KEEP HER IN *YOUR* WORLD FOR LONG.
MY *WORLD* MAY BE ABOUT TO END.
COULD BE.

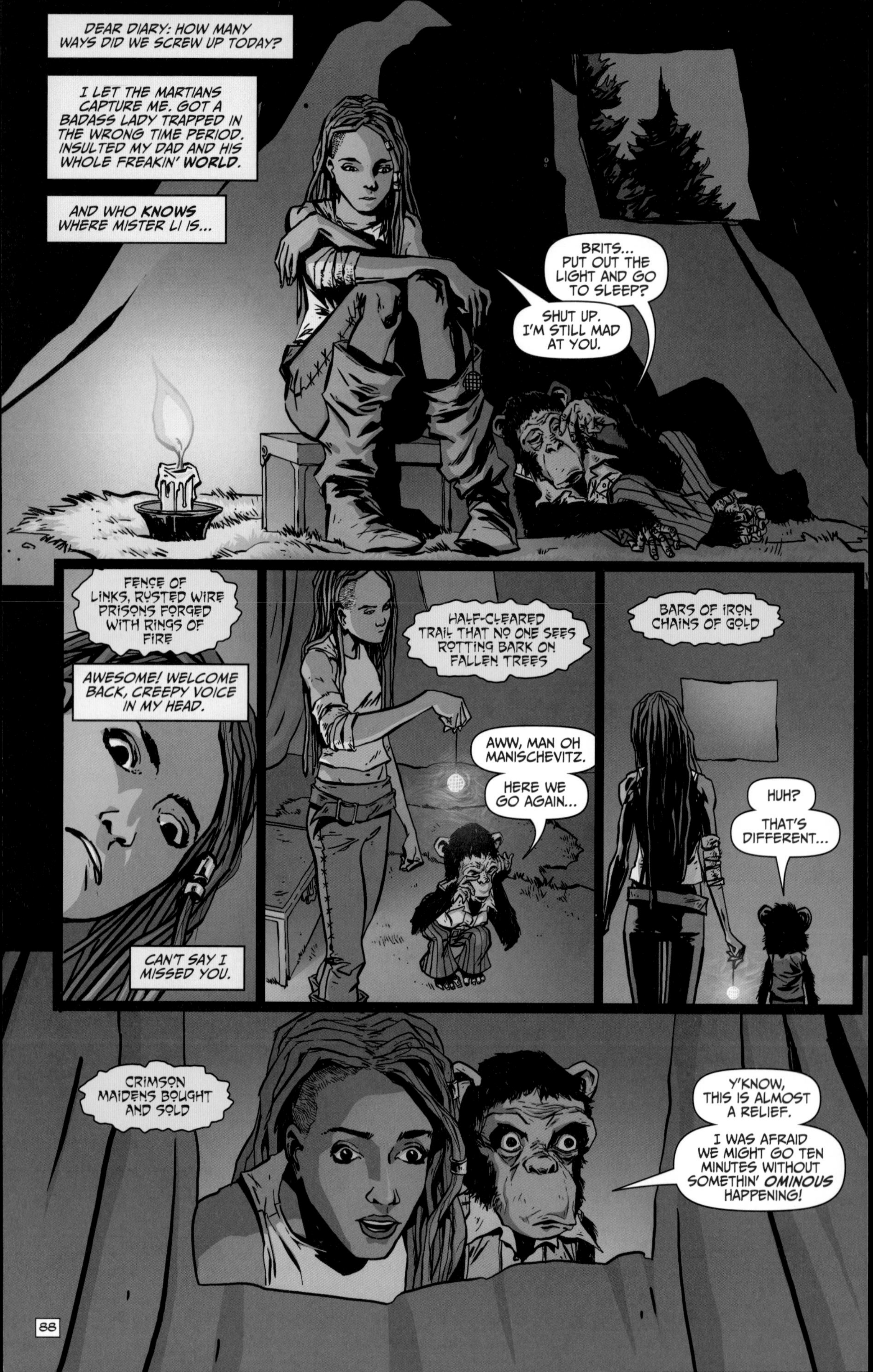
DEAR DIARY: HOW MANY WAYS DID WE SCREW UP TODAY?
I LET THE MARTIANS CAPTURE ME. GOT A BADASS LADY TRAPPED IN THE WRONG TIME PERIOD. INSULTED MY DAD AND HIS WHOLE FREAKIN' WORLD.
AND WHO KNOWS WHERE MISTER LI IS...
BRITS... PUT OUT THE LIGHT AND GO TO SLEEP?
SHUT UP. I'M STILL MAD AT YOU.
FENCE OF LINKS, RUSTED WIRE PRISONS FORGED WITH RINGS OF FIRE
AWESOME! WELCOME BACK, CREEPY VOICE IN MY HEAD.
CAN'T SAY I MISSED YOU.
HALF-CLEARED TRAIL THAT NO ONE SEES ROTTING BARK ON FALLEN TREES
AWW, MAN OH MANISCHEVITZ.
HERE WE GO AGAIN...
BARS OF IRON CHAINS OF GOLD
HUH?
THAT'S DIFFERENT...
CRIMSON MAIDENS BOUGHT AND SOLD
Y'KNOW, THIS IS ALMOST A RELIEF.
I WAS AFRAID WE MIGHT GO TEN MINUTES WITHOUT SOMETHIN' OMINOUS HAPPENING!

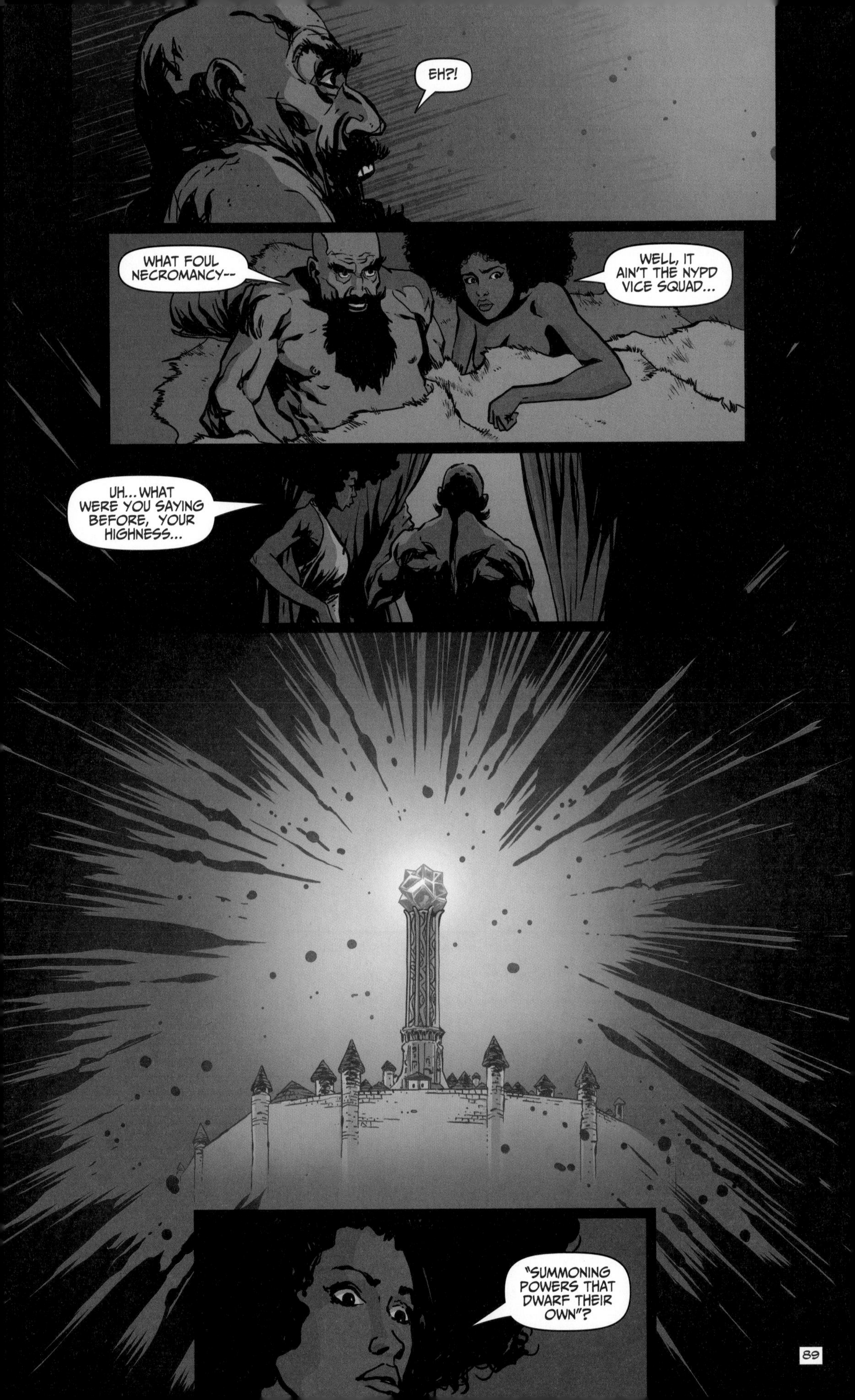
EH?!
WHAT FOUL NECROMANCY--
WELL, IT AIN'T THE NYPD VICE SQUAD...
UH...WHAT WERE YOU SAYING BEFORE, YOUR HIGHNESS...
"SUMMONING POWERS THAT DWARF THEIR OWN"?

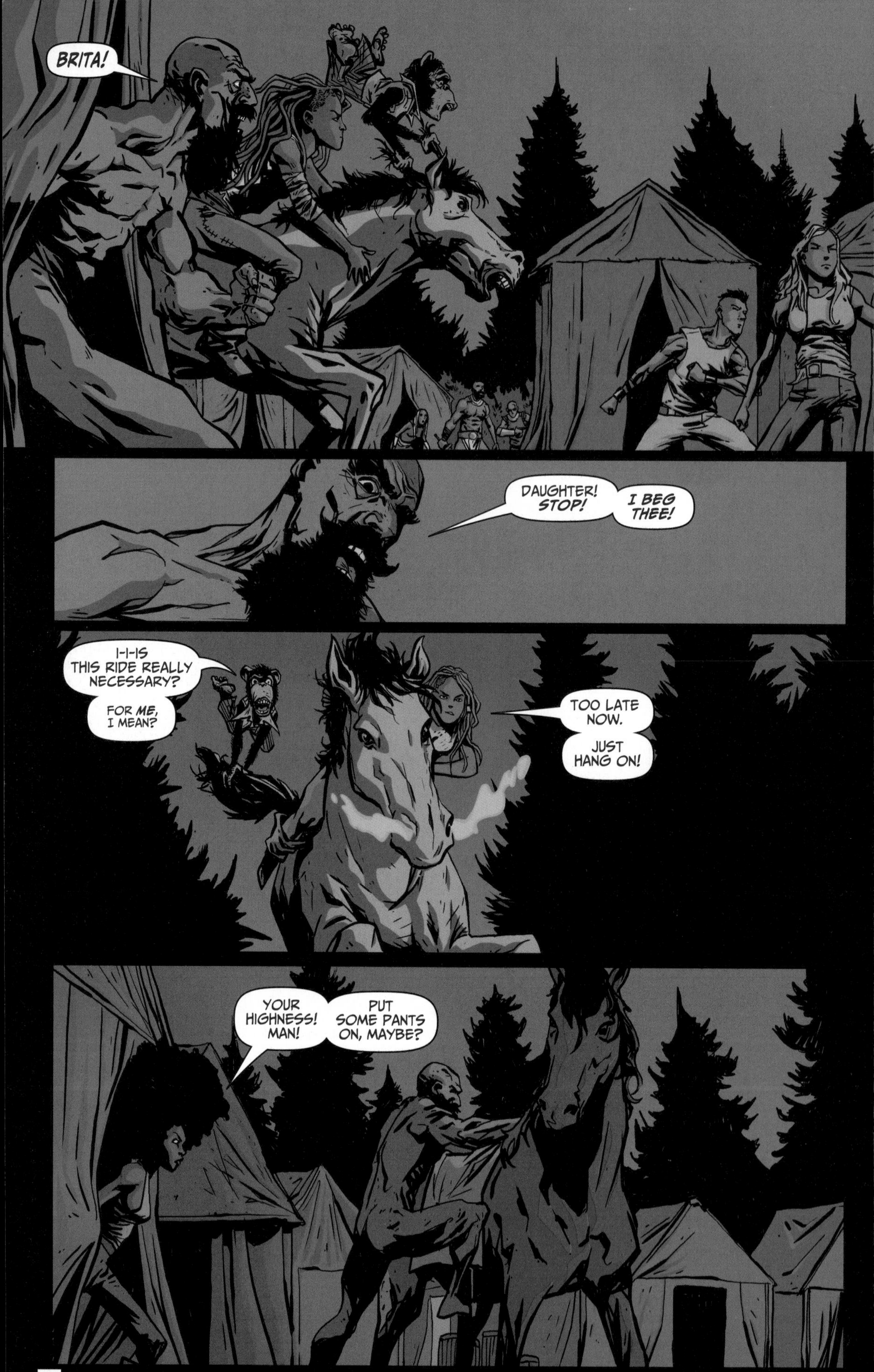
BRITA!
DAUGHTER! STOP!
I BEG THEE!
I-I-IS THIS RIDE REALLY NECESSARY?
FOR ME, I MEAN?
TOO LATE NOW.
JUST HANG ON!
YOUR HIGHNESS! MAN!
PUT SOME PANTS ON, MAYBE?

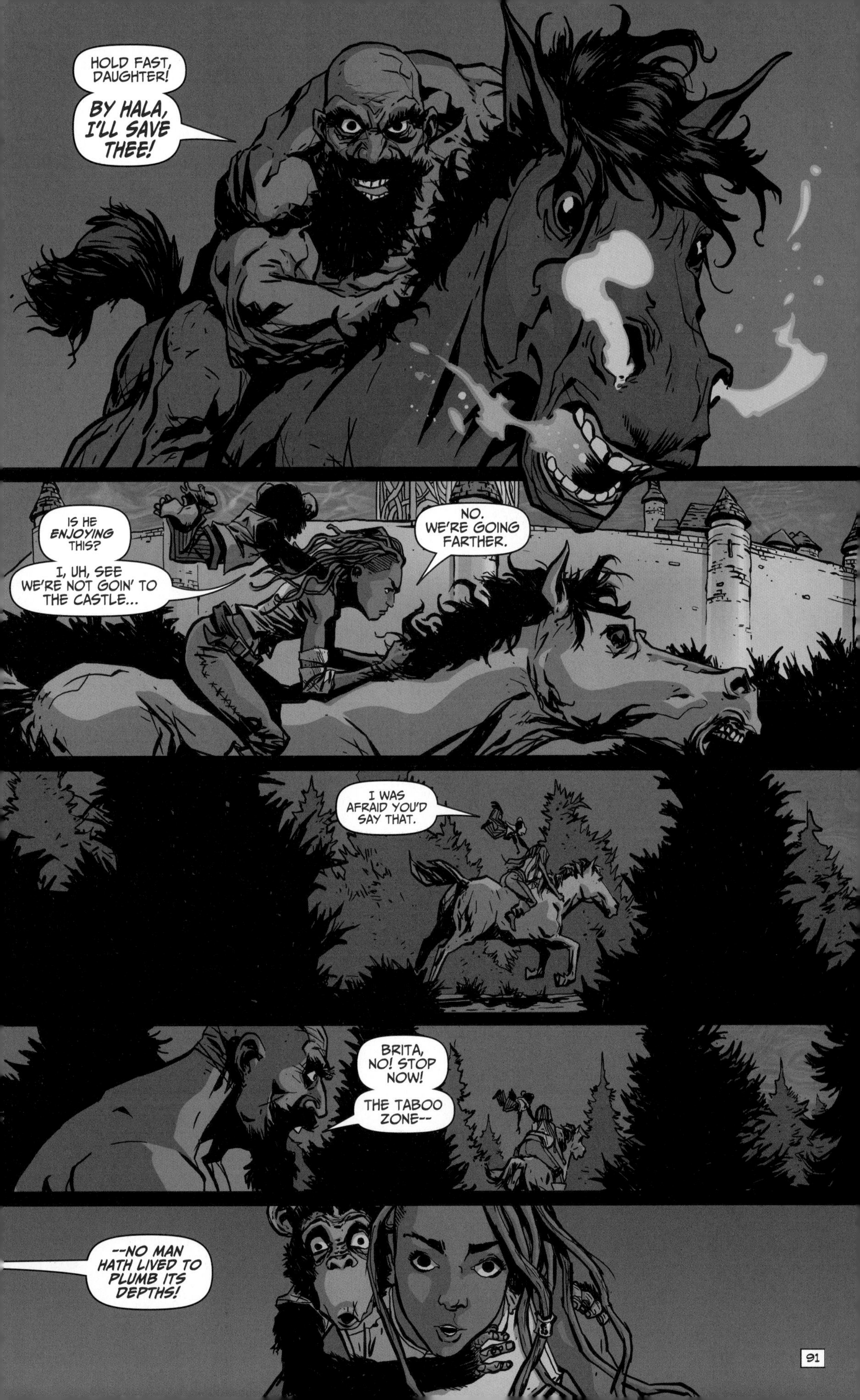
HOLD FAST, DAUGHTER!
BY HALA, I'LL SAVE THEE!
IS HE ENJOYING THIS?
I, UH, SEE WE'RE NOT GOIN' TO THE CASTLE...
NO. WE'RE GOING FARTHER.
I WAS AFRAID YOU'D SAY THAT.
BRITA, NO! STOP NOW!
THE TABOO ZONE--
--NO MAN HATH LIVED TO PLUMB ITS DEPTHS!

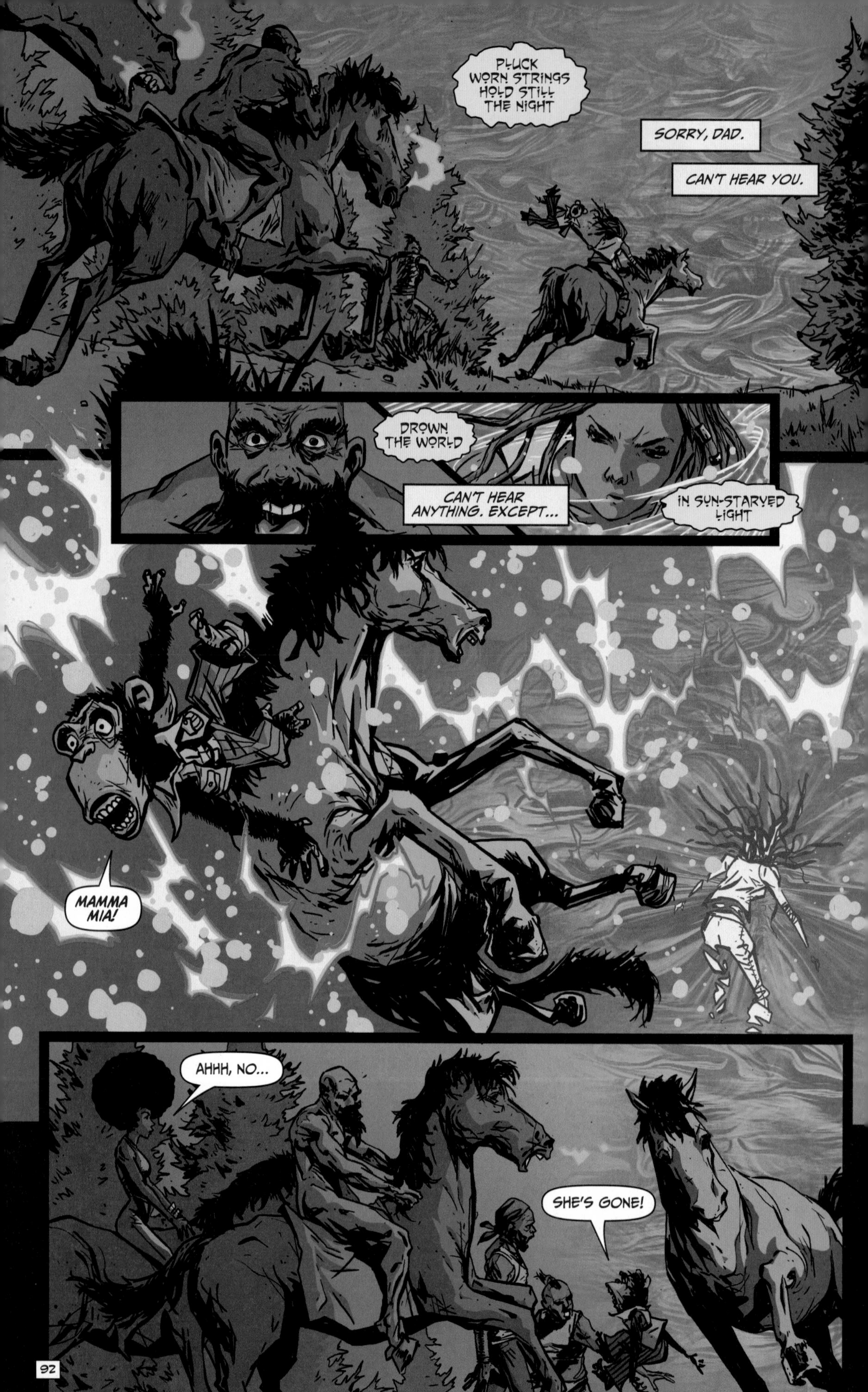
PLUCK WORN STRINGS HOLD STILL THE NIGHT
SORRY, DAD.
CAN'T HEAR YOU.
DROWN THE WORLD
CAN'T HEAR ANYTHING. EXCEPT...
IN SUN-STARVED LIGHT
MAMMA MIA!
AHHH, NO...
SHE'S GONE!

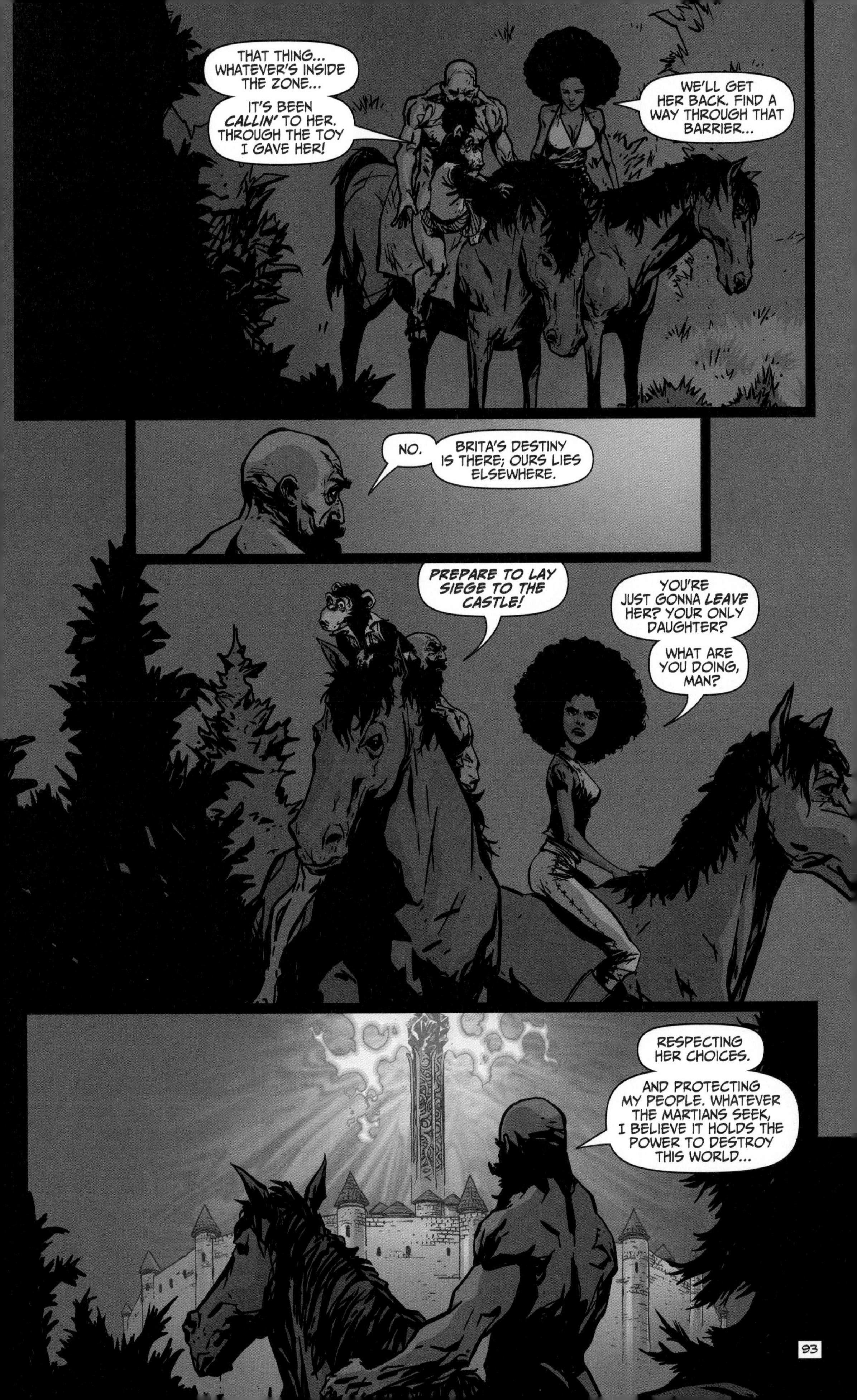
THAT THING... WHATEVER'S INSIDE THE ZONE...
IT'S BEEN CALLIN' TO HER. THROUGH THE TOY I GAVE HER!
WE'LL GET HER BACK. FIND A WAY THROUGH THAT BARRIER...
NO.
BRITA'S DESTINY IS THERE; OURS LIES ELSEWHERE.
PREPARE TO LAY SIEGE TO THE CASTLE!
YOU'RE JUST GONNA LEAVE HER? YOUR ONLY DAUGHTER?
WHAT ARE YOU DOING, MAN?
RESPECTING HER CHOICES.
AND PROTECTING MY PEOPLE. WHATEVER THE MARTIANS SEEK, I BELIEVE IT HOLDS THE POWER TO DESTROY THIS WORLD...

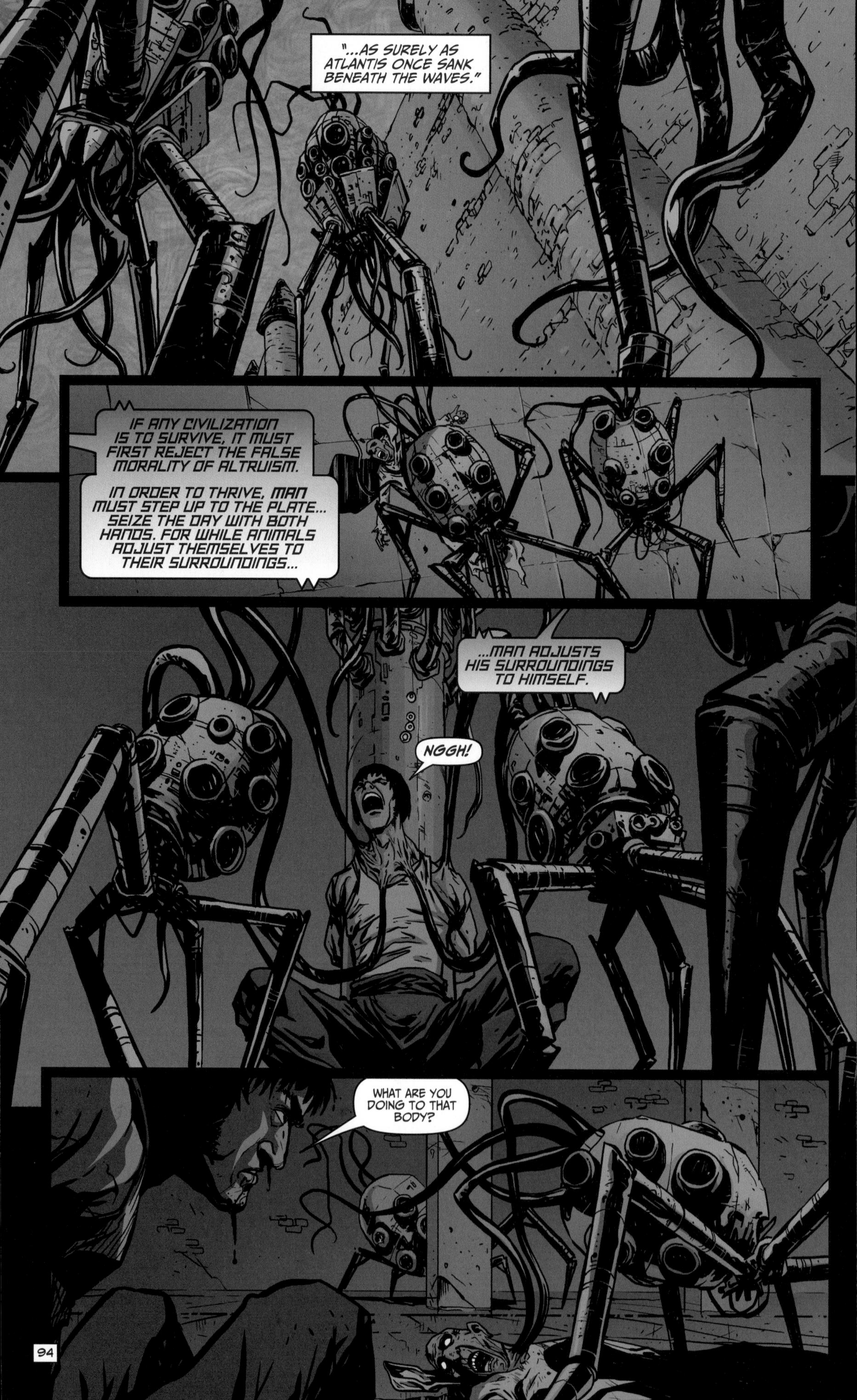
"...AS SURELY AS ATLANTIS ONCE SANK BENEATH THE WAVES."
IF ANY CIVILIZATION IS TO SURVIVE, IT MUST FIRST REJECT THE FALSE MORALITY OF ALTRUISM.
IN ORDER TO THRIVE, MAN MUST STEP UP TO THE PLATE... SEIZE THE DAY WITH BOTH HANDS. FOR WHILE ANIMALS ADJUST THEMSELVES TO THEIR SURROUNDINGS...
...MAN ADJUSTS HIS SURROUNDINGS TO HIMSELF.
NGGH!
WHAT ARE YOU DOING TO THAT BODY?

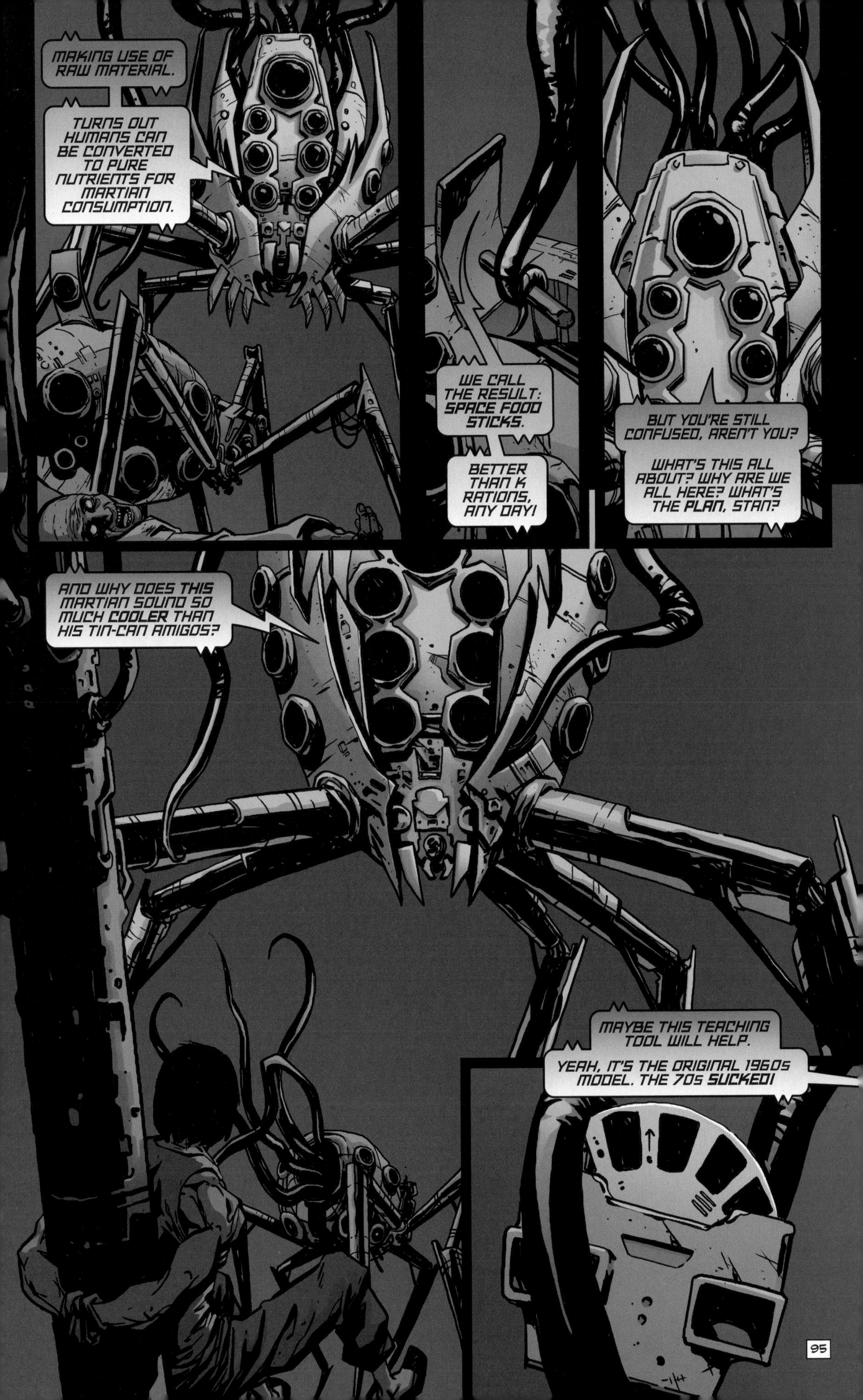
MAKING USE OF RAW MATERIAL.
TURNS OUT HUMANS CAN BE CONVERTED TO PURE NUTRIENTS FOR MARTIAN CONSUMPTION.
WE CALL THE RESULT: SPACE FOOD STICKS.
BETTER THAN K RATIONS, ANY DAY!
BUT YOU'RE STILL CONFUSED, AREN'T YOU?
WHAT'S THIS ALL ABOUT? WHY ARE WE ALL HERE? WHAT'S THE PLAN, STAN?
AND WHY DOES THIS MARTIAN SOUND SO MUCH COOLER THAN HIS TIN-CAN AMIGOS?
MAYBE THIS TEACHING TOOL WILL HELP.
YEAH, IT'S THE ORIGINAL 1960s MODEL. THE 70s SUCKED!

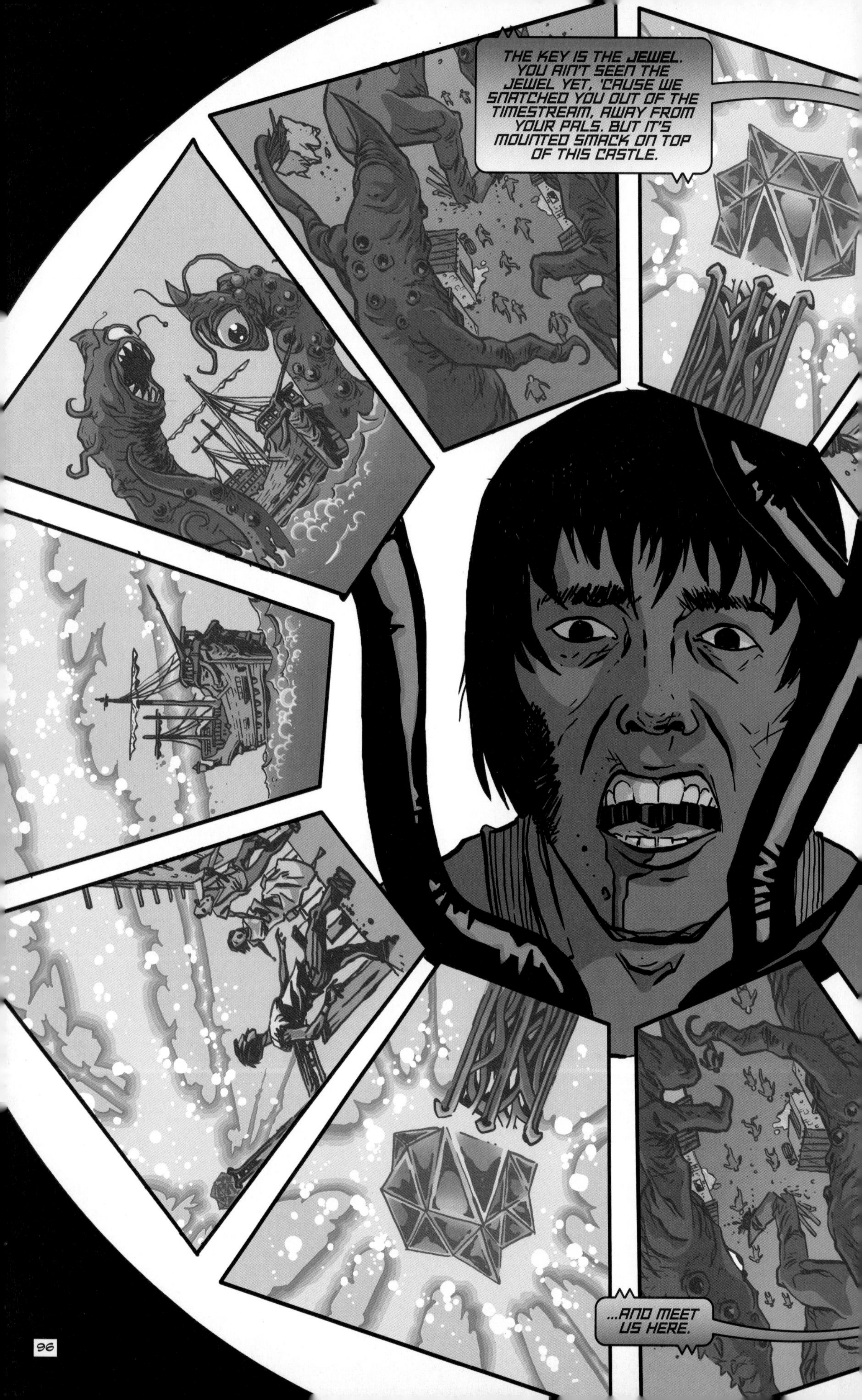
THE KEY IS THE JEWEL. YOU AIN'T SEEN THE JEWEL YET, 'CAUSE WE SNATCHED YOU OUT OF THE TIMESTREAM, AWAY FROM YOUR PALS. BUT IT'S MOUNTED SMACK ON TOP OF THIS CASTLE.
...AND MEET US HERE.

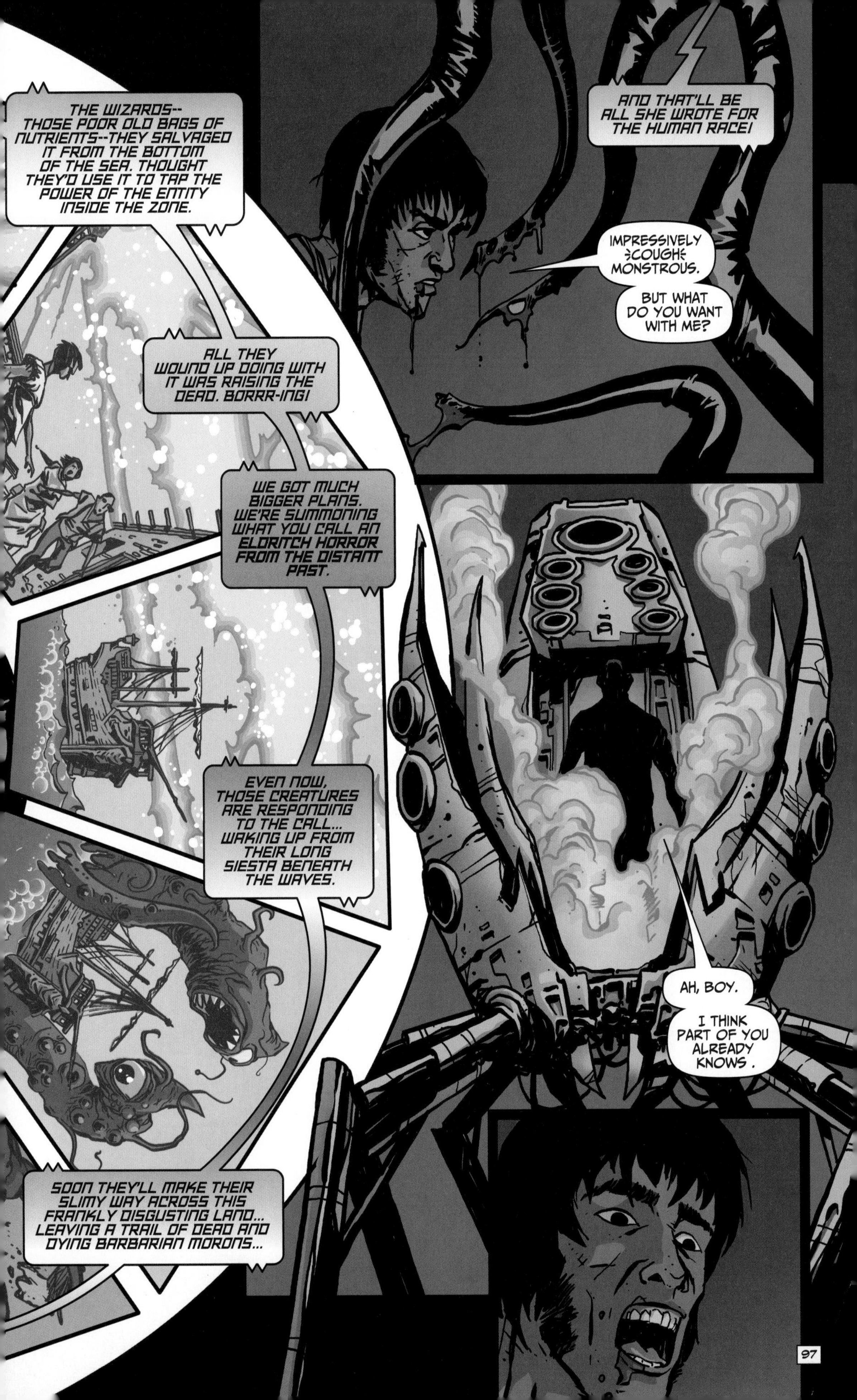

THE WIZARDS-- THOSE POOR OLD BAGS OF NUTRIENTS--THEY SALVAGED IT FROM THE BOTTOM OF THE SEA. THOUGHT THEY'D USE IT TO TAP THE POWER OF THE ENTITY INSIDE THE ZONE.
AND THAT'LL BE ALL SHE WROTE FOR THE HUMAN RACE!
IMPRESSIVELY *COUGH* MONSTROUS.
BUT WHAT DO YOU WANT WITH ME?
ALL THEY WOUND UP DOING WITH IT WAS RAISING THE DEAD. BORRR-ING!
WE GOT MUCH BIGGER PLANS. WE'RE SUMMONING WHAT YOU CALL AN ELDRITCH HORROR FROM THE DISTANT PAST.
EVEN NOW, THOSE CREATURES ARE RESPONDING TO THE CALL... WAKING UP FROM THEIR LONG SIESTA BENEATH THE WAVES.
SOON THEY'LL MAKE THEIR SLIMY WAY ACROSS THIS FRANKLY DISGUSTING LAND... LEAVING A TRAIL OF DEAD AND DYING BARBARIAN MORONS...
AH, BOY.
I THINK PART OF YOU ALREADY KNOWS .

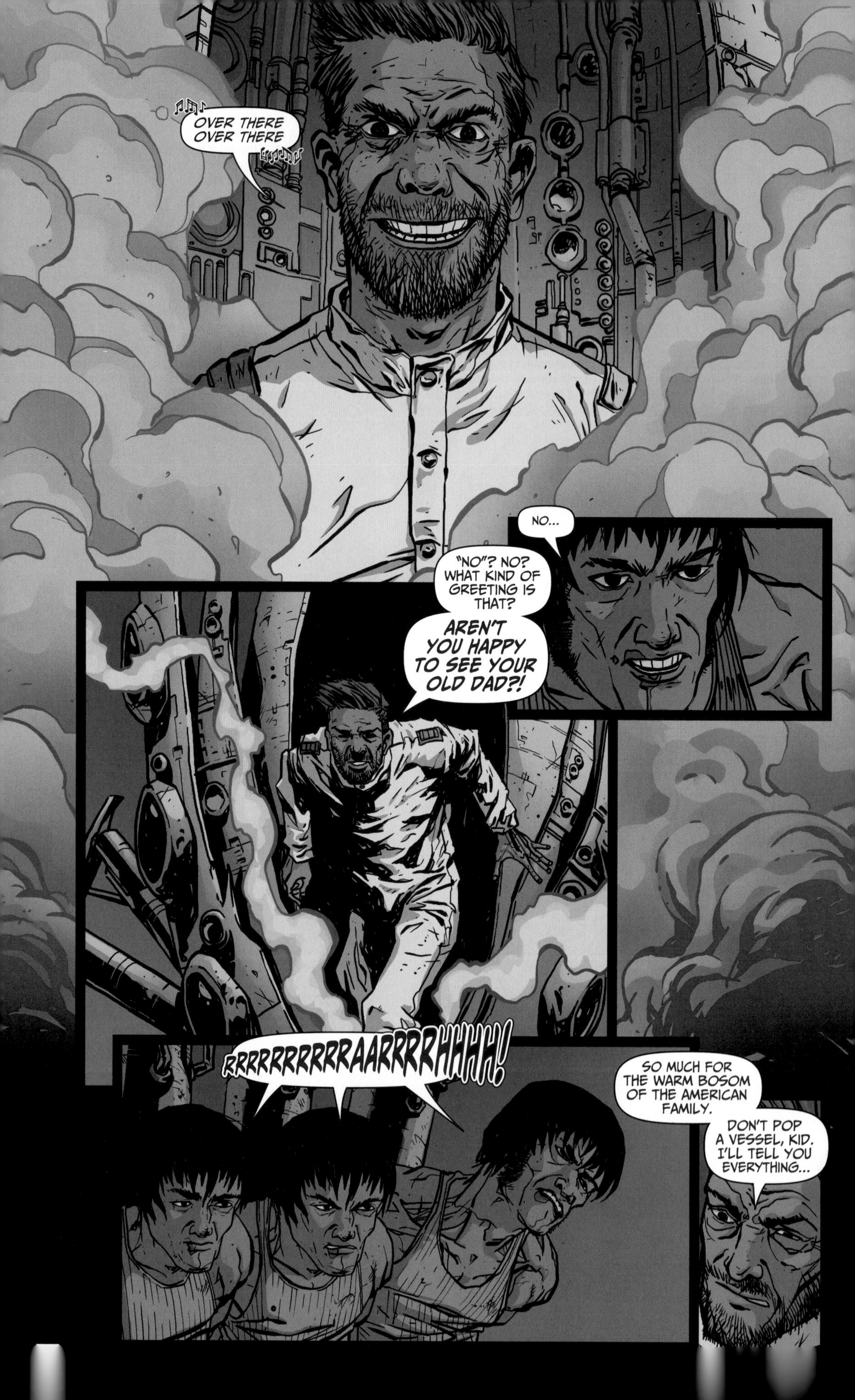
OVER THERE
OVER THERE
NO...
"NO"? NO? WHAT KIND OF GREETING IS THAT?
AREN'T YOU HAPPY TO SEE YOUR OLD DAD?!
RRRRRRRRRRAARRRRHHHH!
SO MUCH FOR THE WARM BOSOM OF THE AMERICAN FAMILY.
DON'T POP A VESSEL, KID. I'LL TELL YOU EVERYTHING...

You twist against your bonds, struggle to turn away. You've never known this man, you care nothing for what he has to say. He smells of musk, whiskey, and tobacco…a nauseating contrast to the machine-oil stench of the Martians.

You can almost hear your late mother's voice, spitting his name like a curse: *Theodore Roosevelt Eckhart.*

"I guess it starts with my own dad," Eckhart begins. "Your grandpa. He was a real rough rider…a man's man.

"Pappy was the one that made the deal with the Martians. He hooked up with 'em when they invaded Surrey, tail end of the 19th century. I don't know what favors he did for them, but they helped him amass the family fortune. One tentacle washes the other, I guess.

"He was kind of a bastard, old dad. When WWII broke out I beat a path to enlist, just to get away from him. That was a sh*t-awful mistake. Screwed me up in the head…so bad I went looking for some *Eastern enlightenment* afterward.

"But things didn't work out with your mom. Women, right? So I found myself back in the States. Pappy had the good manners to die of a septic infection soon after. On his deathbed, he told me *They'll be back. The Martians. Beware of them.*

"I told him off good. Let him know what I thought of him, his Martians, and the whole grimy deal he'd got me into. He just looked away, all sad, and handed me a glowing locket with a strange inscription on it. Then he croaked.

"Sure as shooting, not more'n a year later, the Martians came back. In secret, this time. Just one of the creepy buggers, actually—an advance scout, clankin' and hissing around the family mansion. He told me all about their history, how they'd tried to invade Earth a bunch of times before. This time he was sure they'd pull it off.

"Then he saw the locket. He told me what it was for: traveling through time. Said it had just enough charge to carry a man back and forth a few times before it crumbled to dust.

"I thanked him, pulled out dad's old Colt Browning, and shot him dead.

"Then I got to thinkin'. What if I used the locket to go back in time, to one of them earlier Martian invasions? With my knowledge of the future, I could lead 'em to an easy victory against the toothless yokels of this time.

"You could call it collusion, I guess. Treason against your own kind. But I just call it…"

He leans in close, whiskey-breath filling the air. That smug grin of his turns your stomach.

"…like father, like son."

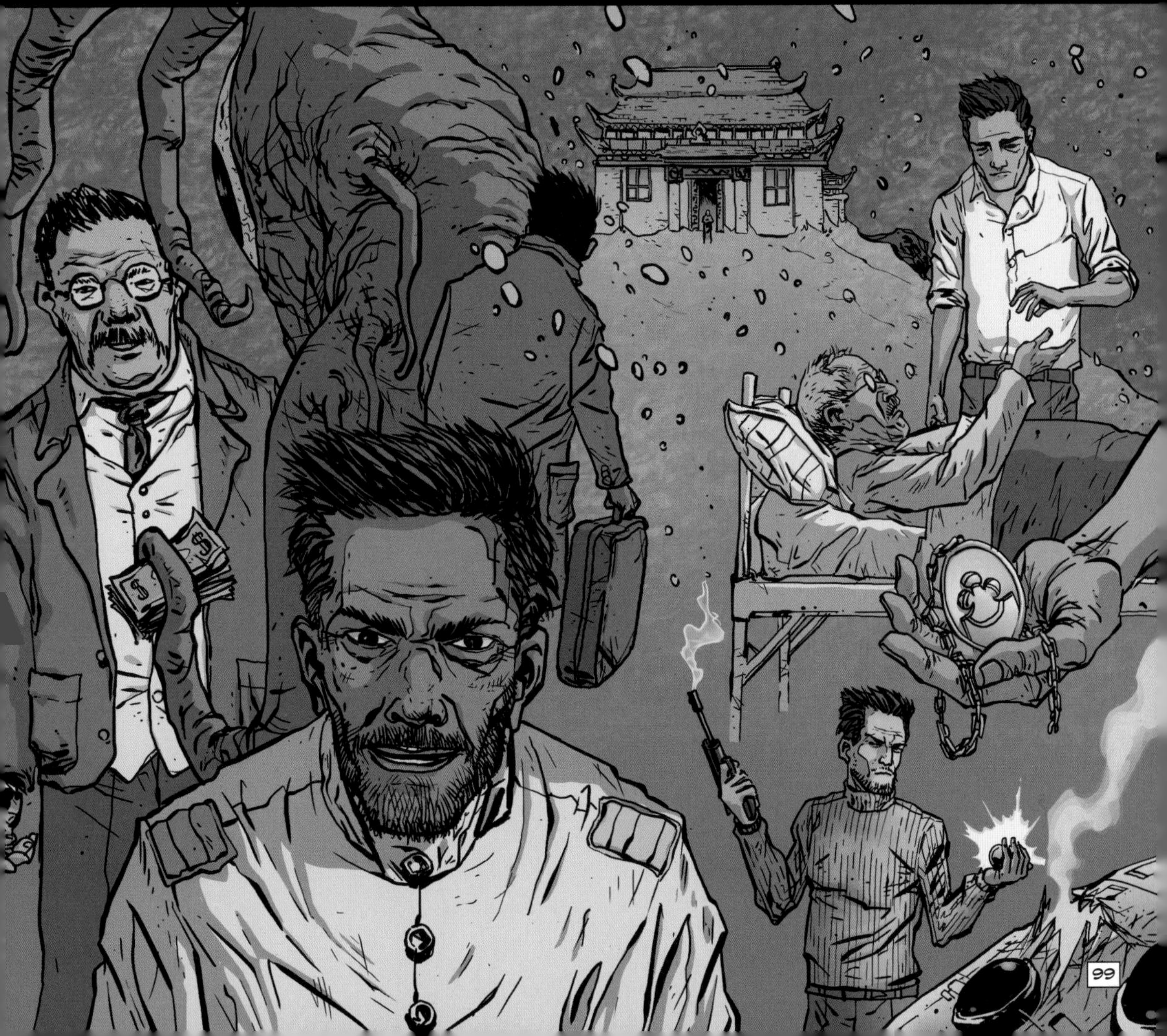

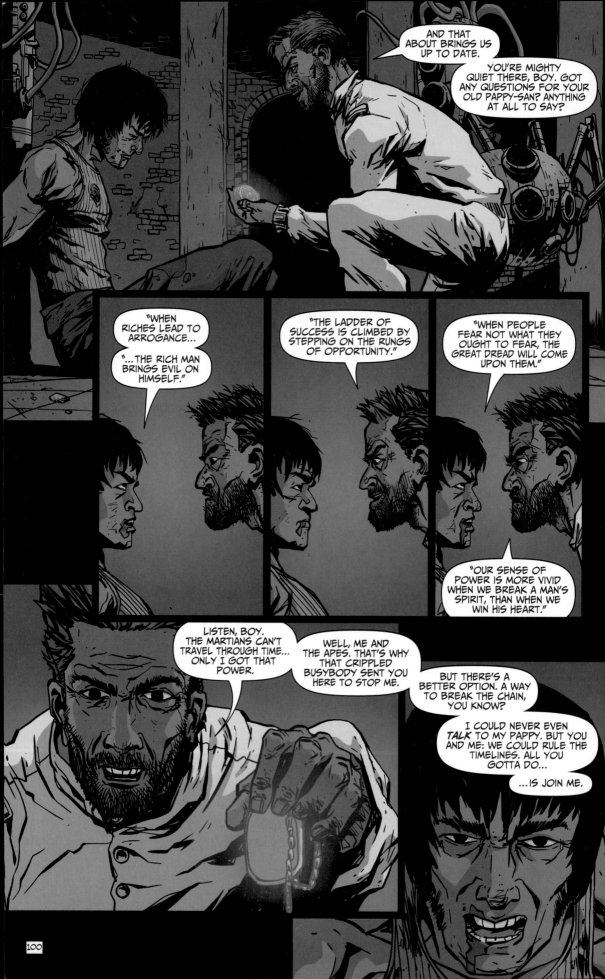

AND THAT ABOUT BRINGS US UP TO DATE.

YOU'RE MIGHTY QUIET THERE, BOY. GOT ANY QUESTIONS FOR YOUR OLD PAPPY-SAN? ANYTHING AT ALL TO SAY?

"WHEN RICHES LEAD TO ARROGANCE...

"...THE RICH MAN BRINGS EVIL ON HIMSELF."

"THE LADDER OF SUCCESS IS CLIMBED BY STEPPING ON THE RUNGS OF OPPORTUNITY."

"WHEN PEOPLE FEAR NOT WHAT THEY OUGHT TO FEAR, THE GREAT DREAD WILL COME UPON THEM."

"OUR SENSE OF POWER IS MORE VIVID WHEN WE BREAK A MAN'S SPIRIT, THAN WHEN WE WIN HIS HEART."

LISTEN, BOY. THE MARTIANS CAN'T TRAVEL THROUGH TIME... ONLY I GOT THAT POWER.

WELL, ME AND THE APES. THAT'S WHY THAT CRIPPLED BUSYBODY SENT YOU HERE TO STOP ME.

BUT THERE'S A BETTER OPTION. A WAY TO BREAK THE CHAIN, YOU KNOW?

I COULD NEVER EVEN *TALK* TO MY PAPPY. BUT YOU AND ME: WE COULD RULE THE TIMELINES. ALL YOU GOTTA DO...

...IS JOIN ME.

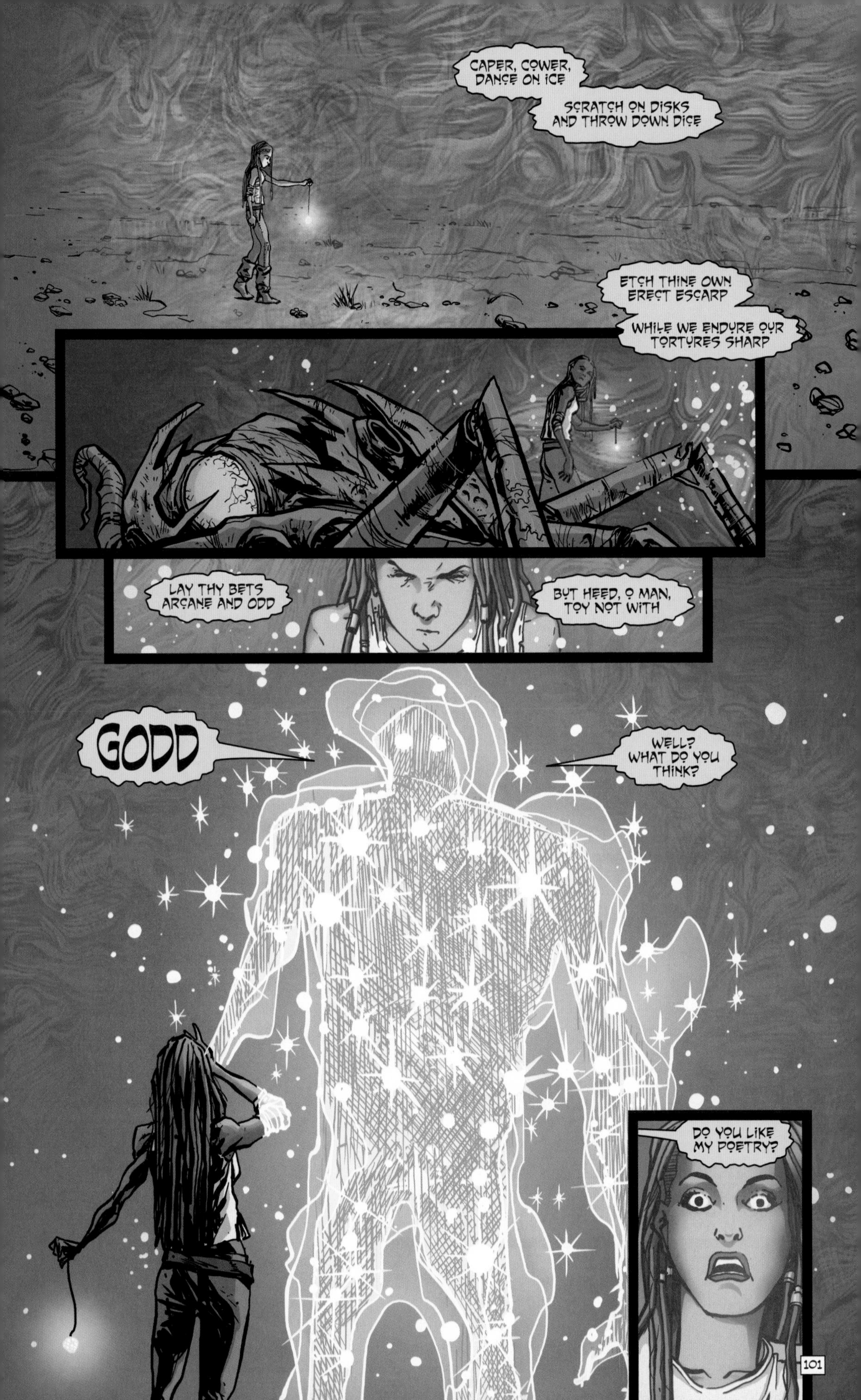
CAPER, COWER,
DANCE ON ICE
SCRATCH ON DISKS
AND THROW DOWN DICE
ETCH THINE OWN
ERECT ESCARP
WHILE WE ENDURE OUR
TORTURES SHARP
LAY THY BETS
ARCANE AND ODD
BUT HEED, O MAN,
TOY NOT WITH
GODD
WELL?
WHAT DO YOU
THINK?
DO YOU LIKE
MY POETRY?

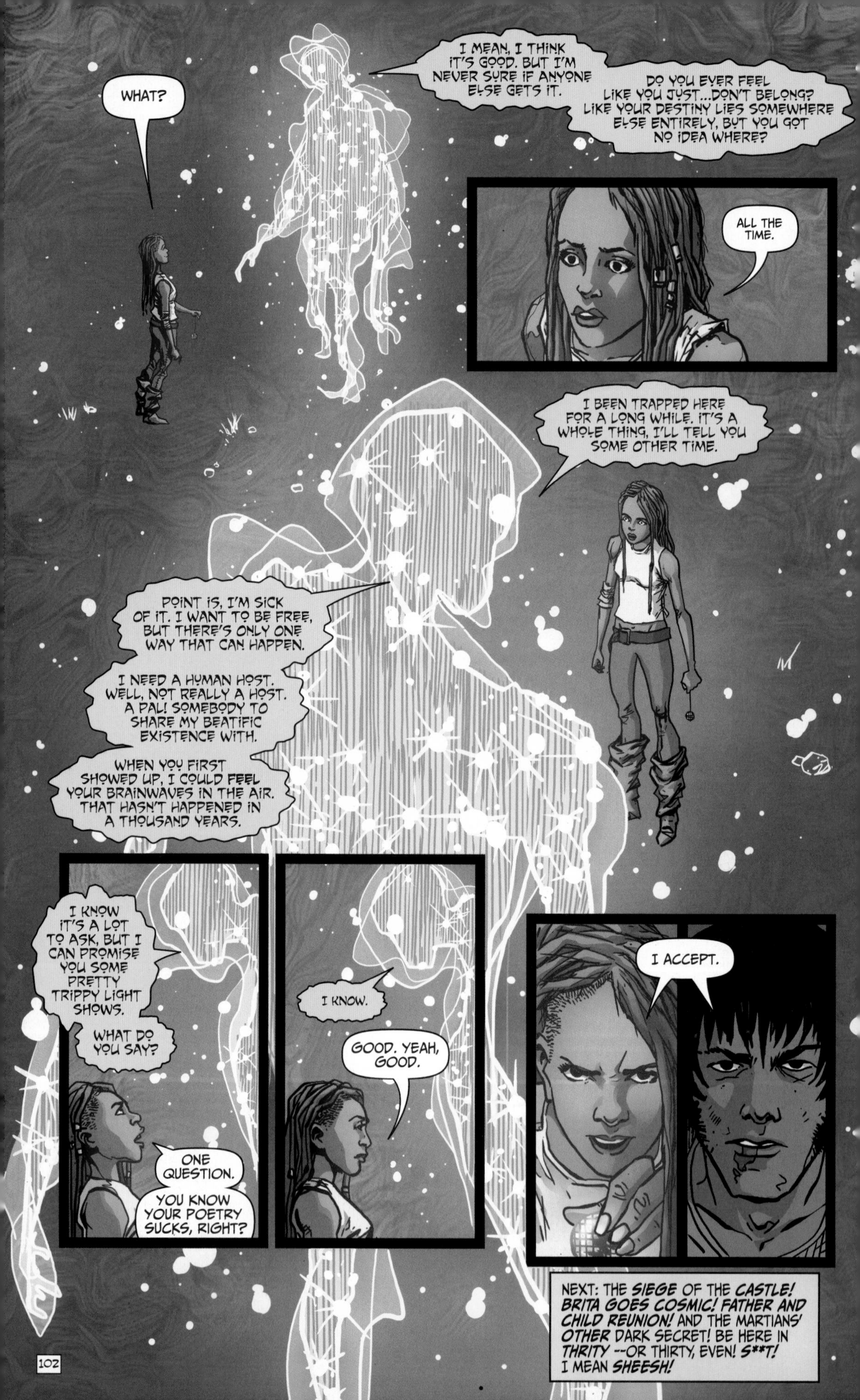
WHAT?
I MEAN, I THINK IT'S GOOD. BUT I'M NEVER SURE IF ANYONE ELSE GETS IT.
DO YOU EVER FEEL LIKE YOU JUST...DON'T BELONG? LIKE YOUR DESTINY LIES SOMEWHERE ELSE ENTIRELY, BUT YOU GOT NO IDEA WHERE?
ALL THE TIME.
I BEEN TRAPPED HERE FOR A LONG WHILE. IT'S A WHOLE THING, I'LL TELL YOU SOME OTHER TIME.
POINT IS, I'M SICK OF IT. I WANT TO BE FREE, BUT THERE'S ONLY ONE WAY THAT CAN HAPPEN.
I NEED A HUMAN HOST. WELL, NOT REALLY A HOST. A PAL! SOMEBODY TO SHARE MY BEATIFIC EXISTENCE WITH.
WHEN YOU FIRST SHOWED UP, I COULD FEEL YOUR BRAINWAVES IN THE AIR. THAT HASN'T HAPPENED IN A THOUSAND YEARS.
I KNOW IT'S A LOT TO ASK, BUT I CAN PROMISE YOU SOME PRETTY TRIPPY LIGHT SHOWS.
WHAT DO YOU SAY?
ONE QUESTION.
YOU KNOW YOUR POETRY SUCKS, RIGHT?
I KNOW.
GOOD. YEAH, GOOD.
I ACCEPT.
NEXT: THE SIEGE OF THE CASTLE! BRITA GOES COSMIC! FATHER AND CHILD REUNION! AND THE MARTIANS' OTHER DARK SECRET! BE HERE IN THIRTY --OR THIRTY, EVEN! S**T! I MEAN SHEESH!

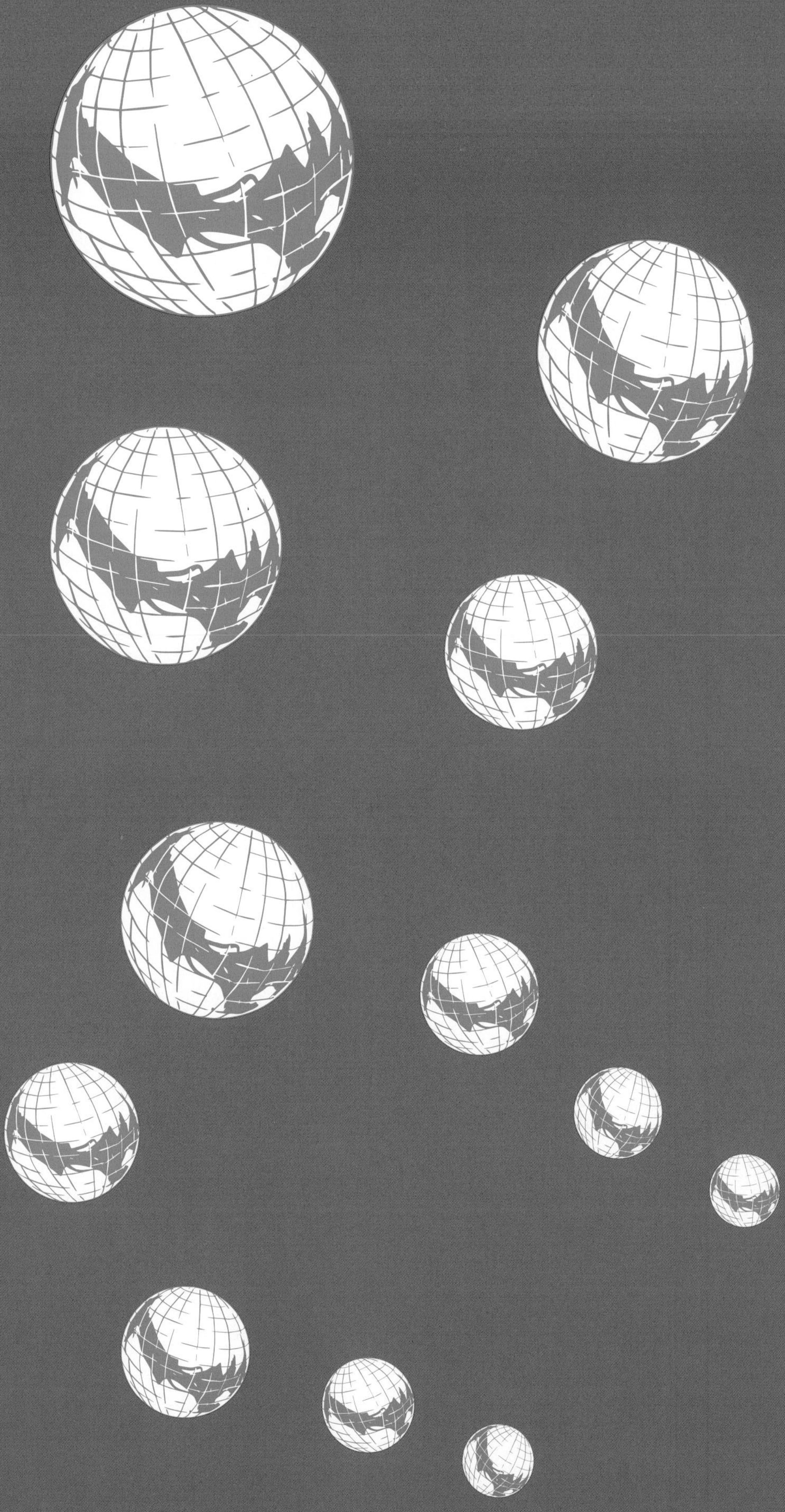

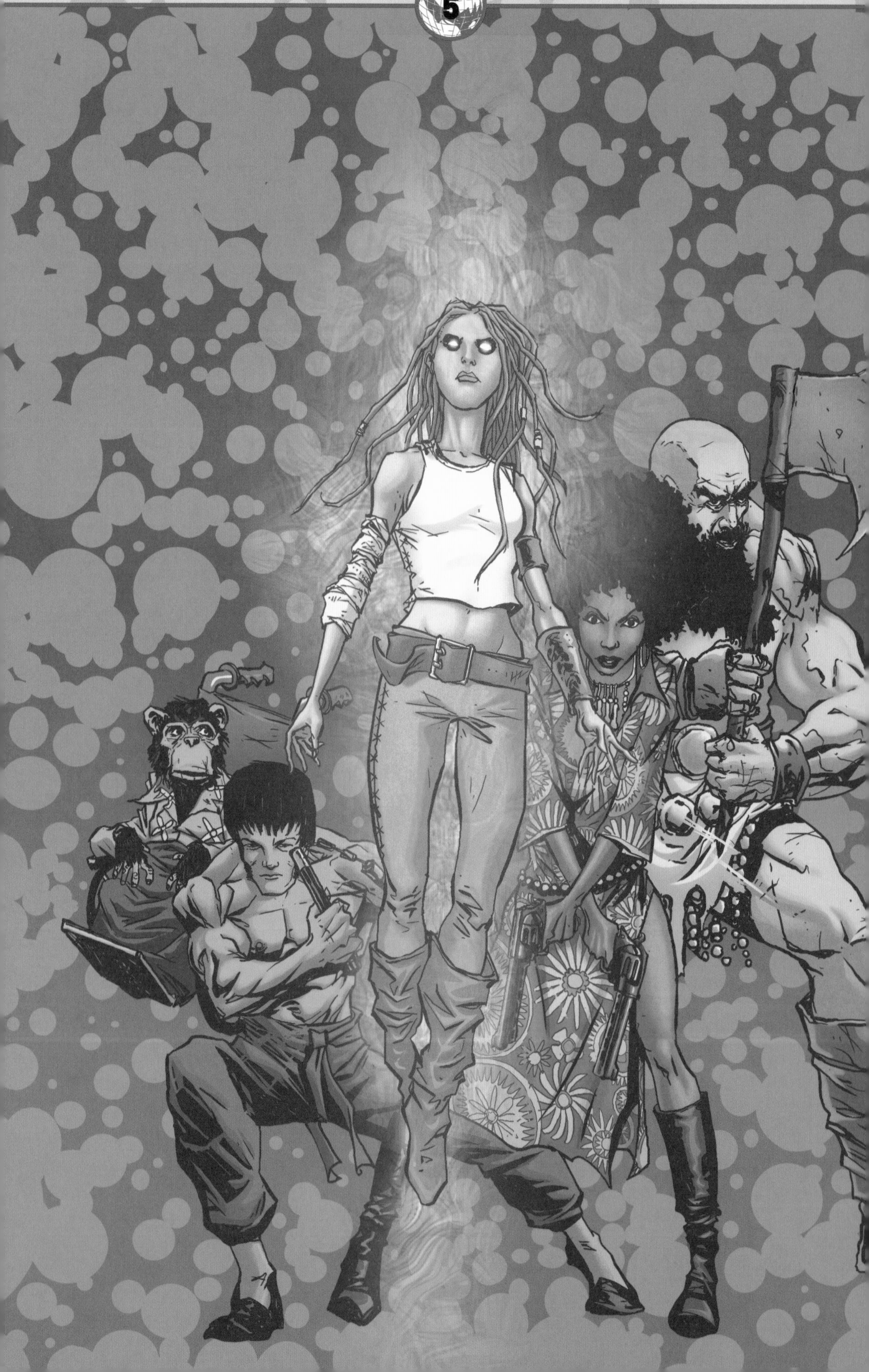

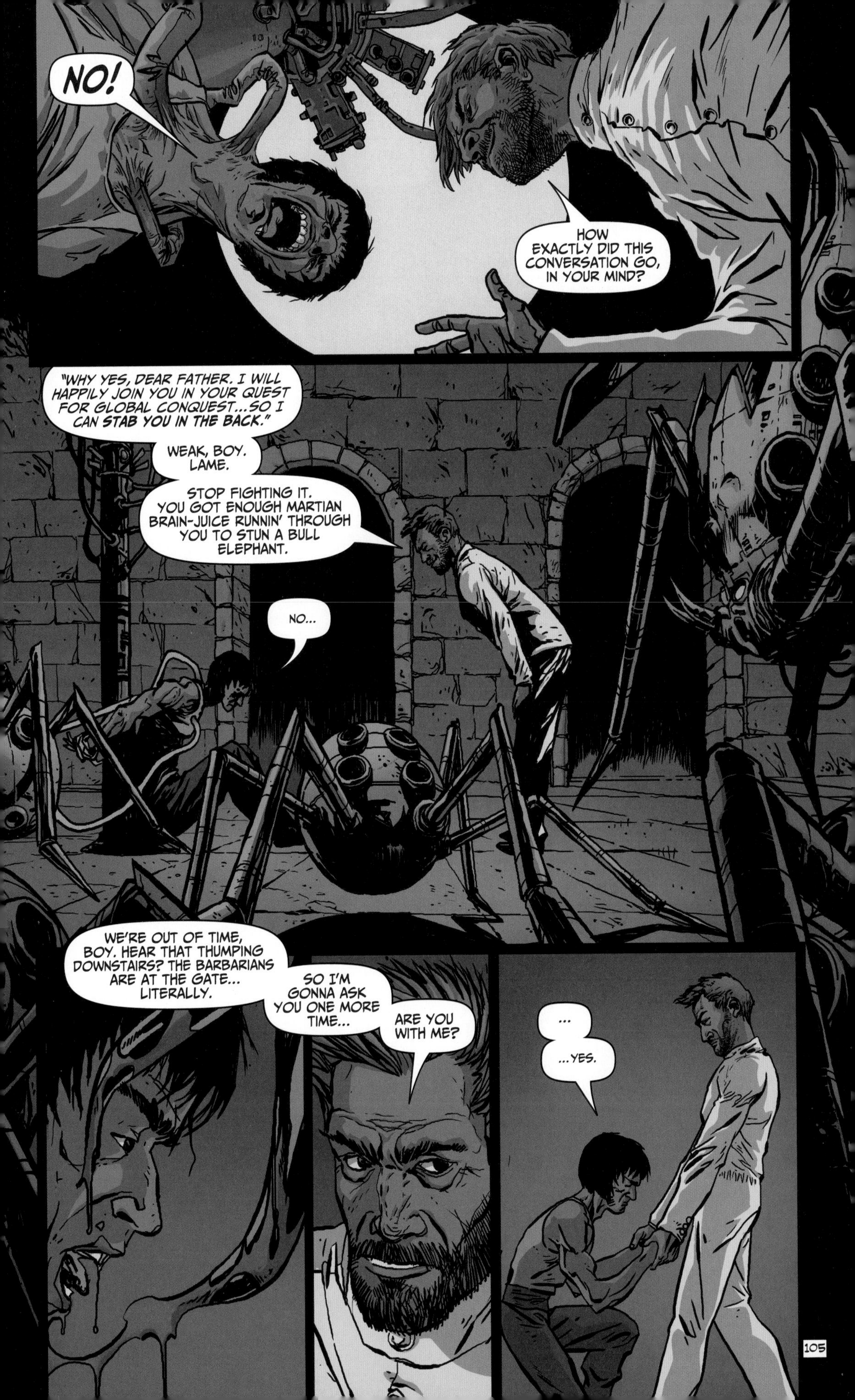
NO!
HOW EXACTLY DID THIS CONVERSATION GO, IN YOUR MIND?
"WHY YES, DEAR FATHER. I WILL HAPPILY JOIN YOU IN YOUR QUEST FOR GLOBAL CONQUEST...SO I CAN STAB YOU IN THE BACK."
WEAK, BOY. LAME.
STOP FIGHTING IT. YOU GOT ENOUGH MARTIAN BRAIN-JUICE RUNNIN' THROUGH YOU TO STUN A BULL ELEPHANT.
NO...
WE'RE OUT OF TIME, BOY. HEAR THAT THUMPING DOWNSTAIRS? THE BARBARIANS ARE AT THE GATE... LITERALLY.
SO I'M GONNA ASK YOU ONE MORE TIME...
ARE YOU WITH ME?
...
...YES.

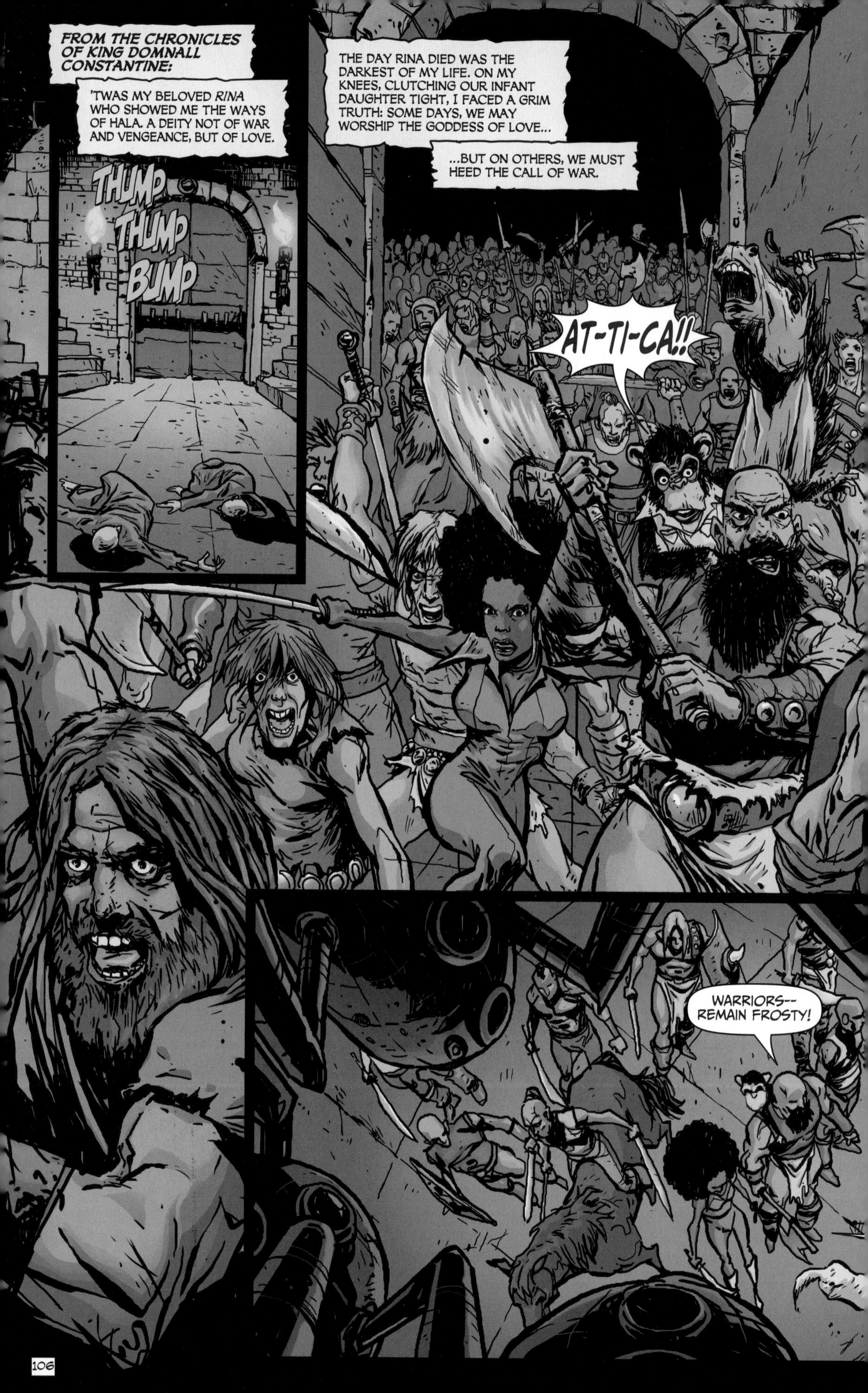
FROM THE CHRONICLES OF KING DOMNALL CONSTANTINE:
'TWAS MY BELOVED *RINA* WHO SHOWED ME THE WAYS OF HALA. A DEITY NOT OF WAR AND VENGEANCE, BUT OF LOVE.
THUMP THUMP BUMP
THE DAY RINA DIED WAS THE DARKEST OF MY LIFE. ON MY KNEES, CLUTCHING OUR INFANT DAUGHTER TIGHT, I FACED A GRIM TRUTH: SOME DAYS, WE MAY WORSHIP THE GODDESS OF LOVE...
...BUT ON OTHERS, WE MUST HEED THE CALL OF WAR.
AT-TI-CA!!
WARRIORS-- REMAIN FROSTY!

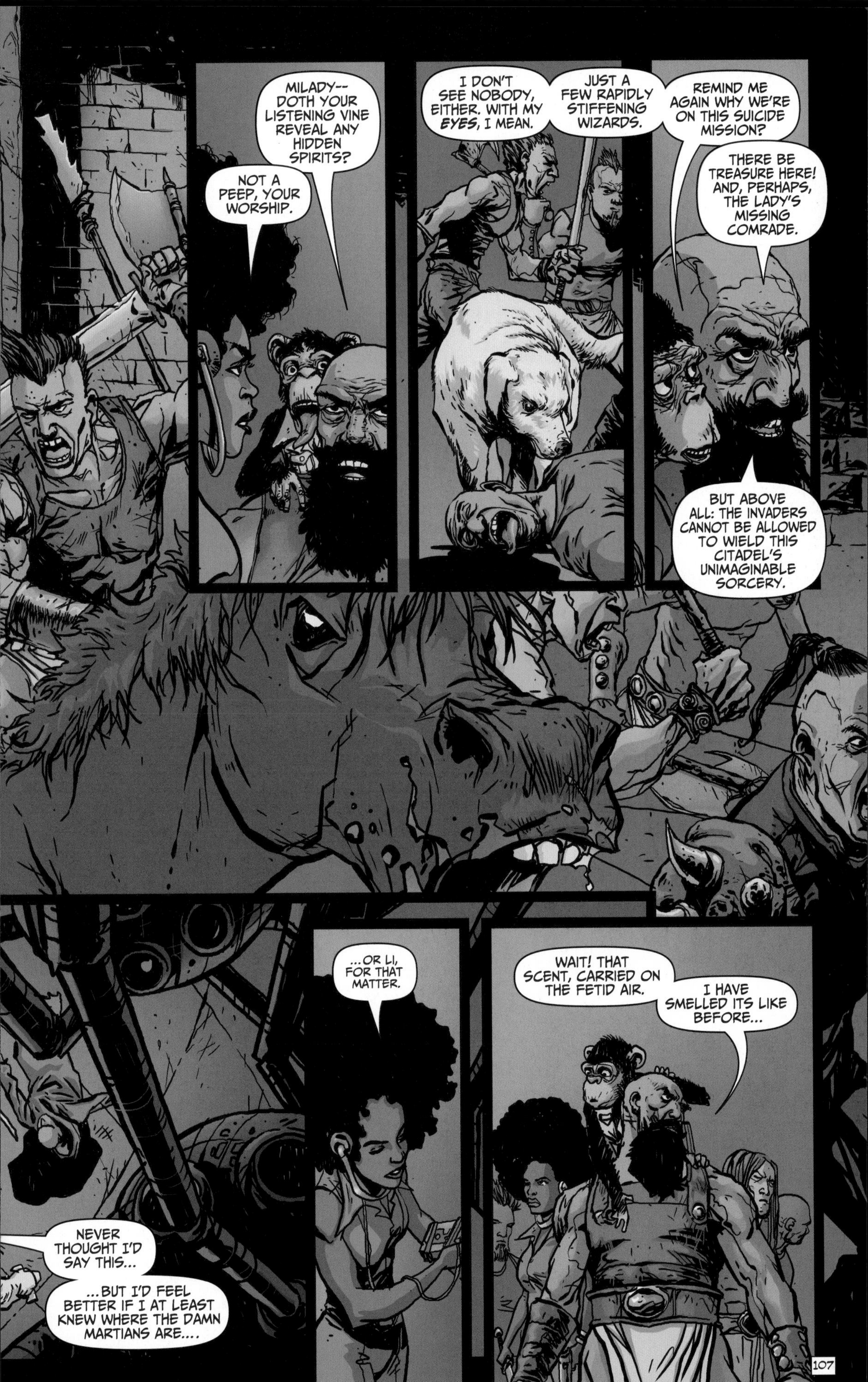
MILADY-- DOTH YOUR LISTENING VINE REVEAL ANY HIDDEN SPIRITS?
NOT A PEEP, YOUR WORSHIP.
I DON'T SEE NOBODY, EITHER. WITH MY EYES, I MEAN.
JUST A FEW RAPIDLY STIFFENING WIZARDS.
REMIND ME AGAIN WHY WE'RE ON THIS SUICIDE MISSION?
THERE BE TREASURE HERE! AND, PERHAPS, THE LADY'S MISSING COMRADE.
BUT ABOVE ALL: THE INVADERS CANNOT BE ALLOWED TO WIELD THIS CITADEL'S UNIMAGINABLE SORCERY.
NEVER THOUGHT I'D SAY THIS...
...BUT I'D FEEL BETTER IF I AT LEAST KNEW WHERE THE DAMN MARTIANS ARE....
...OR LI, FOR THAT MATTER.
WAIT! THAT SCENT, CARRIED ON THE FETID AIR.
I HAVE SMELLED ITS LIKE BEFORE...

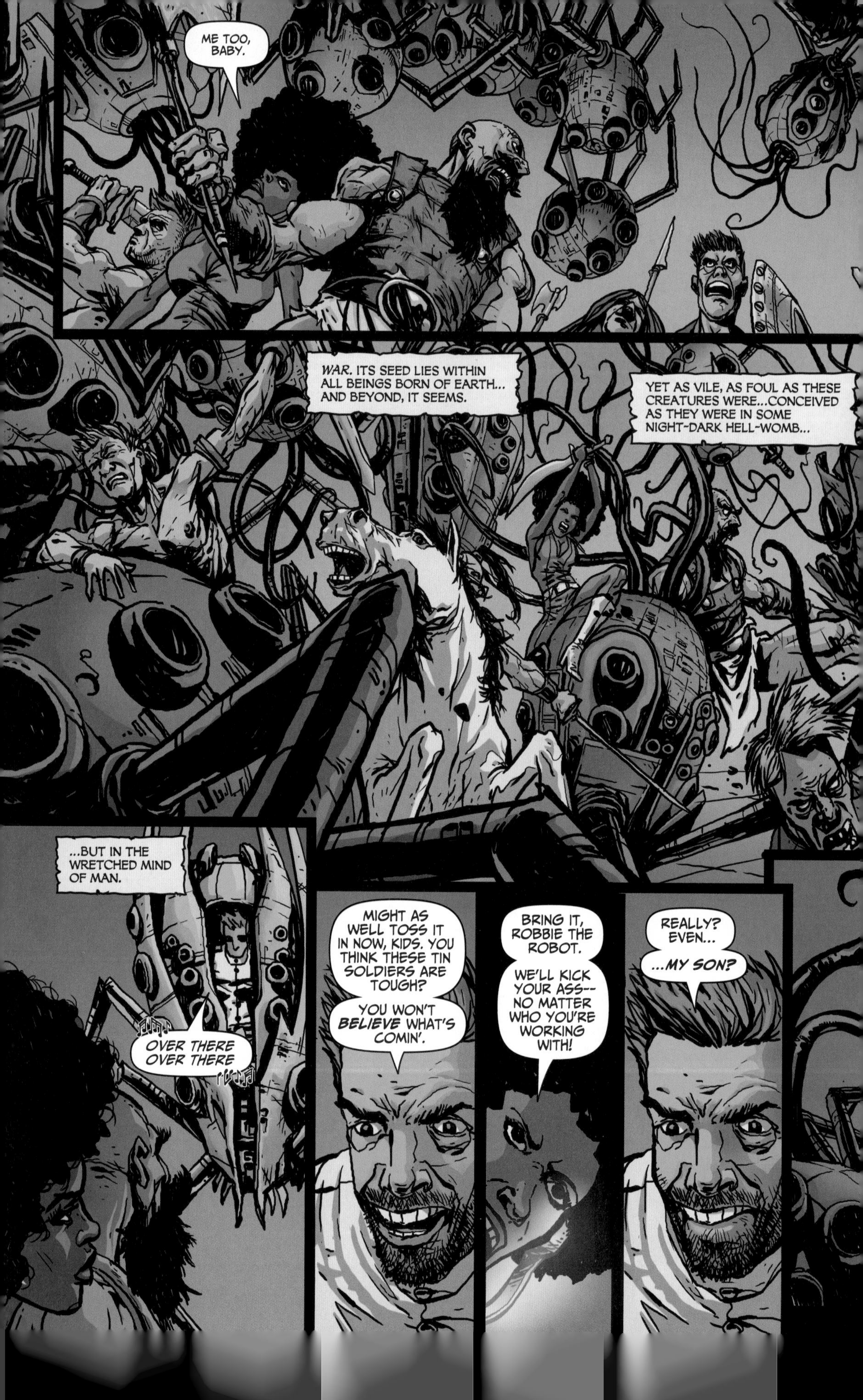
ME TOO, BABY.
WAR. ITS SEED LIES WITHIN ALL BEINGS BORN OF EARTH... AND BEYOND, IT SEEMS.
YET AS VILE, AS FOUL AS THESE CREATURES WERE...CONCEIVED AS THEY WERE IN SOME NIGHT-DARK HELL-WOMB...
...BUT IN THE WRETCHED MIND OF MAN.
OVER THERE OVER THERE
MIGHT AS WELL TOSS IT IN NOW, KIDS. YOU THINK THESE TIN SOLDIERS ARE TOUGH?
YOU WON'T BELIEVE WHAT'S COMIN'.
BRING IT, ROBBIE THE ROBOT.
WE'LL KICK YOUR ASS-- NO MATTER WHO YOU'RE WORKING WITH!
REALLY? EVEN...
...MY SON?

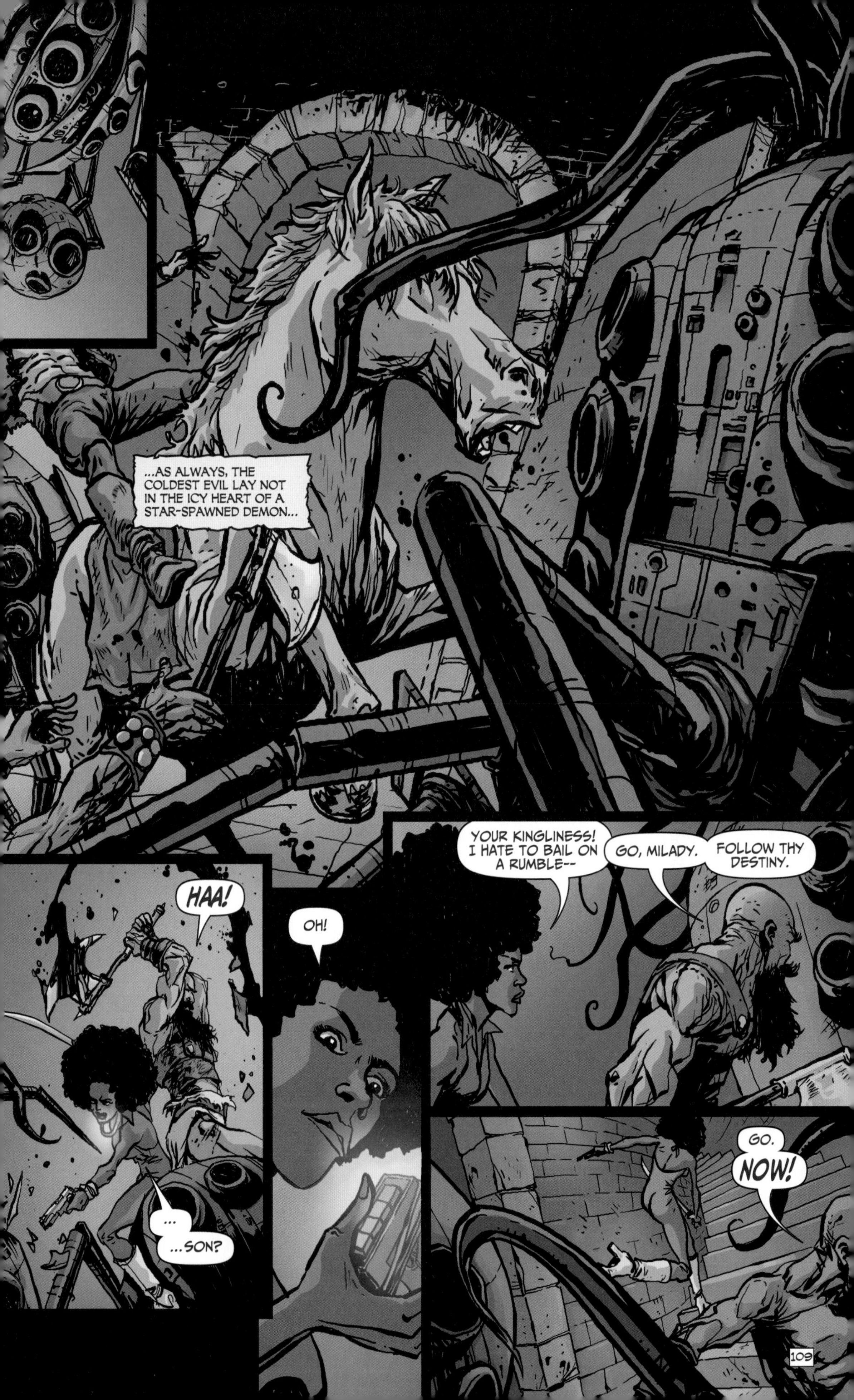
...AS ALWAYS, THE COLDEST EVIL LAY NOT IN THE ICY HEART OF A STAR-SPAWNED DEMON...
HAA!
...
...SON?
OH!
YOUR KINGLINESS! I HATE TO BAIL ON A RUMBLE--
GO, MILADY.
FOLLOW THY DESTINY.
GO.
NOW!

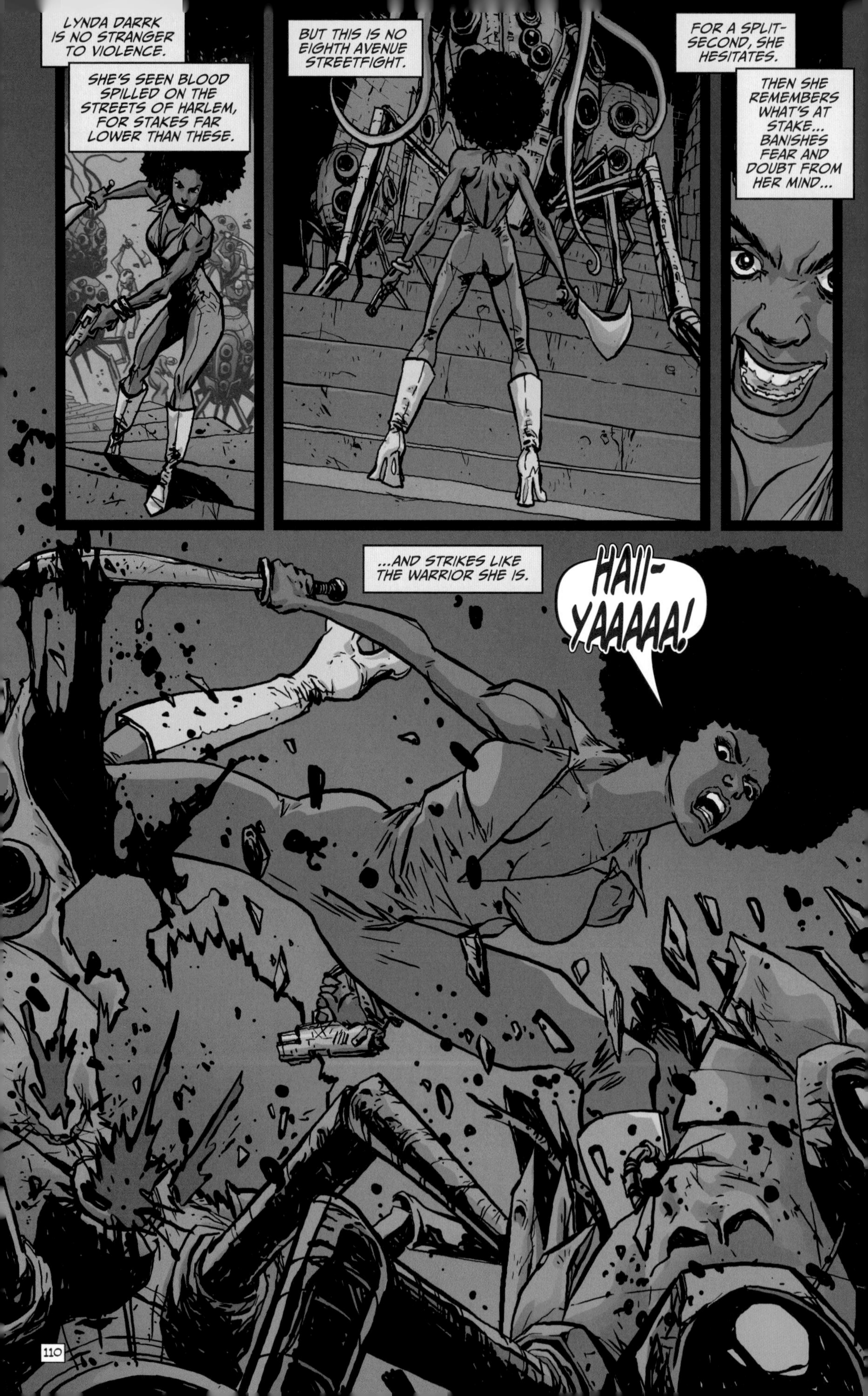
LYNDA DARRK IS NO STRANGER TO VIOLENCE.
SHE'S SEEN BLOOD SPILLED ON THE STREETS OF HARLEM, FOR STAKES FAR LOWER THAN THESE.
BUT THIS IS NO EIGHTH AVENUE STREETFIGHT.
FOR A SPLIT-SECOND, SHE HESITATES.
THEN SHE REMEMBERS WHAT'S AT STAKE... BANISHES FEAR AND DOUBT FROM HER MIND...
...AND STRIKES LIKE THE WARRIOR SHE IS.
HAII-YAAAAA!

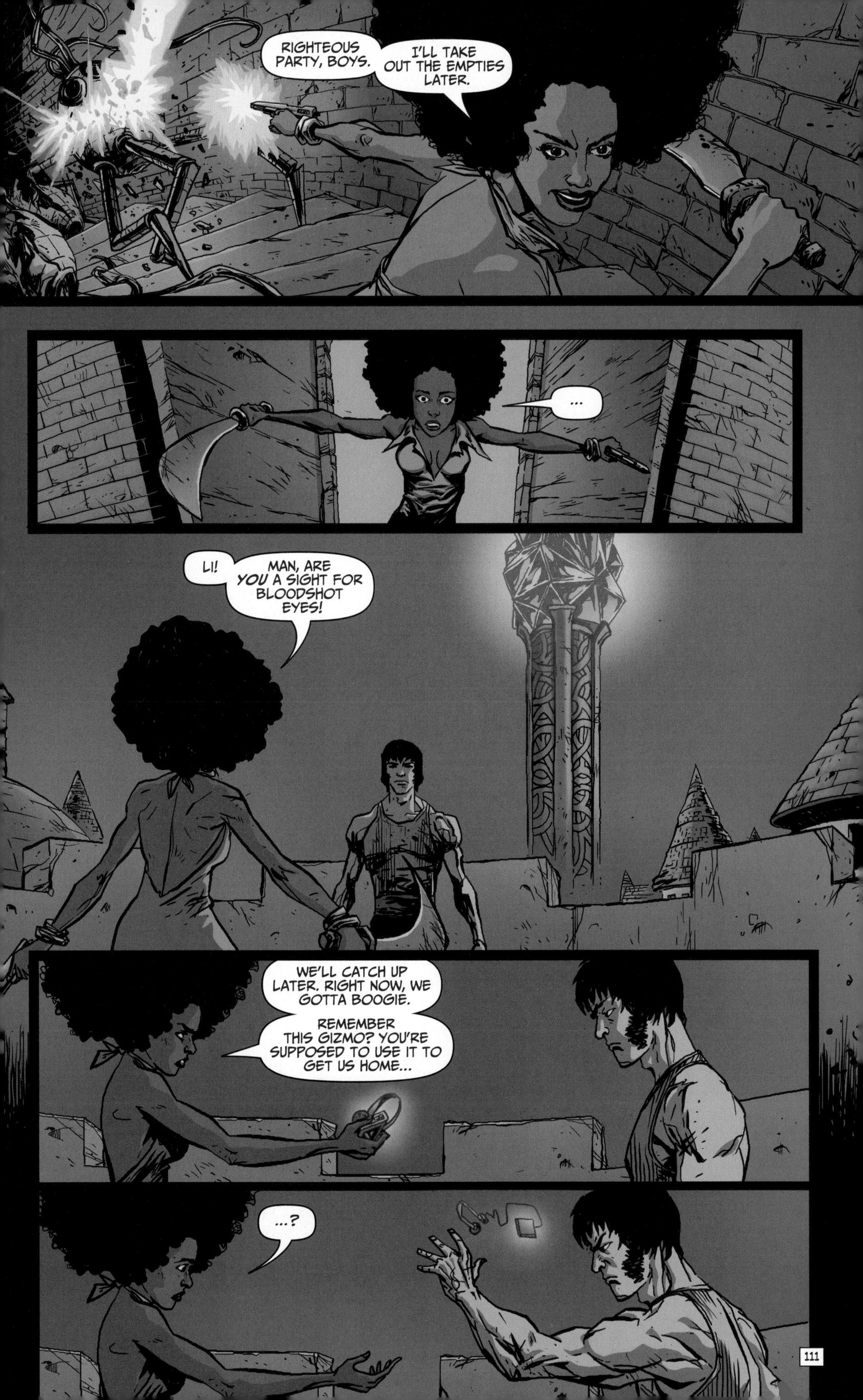
RIGHTEOUS PARTY, BOYS.
I'LL TAKE OUT THE EMPTIES LATER.
...
LI!
MAN, ARE *YOU* A SIGHT FOR BLOODSHOT EYES!
WE'LL CATCH UP LATER. RIGHT NOW, WE GOTTA BOOGIE.
REMEMBER THIS GIZMO? YOU'RE SUPPOSED TO USE IT TO GET US HOME...
...?

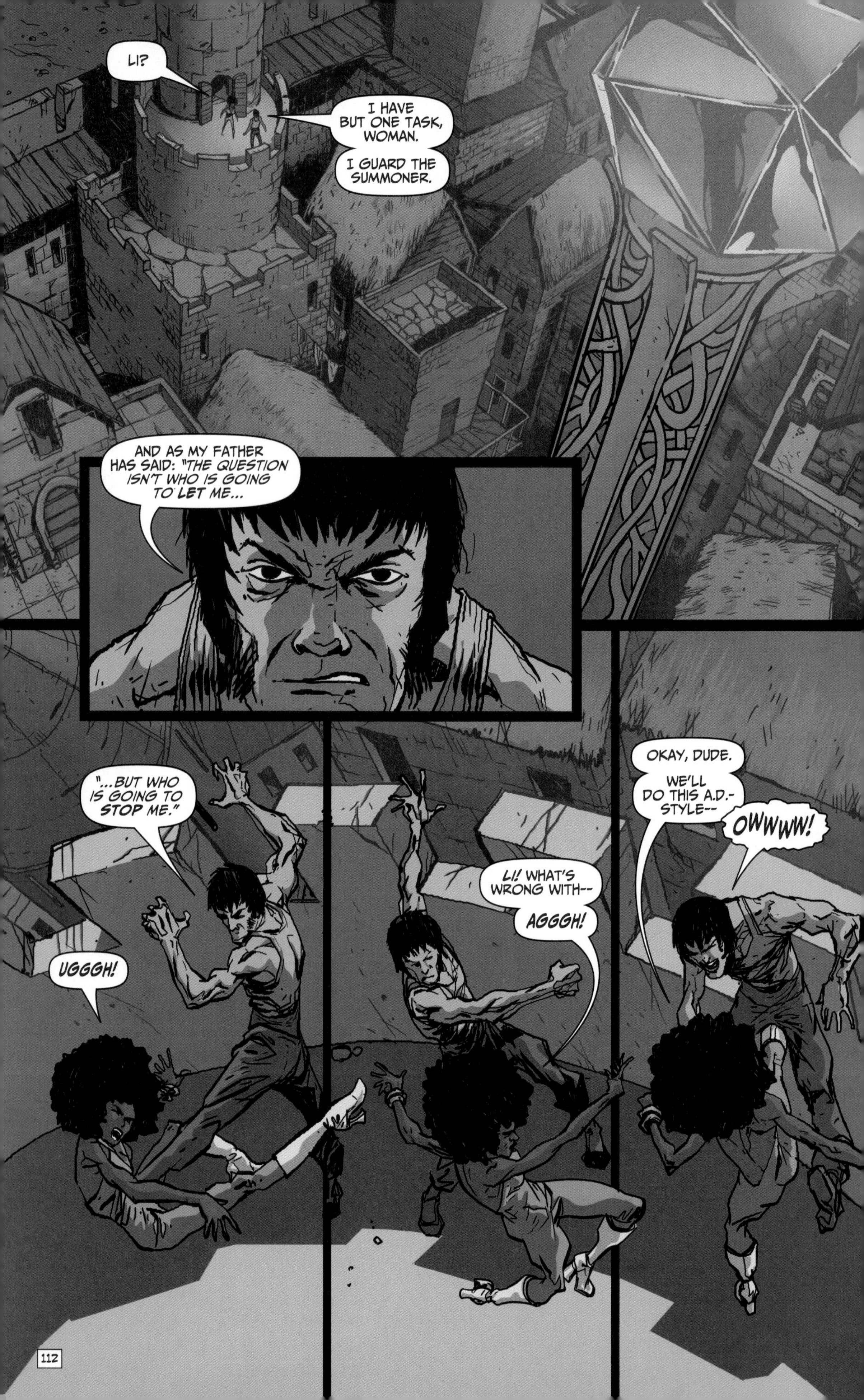
LI?
I HAVE BUT ONE TASK, WOMAN.
I GUARD THE SUMMONER.
AND AS MY FATHER HAS SAID: "THE QUESTION ISN'T WHO IS GOING TO LET ME...
"...BUT WHO IS GOING TO STOP ME."
UGGGH!
LI! WHAT'S WRONG WITH--
AGGGH!
OKAY, DUDE.
WE'LL DO THIS A.D.-STYLE--
OWWWW!

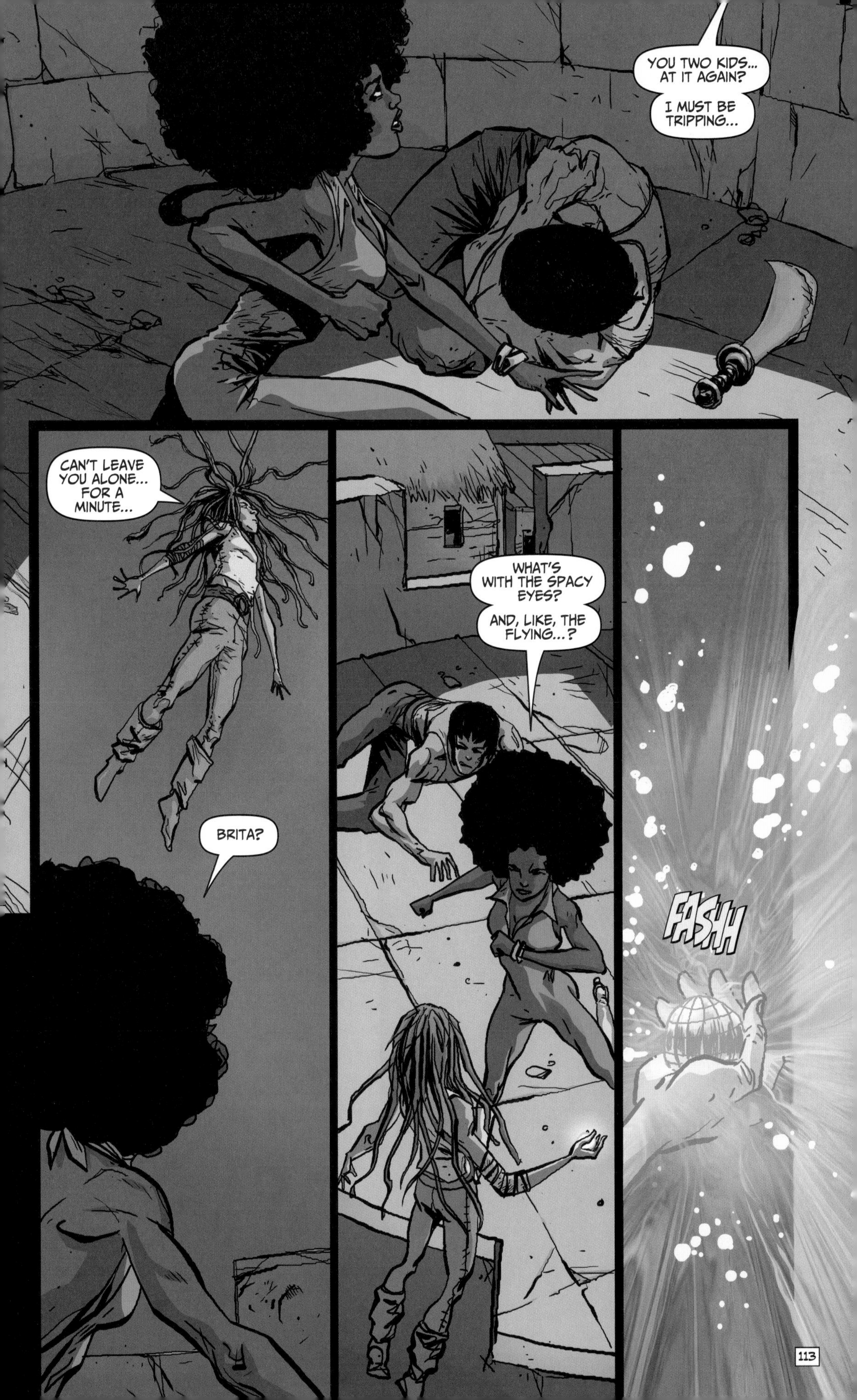

YOU TWO KIDS... AT IT AGAIN?
I MUST BE TRIPPING...
CAN'T LEAVE YOU ALONE... FOR A MINUTE...
BRITA?
WHAT'S WITH THE SPACY EYES?
AND, LIKE, THE FLYING...?
FASHH

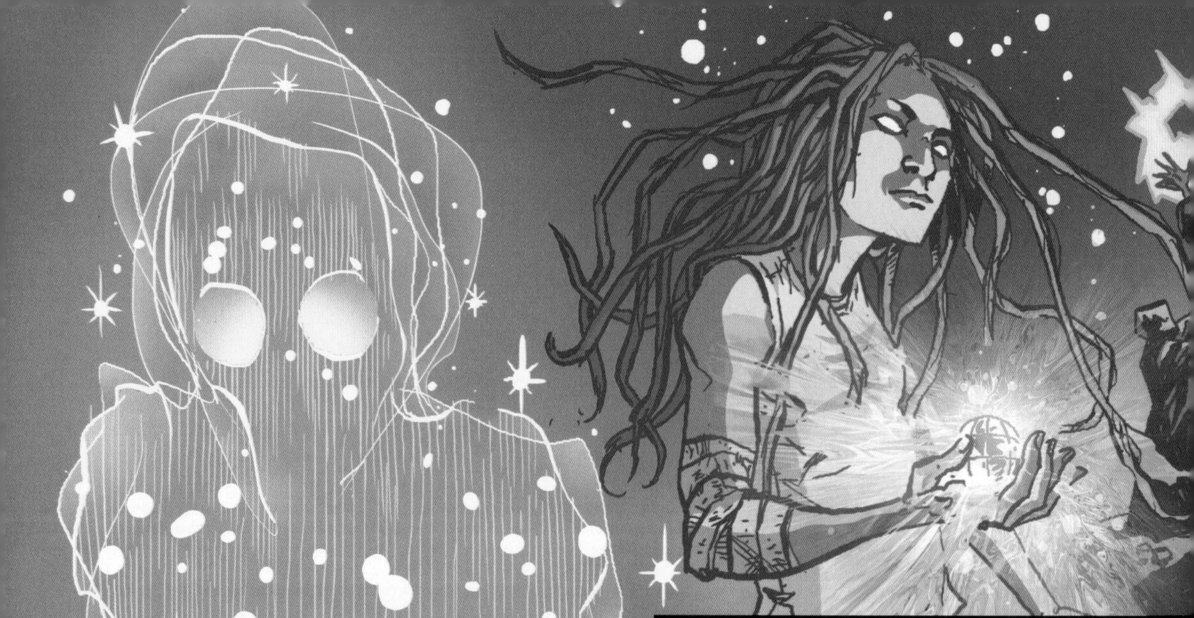

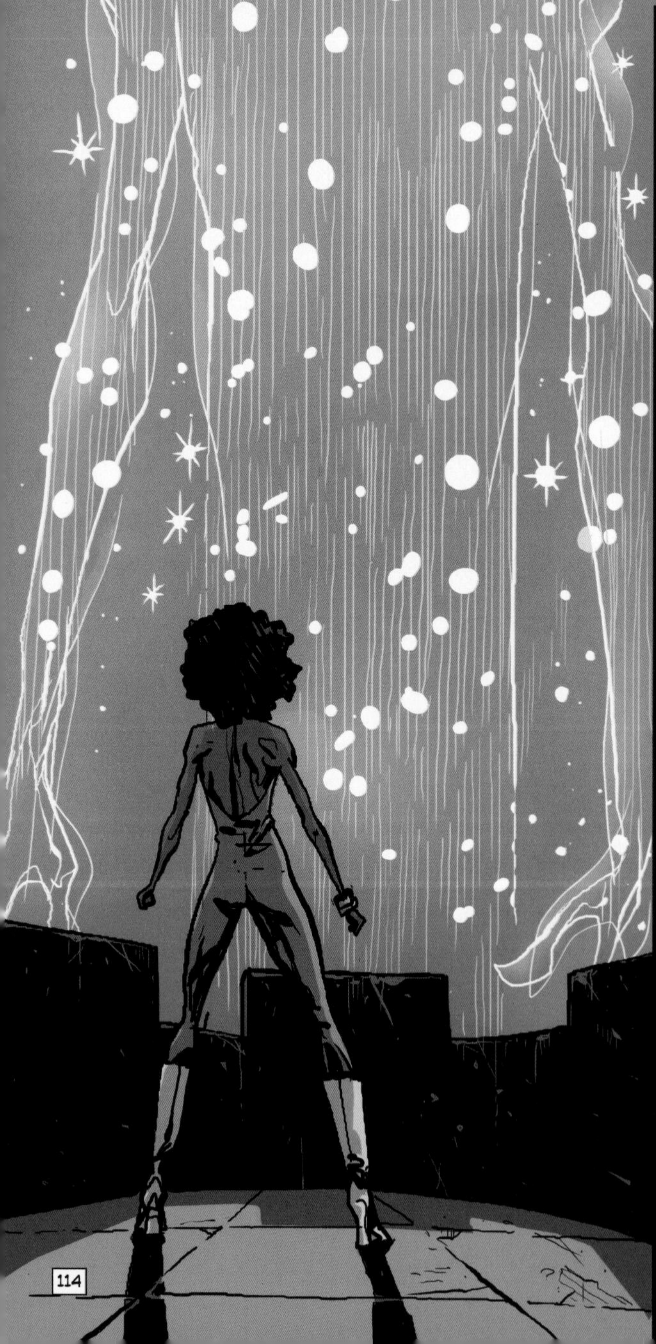

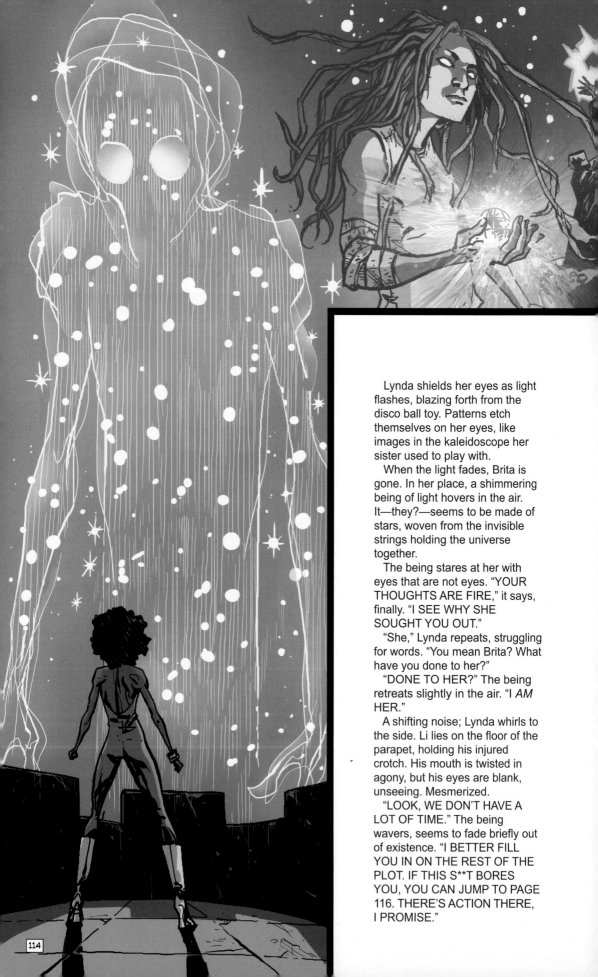

Lynda shields her eyes as light flashes, blazing forth from the disco ball toy. Patterns etch themselves on her eyes, like images in the kaleidoscope her sister used to play with.

When the light fades, Brita is gone. In her place, a shimmering being of light hovers in the air. It—they?—seems to be made of stars, woven from the invisible strings holding the universe together.

The being stares at her with eyes that are not eyes. “YOUR THOUGHTS ARE FIRE,” it says, finally. “I SEE WHY SHE SOUGHT YOU OUT.”

“She,” Lynda repeats, struggling for words. “You mean Brita? What have you done to her?”

“DONE TO HER?” The being retreats slightly in the air. “I *AM* HER.”

A shifting noise; Lynda whirls to the side. Li lies on the floor of the parapet, holding his injured crotch. His mouth is twisted in agony, but his eyes are blank, unseeing. Mesmerized.

“LOOK, WE DON’T HAVE A LOT OF TIME.” The being wavers, seems to fade briefly out of existence. “I BETTER FILL YOU IN ON THE REST OF THE PLOT. IF THIS S**T BORES YOU, YOU CAN JUMP TO PAGE 116. THERE’S ACTION THERE, I PROMISE.”

Lynda blinks.

"OKAY, LISTEN. I'M THE ONE THAT SENT BRIT-TA INTO THE FUTURE, TO MEET YOU. TROUBLE IS, I WASN'T STRONG ENOUGH TO BRING HER BACK. GOOD THING YOU FOUND ANOTHER WAY."

"Uh-*huh*..."

"BUT WHAT YOU NEED TO KNOW IS WHY I DID IT IN THE FIRST PLACE. I TRIED TELLING BRIT ABOUT IT IN VERSE, BUT THAT DIDN'T WORK. SHE SAYS I SHOULD JUST GIVE IT TO YOU STRAIGHT, WHICH IS *BORING*, BUT HERE GOES.

"A LONG TIME AGO—AND I MEAN A LONG TIME FROM *NOW*, WHICH IS ALREADY A LONG TIME AGO TO YOU—THERE WAS THIS WAR. OLD ONES, HIDEOUS CREATURES FROM BEYOND THE STARS, FOUGHT TO THE DEATH AGAINST WIZARDS. AND WE'RE TALKING *WIZARDS*, MAGES WITH A LOT MORE POWER THAN ANYBODY LEFT ON EARTH TODAY.

"THE RESULTING CATACLYSM SANK ATLANTIS LIKE A ROCK. AND THE AFORE-MENTIONED OLD ONES SANK WITH 'EM.

"ALONG THE WAY, ONE SIDE OR THE OTHER—I HONESTLY CAN'T REMEMBER—BUILT THE TABOO ZONE AS A KIND OF PRISON. THEY PENNED UP A BEING OF UNIMAGINABLE POWER INSIDE, TO KEEP THE ENEMY FROM USING IT AGAINST THEM. GUESS WHO?

"THE HANDLE'S *GODD*, BY THE WAY. YOU KNOW, LIKE THE DEITY. NOT THAT I'M, Y'UNDERSTAND, PRESUMING…"

The entity—GODD—flickers again, falters. Lynda steps closer to the edge. "Are you okay?"

"I'M…NOT AT FULL STRENGTH HERE," GODD explains. "I CAN ONLY EXIST ON THIS WORLD FOR SHORT PERIODS OF TIME…IT'S DISORIENTING, EVEN KIND OF PAINFUL. THANKS FOR ASKING, THAT'S VERY COOL OF YOU.

"BRIT-TA, SHE BUSTED ME OUT OF STIR," they continue. "LIKE I TOLD HER, I NEED A HUMAN HOST TO FUNCTION HERE AT ALL. AND THAT CRACKER JACK PRIZE UP THERE ISN'T HELPING EITHER."

Lynda glances past GODD, up at the jewel—still blazing bright, atop the highest tower of the castle. What did Li say? *I guard the Summoner…*

"IT WAS CREATED BY THE ANCIENT ATLANTEANS. THEY USED IT TO BATTLE AND CONTROL THE OLD ONES, EONS AGO."

"Look," Lynda says, "I appreciate the history lesson, but this mystical jazz is gonna have to wait. Right now, we got to stop the *Martians*."

The energy within GODD seems to sizzle, to surge brighter. They lean in closer, their enormous head moving very close to Lynda's. She tries not to flinch.

"DON'T YOU KNOW?"

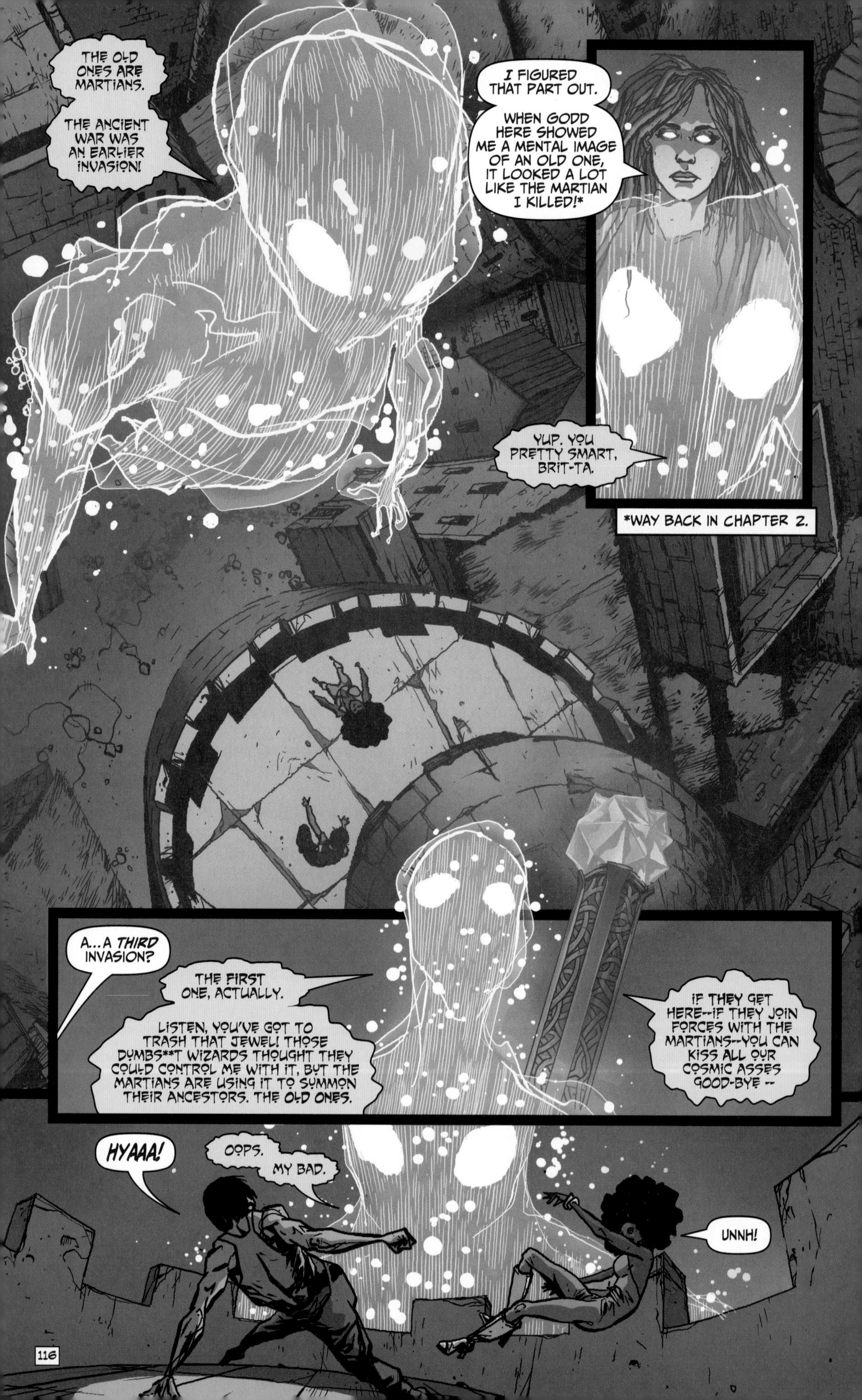
THE OLD ONES ARE MARTIANS.
THE ANCIENT WAR WAS AN EARLIER INVASION!
I FIGURED THAT PART OUT.
WHEN GODD HERE SHOWED ME A MENTAL IMAGE OF AN OLD ONE, IT LOOKED A LOT LIKE THE MARTIAN I KILLED!*
YUP. YOU PRETTY SMART, BRIT-TA.
*WAY BACK IN CHAPTER 2.
A...A *THIRD* INVASION?
THE FIRST ONE, ACTUALLY.
LISTEN, YOU'VE GOT TO TRASH THAT JEWEL! THOSE DUMBS**T WIZARDS THOUGHT THEY COULD CONTROL ME WITH IT, BUT THE MARTIANS ARE USING IT TO SUMMON THEIR ANCESTORS. THE OLD ONES.
IF THEY GET HERE--IF THEY JOIN FORCES WITH THE MARTIANS--YOU CAN KISS ALL OUR COSMIC ASSES GOOD-BYE --
HYAAA!
OOPS.
MY BAD.
UNNH!

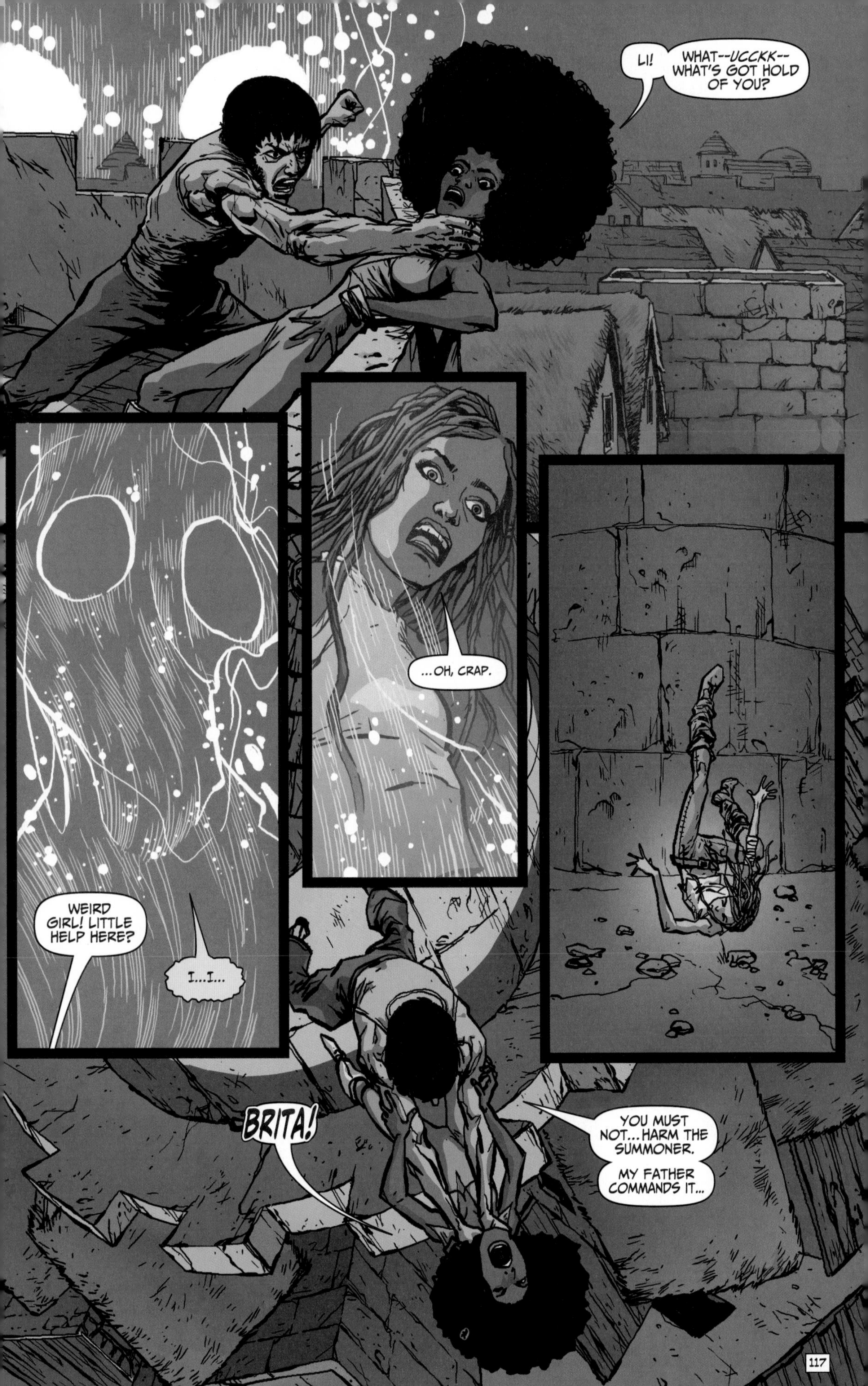
LI!
WHAT--UCCKK--
WHAT'S GOT HOLD
OF YOU?
...OH, CRAP.
WEIRD
GIRL! LITTLE
HELP HERE?
I...I...
BRITA!
YOU MUST
NOT...HARM THE
SUMMONER.
MY FATHER
COMMANDS IT...

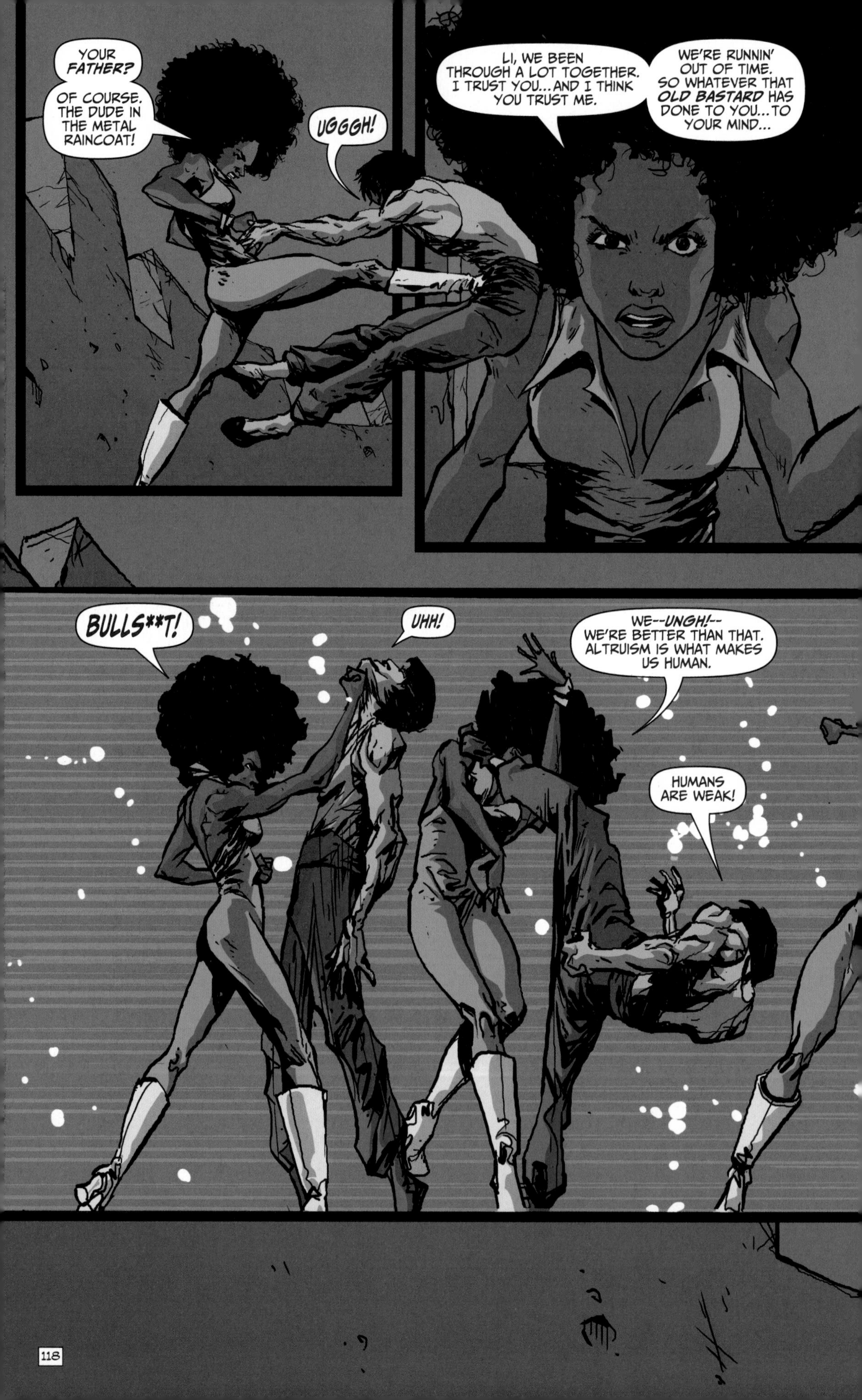
YOUR FATHER?
OF COURSE. THE DUDE IN THE METAL RAINCOAT!
UGGGH!
LI, WE BEEN THROUGH A LOT TOGETHER. I TRUST YOU...AND I THINK YOU TRUST ME.
WE'RE RUNNIN' OUT OF TIME. SO WHATEVER THAT OLD BASTARD HAS DONE TO YOU...TO YOUR MIND...
BULLS**T!
UHH!
WE--UNGH!-- WE'RE BETTER THAN THAT. ALTRUISM IS WHAT MAKES US HUMAN.
HUMANS ARE WEAK!

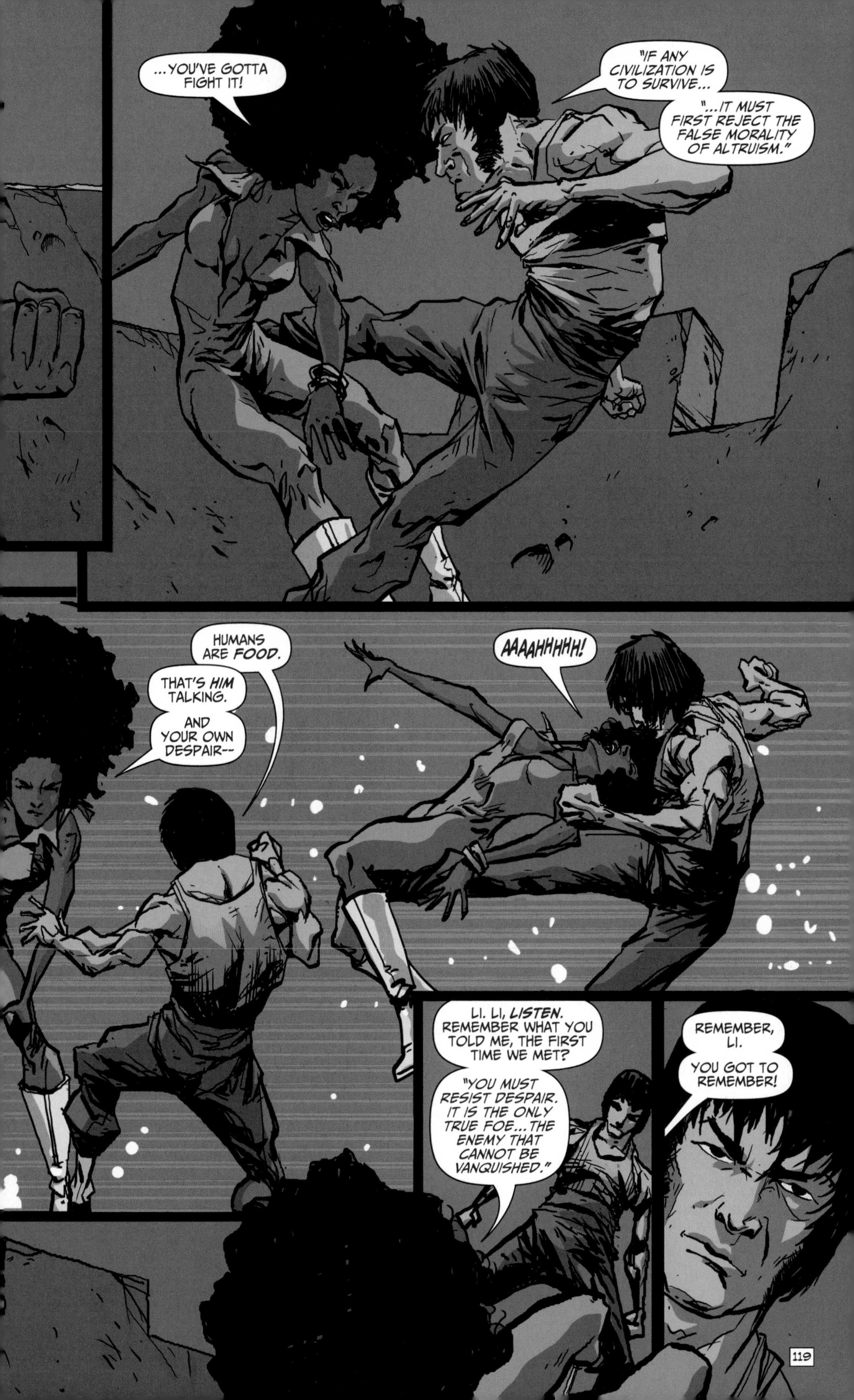
...YOU'VE GOTTA FIGHT IT!
"IF ANY CIVILIZATION IS TO SURVIVE...
"...IT MUST FIRST REJECT THE FALSE MORALITY OF ALTRUISM."
HUMANS ARE FOOD.
AAAAHHHHH!
THAT'S HIM TALKING.
AND YOUR OWN DESPAIR--
LI. LI, LISTEN. REMEMBER WHAT YOU TOLD ME, THE FIRST TIME WE MET?
"YOU MUST RESIST DESPAIR. IT IS THE ONLY TRUE FOE...THE ENEMY THAT CANNOT BE VANQUISHED."
REMEMBER, LI.
YOU GOT TO REMEMBER!

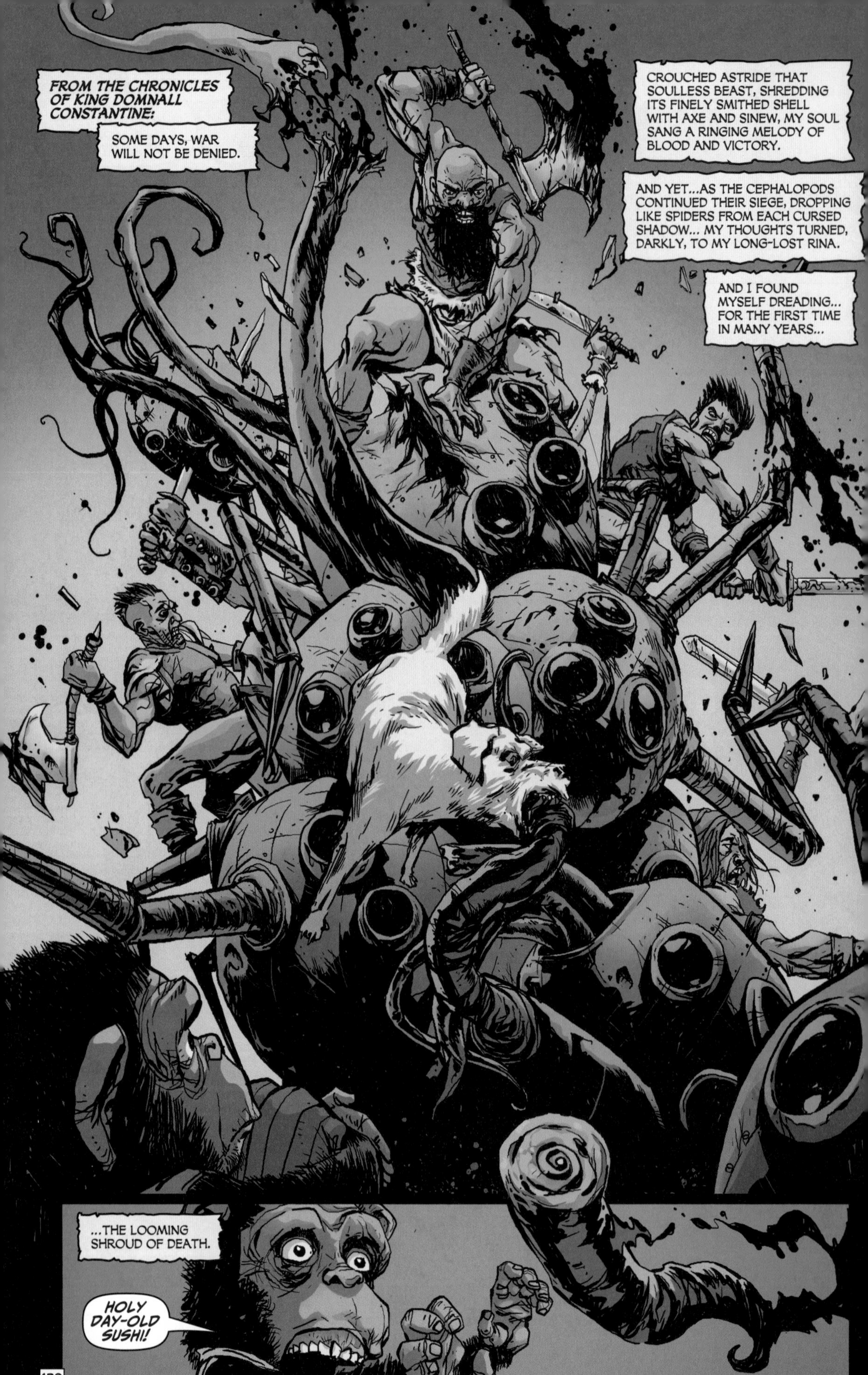
FROM THE CHRONICLES OF KING DOMNALL CONSTANTINE:
SOME DAYS, WAR WILL NOT BE DENIED.
CROUCHED ASTRIDE THAT SOULLESS BEAST, SHREDDING ITS FINELY SMITHED SHELL WITH AXE AND SINEW, MY SOUL SANG A RINGING MELODY OF BLOOD AND VICTORY.
AND YET...AS THE CEPHALOPODS CONTINUED THEIR SIEGE, DROPPING LIKE SPIDERS FROM EACH CURSED SHADOW... MY THOUGHTS TURNED, DARKLY, TO MY LONG-LOST RINA.
AND I FOUND MYSELF DREADING... FOR THE FIRST TIME IN MANY YEARS...
...THE LOOMING SHROUD OF DEATH.
HOLY DAY-OLD SUSHI!

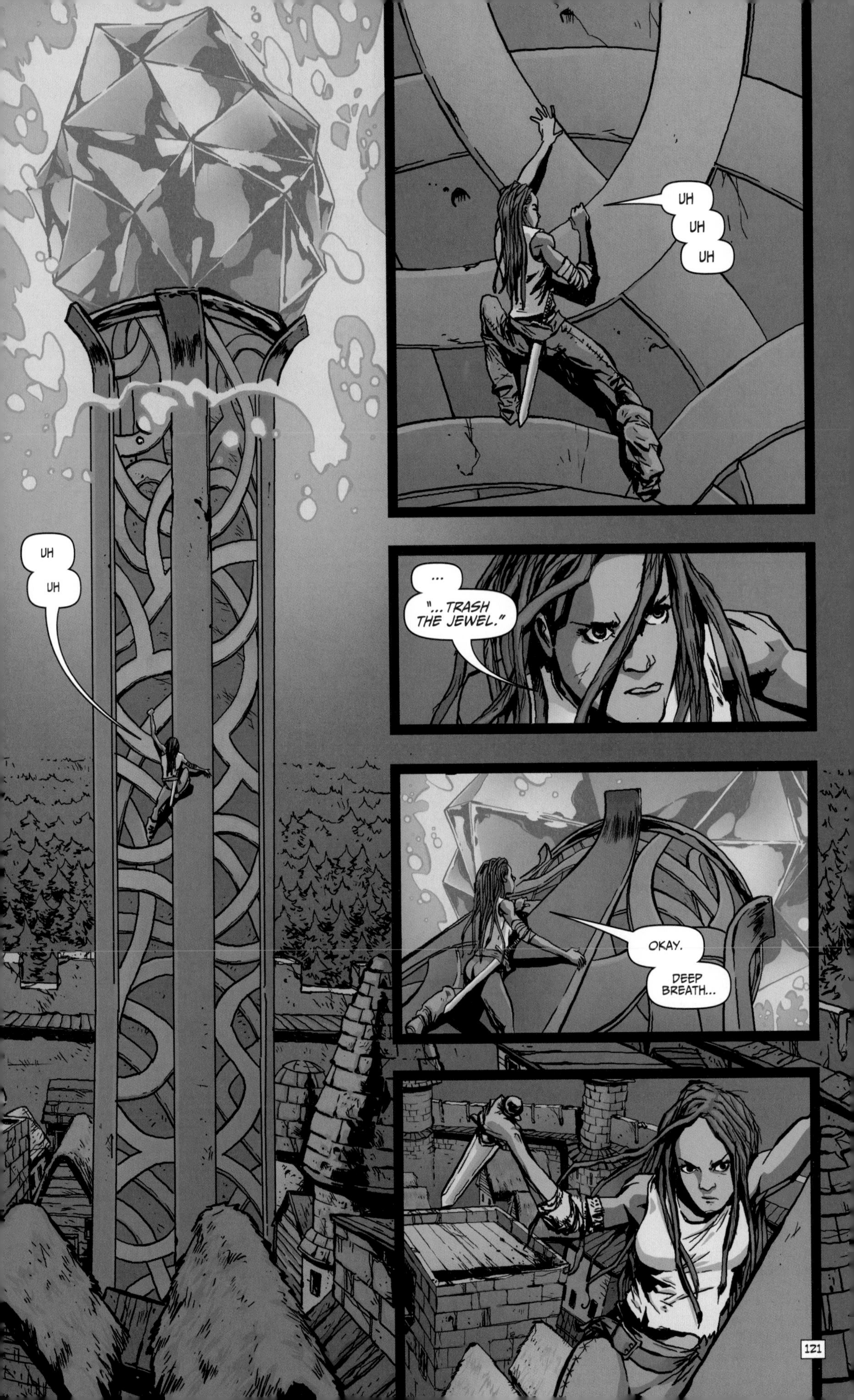
UH
UH
UH
UH
UH
...
"...TRASH THE JEWEL."
OKAY.
DEEP BREATH...

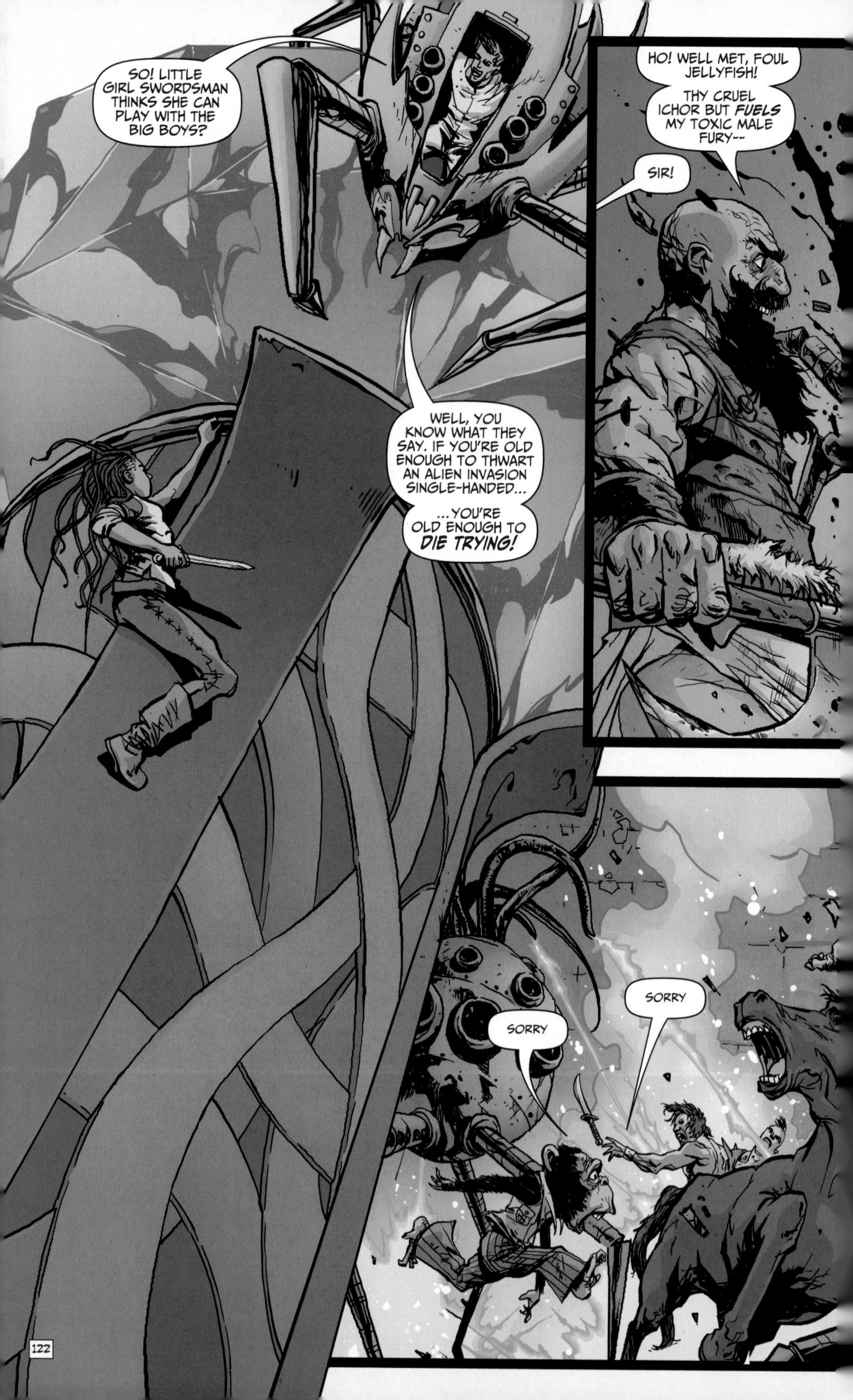
SO! LITTLE GIRL SWORDSMAN THINKS SHE CAN PLAY WITH THE BIG BOYS?
HO! WELL MET, FOUL JELLYFISH!
THY CRUEL ICHOR BUT FUELS MY TOXIC MALE FURY--
SIR!
WELL, YOU KNOW WHAT THEY SAY. IF YOU'RE OLD ENOUGH TO THWART AN ALIEN INVASION SINGLE-HANDED...
...YOU'RE OLD ENOUGH TO DIE TRYING!
SORRY
SORRY

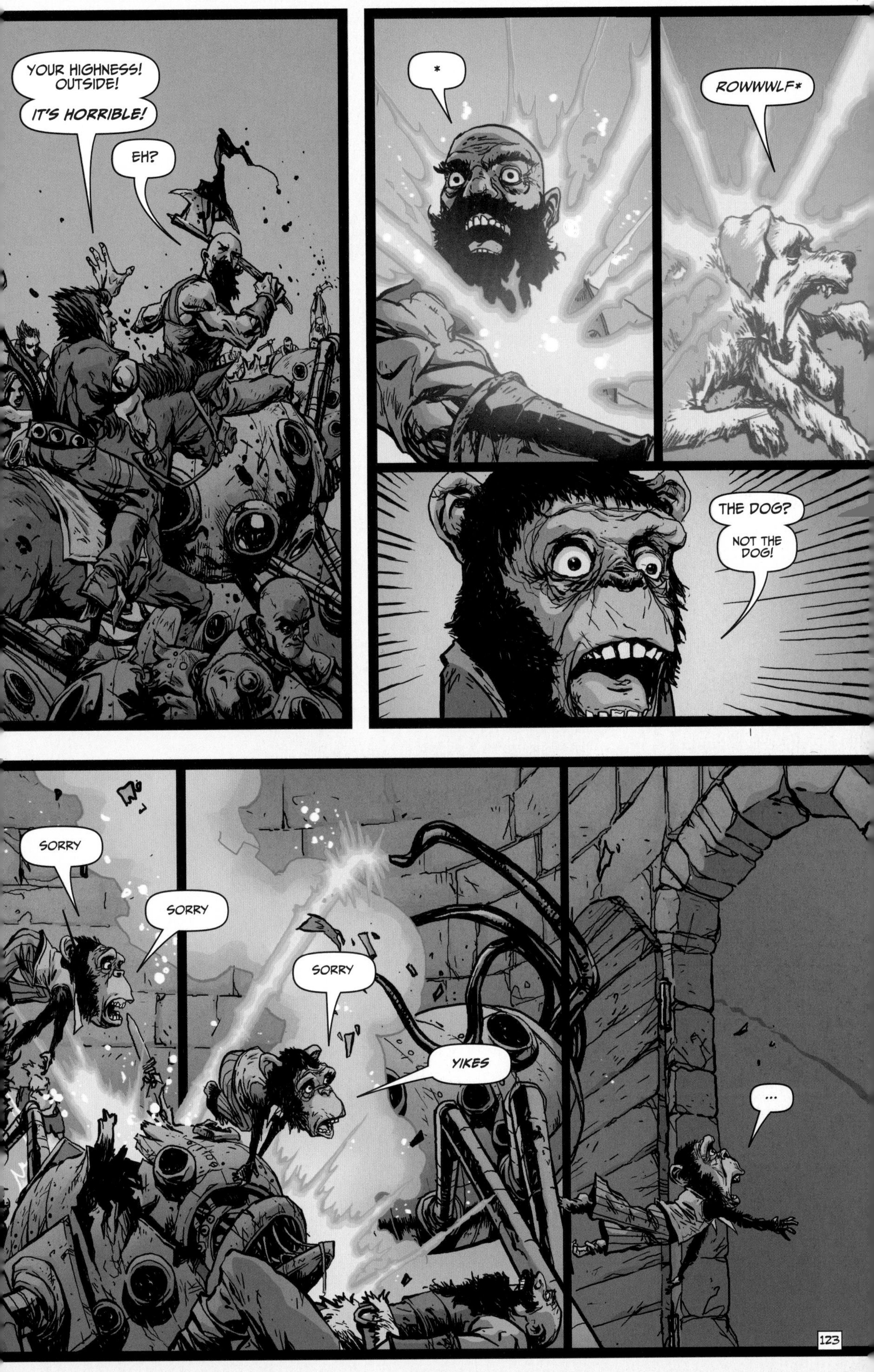
YOUR HIGHNESS! OUTSIDE!
IT'S HORRIBLE!
EH?
*
ROWWWLF*
THE DOG?
NOT THE DOG!
SORRY
SORRY
SORRY
YIKES
...

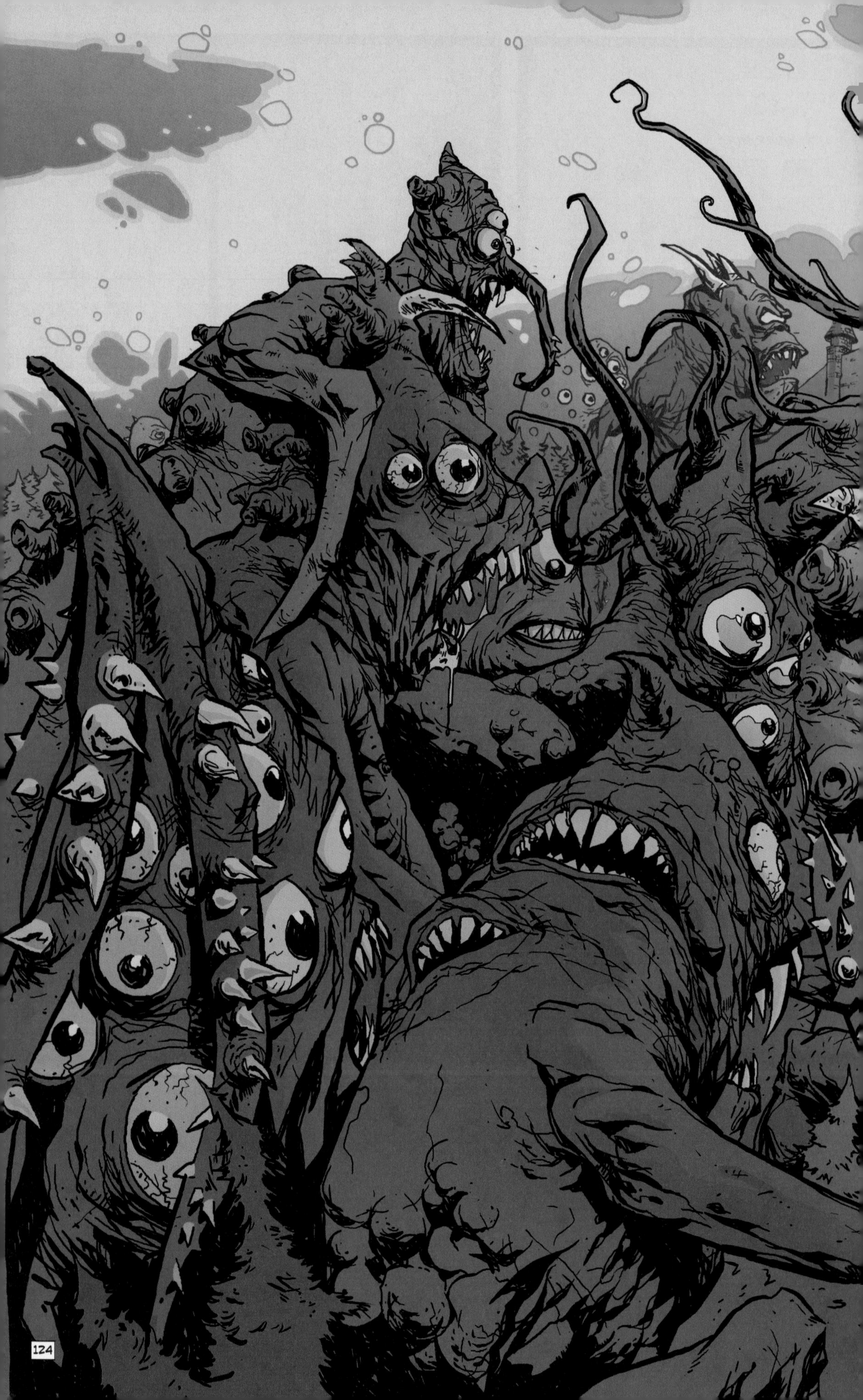

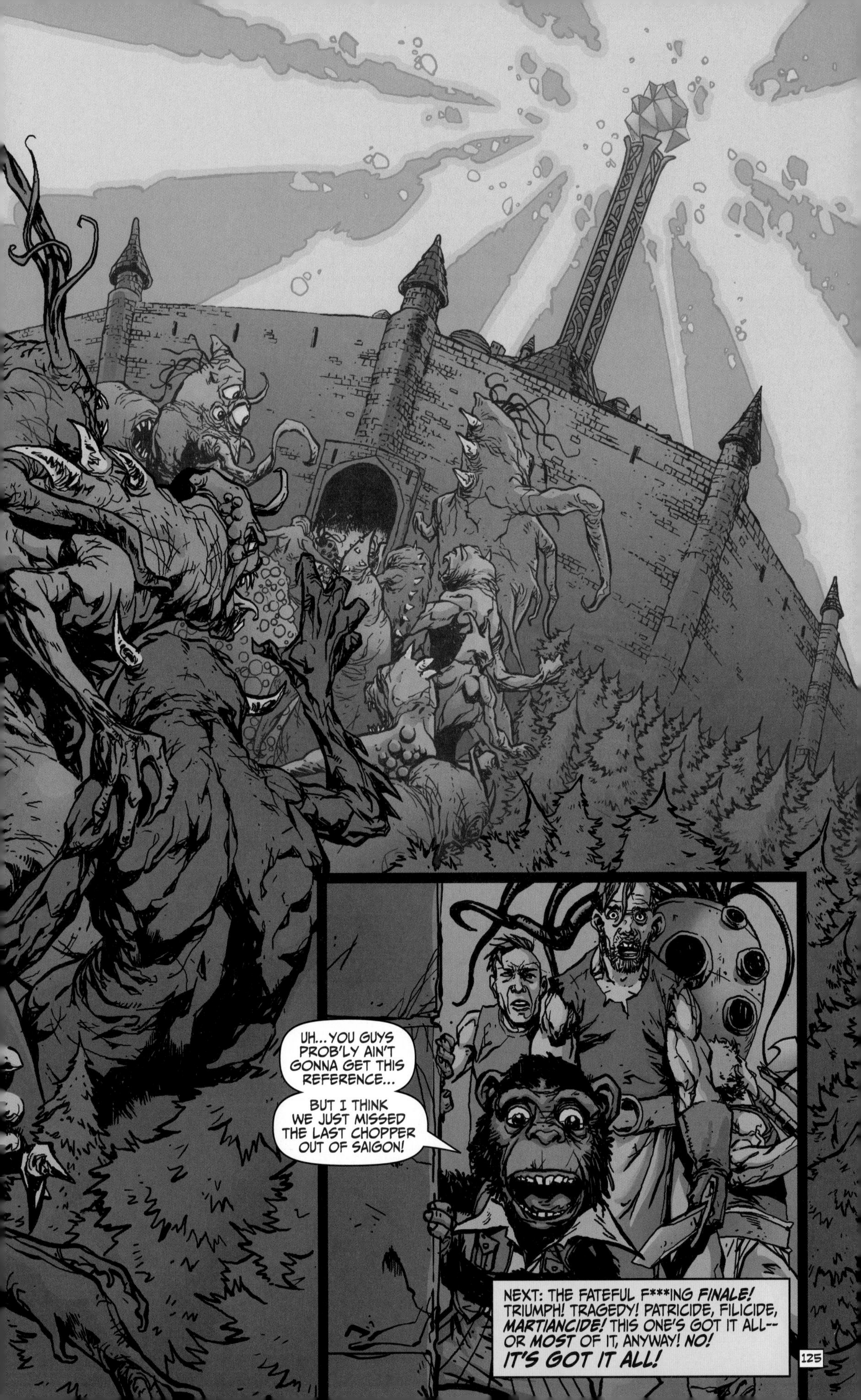
UH...YOU GUYS PROB'LY AIN'T GONNA GET THIS REFERENCE...
BUT I THINK WE JUST MISSED THE LAST CHOPPER OUT OF SAIGON!
NEXT: THE FATEFUL F***ING *FINALE!* TRIUMPH! TRAGEDY! PATRICIDE, FILICIDE, *MARTIANCIDE!* THIS ONE'S GOT IT ALL-- OR *MOST* OF IT, ANYWAY! *NO!* ***IT'S GOT IT ALL!***

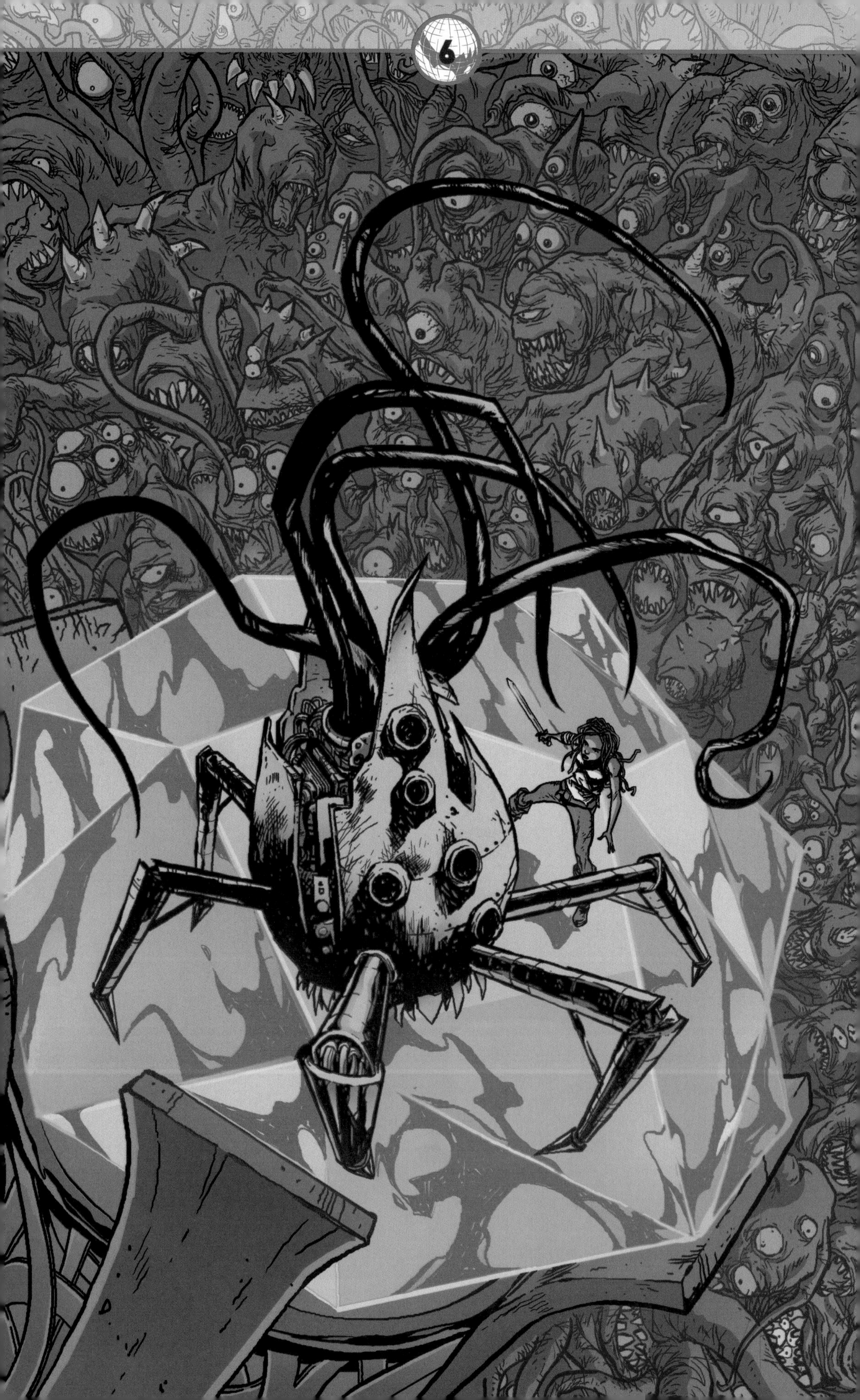

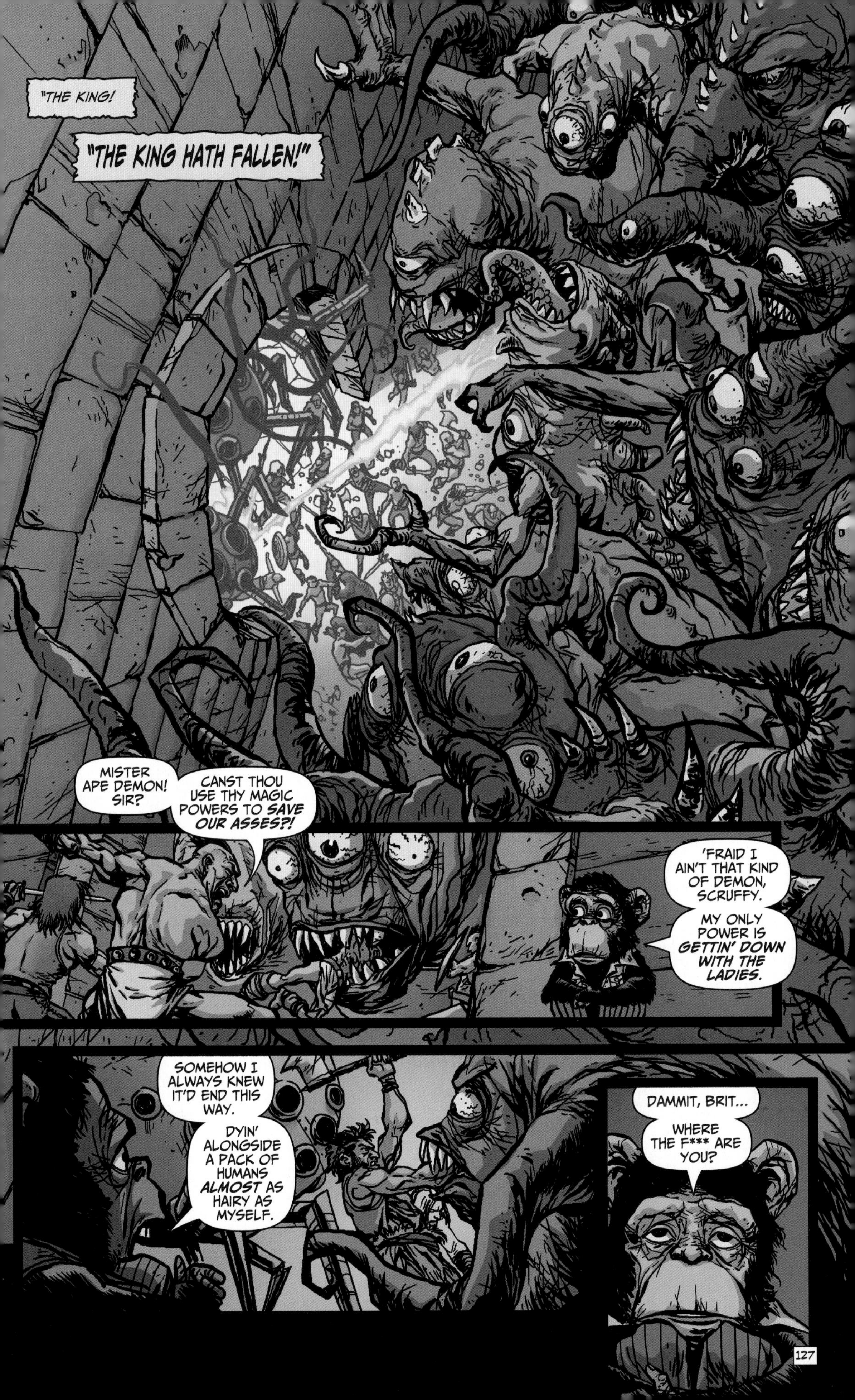
"THE KING!
"THE KING HATH FALLEN!"
MISTER APE DEMON! SIR?
CANST THOU USE THY MAGIC POWERS TO SAVE OUR ASSES?!
'FRAID I AIN'T THAT KIND OF DEMON, SCRUFFY.
MY ONLY POWER IS GETTIN' DOWN WITH THE LADIES.
SOMEHOW I ALWAYS KNEW IT'D END THIS WAY.
DYIN' ALONGSIDE A PACK OF HUMANS ALMOST AS HAIRY AS MYSELF.
DAMMIT, BRIT...
WHERE THE F*** ARE YOU?

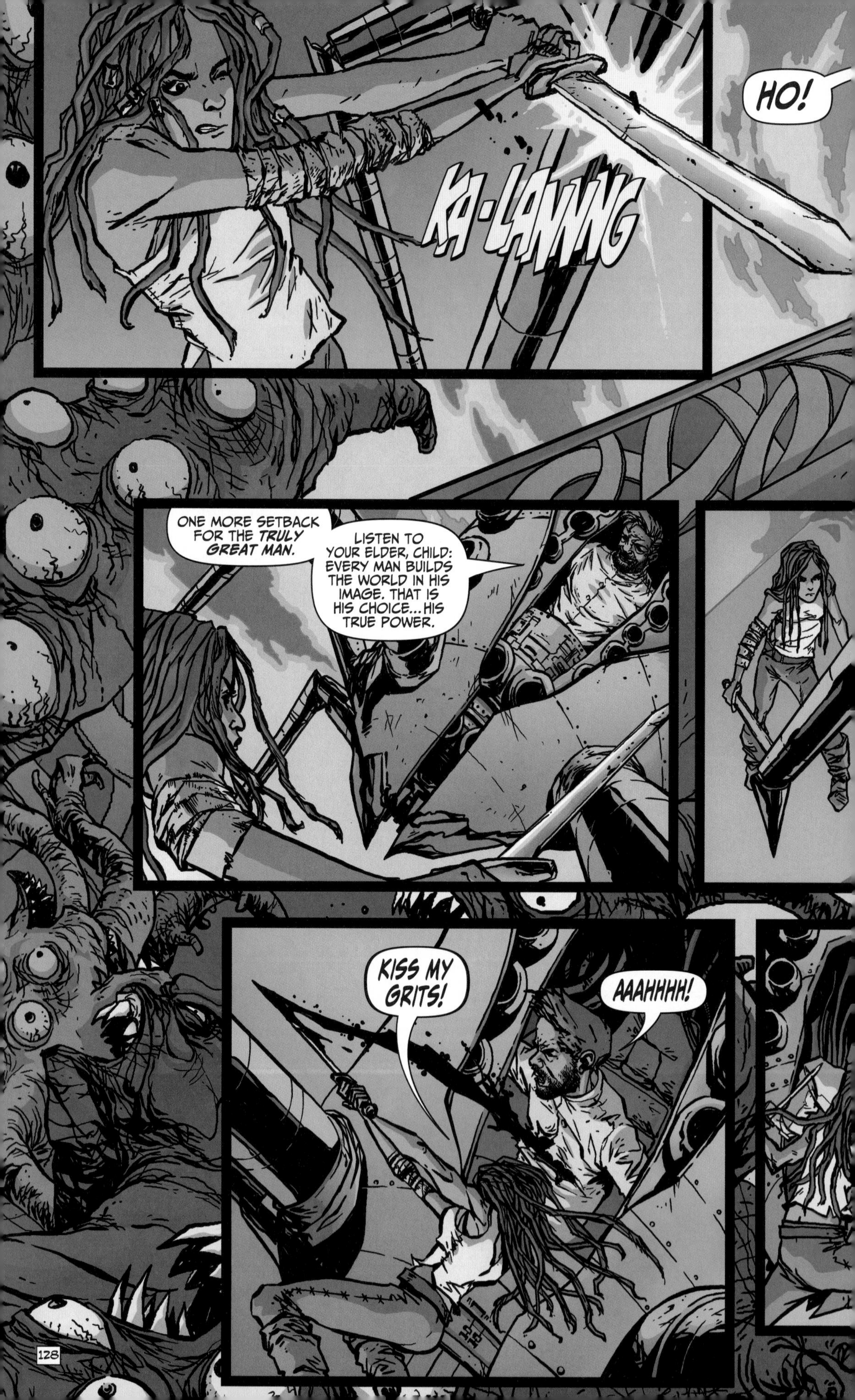
KA-LANNNG
HO!
ONE MORE SETBACK FOR THE *TRULY GREAT MAN*.
LISTEN TO YOUR ELDER, CHILD: EVERY MAN BUILDS THE WORLD IN HIS IMAGE. THAT IS HIS CHOICE...HIS TRUE POWER.
KISS MY GRITS!
AAAHHHH!

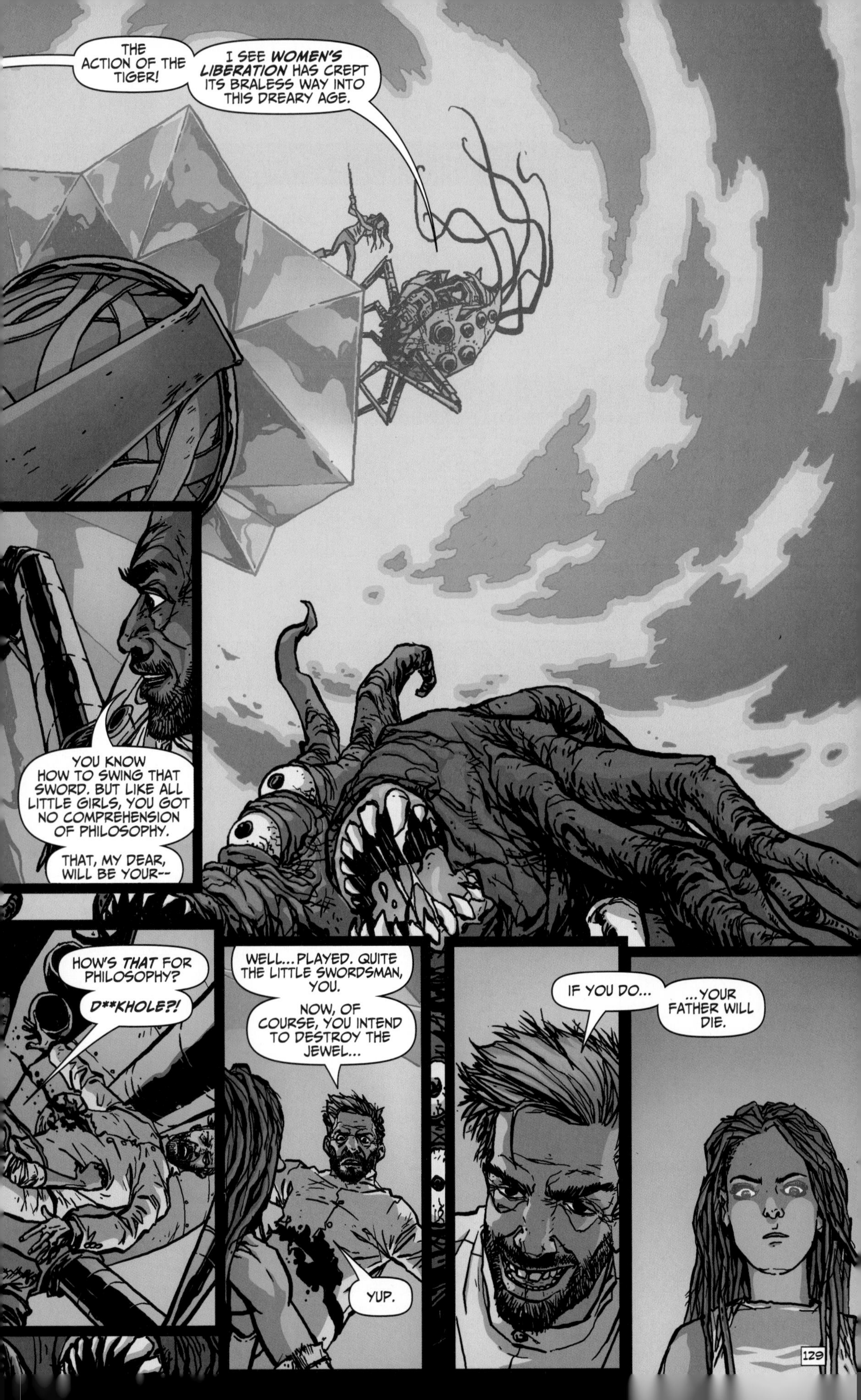
THE ACTION OF THE TIGER!
I SEE WOMEN'S LIBERATION HAS CREPT ITS BRALESS WAY INTO THIS DREARY AGE.
YOU KNOW HOW TO SWING THAT SWORD. BUT LIKE ALL LITTLE GIRLS, YOU GOT NO COMPREHENSION OF PHILOSOPHY.
THAT, MY DEAR, WILL BE YOUR--
HOW'S THAT FOR PHILOSOPHY?
D**KHOLE?!
WELL...PLAYED. QUITE THE LITTLE SWORDSMAN, YOU.
NOW, OF COURSE, YOU INTEND TO DESTROY THE JEWEL...
YUP.
IF YOU DO...
...YOUR FATHER WILL DIE.

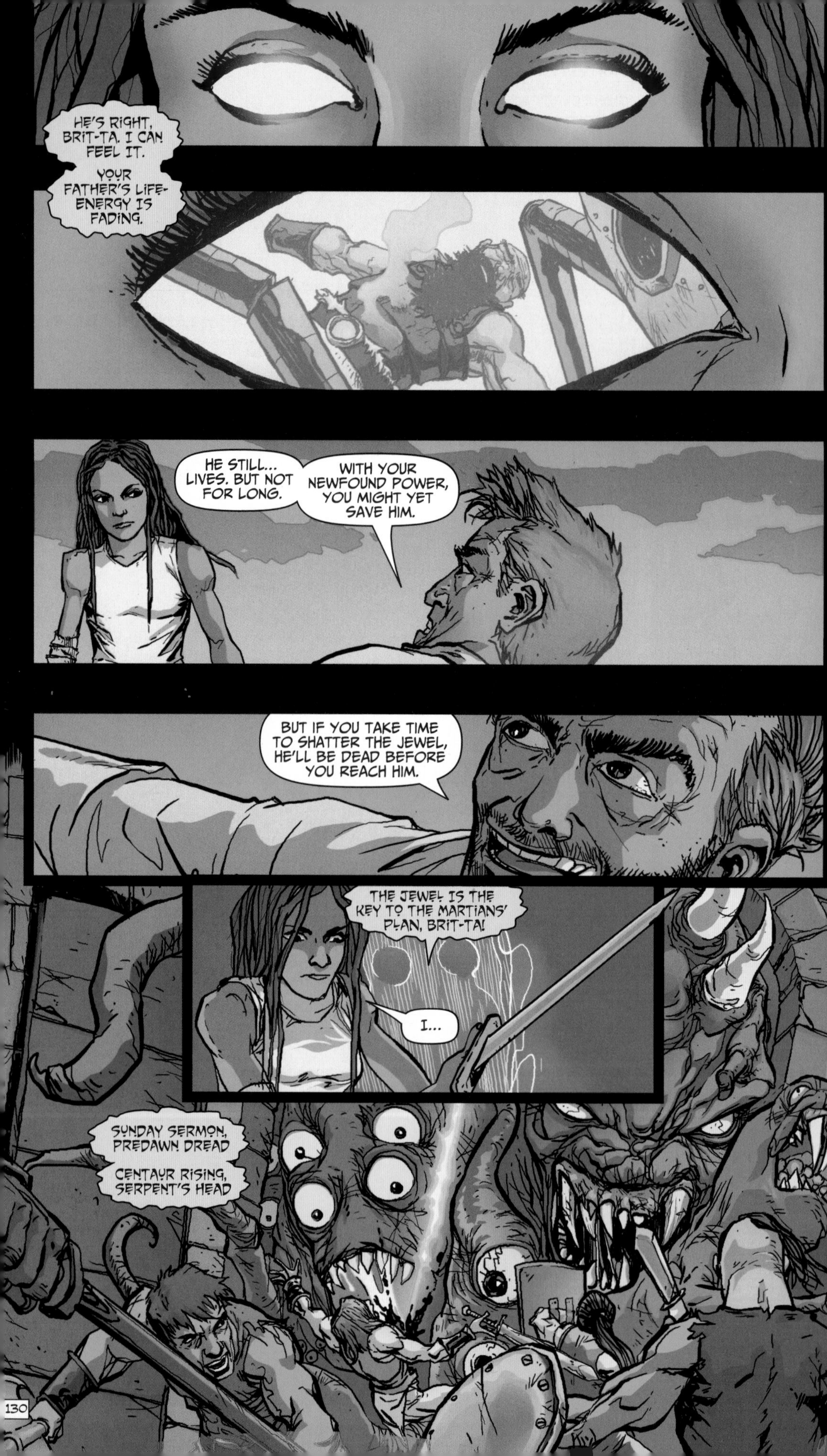
HE'S RIGHT, BRIT-TA. I CAN FEEL IT.
YOUR FATHER'S LIFE-ENERGY IS FADING.
HE STILL... LIVES. BUT NOT FOR LONG.
WITH YOUR NEWFOUND POWER, YOU MIGHT YET SAVE HIM.
BUT IF YOU TAKE TIME TO SHATTER THE JEWEL, HE'LL BE DEAD BEFORE YOU REACH HIM.
THE JEWEL IS THE KEY TO THE MARTIANS' PLAN, BRIT-TA!
I...
SUNDAY SERMON, PREDAWN DREAD
CENTAUR RISING, SERPENT'S HEAD

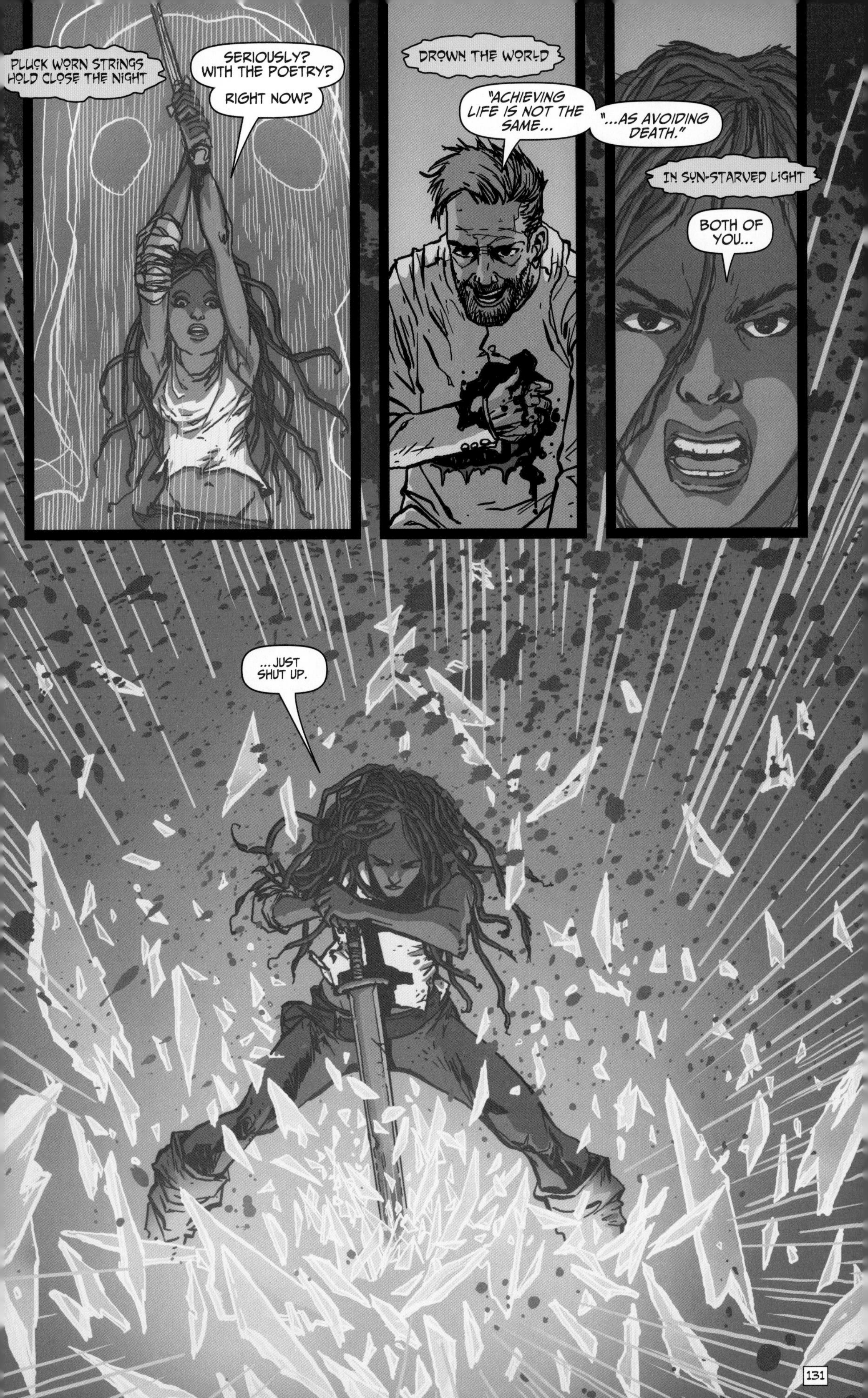
PLUCK WORN STRINGS HOLD CLOSE THE NIGHT
SERIOUSLY? WITH THE POETRY?
RIGHT NOW?
DROWN THE WORLD
"ACHIEVING LIFE IS NOT THE SAME...
"...AS AVOIDING DEATH."
IN SUN-STARVED LIGHT
BOTH OF YOU...
...JUST SHUT UP.

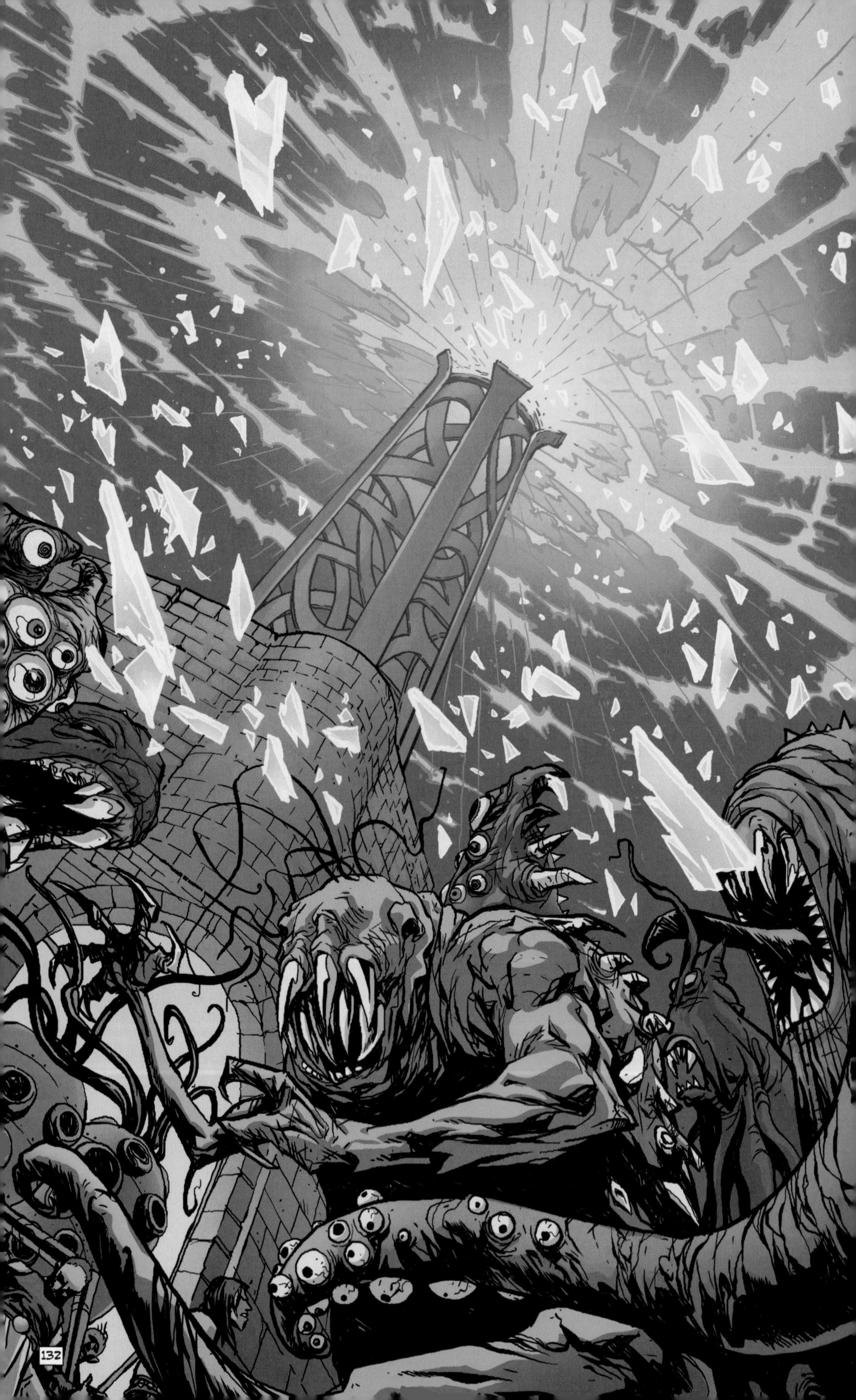

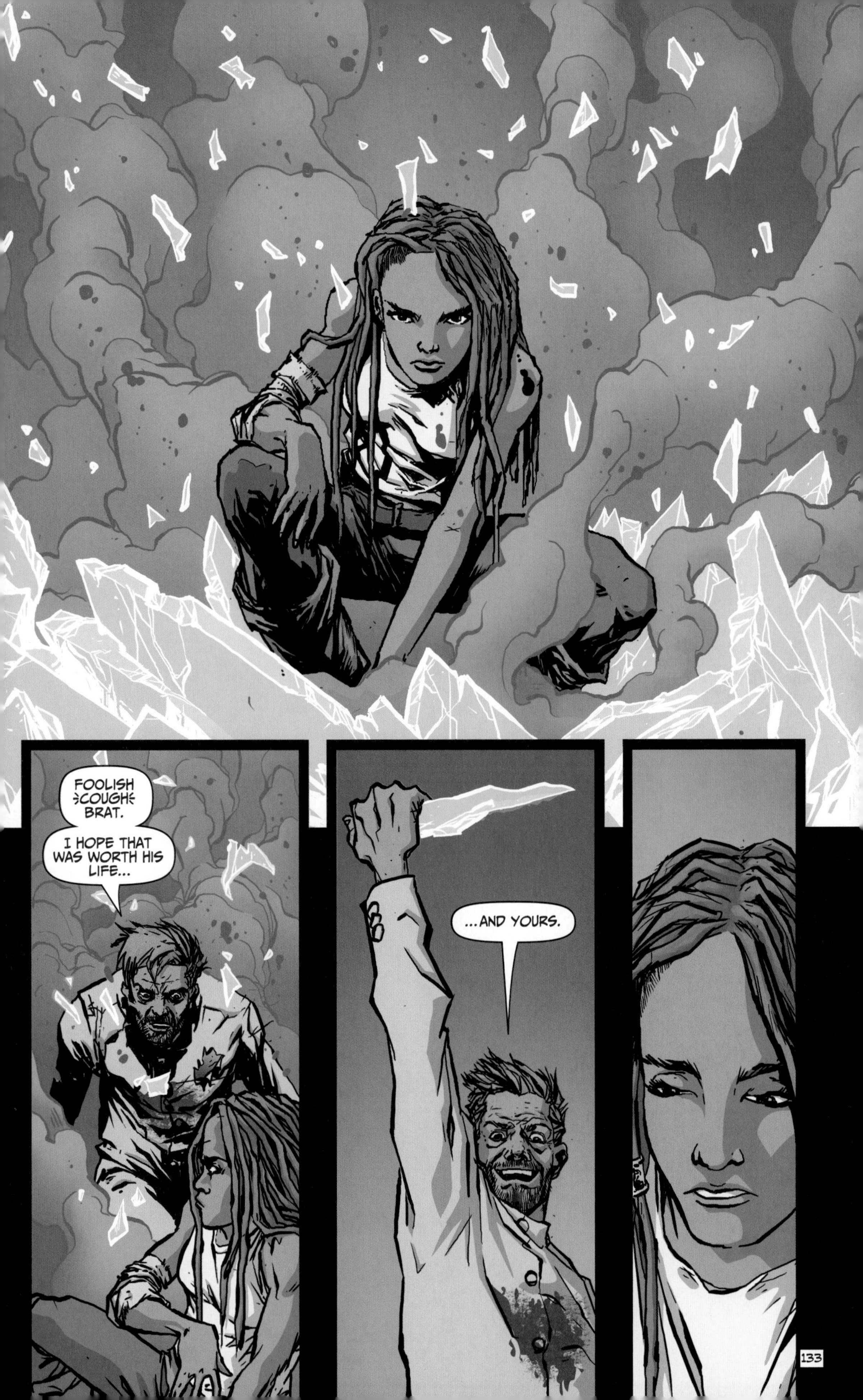
FOOLISH
COUGH
BRAT.
I HOPE THAT WAS WORTH HIS LIFE...
...AND YOURS.

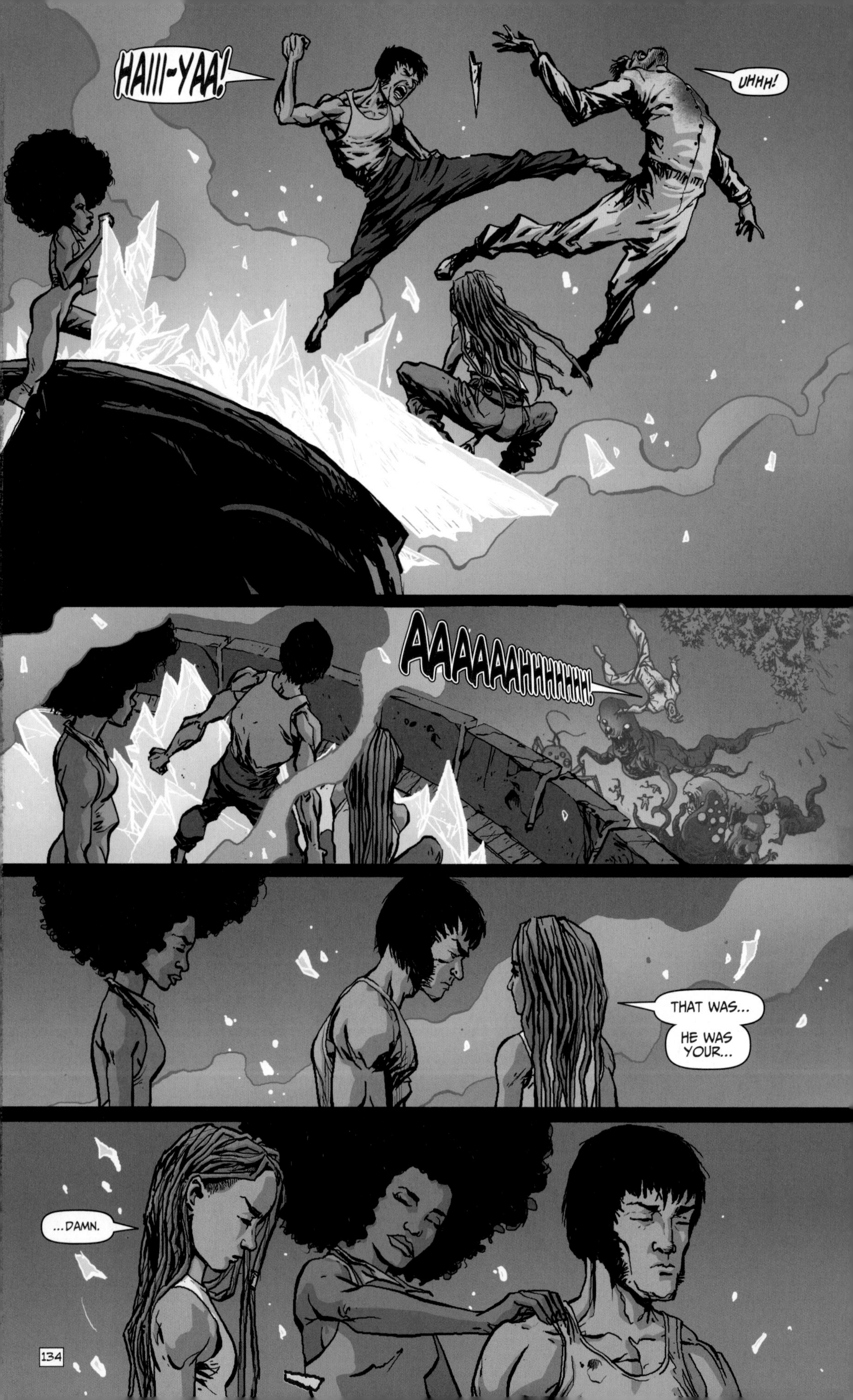
HAIII-YAA!
UHHH!
AAAAAAHHHHHHH!
THAT WAS...
HE WAS YOUR...
...DAMN.

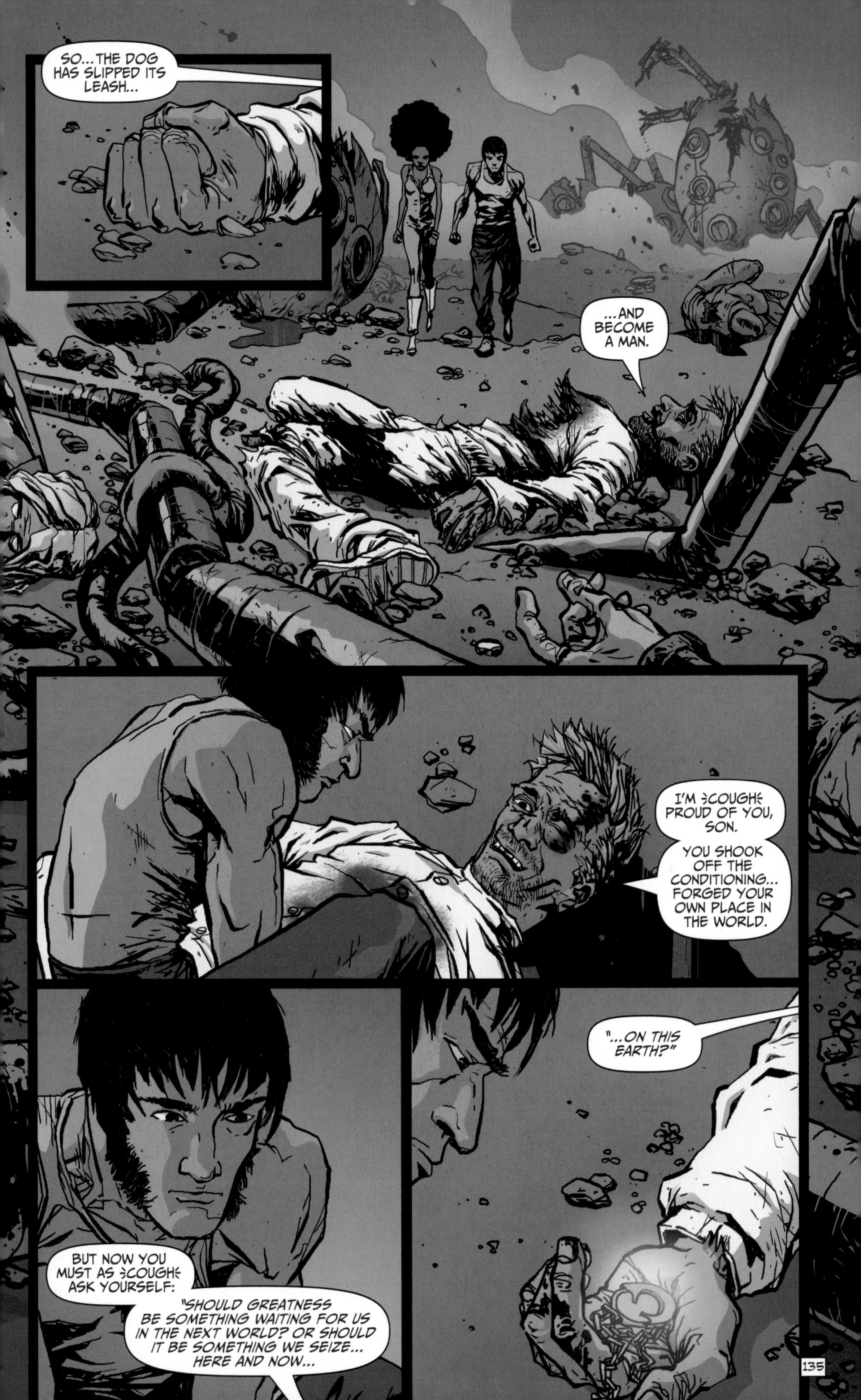
SO... THE DOG HAS SLIPPED ITS LEASH...
...AND BECOME A MAN.
I'M ⸗COUGH⸗ PROUD OF YOU, SON.
YOU SHOOK OFF THE CONDITIONING... FORGED YOUR OWN PLACE IN THE WORLD.
BUT NOW YOU MUST AS ⸗COUGH⸗ ASK YOURSELF:
"SHOULD GREATNESS BE SOMETHING WAITING FOR US IN THE NEXT WORLD? OR SHOULD IT BE SOMETHING WE SEIZE... HERE AND NOW...
"...ON THIS EARTH?"

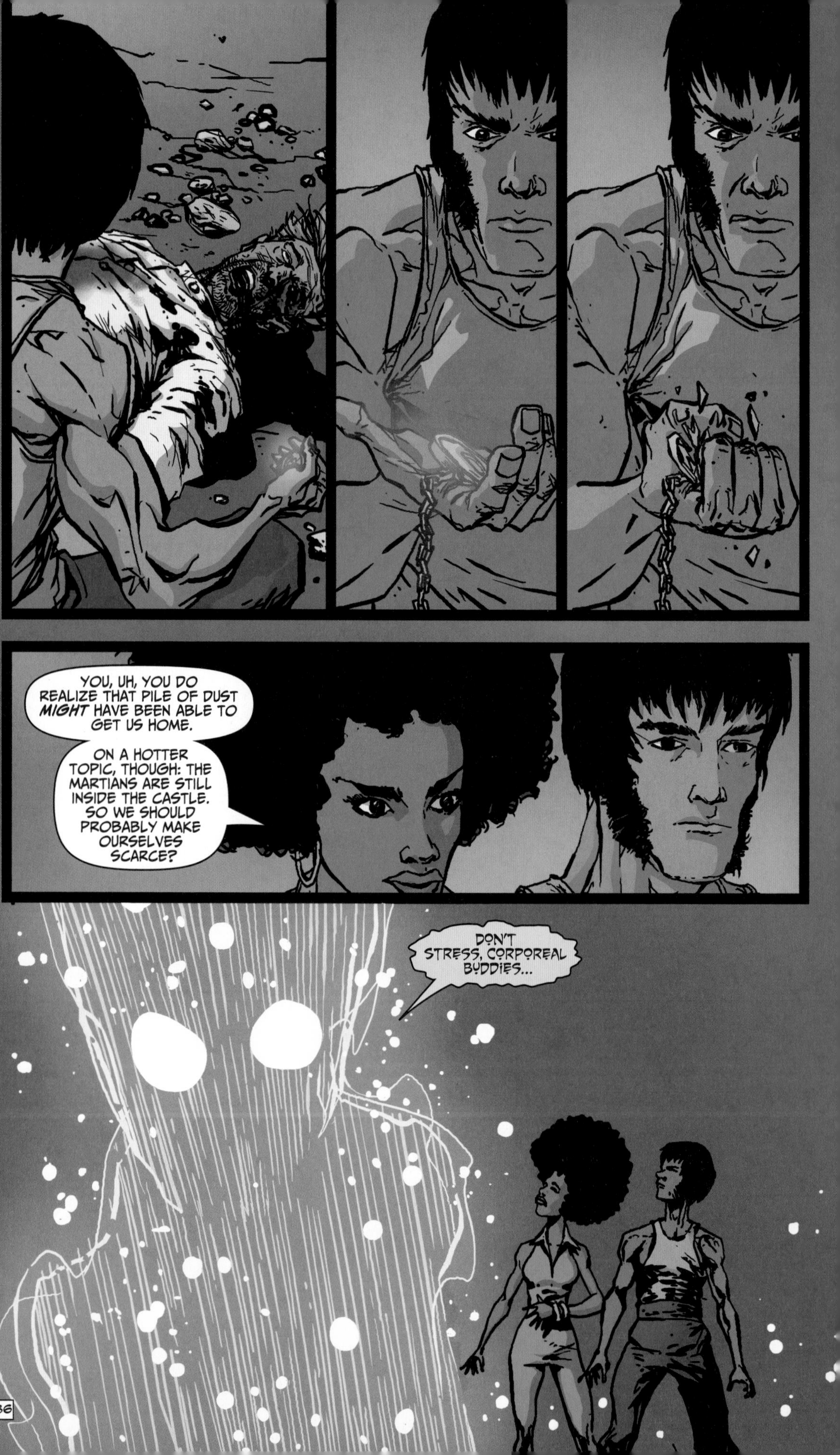
YOU, UH, YOU DO REALIZE THAT PILE OF DUST *MIGHT* HAVE BEEN ABLE TO GET US HOME.
ON A HOTTER TOPIC, THOUGH: THE MARTIANS ARE STILL INSIDE THE CASTLE. SO WE SHOULD PROBABLY MAKE OURSELVES SCARCE?
DON'T STRESS, CORPOREAL BUDDIES...

You stand perfectly still, listening to the eerie voice of the being hovering above. Your father's corpse lies fresh on the ground; your hand bleeds from the shards of his shattered locket. But you will not share your pain. You have been trained, by the monks and western society alike, to hold your feelings close.

"...IT'S LIKE THIS," the being—GODD—continues. "THE JEWEL WASN'T JUST *SUMMONING* THE OLD ONES FROM THEIR THOUSAND-YEAR SIESTA UNDER THE WAVES. IT WAS ACTIVELY CONTROLLING THEM...THE SAME WAY IT LURED ME HERE, EONS AGO."

"The Taboo Zone," Lynda murmurs.

You can feel her warmth, her hand reaching out to brush against yours. But as always, you pull away.

"RIGHT," GODD says. "BUT MY GIRL HERE DESTROYED THE JEWEL...WHICH MEANS THE OLD ONES ARE FREE OF ITS POWER. AND IT TURNS OUT THEY DON'T MUCH LIKE BEING TOLD WHAT TO DO."

"Hold up." Lynda turns to stare at the castle. "You're tellin' me that right now, inside that stone tenement..."

"...THE OLD ONES ARE SLAUGHTERING THE MARTIANS."

Something cold begins to form in your gut. "The Martians," you say, "are the Old Ones' *descendants*."

"YEAH, WELL. EVERYBODY HATES THEIR KIDS."

"Not everybody!"

You look up sharply at the sound of Brita's voice. In the shimmering atoms of GODD's energy-form, you think you can make out the ghost of her smile. For a brief moment, it warms your spirit.

Then you glance down at your father's body, cold and empty, and you know: Some pain is universal. And some sins are worse, harder to forgive, when committed by one's own blood.

No words—no philosophy in all the world—will ever change that.

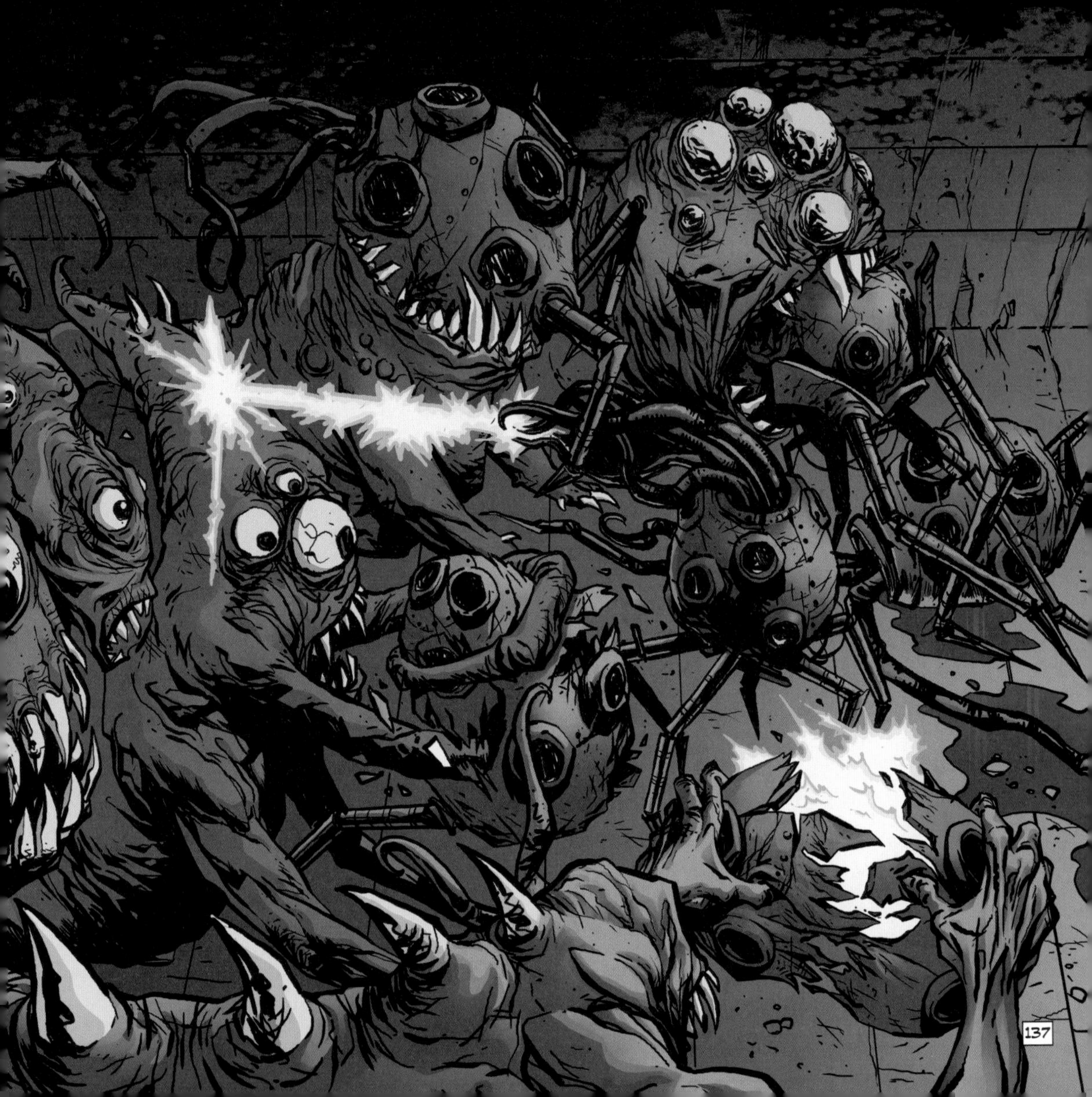

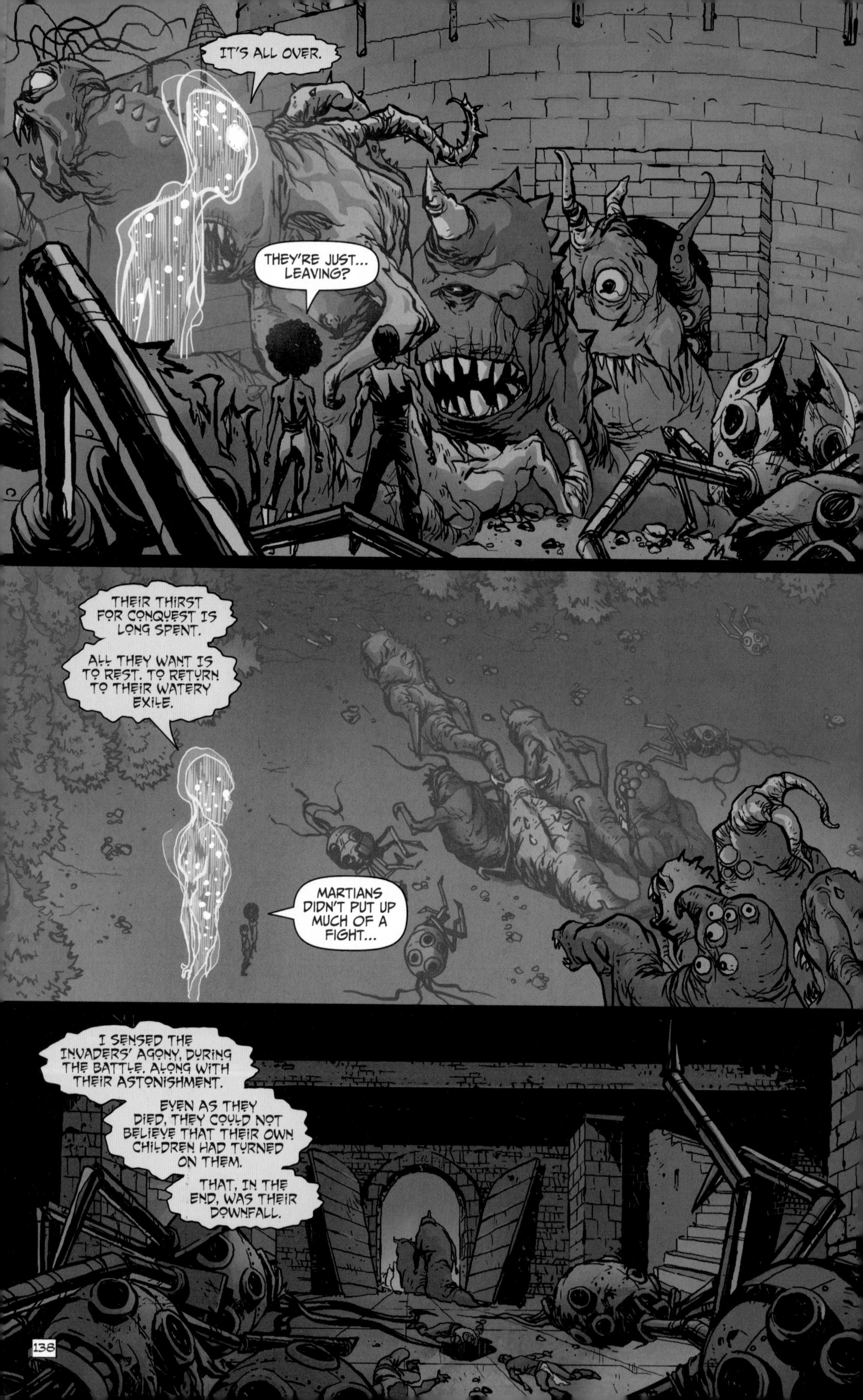
IT'S ALL OVER.
THEY'RE JUST... LEAVING?
THEIR THIRST FOR CONQUEST IS LONG SPENT.
ALL THEY WANT IS TO REST. TO RETURN TO THEIR WATERY EXILE.
MARTIANS DIDN'T PUT UP MUCH OF A FIGHT...
I SENSED THE INVADERS' AGONY, DURING THE BATTLE. ALONG WITH THEIR ASTONISHMENT.
EVEN AS THEY DIED, THEY COULD NOT BELIEVE THAT THEIR OWN CHILDREN HAD TURNED ON THEM.
THAT, IN THE END, WAS THEIR DOWNFALL.

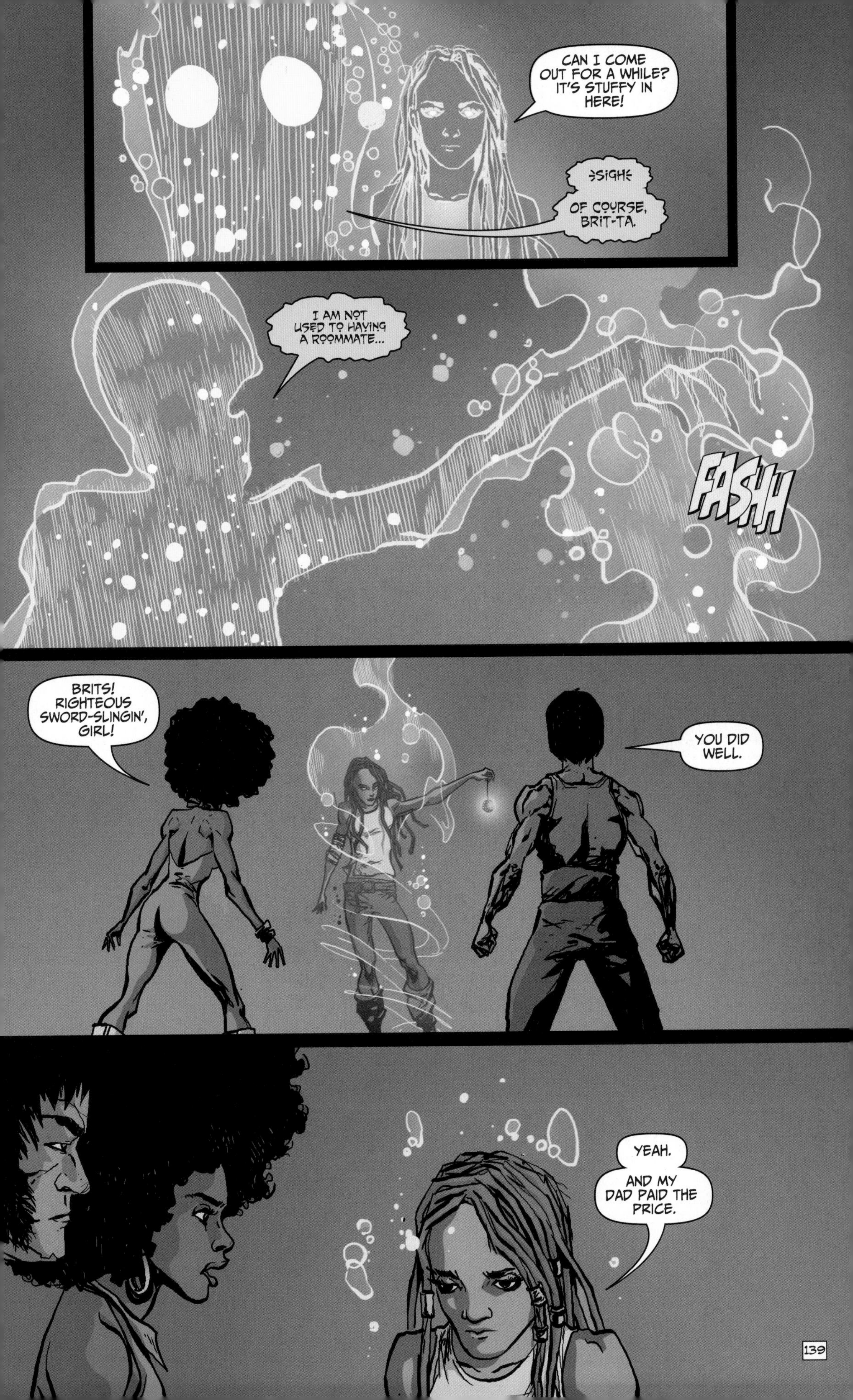
CAN I COME OUT FOR A WHILE? IT'S STUFFY IN HERE!
≶SIGH≷
OF COURSE, BRIT-TA.
I AM NOT USED TO HAVING A ROOMMATE...
FASHH
BRITS! RIGHTEOUS SWORD-SLINGIN', GIRL!
YOU DID WELL.
YEAH.
AND MY DAD PAID THE PRICE.

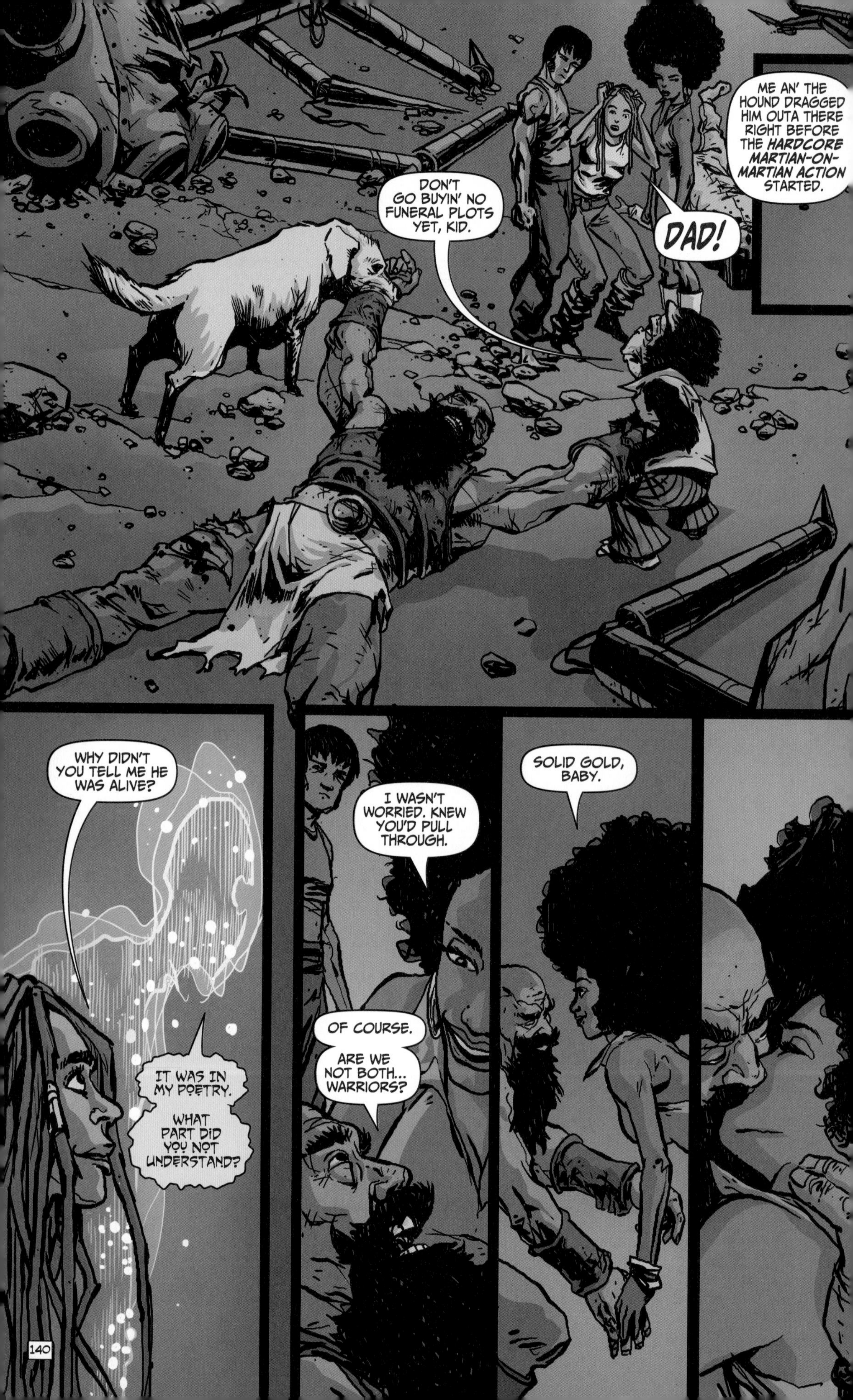

ME AN' THE HOUND DRAGGED HIM OUTA THERE RIGHT BEFORE THE HARDCORE MARTIAN-ON-MARTIAN ACTION STARTED.
DAD!
DON'T GO BUYIN' NO FUNERAL PLOTS YET, KID.
WHY DIDN'T YOU TELL ME HE WAS ALIVE?
IT WAS IN MY POETRY.
WHAT PART DID YOU NOT UNDERSTAND?
I WASN'T WORRIED. KNEW YOU'D PULL THROUGH.
OF COURSE.
ARE WE NOT BOTH... WARRIORS?
SOLID GOLD, BABY.

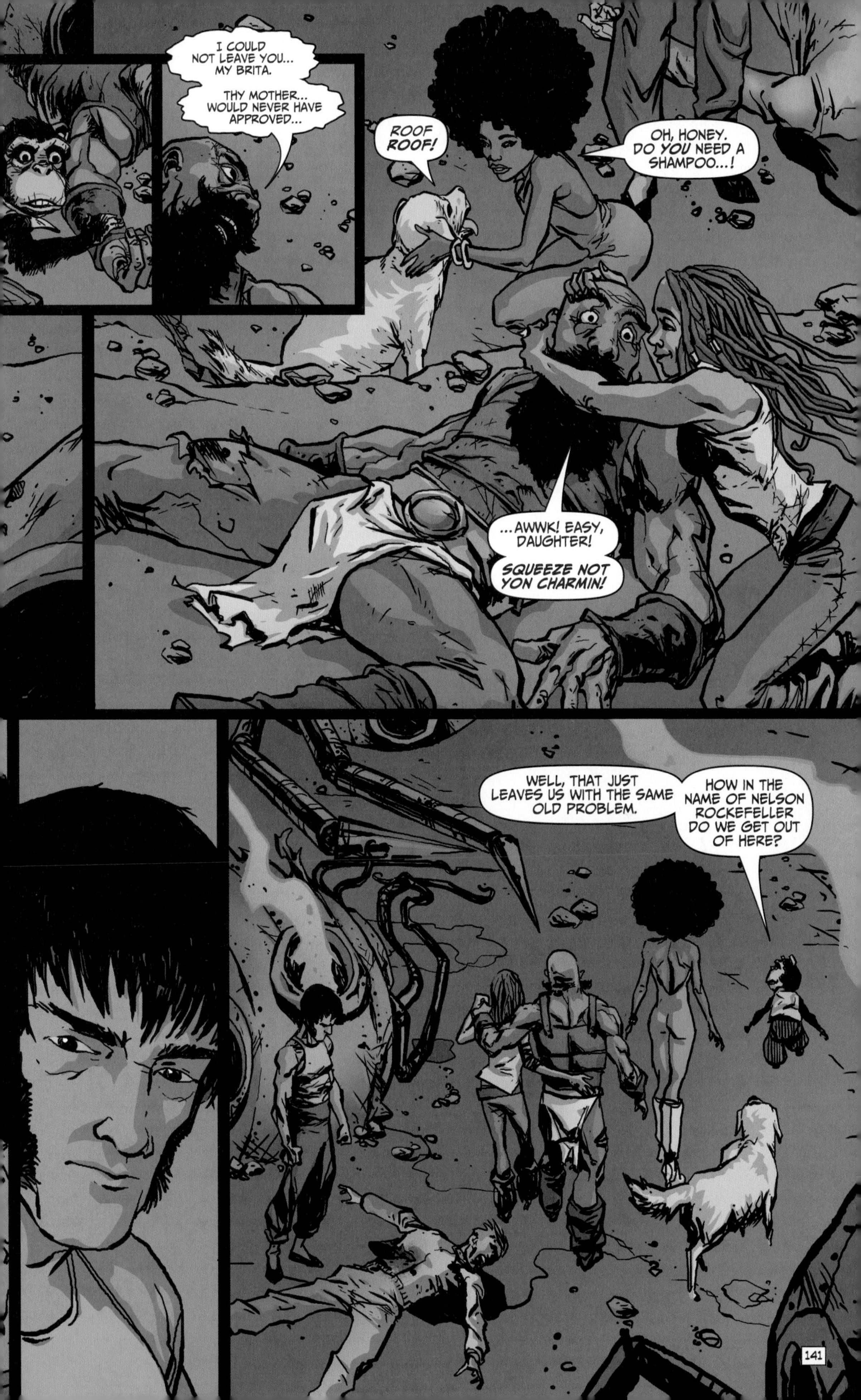
I COULD NOT LEAVE YOU... MY BRITA.
THY MOTHER... WOULD NEVER HAVE APPROVED...
ROOF ROOF!
OH, HONEY. DO YOU NEED A SHAMPOO...!
...AWWK! EASY, DAUGHTER!
SQUEEZE NOT YON CHARMIN!
WELL, THAT JUST LEAVES US WITH THE SAME OLD PROBLEM.
HOW IN THE NAME OF NELSON ROCKEFELLER DO WE GET OUT OF HERE?

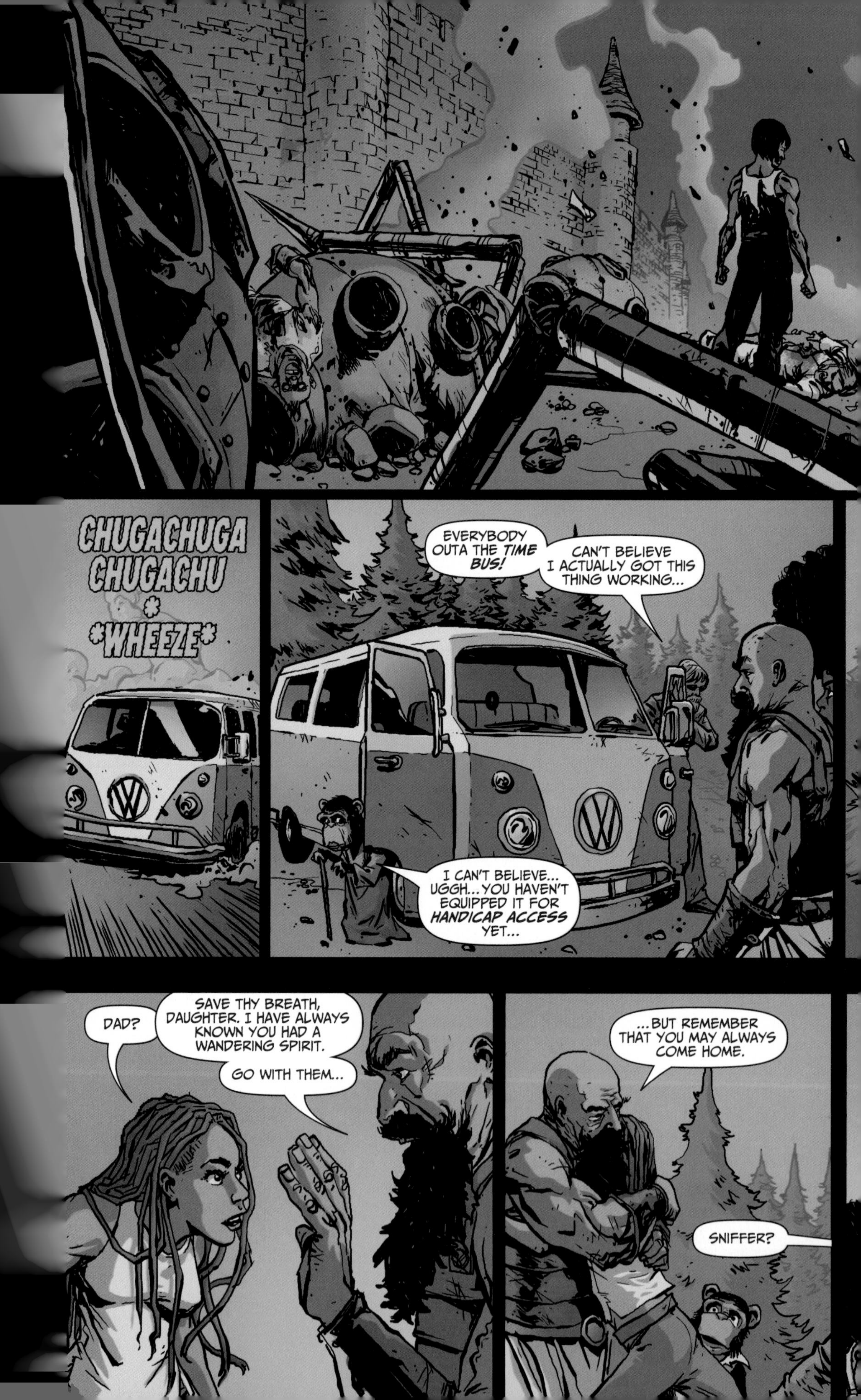
CHUGACHUGA CHUGACHU
WHEEZE
EVERYBODY OUTA THE TIME BUS!
CAN'T BELIEVE I ACTUALLY GOT THIS THING WORKING...
I CAN'T BELIEVE... UGGH...YOU HAVEN'T EQUIPPED IT FOR HANDICAP ACCESS YET...
DAD?
SAVE THY BREATH, DAUGHTER. I HAVE ALWAYS KNOWN YOU HAD A WANDERING SPIRIT.
GO WITH THEM...
...BUT REMEMBER THAT YOU MAY ALWAYS COME HOME.
SNIFFER?

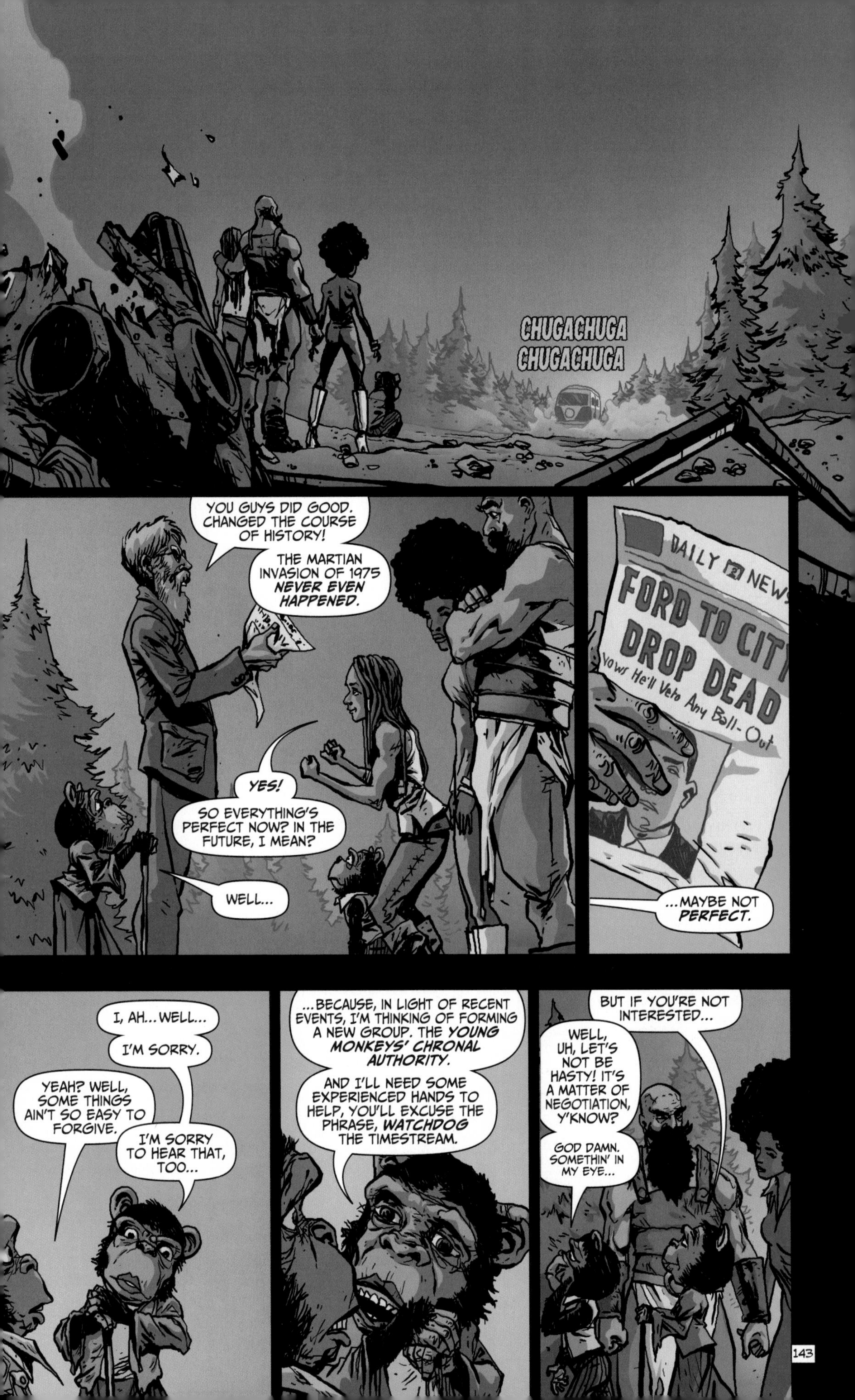
CHUGACHUGA
CHUGACHUGA
YOU GUYS DID GOOD. CHANGED THE COURSE OF HISTORY!
THE MARTIAN INVASION OF 1975 NEVER EVEN HAPPENED.
YES!
SO EVERYTHING'S PERFECT NOW? IN THE FUTURE, I MEAN?
WELL...
DAILY 2 NEWS
FORD TO CITY DROP DEAD
Vows He'll Veto Any Bail-Out
...MAYBE NOT PERFECT.
I, AH... WELL...
I'M SORRY.
YEAH? WELL, SOME THINGS AIN'T SO EASY TO FORGIVE.
I'M SORRY TO HEAR THAT, TOO...
...BECAUSE, IN LIGHT OF RECENT EVENTS, I'M THINKING OF FORMING A NEW GROUP. THE YOUNG MONKEYS' CHRONAL AUTHORITY.
AND I'LL NEED SOME EXPERIENCED HANDS TO HELP, YOU'LL EXCUSE THE PHRASE, WATCHDOG THE TIMESTREAM.
BUT IF YOU'RE NOT INTERESTED...
WELL, UH, LET'S NOT BE HASTY! IT'S A MATTER OF NEGOTIATION, Y'KNOW?
GOD DAMN. SOMETHIN' IN MY EYE...

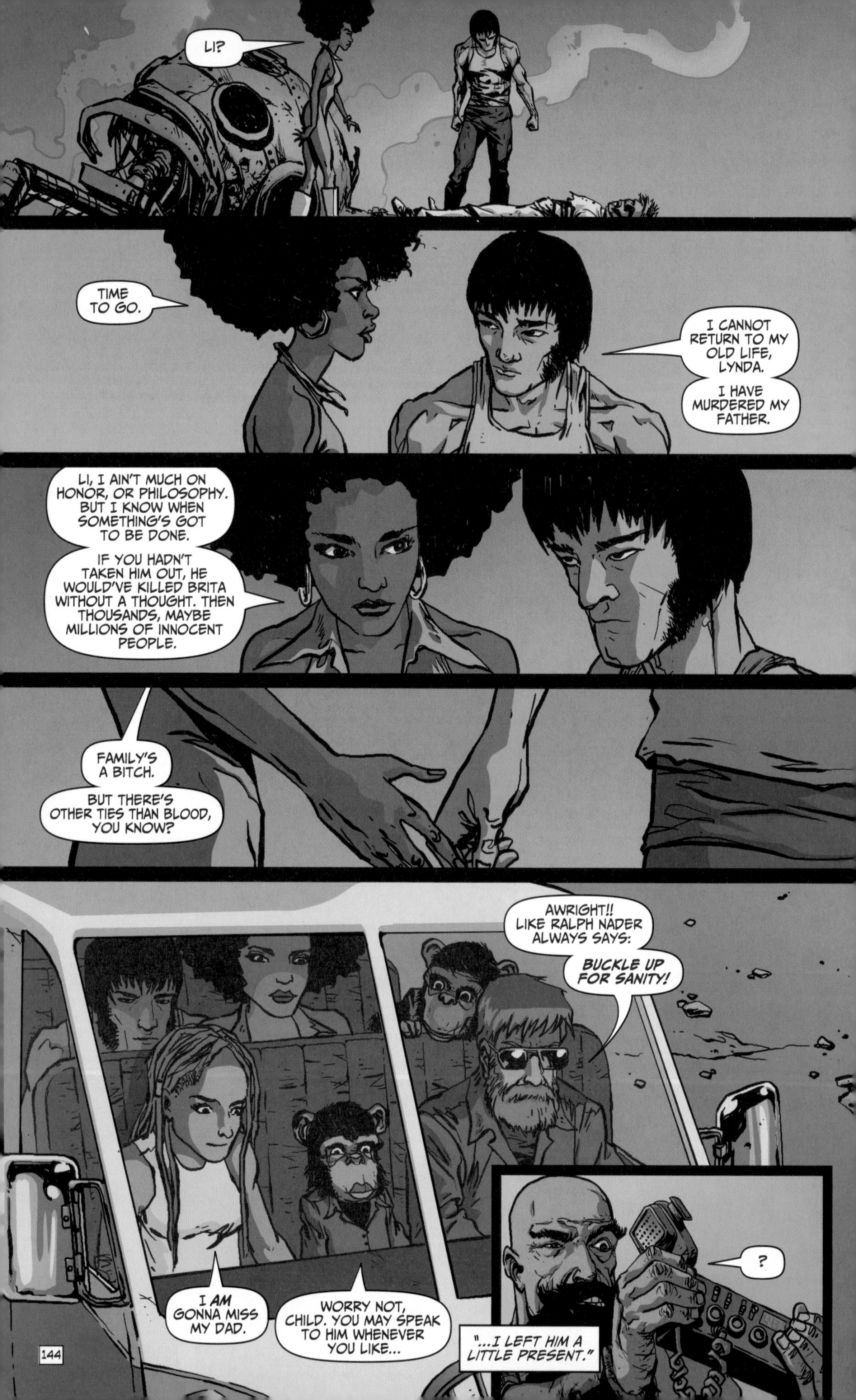
LI?
TIME TO GO.
I CANNOT RETURN TO MY OLD LIFE, LYNDA.
I HAVE MURDERED MY FATHER.
LI, I AIN'T MUCH ON HONOR, OR PHILOSOPHY. BUT I KNOW WHEN SOMETHING'S GOT TO BE DONE.
IF YOU HADN'T TAKEN HIM OUT, HE WOULD'VE KILLED BRITA WITHOUT A THOUGHT. THEN THOUSANDS, MAYBE MILLIONS OF INNOCENT PEOPLE.
FAMILY'S A BITCH.
BUT THERE'S OTHER TIES THAN BLOOD, YOU KNOW?
AWRIGHT!! LIKE RALPH NADER ALWAYS SAYS:
BUCKLE UP FOR SANITY!
I AM GONNA MISS MY DAD.
WORRY NOT, CHILD. YOU MAY SPEAK TO HIM WHENEVER YOU LIKE...
"...I LEFT HIM A LITTLE PRESENT."
?

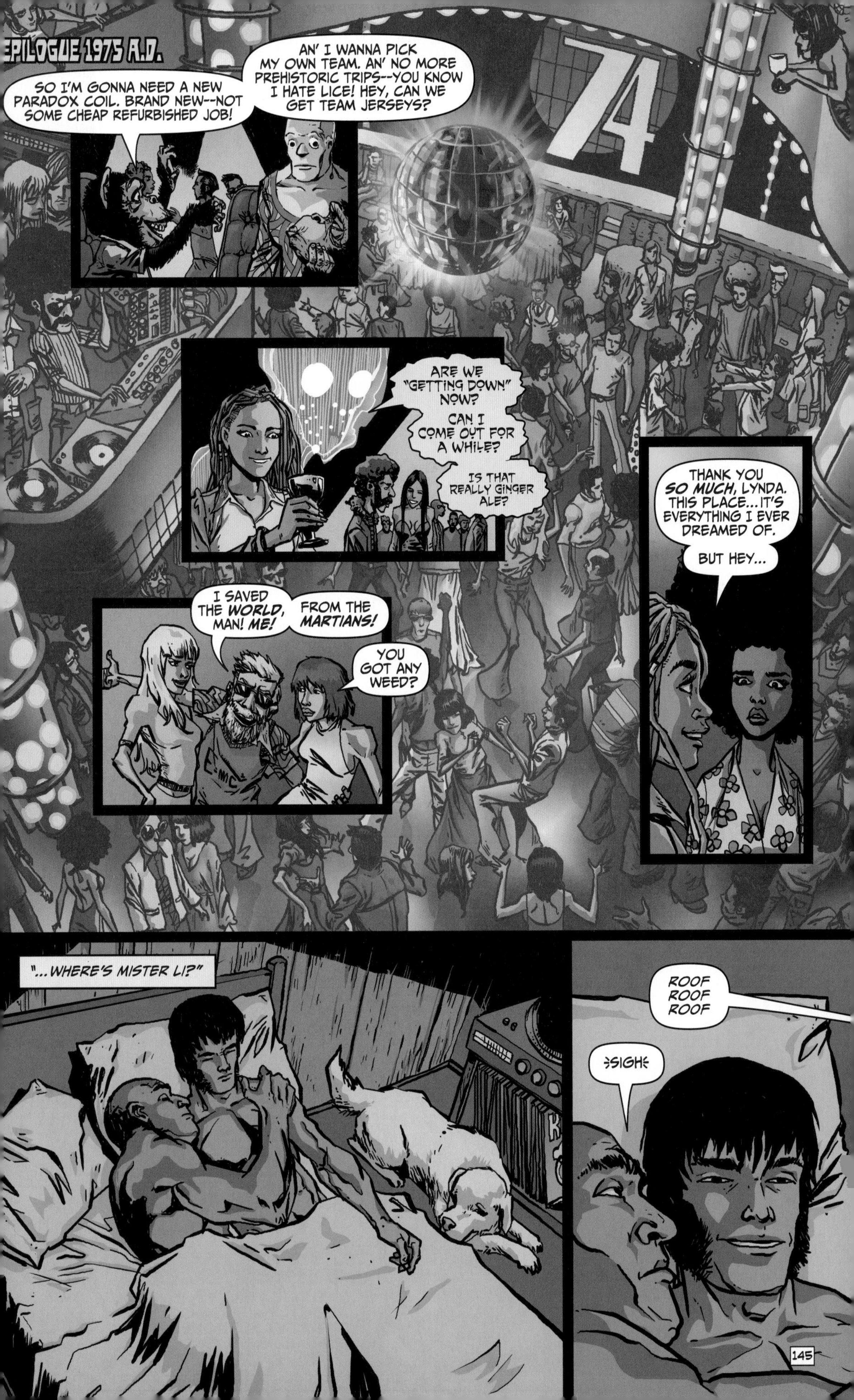
EPILOGUE 1975 A.D.
SO I'M GONNA NEED A NEW PARADOX COIL. BRAND NEW--NOT SOME CHEAP REFURBISHED JOB!
AN' I WANNA PICK MY OWN TEAM. AN' NO MORE PREHISTORIC TRIPS--YOU KNOW I HATE LICE! HEY, CAN WE GET TEAM JERSEYS?
74
ARE WE "GETTING DOWN" NOW?
CAN I COME OUT FOR A WHILE?
IS THAT REALLY GINGER ALE?
I SAVED THE WORLD, MAN! ME!
FROM THE MARTIANS!
YOU GOT ANY WEED?
THANK YOU SO MUCH, LYNDA. THIS PLACE... IT'S EVERYTHING I EVER DREAMED OF.
BUT HEY...
"...WHERE'S MISTER LI?"
ROOF ROOF ROOF
SIGH

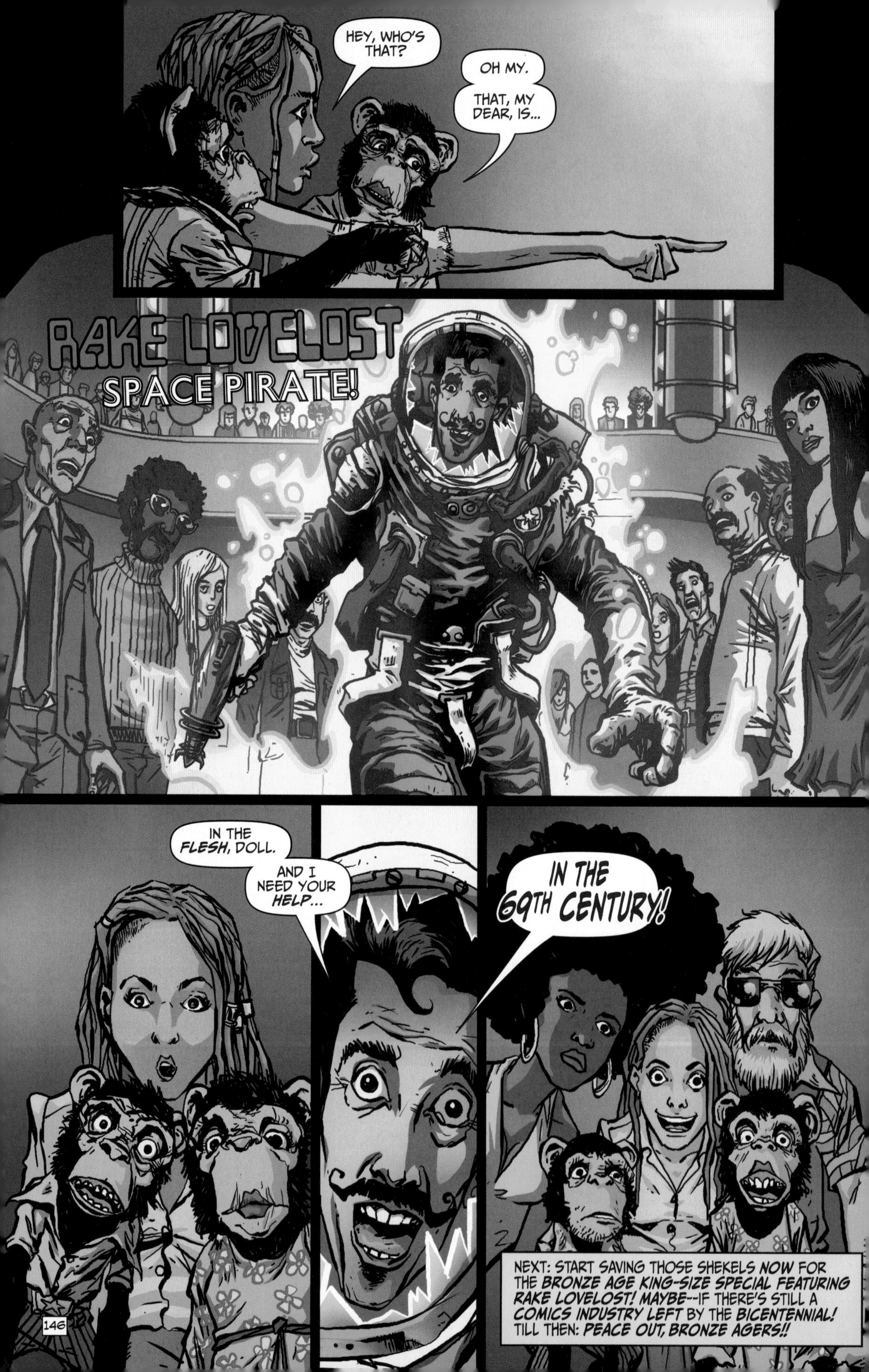
HEY, WHO'S THAT?
OH MY.
THAT, MY DEAR, IS...
RAKE LOVELOST
SPACE PIRATE!
IN THE FLESH, DOLL.
AND I NEED YOUR HELP...
IN THE 69TH CENTURY!
NEXT: START SAVING THOSE SHEKELS NOW FOR THE BRONZE AGE KING-SIZE SPECIAL FEATURING RAKE LOVELOST! MAYBE--IF THERE'S STILL A COMICS INDUSTRY LEFT BY THE BICENTENNIAL! TILL THEN: PEACE OUT, BRONZE AGERS!!

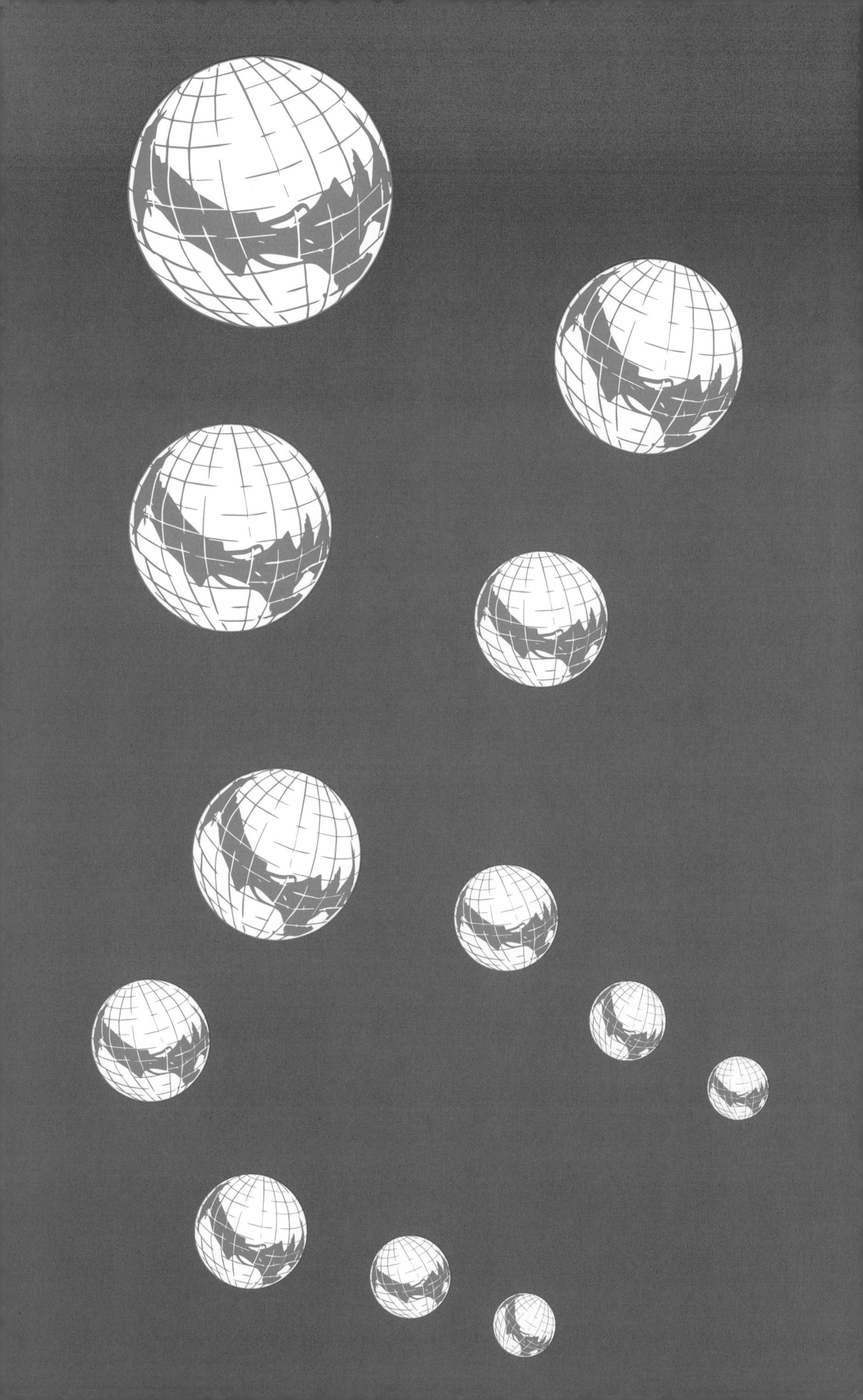

BRONZE AGE BOOGIE
SKETCHBOOK

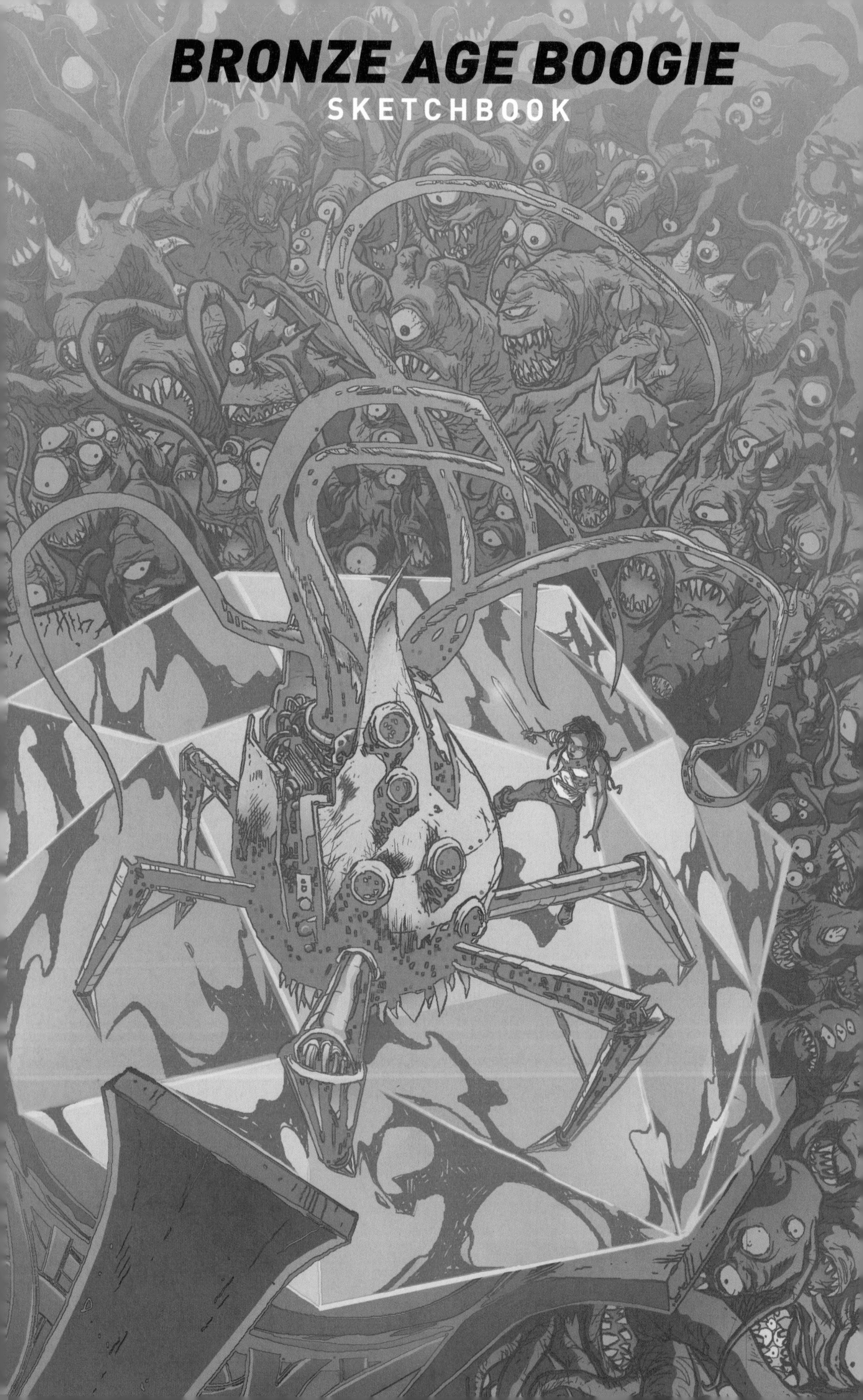

Alberto Ponticelli isn't just a talented artist; he's extremely prolific! Here's a selection of cover sketches he did for *BRONZE AGE BOOGIE*. Elements of Alberto's sketches for issue #1 were used in the first cover and elsewhere in the series.

— *Stuart Moore*

1

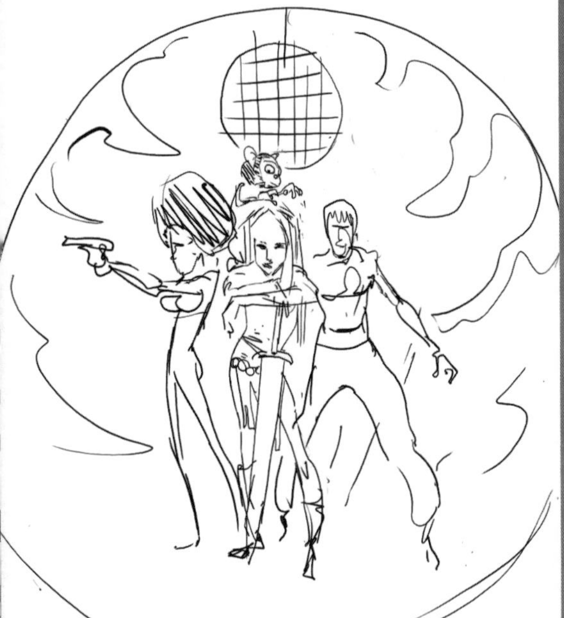

2

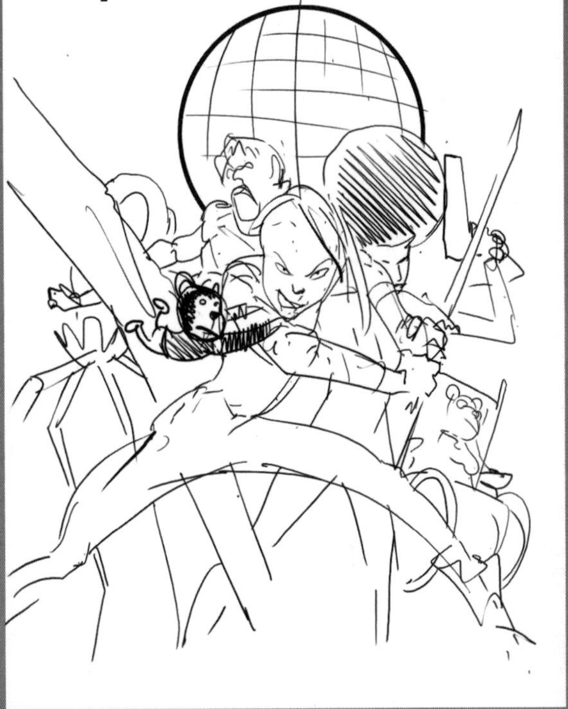

3

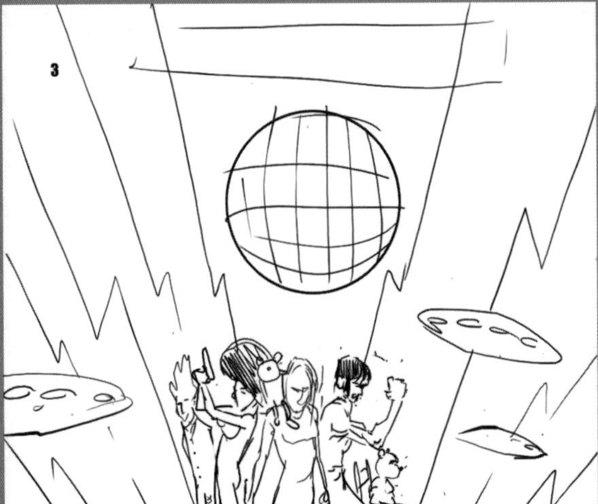

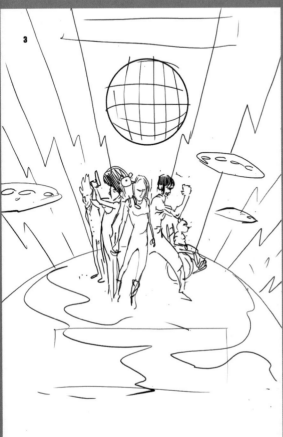

4

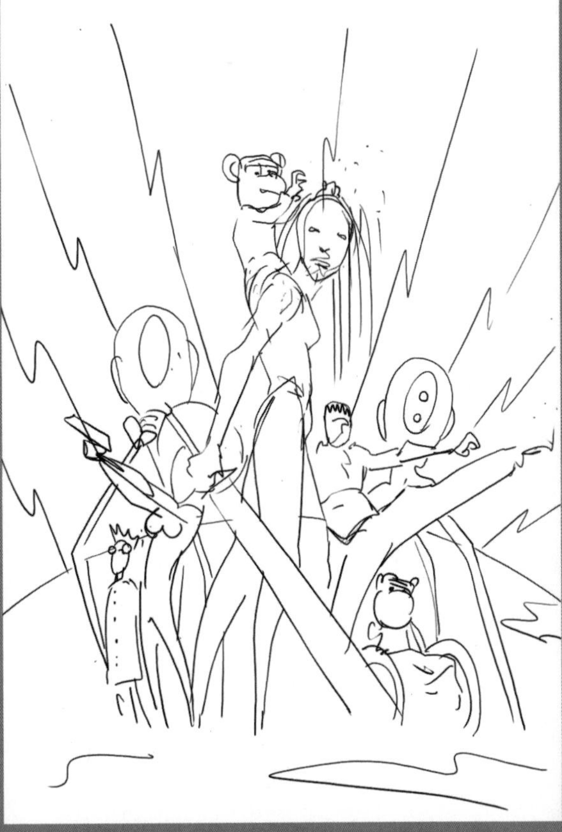

BRONZE AGE BOOGIE #1 REVISED COVER SKETCHES by Alberto Ponticelli

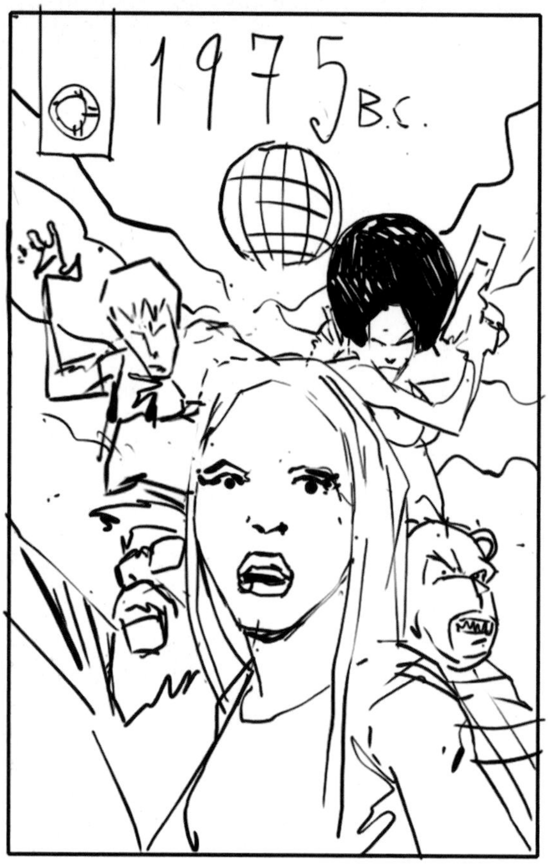
1975 B.C.

These are closer to the published cover, as seen on page six. I asked him to add the sword seen in his final artwork (at right).

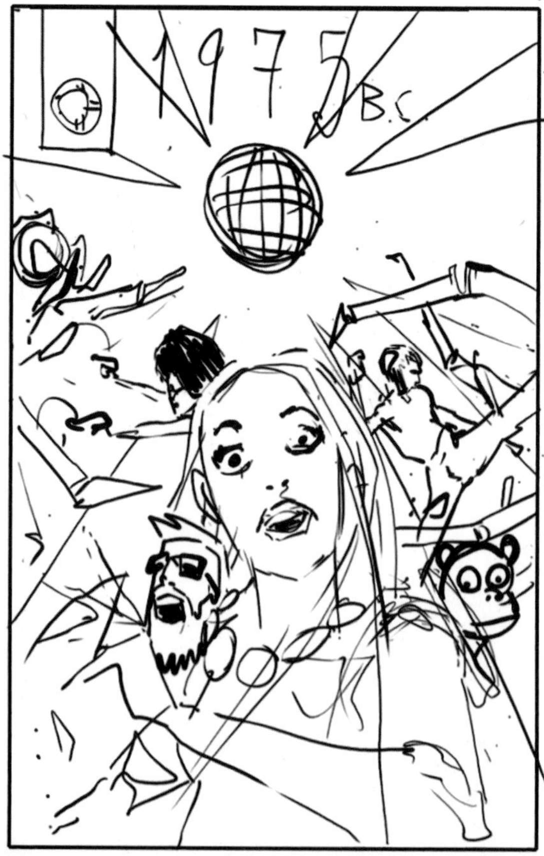
1975 B.C

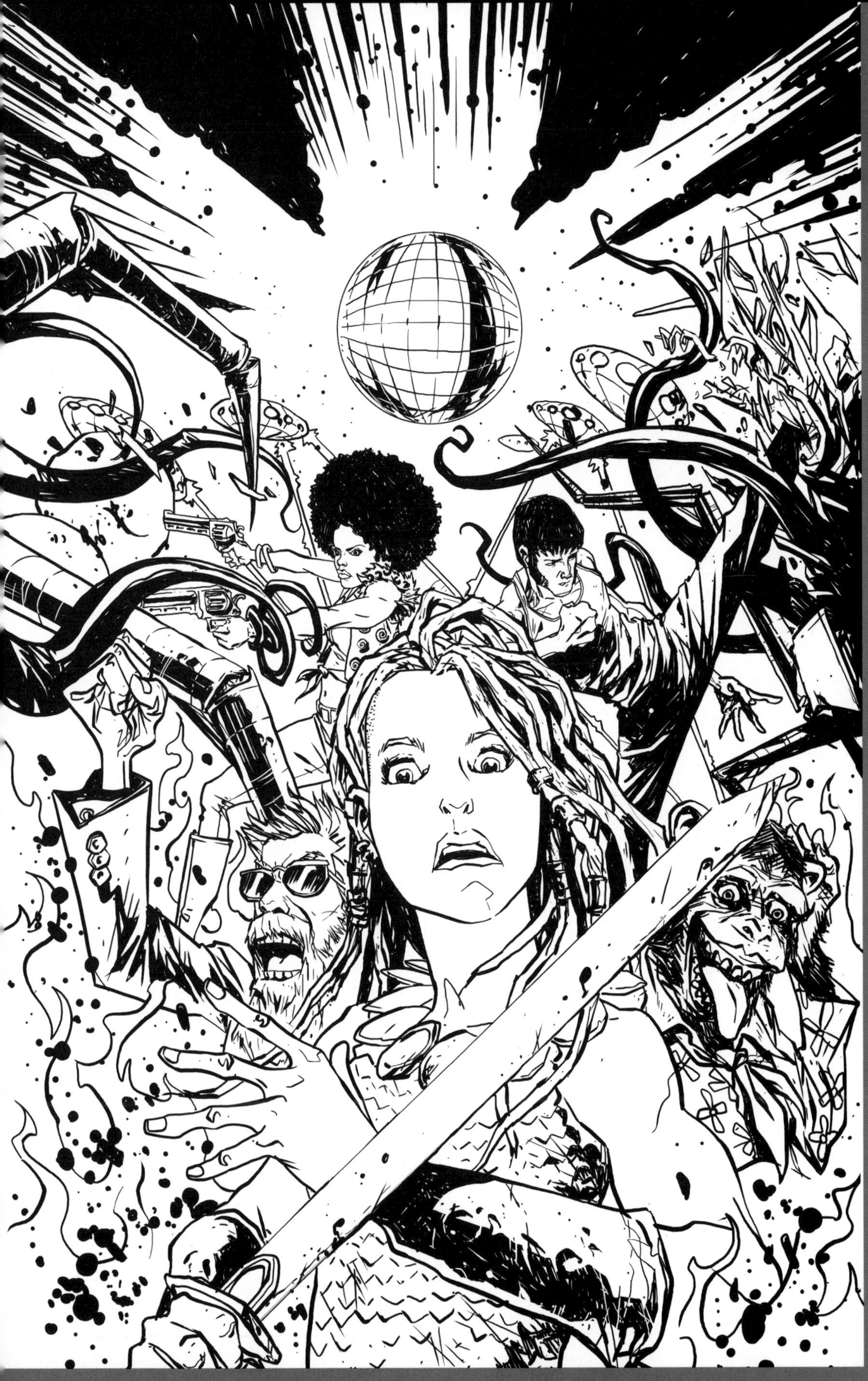

Several takes on cover #3, including one that's very close to the final version.

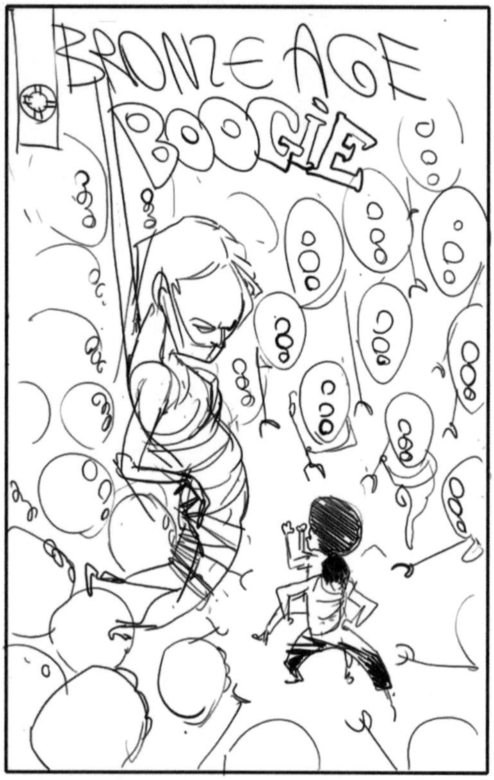
BRONZE AGE
BOOGIE

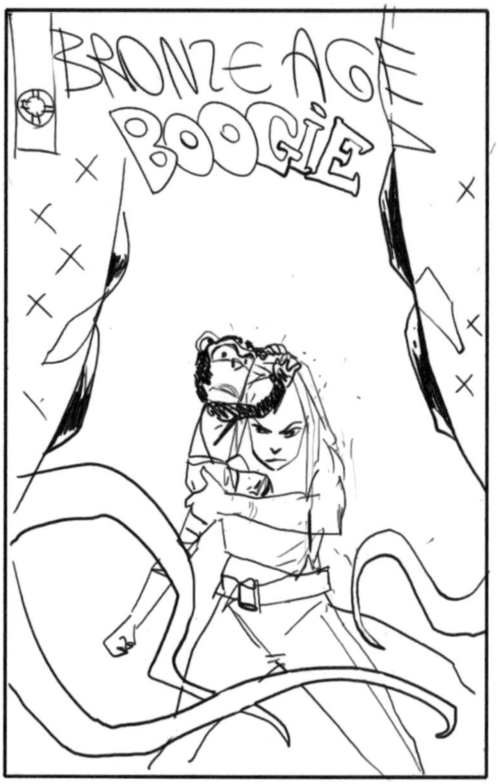
BRONZE AGE
BOOGIE

Cover 3C

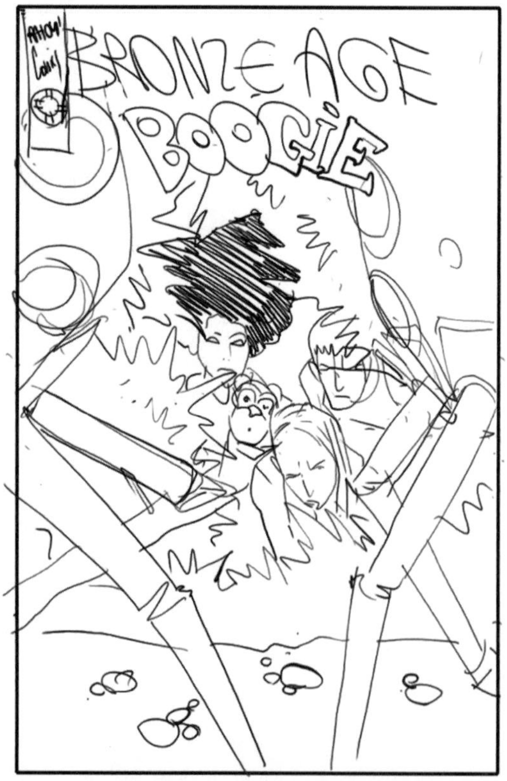
BRONZE AGE
BOOGIE

Cover 3D

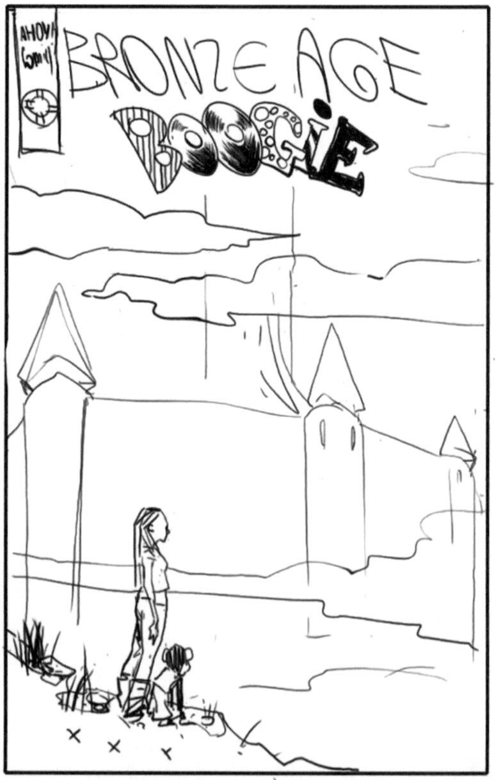
BRONZE AGE
BOOGIE

Because Alberto is co-owner of *BRONZE AGE BOOGIE*, we asked him to design the Moon-Thing character, even though he wasn't going to draw that story. Here are some early stabs at the design...

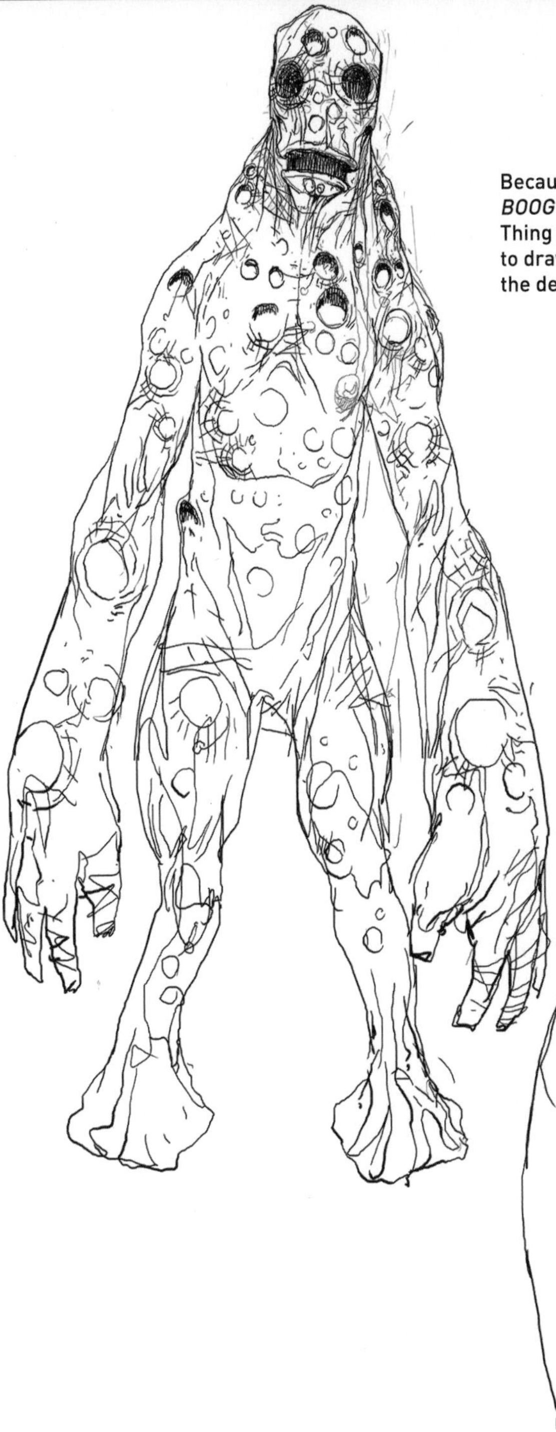

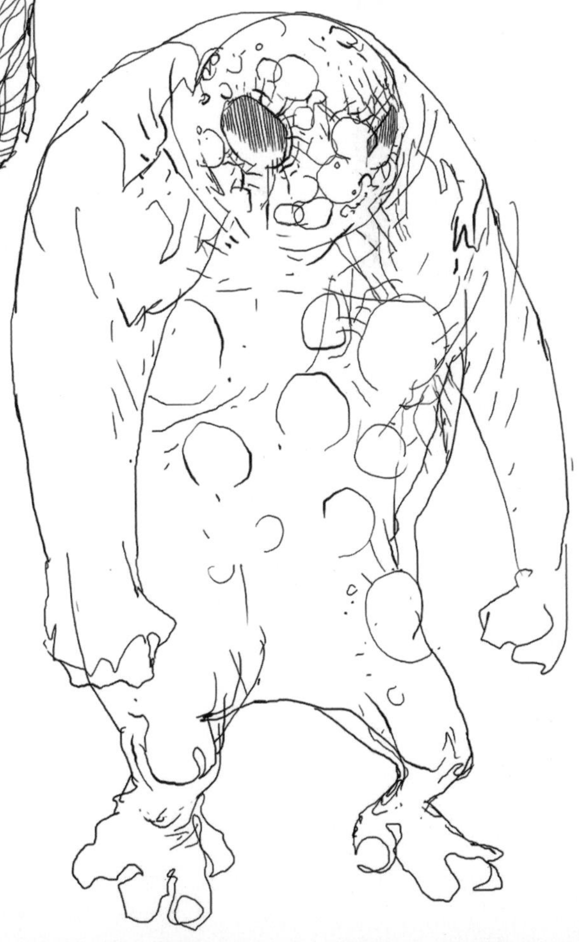

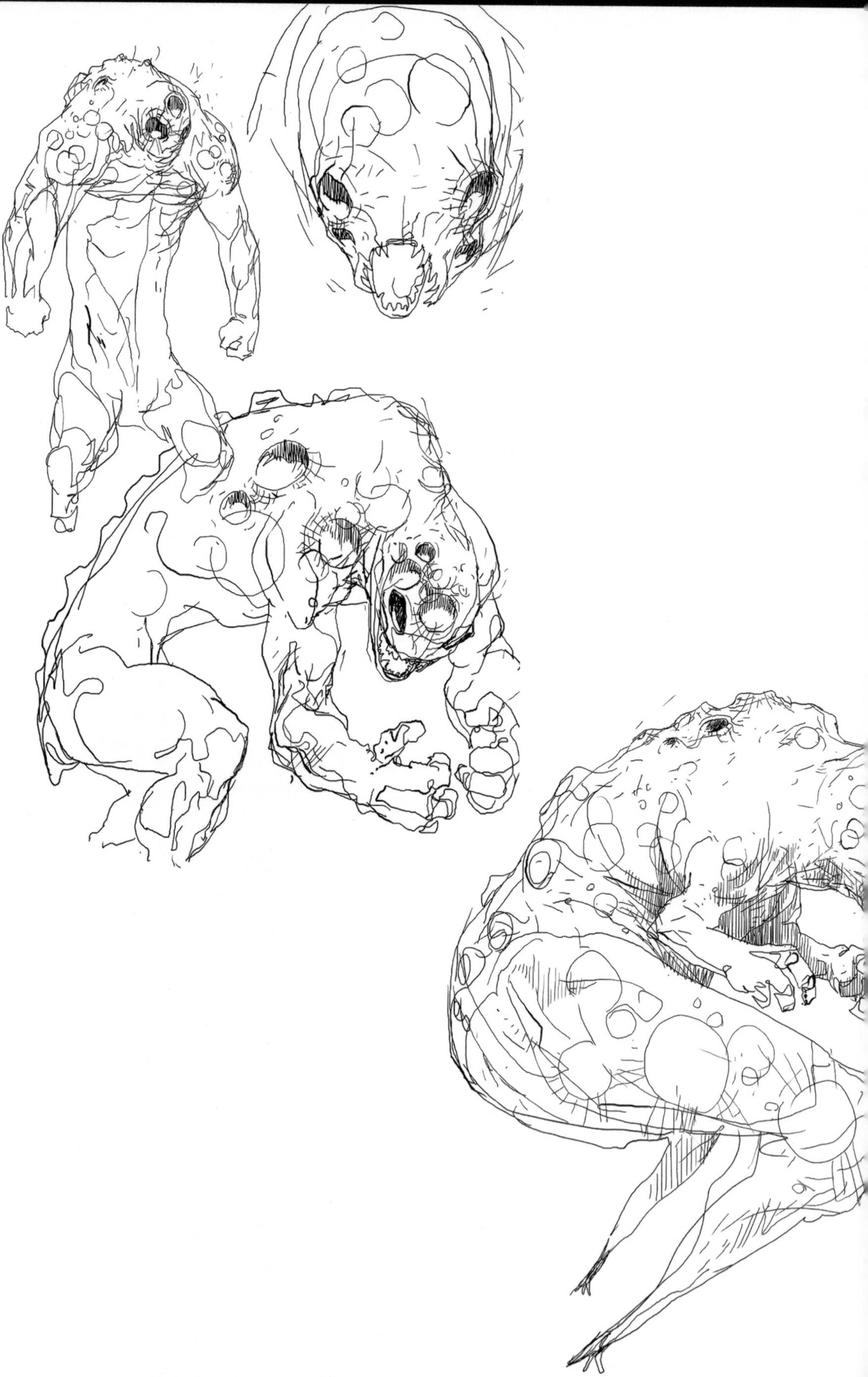

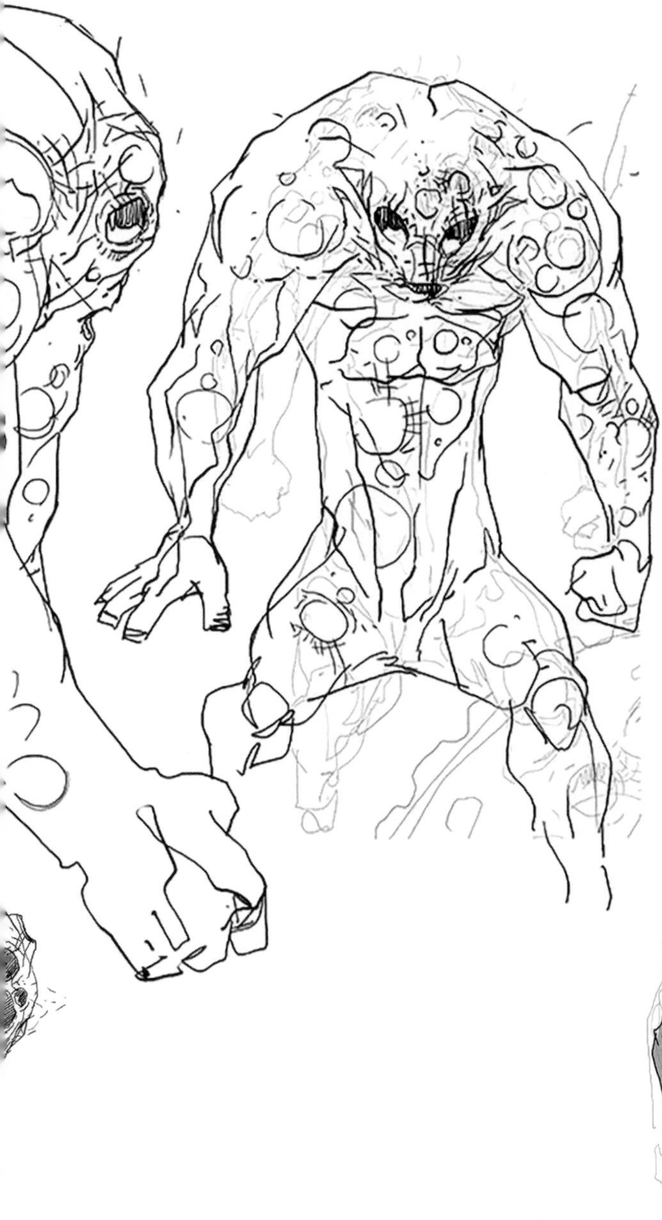

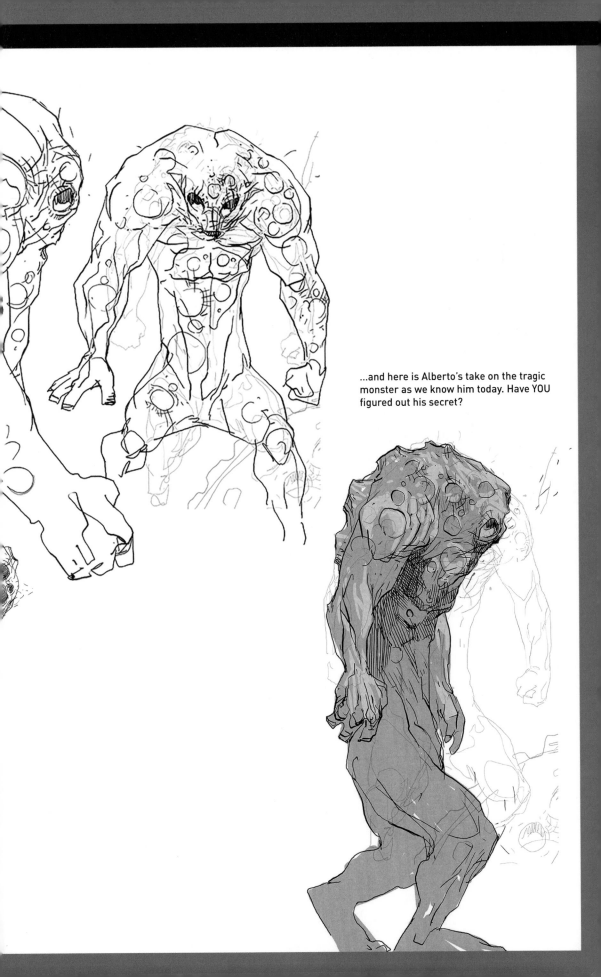

...and here is Alberto's take on the tragic monster as we know him today. Have YOU figured out his secret?

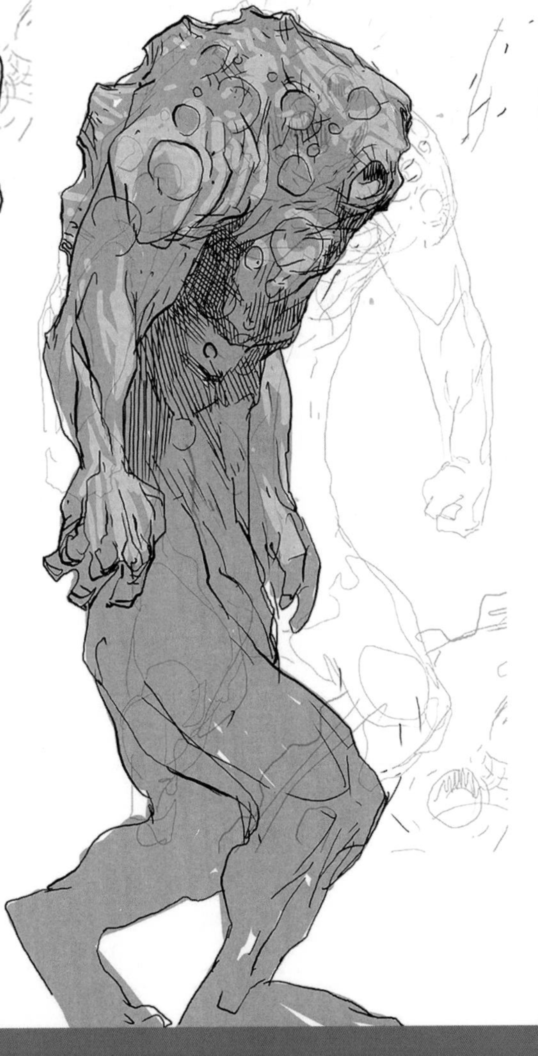

BRONZE AGE BOOGIE #4 COVER SKETCHES by Alberto Ponticelli

A stunning array of sketches for cover #4. Note the three different takes on the final cover, with Lynda and the King gazing into the Taboo Zone.

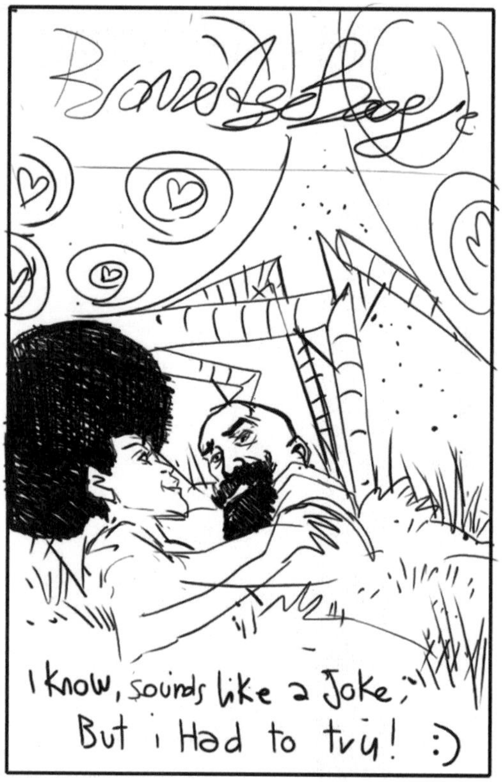
I know, sounds like a Joke;
But i Had to try! :)

4B

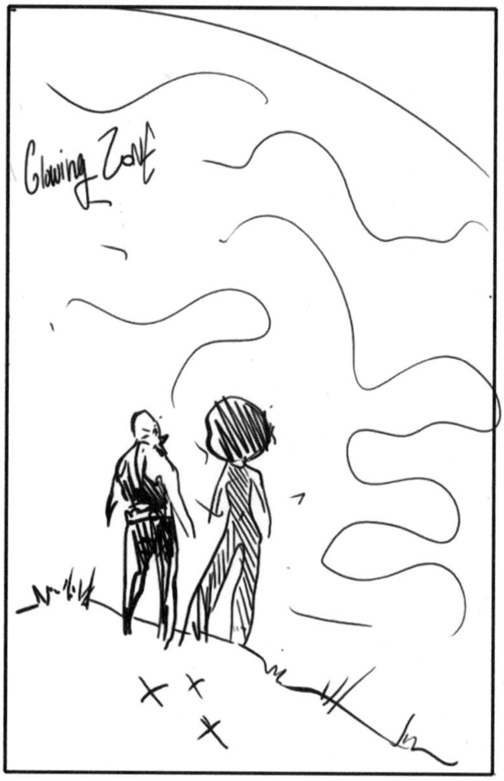
Glowing Zone

4C

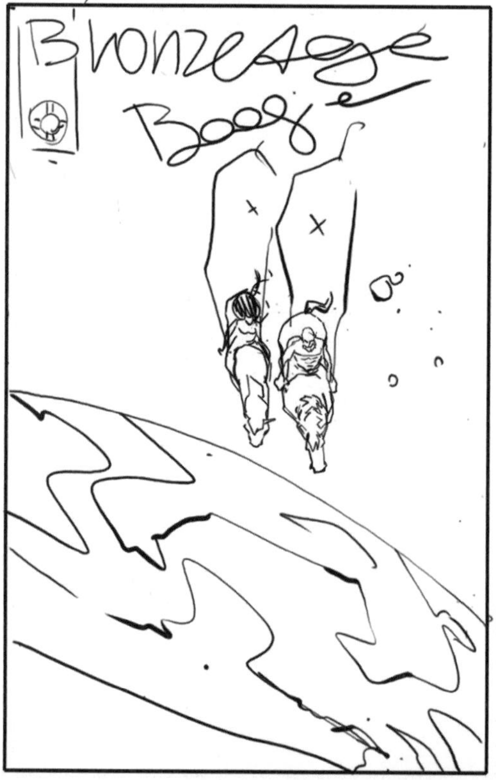
Bronze Age
Boogie

4D

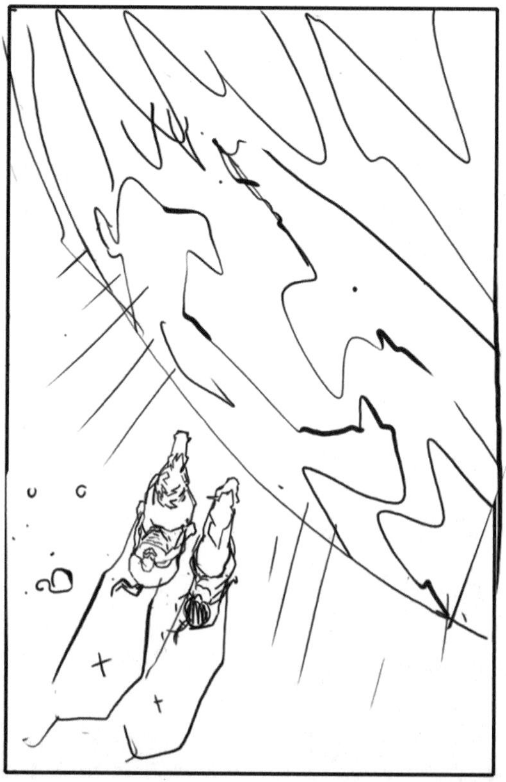

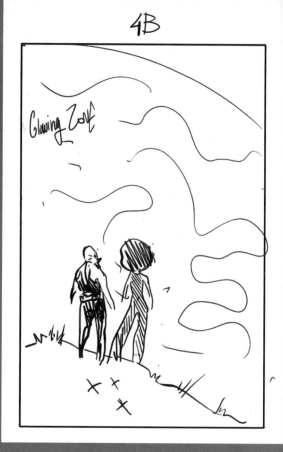

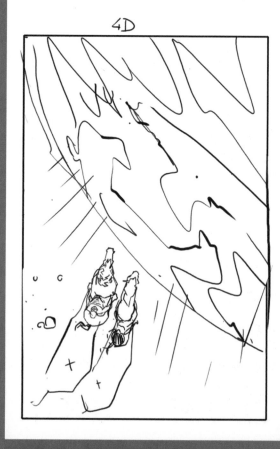

4E

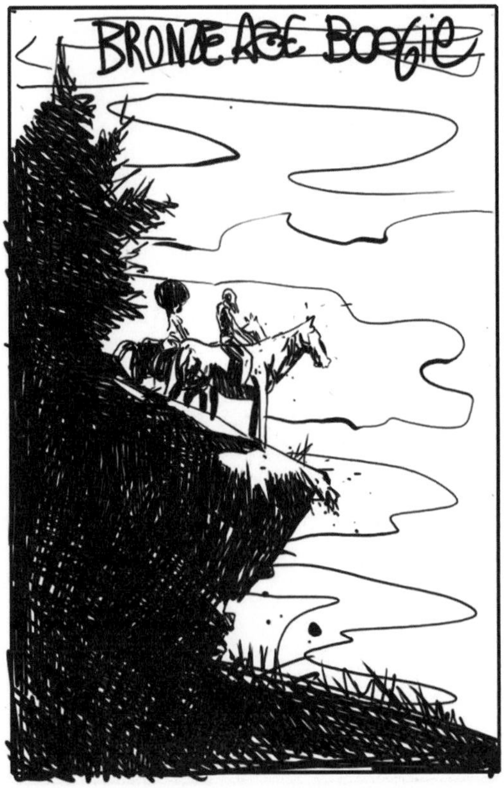
BRONZE AGE BOOGIE

4F

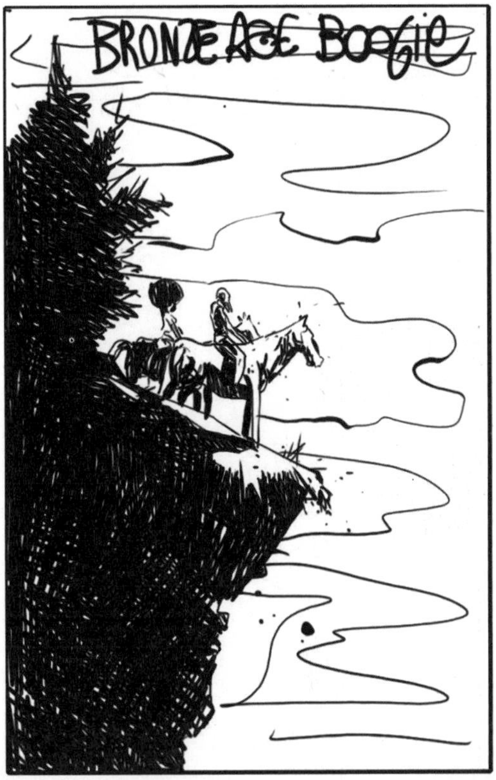
BRONZE AGE BOOGIE

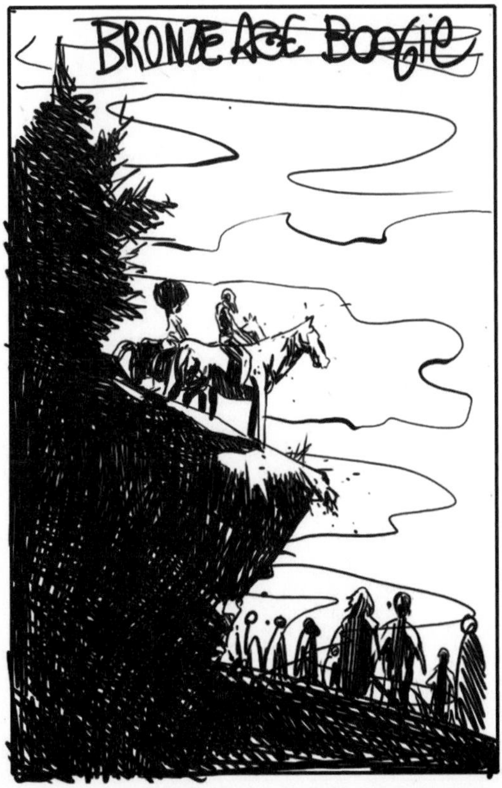
BRONZE AGE BOOGIE

ALL THE TRIBE?

4G

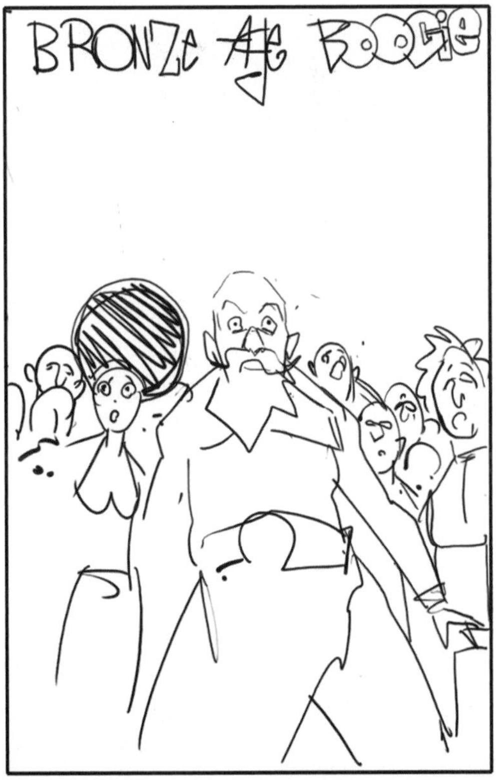
BRONZE AGE BOOGIE

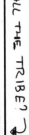

BRONZE AGE BOOGIE #6 COVER SKETCHES by Alberto Ponticelli

For issue #6: four different angles, all dynamic and powerful, depicting Brita's assault on the Martian with Eckhart in the driver's seat.

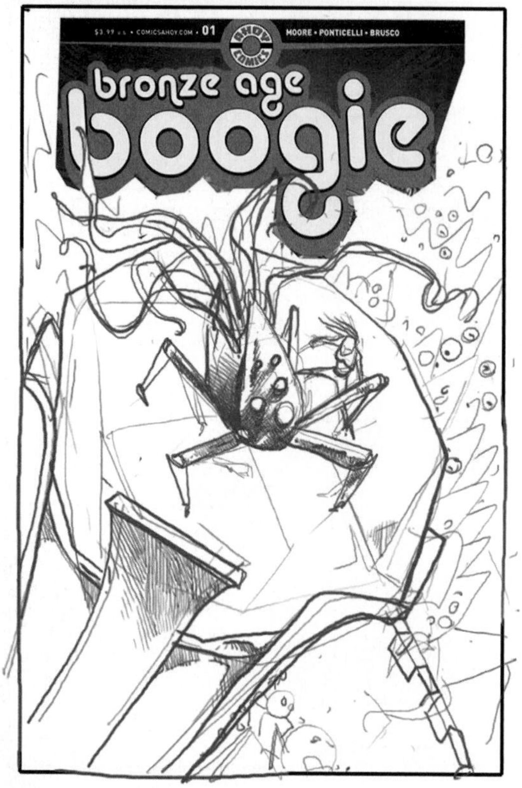
MOORE • PONTICELLI • BRUSCO
bronze age
boogie

Cover 2

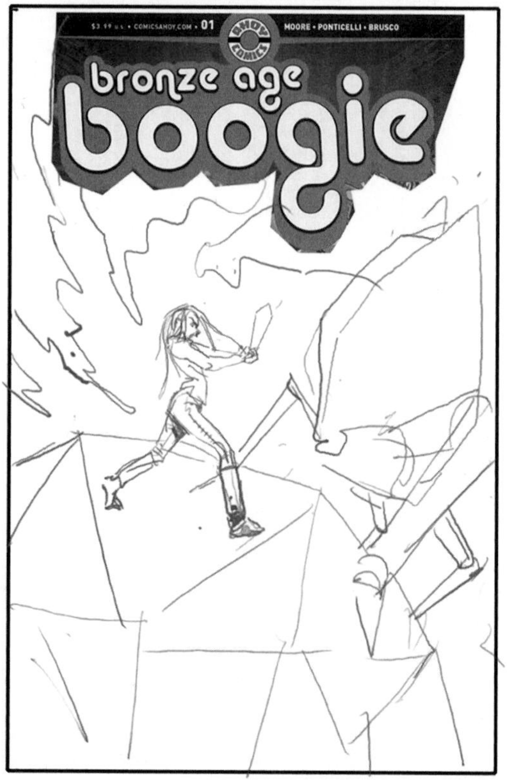
MOORE • PONTICELLI • BRUSCO
bronze age
boogie

Cover 3

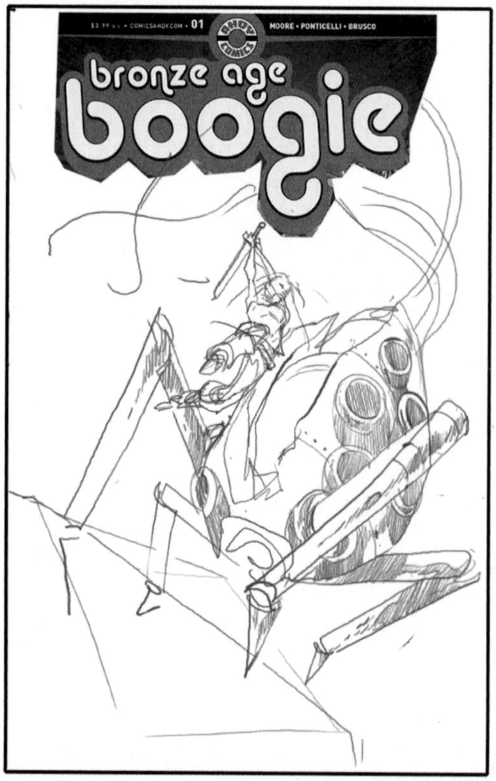
MOORE • PONTICELLI • BRUSCO
bronze age
boogie

Cover 4

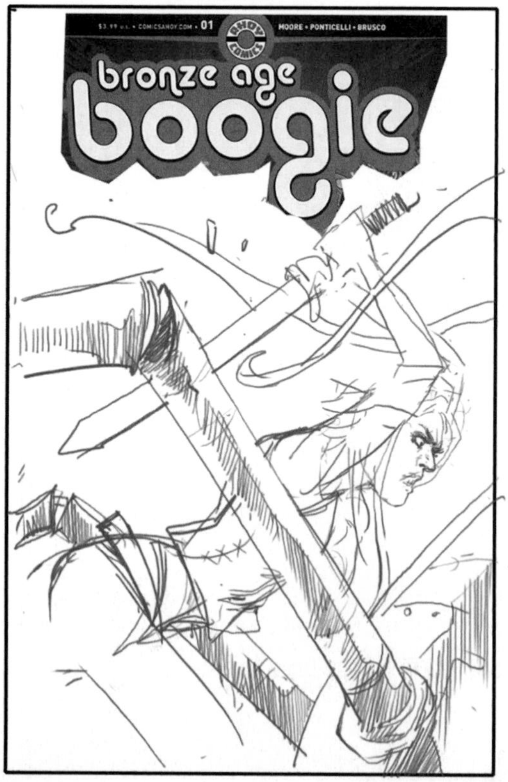
MOORE • PONTICELLI • BRUSCO
bronze age
boogie

BRONZE AGE BOOGIE #5 COVER, ALTERNATE COLOR TREATMENT by Guilia Brusco

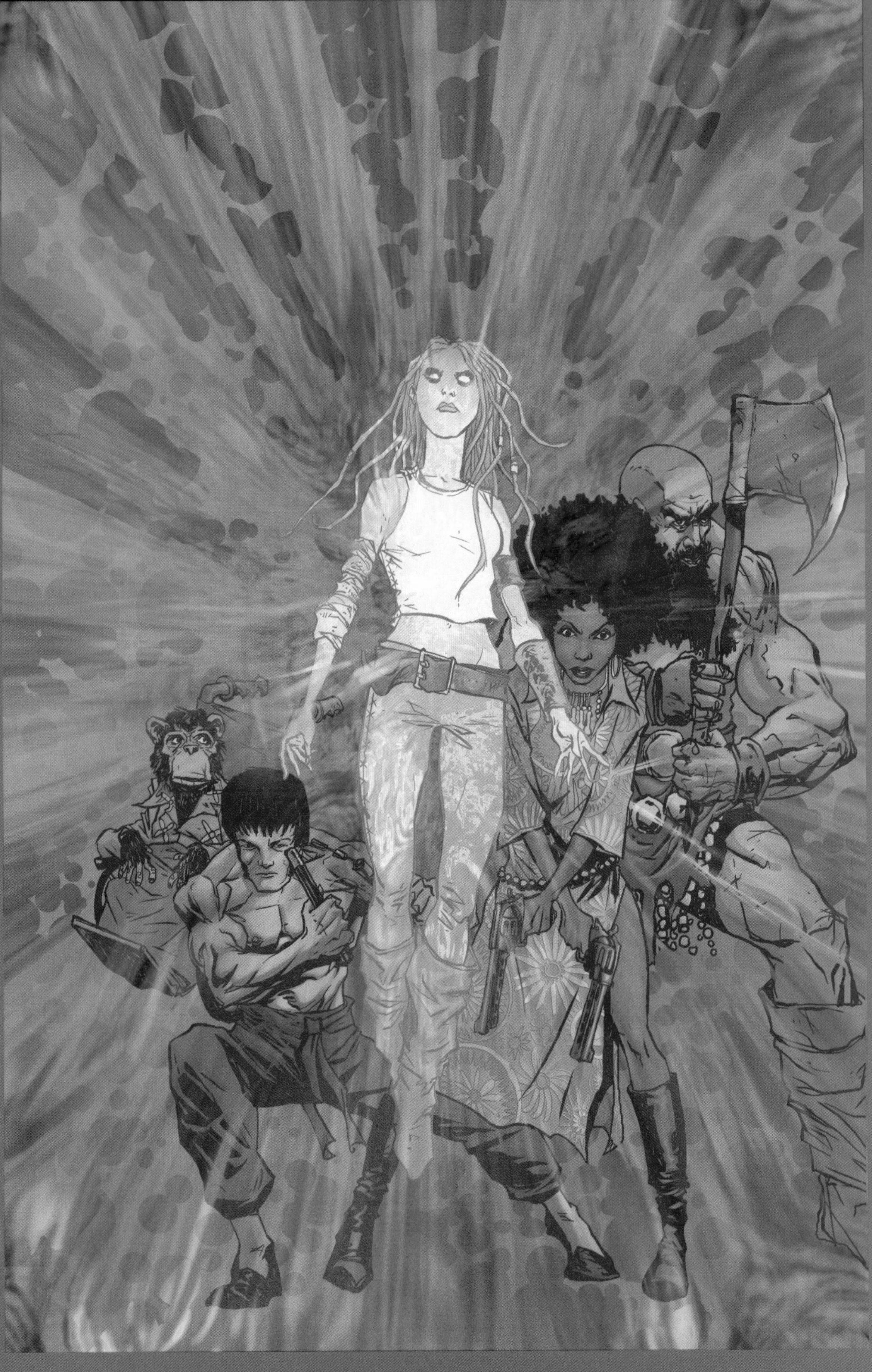

B I O G R A P H I E S

GUILIA BRUSCO has lent her talent as a color artist to numerous titles throughout the U.S. and European marketplace including Vertigo's *Scalped* and the Marvel's *Punisher MAX* storyline introducing the infamous Barracuda.

SHAWN CRYSTAL was born to draw. Not even his love for hardcore, hip-hop and skateboarding could stop him from pursuing a career in art. He has illustrated series for Wildstorm, DC and Marvel and has also worked in animation and video game concept design.

LEE LOUGHRIDGE is a color artist who has created award-winning work for Marvel, DC, Dark Horse and Image Comics throughout his 25-year career.

STUART MOORE is a writer, a book editor, and an award-winning comics editor. His recent comics writing includes *Deadpool the Duck* (Marvel), *EGOs* (Image), and *CAPTAIN GINGER* (AHOY). His novels include three volumes of *The Zodiac Legacy*, a bestselling Disney Press series created and cowritten by Stan Lee, *Thanos: Death Sentence* (Marvel), and *X-Men: The Dark Phoenix Saga* (Titan). Stuart also handles Publishing Ops for AHOY on a freelance basis from his home in Brooklyn, New York, where he lives with two of the most spoiled cats on this or any other planet.

ALBERTO PONTICELLI developed a passion for illustration at a young age and pursued his dream of being a comic book artist through a self-publishing collaborative, Shok Studios, in his native Italy. His work was quickly recognized and reprinted by Dark Horse, launching his career in American comics. Since, Ponticelli has done work for Marvel, DC, Image and IDW as well as his award-winning graphic novel *Blatta* for Leopoldo Bloom Editore.

ROB STEEN is the illustrator of *Flanimals*, the best-selling series of children's books written by Ricky Gervais, and *Erf*, a children's book written by Garth Ennis.